RECKLESS ABANDON

JEANNINE COLETTE

This is a work of fiction. The names, characters, places, and incidents are products of the author's imagination or have been used fictitiously. Any resemblance to actual persons, living or dead, events, or locales is entirely coincidental.

Cover Design by Sarah Hansen, Okay Creations, www.okaycreations.com
Formatting by Jovana Shirley, Unforeseen Editing, www.unforeseenediting.com

Printed in the United States of America
First Printing, 2015
ISBN-13: 978-0-9964997-4-3

www.JeannineColette.com

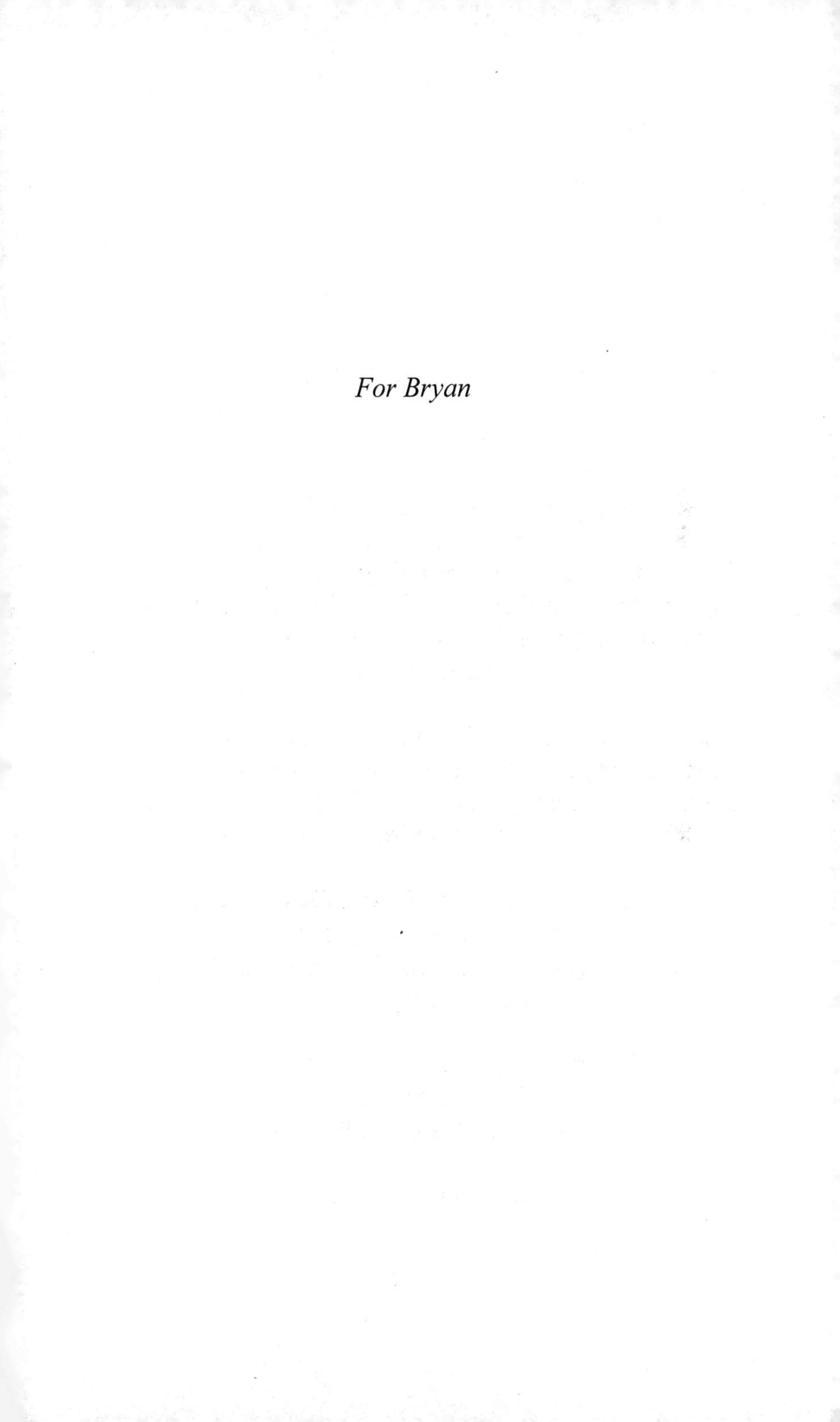

For Bryan

PROLOGUE

I open the car door, begging entrance into a world of speed and carelessness. I've always done things by the book. Tonight, I want to be reckless.

It could be the liquor talking, but I don't care.

"Where are we going next?" Luke turns up the stereo. All the way up to the point your eardrums try to close in protection of the onslaught of erratic beats and heavy metal.

"Anywhere you want, baby bro! Tonight I feel like flying!" I bang my head on the doorframe as my butt falls hard onto the passenger seat of his Mustang. I raise my hand to the spot that should hurt but surprisingly doesn't.

Luke shakes his head and laughs. "You're gonna feel that in the morning. You're numb drunk."

I twist my face and think about how drunk I possibly am.

Do I know where I am? Yes. I am in Luke's car.

Where did we just come from? The bar? Yes. The bar.

I'm not too sure how many drinks I had. My guess is three, four, seven . . . wait.

My mouth pulls in and my throat clenches as I release a warm air belch. The quiet kind that leaves a liquor aftertaste in your mouth.

Positive assessment: I am drunk. Just enough to feel really fucking good, but not enough to drive. That is why my baby brother is bringing my ass home.

"Drive." I order.

"Yes, Ma'am!" Luke salutes me and puts the car in gear.

When you live in a rural town, driving at night can be dangerous. With dark winding back roads and the only light coming from your own vehicle, you have to proceed with caution.

Not tonight.

"Let's run the night!"

Luke changes gears and we zip down the roads he knows like the back of his hand.

"I like drunk Emma!" he shouts over the music, and I just close my eyes and smile.

I like drunk Emma too.

Sober Emma does everything right. Practices every day. Follows the rules. Dates the right boys.

Boys. Fucking boys.

I almost forgot about the douche who broke my goddamn heart. I spent the entire day torn up over him. I wasted years of my life being there for him.

And then he left me.

Just. Like. That.

"Faster!" I hear the words pour out of my mouth but don't actually feel my mouth move.

"Really?" Luke asks.

I open my eyes and look over at him. My eyebrows scrunch close together and give my best stare down. "Faster!"

With a lead foot, Luke drives. Rapid, thoughtless, and uninhibited.

The heavy bass shouting through the sound system makes the car vibrate and my pulse race. I hear Luke sing along. My mind is a rush of adrenaline and my fingertips rise above my head and then out the open window. The passing wind makes me feel alive and wild.

Luke takes a turn and the tires of the car screech, my body slightly rises from the seat. I have to grab the door to get my bearings. He straightens out with precision and my heart pounds.

That felt so fucking good.

With his hand on the gear he shifts with each sharp turn, losing ground over hills. The wooded confines become a blur in the black night. The fast passing gravel ahead is all I see.

The world around me starts to move. Fixing my eyes on the dash, I try to ground myself but it's not working. The wild movements make my head feel dizzy. My stomach rolls up and away from itself. I think I'm going to puke. We should stop.

We should . . .

The tires squeal. A loud bang comes from Luke's side of the car and the force of the impact slams me into my door.

Spinning.

We're spinning.

Luke's hands are grabbing violently at the steering wheel. He's out of control.

It's happening too fast.

My head smacks against the door and then toward the windshield. Like a rag doll, my body is shifted. I have to grab hold of something but I can't reach anything.

The glass implodes. I raise my hands to cover my face from the shattering shards. My arms are covering my eyes. I can't see anything but I feel the weightlessness of antigravity.

I start to pray but the words can't get out of my mouth fast enough.

The car crashes hard into the ground with a force so powerful . . . so fierce . . . so . . .

Silent.

PART I
CAPRI, ITALY

chapter ONE

"How much further to the top?" Leah whines, clenching onto her roller suitcase. The casters make a thumping sound, banging against each step as she pulls it up the mountain of stairs.

"We could have taken the bus." My voice is an I-told-you-so singsong, slightly wincing, as I try to tame the ache shooting up my left arm. It's my less-dominant one and not made for lifting a suitcase vertically up a hill.

We're both a little snippy from our long day of travel. It has been an episode of planes, trains, and automobiles to get us here. Yesterday morning, we woke up in Columbus and boarded a plane to New York, only to transfer to another flight to Dublin. After a serious layover and a few pints of Guinness, we boarded our third and final flight to Naples, Italy. With seventeen hours of travel behind us, we were elated to board a hydrofoil to take us to the island of Capri.

We are tired, we want showers, and a glass of Prosecco wouldn't hurt either.

I raise my gaze to the incredible surroundings. When the boat pulled up to the Grande Marina of Capri, I had to blink to make sure I wasn't dreaming. The sight so surreal, Schubert's Ninth Symphony played in my head as a virtual theme song.

Capri is a massive rock, shooting out from the Tyrrhenian Sea. Rocky caves around the island can be made out as the water crashes at the base. Up top, a cloud hides the peak of the mountain, making it seem as if heaven is just beyond the fog. Cascading down the slope is fresh green, hugging the landscape like a blanket.

As you get closer to the island, the definition and vibrant colors of homes and hotels peering up from the greenery becomes clearer. Shades of gold, red, and orange reflect off the rooftops. At the foreground, vendors and shops are bustling with activity. Tourists are buying souvenirs or trying to get a glimpse of Mt. Vesuvius, while others are walking to the various restaurants that line the marina.

Stepping off the boat, Leah and I had rolled our suitcases along the stone path of the dock and over to where my map said we could hail a taxi or take a bus to our hotel. Leah being Leah, hell bent on living life to the fullest, decided we should walk to our hotel, taking the narrow stairway paths that cut through the island. She said it would be "exciting" and would help us "stretch our legs." She had no idea how many hundreds of stairs we would have to climb.

"Buses are for tourists. We are here to enjoy this magnificent island and the only way to do it is on foot!" Leah gives a loud huff at the end of her sentence, as she wraps two hands around the lever of her large suitcase and hoists it up.

"Switch bags with me," I say. My bag is much smaller and easier to maneuver. I pack light. We're spending a week in the exotic Mediterranean. How many pieces of clothing could you need?

Apparently for Leah, it's a lot.

I extend my arm, then quickly pull it back, realizing the one I was offering wouldn't be of any use.

"No, Emma, your hand." She stops her progression and looks down at me. "You must be having enough trouble lifting your own. I wasn't thinking. I shouldn't—"

"It's fine." I cut her off, stretching out my right hand, a constant reminder of the worst year of my life and all the dreams that faded in one awful weekend.

A heart-wrenching breakup with the man I thought I was going to marry?

Check.

The devastating loss of a family member that left my soul aching so hard I found it hard to breathe?

Check. Check.

An accident that crushed my desires and everything I'd worked my entire life for, leaving me virtually numb?

Triple check.

Yes, it has been the worst year of my life and we're only halfway through it. I've been so anesthetized and empty that my family pushed their own grieving aside to make sure I'm okay. All they want to do is talk, when it's the last thing I need. That, and have them worry about me. They worry too much.

I shake off the thought and brush away Leah's concerns. "It's fine. I'm using my left hand. Keep going. This should be the last set of stairs and then our hotel is on the left."

With a nod, Leah continues up, me following, until we reach a road. Sure enough, our hotel is just to the left. I have never been more excited to see a hotel in my life.

I love vacations, don't get me wrong. But for the amount of travel and manual labor it just took to get us here, this better be the best vacation of my life. At least I hope it is. Leah gave up a lot for us to experience this together.

We enter the sliding glass doors of the Villa Marina Capri and a lovely receptionist who speaks perfect English greets us. She takes our passports to make copies, as per Italian custom, and when she returns them she escorts us to an outdoor waiting area while our room is readied.

I'm a bit unsure about leaving my bag. Ever since my luggage was stolen on a college trip to Cancún, I refuse to let other people handle my belongings. After Leah assures me this five-star resort is a far cry from that rum-soaked

Mexican hotel, I concede, but only after making sure my purse, along with my money and valuables, is with me.

Leah just laughs at my one OCD trait and heads outside with me.

"Oh my God." The words escape my mouth.

"Oh my God is right." Leah repeats, sliding her sunglasses up her perfect button nose.

The two of us stand in awe, gawking over the incredible sight before us. If I thought the view coming into port was phenomenal, I was mistaken. This is the most incredible view I have ever seen in my life.

Standing about a third up the mountain, the island below us, and the sea beyond it, is the true answer of why God created the earth. So we can marvel at its beauty.

The afternoon sun is shining bright. The sky is a perfect shade of blue with a few stray clouds. The whiteness of them only illuminates the color of the sky. The rooftops below are a gorgeous copper color and the sea is all but breathtaking.

With a slight breeze in the air, Leah's hair blows away from her cheek. Looking over at her, I see a look of melancholy on her face. A look so un-Leah, it makes my stomach drop.

"I knew this was a bad idea. I shouldn't be here. Adam . . ." The words choke in my throat.

"Adam is the most amazing man in the world." She finishes my sentence for me. It's not what I was going to say, but she's right. Leah's fiancé, Adam Reingold, is by far the most caring, understanding, and perfect man in the world. He is the kind of guy you want your sister to marry. It's exactly why I feel awful being the one standing here with her and not him.

Leah gives me this knowing look that she's been giving me a lot lately, followed by a hug. "Stop it. We're here and this is happening. This week is about you and me. We are going to have the most spectacular vacation of our lives and

I don't want you feeling bad for one second. You hear me?" She holds me tighter and I return her embrace.

Sometimes it's hard to accept she's the little sister. Not that she's younger by a lot. Hell, we're born in the same year, she arriving the day before New Years Eve. Irish twins. Most days she's the wacky, wild sister who dances on bars and runs into oncoming traffic to get across the street. She never returns things she borrows and loves to sing karaoke, even when the establishment doesn't have karaoke. It can get quite embarrassing.

Back in Cedar Ridge, Leah owns a bar called McConaughey's. Yes, it's named after the famed actor and has Matthew McConaughey paraphernalia all around. There's no good explanation for why the bar exists, other than the fact she is a die-hard fan and the cliental love to get drunk and chant, "Alright, alright, alright."

Leah is usually the crazy one getting the crowd riled up.

Yet there are times like this—like this entire year—when she shows more maturity and composure than you would expect from the wild child with the platinum blonde bob and sheared jeans. This year had to be hard on her as well, yet she gave up so much for me, for our family.

Pulling back from her, I let out a large sigh and am relieved to see a waiter approach us with a platter of prosciutto and a bottle of Prosecco, compliments of the hotel. We clink glasses and salute the start of our sisters sabbatical.

"Do you know how much sex can be had in a tub like this?"

Leah is sitting, fully clothed in the empty bathtub in our hotel suite. The large porcelain tub is yet another reminder of the honeymoon this was supposed to be.

"Too bad it will be sexless for the next week." I say, putting my clothes away in the large wardrobe that sits opposite the massive king-size bed.

"Just because I won't be getting foamed up in here doesn't mean you can't." She wiggles her eyebrows.

"No." I shoot her an evil glare.

"What happens in Italy, stays in Italy." Leah sings, resting her head on the back of the tub and kicking up her feet.

I let out a laugh knowing that is not true. My sister has the biggest mouth in Cedar Ridge. The fact she is marrying a state trooper means Leah not only knows everyone's business from the bar, but she also gets the lowdown on every speeding ticket and arrest in town. If I hook up with a random Italian on vacation, everyone within a ten-mile radius will know, and I don't need my dad hearing about my rendezvous. My poor dad. He still has a hard time believing I'm twenty-five-years-old.

"I didn't travel five thousand miles for a random hookup." Placing my sundresses delicately on each hanger, I look over at Leah's suitcase, open on the sofa, in the seating area by the door. I'm sure that's exactly where it will stay.

"I didn't give up my honeymoon so you could wallow the entire trip." Her head peeks up from the tub's headrest, one eyebrow slanted up, her mouth in a lopsided smirk.

She's a conniving one. In one breath she tells me not to worry about hijacking her honeymoon and in the next she's guilting me over it. Nice to see she hasn't lost her sense of humor.

I shake my head and grin. Leah catches my laugh and points it out. "You're getting some action this week, lady. It's your debt to me. If you don't pick him, I will."

I turn around from my place at the closet, placing my hands on my hips. "Why are you so hell-bent on getting me laid?"

"Because it pisses me off the last guy in your pants was that jerk Parker. He's an asshole, he fucked with your head, and it's been six months since you've been with anyone else."

I can't argue with her there. Six months ago I thought I was in love with Parker Ryles. We met at Carnegie Mellon, where he was studying the flute, and I was on the violin. He was smart and sweet and made that instrument look super sexy.

After four years of dating, I was practically picking out bridesmaid dresses. That is, until he dumped me because he wasn't ready to settle down. That would have been fine and dandy if we hadn't started having "the talk." You know, the one where you discuss how many children you want and where you'll live. We were on the same page, or at least I thought we were. Now I know there is no way I could have married someone so selfish. My life has been destroyed and I blame him every day for what happened.

At least it's easier to blame him than myself.

And right now I'd really like to tell him what he could do with that flute.

For some reason Leah feels it's imperative that I meet someone new. As if going out on a date is going to make the pain go away. Well, it's not. I'm broken and loving someone or something is just not worth it because when you lose it . . . when you lose them . . . the pain is too much to bear.

Leah rises from the tub and stalks over to her suitcase. "Let's put on our sexiest outfits and hit this town."

I let out a stretch, arching my fingertips toward the ceiling. "Can we sleep first? I am jet-lagged and still on Ohio time."

Unzipping her bag, Leah moves some clothes around and talks over her shoulder. "No prob. I heard Italians like to eat really late anyway. You doze for a few. I'm too wired to sleep."

Leah pulls the largest pair of binoculars I've ever seen out of her suitcase and holds them up to her face.

"What the hell are those?" They look like they belong to the CIA.

"They're Adam's. He uses them for surveillance. I borrowed them for our trip." She walks over to the glass door that acts as the main entrance into our suite. Opening the door, Leah steps out onto the veranda facing the marina and the view we were admiring earlier.

"Those things are huge. There's no way you're carrying them around. And if you lose them, I don't care how much Adam loves you. He'll flip."

Leah lets out a loud laugh. I return it. We both know Adam staying mad at Leah is about as likely as me befriending an octopus who speaks French.

See? Unlikely.

I walk over to the bed and fall into it. My body sinks into the duvet and I actually sigh, it feels so good. My eyes are just about to set into sleepyland when Leah lets out a loud gasp.

I prop open an eye.

"Ems, Ems—come here, you have to see this." She's still on the veranda, her hand flapping at a million miles a second. Her eyes still glued to the binoculars.

I let out a grunt and fall further into the pillow.

"Emma!" She shrieks. It's a hurry-up shriek, not a I'm-being-kidnapped shriek.

Unwillingly and very tiredly, I roll off the bed and pad over to where she's standing. When I reach her side, she hands the binoculars over to me and positions my body and the binoculars in the direction she was gawking at. I lift the binoculars to my face and look out on the marina.

"What am I looking at?" I ask.

"The boat. Do you see the boat?"

"I see, like, a million boats." I reply.

"The ginormous boat, Ems. It's huge. You can't miss."

I pan the area where she's positioned me to look. Sailboat, sailboat, sailboat, smaller vessel, smaller vessel, motorboat, hydrofoil . . . Ahh, I see it. Ginormous isn't even the word. It's twice the size of the ferry we took from Naples this morning. It's impressive, I'll give her that, but so not worth getting out of bed for.

I hand the binoculars back to Leah. "It's very nice. Now, if you'll excuse me, I have some sleep to catch up on."

Leah pushes the binoculars back to my chest.

"Look at the upper deck, spaz."

With an eye roll, I take the binoculars back. There's the boat again. I see windows. I see a double staircase off the back of the boat. I see a seating area. I see . . . oh. *Oh, have mercy.*

I see a man. Not just any man. I see a naked man. Naked in all his glory.

Yup, I'm awake now.

These binoculars are really powerful because from the incredible distance we are from the yacht, I can see the clear definition of his ass.

It's a good ass.

It's a gladiator ass.

And that's not all. His back is rumbling with muscle, cascading with each movement of his incredible body.

Sweet Jesus, hallelujah.

I can't see his face because his back is to us as he is pounding into a woman. Maybe pounding isn't the word. Grinding, thrusting, plunging—take your pick. I can't see her at all because his masculine frame is blocking my view. All I can see of her is two legs wrapped around his lean torso. With each thrust, his gluts flex in and the lats muscles on his back pump out.

These two are having sex. And it's the really dirty kind.

A pool of heat settles between my legs. The nerve endings in my chest spark alive and my cheeks flush with heat.

It's like the first time I watched soft porn. My friends wanted to see what it was about so they turned on Cinemax and we sat there in silence pretending we weren't being affected. The truth was I was sitting there with a throbbing between my legs and the very strong desire to do something about it.

I have that exact feeling right now.

"My turn." Leah says, grabbing the binoculars from my face.

I breathe out through my puckered lips. That was hot. Really hot.

And really sick of us to watch.

"Leah, there has to be some law against you watching them have sex. Aren't there, like, stalker laws?" I ask.

"They're having sex in the open. If we were home, they'd be the ones getting arrested." She licks her lips and bites down on her lower lip. "I love Italy already."

Shaking my head, I walk back over to the bed and try to fall asleep.

My mind racing with visions of naked men, it's not so easy for me to fall into sleepy land as it was before.

chapter TWO

The first night of our sister sabbatical was more than I was ready for. After sleeping for five hours, Leah threw me out of bed and made me put on a very sparkly halter top and black capri pants for dinner. She insisted we wear capris in Capri. I couldn't argue with her logic.

After dinner, we went to the Piazetta Umberto I, the town square, got tipsy on limoncello and then followed a group of other twentysomethings to a club in town. Leah's idea, not mine. There we drank more limoncello, and by the end of the night Leah had the entire club singing a Katy Perry song.

Because that's what Leah does.

And apparently, even non-English–speaking Italians know the words to Katy Perry songs.

While they sang and danced, I sat at a table and sucked down my drinks, plastering a fake smile on my face, trying not to ruin Leah's "honeymoon" or elicit one of those looks from her.

I caught her inspecting me a few times, making sure I wasn't falling into a mood or withdrawing myself. She thought she was being sly, asking me if I wanted another drink when it was still full and hers was drained, encouraging me to drink up or telling me a joke and making sure I laughed at it, because, if I didn't, then something must be wrong. Each time her eyes drifted over to mine, I'd bob my head to the music pretending I'm into whatever song the DJ is playing when I'd rather have been back in the room.

This morning, my brain does not like the Teenage Dream lived last night and feels like I have fireworks going off in my head.

Thank you, Leah, and thank you, Katy Perry.

And thank you, limoncello.

"Rise and shine." My chipper roommate bounces on the bed. Since I don't drink as much as she does on a daily basis, my body doesn't process liquor as fast as hers does. I think I'm still a little drunk.

"Go away." My voice is deep and hoarse.

"'Morning, Emma." A male voice echoes from Leah's speakerphone.

I glance up at the clock beside the bed. "'Morning Adam. Holy God, what time is it over there?"

Adam's chuckle pours out of the phone. "Four in the morning. Just getting off the nightshift. You sound like you had fun last night."

I grumble at his reference to my morning man-voice.

"You keeping my girl from getting into trouble?" he asks, knowing his fiancé oh-so-well.

"Her talents for entertainment have rose to international capabilities."

Adam laughs again. "That's my girl."

Leah talks back into the phone. "Okay, baby, let me go. I have to get this lazy ass out of bed or else she'll sleep the day away."

Leah lets out a loud air kiss and Adam does the same before they hang up. With her knees still on the bed, she rocks back and forth making the bed move beneath me. "Let's drink espresso and eat croissants. You'll feel like new in no time."

I look up from the sheets I pulled over my head. She is dressed in a denim miniskirt and a white peasant shirt. Her hair is blown out in her signature bob but the front is pulled up in a mini poof and secured to her head with a red barrette. Her pale eyes are light and bright; a far cry from what she should be looking like this morning after drinking her weight in lemon oil and sugar.

"Ten more minutes," I plead.

"Nope." She lifts the sheets off my body. "We have an island to explore."

"We're gonna be here for seven more days." My voice is starting to get back its natural characteristics. More feminine, less mannish.

"And I don't want to waste a second. Now, get out of bed and spend my honeymoon with me!"

I peer up from her with vulture eyes. She really knows how to guilt trip me.

I bang my fists on the bed and get up, not before getting my bearings and making sure the room isn't spinning. When I'm sure the ground is even, I straighten my back and walk to the bathroom.

There's a shower, a stall and a sink for two in here. Since the bathtub is near the bed, there is plenty room for a large shower made for—you got it—two. I head straight into the shower and let the hot water hit my head and my back until I feel normal again.

Out of the shower, I wrap my body in a towel and dry my hair over the double vanity made of rock. Like, literal rock that is jutting out of the mountain. It's crazy cool.

Looking at my reflection I see a girl who looks like Leah but so very different. Our faces are fairly similar. Almond-shaped eyes, nice noses, and a heart-shaped face. But that's where the similarities end. Where her eyes are blue, mine are a light brown. She has Dad's eyes; I have Mom's. Leah also has this adorable cupid mouth that bows at the top. Yeah, mine doesn't do that at all.

And while Leah's hair is almost white, my hair is an ashy color. It's the kind of hair that's too dark to be called blonde but absolutely not brown. It's just ashy.

Some people say I should get highlights but my schedule was always too busy to spend hours at a salon.

When you've been playing the violin since you were ten, there isn't much your life offers in the form of time. If I wasn't at school, doing homework, or grooming my career, I was practicing.

Well, now that that dream has died, I guess I have time to change my hair.

I look down at my right hand and flip it over repeatedly, flexing the nerve. Biting at my jaw, I look back up at myself in the mirror and continue to get ready. I don't want to think about that right now.

"She's doing fine." Leah is in our room talking to someone. I turn the sink water on low and prop my ear to the door to listen in on her conversation. "Yes, Mom, she's out of bed and in the shower . . . yes . . . yes . . . I'm making sure she's eating."

Being thousands of miles away from my family doesn't seem to change anything.

"She thought I didn't notice but she didn't want to be out last night. She was a trooper. She's trying." Leah's voice is so hushed; I have to strain against the door to hear her muffled words. "I have her meds just in case."

My stomach rolls at the thought of those damn pills, which I spent three months on. I didn't know I was depressed. I just thought I was sad.

And tired. So very, very tired.

I didn't know it had been three weeks since I got out of bed. I didn't know I wasn't eating. Who needs a shower when you have nowhere to go?

My behavior led to a meeting with a Dr. Schueler, who had a lovely parting gift in the form of antidepressants. I didn't want to take them. I'm strong. I'm an accomplished musician with a world-renowned orchestra. I have a boyfriend, a happy family and the world at my fingertips.

At least, I did.

Not anymore.

So I took the damn pills and spent the next three months numb. So numb that I was void of myself. I hated taking them but only did so I didn't have to see the look in my family's eyes. The one that said they can't move on until I do.

Two months ago, I told Dr. Schueler I didn't want the pills anymore. I wanted to do this on my own. She didn't think it was a good idea but I stopped them anyway. I've been doing really well for the last eight weeks. It drives me insane that Leah felt the need to bring them with her.

She probably did it for Mom.

When I hear Leah hang up, I grab the sun block and walk it into the bedroom, motioning for Leah to apply some. She doesn't even mention she was on the phone with our mom, and I don't bring it up.

Turning to the wardrobe, I pick out a pair of white shorts and a green tank top, opting for comfort over style. I slide on my Sperry Top-Siders and head out the door.

"You are not wearing a fanny pack!" Leah chides as soon as I step outside.

"Don't knock it. I have our passports, cash, and travelers checks in here. No one is getting away with our stuff." I pat down the bag holstered around my waist to make sure everything is secure.

"There are so many things wrong with that statement, I don't know where to start." Leah's arms flail about her body in mock exaggeration. Or maybe she's being serious?

"What's wrong with my bag?"

"Uh, everything?" She holds up a finger. "*Numero uno*, you are wearing a fanny pack." She stretches out the words *fanny* and *pack* as if I don't understand English and need to hear her diction perfectly. "Those are for tourists at Disney World and marathon runners. Are you riding the teacups or running twenty-six miles today? No. So take it off."

"It's practical and keeps all our stuff safe." It also happens to be super cute. It's gray with white chevron stripes. It's the most adorable fanny pack ever. If it were Gucci Leah probably wouldn't mind. Maybe if I got a Gucci one—

"*Numero dos*, that's what a safe is for. Why are you taking all of our valuables with us?" Her hands are still in front of her body making dramatic gestures. I think talking to the Italians last night rubbed off on her.

"It's *due*, not *dos*," I say.

Leah just taps her foot and waits for an answer.

"I am not leaving our money in some chintzy safe where anyone can walk out with it. Been there done that." Fool me once, shame on you. Fool me twice . . . you know how it goes. "If you want to get stranded in a foreign country with no way to get home, be my guest."

She throws her hands up in the air. "Fine. Whatever. Take the stuff. Just leave that horrible pack in the room." She concedes.

Not wanting to cause a fight, I back up into the room and grab my shoulder bag, removing all the items from the fanny pack and inserting them into the new bag. It won't be as comfortable but it will be more stylish. I shouldn't worry. By midweek, Leah won't care what I'm carrying her stuff in. She doesn't carry a bag at all.

Like Leah promised, after some espresso and a croissant, paired with some blood orange juice, my hangover is a dismal headache.

Leah made arrangements for us to take a boat tour of the island, starting with the Blue Grotto and then winding around the island to see the sea caves of Capri. Since the tides don't always cooperate enough for people to view the Grotto, Leah wanted to do this on our first day, just in case we aren't able to during the others.

We walk down to the Grande Marina and pass the vendors and shops we saw yesterday. Past the hydrofoil dock, there is a small area with many boats, anchored idly in the water.

I follow Leah down a concrete path to a boat about fifteen feet long with an Italian flag waving from a pole in the center. The boat is completely open, a day bed taking up half of the boat with a small seating area in the back and motor for the captain to drive. It's a leisure boat made for tours of the island.

I take the gentleman's hand who will be driving us on our tour and take my spot on the day bed, sitting up straight and holding on to my bag. Leah stretches out next to me and leans back on her hands, looking up at the sun.

The gentleman escorting us on our tour speaks a little English, but it is very hard to understand with his thick accent. I know a tiny bit of Italian from taking it in high school, which doesn't amount to much. We nod and pretend we know what he's saying. All we can make out is that his name is Raphael.

Starting the engine, Raphael drives away from the dock and the rocking of the boat in the water forces me to brace myself. I place my hand on the bed behind me and lean back on my side, my back facing the water, my front to Leah.

The boat turns left and drives us past the Grande Marina. Leah points out our hotel and takes a picture of it with her phone. Then, she snaps a few pictures of me and asks me to take a few of her in return.

She slides the phone back in her pocket and goes back to taking in the sun.

Before long, Raphael slows the boat down and Leah and I peer up to see why we've changed speed.

Ahead of us is a sea of boats similar to ours and smaller wooden rowboats. They look like gridlock traffic, all idling in the water, dangerously close to the rock that is the island of Capri.

"Grotto Azzurra," Raphael says as he idles the engine.

Amongst the boats before us, there is a larger one with a sign over it. It looks like a concession stand of sorts.

Squinting my eyes I try to make out what the sign says. It's where people pay their admission to see the Blue Grotto.

Looking around, I notice there is a man to each wooden rowboat and ushering tourists from boats like ours onto the wooden crafts, and then paddling over to the concession to pay an admission.

Leah asks Raphael why we can't take this boat to see the Blue Grotto. He points to a very small opening in the rock. We watch as one at a time, the small wooden boats approach the opening that looks entirely too small for them to fit through. The man on the boat instructs the passengers to lay down on their backs as he pulls himself, and the boat through the opening by a metal chain that is mounted to the rock. The boat and its passengers disappear inside the sea cave.

It looks slightly frightening.

I glance at Leah with an unsure feeling. She shrugs me off and tells me to relax.

Our boat is waiting in a line of sorts. Tourist boats like ours are all gathered in a mosh pit, there's no telling who was here first. When it's our turn, Leah and I will board a small wooden boat and be swallowed up by the sea cave. My stomach drops at the thought.

We slowly inch up, getting closer to the mass of wooden boats. There have to be twenty in line before us.

Craning my neck, I look around at the sea around us. My eyes widen at the sight of a very familiar vessel.

I nudge Leah. "Look."

She turns her head and gawks over at the yacht we were spying on yesterday. It's about a two hundred yards from us, but it's so massive, it feels like it's on top of us.

"Looks like Mr. Sex-a-thon took a break for some culture this morning."

"How long did you watch them yesterday?" I ask.

"Over an hour. It was enough that I had to FaceTime Adam for some afternoon delight."

"Ugh! You did not do that while I was sleeping!"

"Actually, it was more like morning delight for Adam." She grins. "Calm down, I went into the bathroom. You didn't even know, so what do you care?"

I sock Leah in the arm and she laughs.

"Did they seriously go at it that long?" I am so curious. Parker and I never went longer than twenty minutes. And that was on a special occasion.

I once heard Seth Myers tell a joke. "A new study came out that women prefer sleep over sex. Who would want to sleep for two and a half minutes?" When I heard it I thought of Parker and me.

"Ems, he had her in every position. And I mean every position. We're talkin' crazy Kama Sutra stuff."

My hand rises to my face, feeling the heat from my blush. I am not a blusher. Let's make that clear. But just thinking about what I saw through those binoculars yesterday made me hot all over.

"You are so getting laid this week." Leah winks and I glare at her. Getting in bed with someone is so far down on the list of things I want to do.

Thirty minutes later, Leah and I are still drifting in the boat, waiting our turn, when one of the wooden rowboats makes its way over to us.

Leah lets out a huff. "It's about time."

She gets up and waits for me to stand as well. The small boat pulls up next to ours and Raphael holds on to it, trying to keep it positioned as close to ours as possible. The man in the smaller boat holds out his hand and motions for me to grab it and come on board.

I rise and steady my feet to step over the wall and down onto the rowboat. Holding my bag with my left hand, I grab the man's outstretched hand with my right.

"*Nessuna borsa.*" The man says, motioning to the purse I have clenched tightly to the left side of my body.

I blink back at him. There is no way I am leaving my bag and all of its belongings here with some strange man, no matter how nice Raphael may seem.

"Emma, leave the bag. You can't take it with you." Leah translates in case I didn't get the message.

Still holding the man's hand, I turn my head to face her. I try to give her an eye that reads *over my dead body.*

"Give me the bag!" Leah orders and starts to grab it from my hand.

"Stop it." I bite back, pulling the bag back toward me.

Raphael releases the rowboat and stands to say something to the effect of why I can't take the bag. The man in the rowboat is now only connected to our boat by the strength of our hands clasped to one another.

"Seriously, leave the bag. Give it to me." Leah yanks the bag hard.

I release the man's hand and swing my right arm over to grab the bag back out of Leah's grasp. In doing so, I lose my ground and, more importantly, my footing and barrel ass up, backward toward the water.

I try to grab Leah's hand on the way down but when I clasp my hand down on hers, the nerve in my palm bites back and the pain shoots up my arm, forcing me to let go.

My arms flail and I hit the water with a splash, and the searing pain travels from my hand up into to my head.

Black.

All I see is black.

My lungs feel heavy and my body is lifeless. Ashy blonde hair floats around my face. I adjust my eyes and see water . . . everywhere. In front of me, next to me, above and below. The light in front of my eyes goes black again and then backs into focus. My arms reach up to grab onto something, anything, but all I feel is water.

It's dark.

My heart goes into panic mode. I try to spin my body around but there is nowhere to go. I move my arms erratically and try to swim up, but I don't seem to be moving. A burning sensation settles in my throat and my chest grows heavier as the air locked in my lungs begs to get out.

My body is trembling when two arms wrap around my chest from under my arms and pull me back. My body arches forward, my head and feet curving in as I am dragged in retrograde like a rag doll backward and upward. As soon as my head is above water I gasp for air and start coughing from so deep within I sound like a barking seal.

Hair is stuck to the front of my face and I can't see anything as my body continues to be manhandled. One very strong, thick arm wraps around my torso as the other releases its hold on me.

"Can you hold on?" A raspy, deep voice says from behind me. The accent is American.

Trying to process what is happening, I swallow back and attempt to understand what he's saying.

"I need you to hold onto the side of the boat. Can you do that?" The male voice asks again. Taking my right hand, I brush the hair away from my face and reach up with my left hand, securing my body to the boat in question.

When I am in place, the American lets me go and hoists himself onto the boat in a rather rough manner. My body bobs in the water as the boat sways from his weight. No sooner is he on the boat does he reach down and lifts me from under my armpits onto the boat as well. His thumbs leave a prodding feeling in my skin.

He sets me down on a seat and my stomach curls in, hugging my chest to my knees. My clothes are soaked and I've lost a shoe. My body is shaking, frightened from what I can now acknowledge was a near drowning.

Looking around, I notice this is not my boat. It's slightly larger in size to the one I was on and far more luxurious. My eyes widen with panic until I hear Leah's voice yelling over the commotion.

"Emma! Oh my God! Are you okay?" Her voice is close but not coming from the boat I am on. I look around and find her, about thirty feet from where I am. She is standing up and visibly shaken from her place on Raphael's boat. Her clothes are also soaked. I must have pulled her into the water at the same time.

"I'm okay. You?" I assure her.

"Still intact." She calls out. "Where's your bag?"

My bag? I pat my body and then do a quick search at the space around me.

Oh, my God.

"My bag!" I exclaim, standing quickly, I nearly fall overboard again as I launch my body toward the side of the boat to look in the water.

A giant hand pulls me back. "That bag is long gone. No use looking for it."

I turn my head, and finally have a chance to look at the man who rescued me from the water. He, too, is dripping wet and ringing water from his green, linen button down shirt. Quite possible one of the biggest men I've seen in person, he looks like he could be a UFC fighter. His hair is buzzed close to his head and his brown eyes are large to accommodate his wide neck.

He's not fat in any way. To the contrary, he is rock solid with large forearms and a broad chest. His calves look like they're the size of my thighs.

Okay, maybe that's an exaggeration. But he's built. This man is built to protect people.

My bottom lip trembles. The back of my eyes burns as hot water pools along the ridges. "You don't understand. I need that bag. Everything, and I mean *everything* I own is in that bag."

"Sorry to break it to you," he says, pulling his wet shirt away from his chest. "There is no way you're getting your bag back in this water."

My body starts to shiver as this terrible, awful feeling of helplessness pours over me. A dark, thick, sinister cloud of despair settles over my heart and my head fills with thoughts of desolation. It's a familiar feeling. The one that Dr. Schueler told me was from post-traumatic stress. The one that I have fought off but sneaks back to pay a visit every once in a while.

What have I done?

Everything is gone.

I start to cry uncontrollably, my sobs growing bigger and deeper. My lungs feel as if they are being crushed down by a leaded weight. I try to breathe, but I can only gasp.

The stranger in front of me shifts his body to the side, leaning forward a bit and then pulling back. He has no idea how to comfort a woman. And it's a good thing. If he touches me I just might flip out on him. If I can catch my breath, that is.

My daze is slightly lifted by the sound of Leah's voice. She is having Raphael drive her closer to me. When her boat reaches mine, she launches herself over the rails and swings her arms around my convulsing form.

"I was so scared. You didn't come up for air and I thought you were . . ." Her grip gets so tight on me I know exactly how she was going to end that sentence.

She lifts her head and I see her eyes bloodshot. She turns her head to the American sitting across from me, "You saved my sister." Leah launches herself onto the giant man and gives him an impressive hug.

How long was I under that water?

Another shiver runs up my spine as I shake off any thought of what could have been.

"It was no problem." His smile is polite. He acts as if anyone would have done the same.

"I dropped my bag on my way down."

Leah releases her hold on the giant and looks at me. Wiping a tear from her face, she asks, “I know you wanted to bring our things, but what exactly was in the bag?”

I glance up toward the sky and wish the bag would magically float to the surface of the sea. It doesn’t, so I list the items that were in the bag.

“My passport, your passport, our euros that we exchanged at the airport, our credit cards and my phone.”

With the mention of my phone, Leah pats down her skirt and feels for something. She reaches into her pocket and pulls her phone out. It doesn’t turn on. “Shit. Mine might as well be on the ocean floor as well.”

My shoulders lower and the darkness swells in the frontal lobe of my brain.

Leah nods her head and looks at me. “Okay, lets think about this. There has to be a way to get new passports. I’m sure people lose them on vacation all the time.” She’s trying to be positive and I’m trying to appreciate it. “How much money did we have in euros?”

I roll my neck and let out a large breath. “A thousand dollars’ worth.”

Leah swallows; obviously surprised I had that much cash on me. That much unrecoverable cash, that is.

“That sucks. As does your credit card. The good news is my credit card is still in the safe, so we can use that for expenses until we get home.” She pats her knees and offers a cheery smile.

I lift my head and offer her the most grim expression anyone can make.

Leah reads it right.

“Oh no. Oh no no no no no!” She exclaims.

I offer her a shrug.

Her blonde bob, now slicked back on her head, frays out when she stands up. “Are you kidding? Do you mean to tell me we have no passports, and no money whatsoever? Not even a friggin’ credit card to our names?”

All I can do is nod. Slowly.

"Oh, my God, Emma! Because some lowlife in Mexico stole your suitcase eight years ago, you lost every penny we have. We're in a foreign country! We have no phones, no money, no way to get home!"

"I am so sorry." My voice is low and, most certainly, apologetic.

Leah sits down and rocks herself back and forth. I want to do the same.

Raphael says something in Italian that I have a hard time understanding until the giant American pulls a wallet from the cargo pocket of his gray shorts and hands over a soggy hundred-euro note. The American says something back to Raphael in Italian and then thanks him in English.

When Raphael turns the motor on to his boat, Leah and I both come to attention and get our minds back on the problem at hand.

"Did you just send him away?"

"Did you just pay him for our boat ride?"

We say both sentences in unison.

The American nods. "From the sound of it, you two weren't going to be able to pay the man."

Neither of us can argue with that logic.

"We have to get back to our rooms. He was our way back," I say.

"He may not have spoken English well but he understood it and there was no way he was going to take you back without payment. I only gave him a tip for his services."

"So he just left us here?" Leah rubs the sides of her arms with her hands.

"I told him to." He looks back from Leah sitting next to him, to me sitting across from him. "I can help you ladies."

"Thank you but you've already done so much," I say, but am cut off.

"I have a friend at the US consulate in Rome. He can rush you a pair of passports to Naples. While I make that call, you can use my satellite phone to call your credit card companies and see if they can get you a replacement card. Maybe someone back home can wire you some money as well."

His logic is on point. Having a contact at the consulate would be incredible. I don't even know where the nearest one is. That said, this guy is a complete stranger and could hold both Leah and myself down with his pinky if he needed to. The offer is nice but we can handle the situation on our own.

"That would be great," Leah says before I can decline.

"I'm going to take you to my boat. You can dry off there while we make the arrangements." He stands up and starts the engine.

I raise my hand to tell him to take us back to shore but Leah stops me. "No, Emma. You lost our money and you lost our way home. I am not spending the next seven days standing in an embassy, God knows where, getting a new passport issued." Her tone is deep, bossy, and in full lecture mode. "The man saved your life. If he wanted you dead, he would have watched you drown. We are following him back to his boat and that is final."

Her brows are closed in and her button nose is pointed down.

"We don't even know where he's taking us," I whisper entirely too loudly. Obviously he can hear our conversation, but if he is a madman I don't need him knowing I think he's a madman.

"My boat is right there. I'll take you on board, we'll make a few calls, and then I'll take you back to shore." He points his finger at the boat he is talking about.

Leah looks over and I know her mouth is open just as wide as mine is.

The American is taking us to the yacht.

Yes, the yacht.
The sex yacht.
Holy cannoli.
“Ems, we are so going with him.”

chapter THREE

My eyes are bugging out of my head as I stare back at the American who saved me. Is this the guy we saw having crazy freaky sex yesterday?

Flashbacks of an ass pumping and grinding replay in my head. Looking at the guy in front me, he's certainly in shape but he seems much larger than the man I saw through the binoculars. If this man in front of me were on top of a woman I wouldn't have been able to see her at all. He would have engulfed her. Clearly my depth perception is off.

I'm surprised, really. He doesn't seem like the dirty sex kind. I mean, yeah, I just met him, but he is really quite . . . heroic.

I can't believe its taken this long for me to appreciate what he did for me. A complete stranger dove into the water and saved me from drowning.

"Thank you," I say, entirely too late.

Even with the low roar of the engine he can hear me clearly.

"Just doing my job," he says.

I look at him, puzzled by his answer. "Sorry about your wallet. Hope nothing was ruined."

"Nothing that can't be replaced," he says, offering his free hand that is not driving the boat. "Devon."

I shake it back, awkwardly from my seated position. "I'm Emma. And this is my sister, Leah."

"Definitely had you pegged for sisters. You look exactly alike."

Leah smiles at the comment and shakes his hand as well. "Were you hoping to see the Blue Grotto?"

"I can see it another time."

Leah and I don't have a chance to feel terrible for causing Devon to change his plans because we are quickly approaching the yacht and our gazes are drawn elsewhere.

OMEGA.

The name appears in large type across the starboard side of the boat written in black over an omega symbol.

Two grand staircases line the back of the boat. In between the staircases is an area, hidden from us yesterday, where a rectangular pool sits on a covered deck.

We circle the boat and wind around it, getting a closeup view. The ship is unlike anything I've ever seen. It's like a new-age luxury yacht. Almost the length of a football field, the bottom half is all black with two upper decks that look like they're made of steel.

Three quarters through the boat, there's a break in the ship's middle deck to reveal an open seating area, shaded by an upper deck bridge on the third level. Looking up, I see a helicopter parked up top.

There are two garages open in the foreground of the boat. Instead of parking the boat we're on in the garage, Devon pulls up beside an open docking area.

Slowing the engine, he skillfully idles up to the dock, and a much smaller man in a white uniform holds out his hands, helping Leah and I exit the speed boat onto the yacht. Devon follows us as the smaller man switches places with him to park the boat in the garage.

Leah and I follow Devon into the outside seating area on the lowest deck. It looks like a resort, with cabana-style lounge chairs of teak and white surrounding the pool. There is a bar and a dining area as well.

Devon walks inside and we wait on the deck until he returns wearing a dry shirt and shorts, carrying two large white towels with large omega symbols on them. Leah wraps her towel around her shoulders and I tuck mine around my chest, securing it under my armpits.

Leah follows Devon inside the cabin and I am right behind them, walking lopsided from only having one shoe. We walk through a living room bigger than the apartment I had back in Pittsburgh. The walls are paneled in shiny, rich mahogany cut in modern lines. Looking up, I see a honeycombed ceiling illuminated with soft white light. Around the room, furnishings of white creamy leather look like they haven't ever been sat in.

We pass another bar area, a media room, a gym, and down a corridor where two staterooms sit at the end of the hallway. If I wasn't so in awe of my surroundings I'd be nervous about the situation. You know, following a stranger down the hallway of a floating vessel. But if I were to die, this isn't a bad place for it to happen.

Devon stops and holds his hand out, motioning for us to enter one of the bedrooms. Leah and I do, but Devon remains outside.

"There are robes and towels in the bathroom. You can shower and warm up in there. I'll have someone come for your clothes so we can dry them. There's a phone on the nightstand. If you call the hotel, they can get your passport numbers. It will help expedite the process." Devon's voice is authoritative. He's being polite, not entering the room. It's very southern gentleman. I appreciate his boundaries. "Can I get you anything?"

"No. Thank you. This is more than accommodating."

With a curt nod of his head, Devon closes the door, leaving Leah and I inside the stateroom of, what I can only guess is a multimillion-dollar yacht.

"Holy crap, where are we?" Leah starts to laugh.

I let out a huge breath of air and an hour's worth of tension. "When you dragged me out of bed this morning, I was not expecting this. How loaded is this guy?"

"Crazy rich. Did you see the sauna we passed by the pool? It was like a spa."

"What about the artwork that was in the living room, or whatever that was? I'm pretty sure those were originals."

"This is only the bottom floor. I'm dying to see what's upstairs." Leah looks around the room, opening drawers.

"What are you doing?" I pull her hand away from a handle.

"Trying to see how the mega-rich live." She says, and then her eyes bug out as realization strikes her face. "Do you think the girl is still here?"

I blink at her until I understand who she's talking about. "I would hope if he were getting busy with some woman last night, he'd have the decency to let her stay the night."

"Devon was not who I saw yesterday. Trust me. I watched for a long time and that was not him," she says, stressing the word long. "And the girl, if I see her, I'd definitely notice her. She was tall and thin with jet black hair and—"

I snap my fingers to gather Leah out of her trance. "Listen, we can't stay here. You get on the phone and call the hotel. I'll shower and then we'll switch. I need to get out of these clothes. I'm starting to smell like fish."

Leah leans into me and takes a sniff, pinching her nostrils together. "Yeah, you do." She lifts up her arms. "How about me?"

I return the favor and give her a once over. "Same. I'll be quick." I say and turn around and head into the bathroom. Flicking on the light and locking the door, I look around the space.

This is a bathroom. It's a guest bathroom. It's a guest bathroom on a boat. And it's nicer than any latrine I have ever been in my entire life.

I don't know a lot about rich people. Leah and I grew up in a normal, middle-class neighborhood. Our dad is a history teacher and our mom a homemaker. We lived in a three-bedroom house with one full bath. It's the same bathroom I've been using the last six months since having to leave my home and job in Pittsburgh and go home for rehabilitation and mourning. It's a good bathroom. It gets the job done. But what I am quickly learning about rich people is they know how to bathe in style.

A marble steam shower big enough for four, a vanity, a toilet, and a bidet, plus a mahogany dressing table with everything a guest could possibly need during her stay. Deodorants, creams, shampoos, soaps, perfumes . . . yup, it's all here.

On a teak bench there's a plush robe and a pair of slippers. Two of each, actually. After my shower, where I thoroughly scrub using sea salts and lather my face in seaweed, I wrap my hair in a fresh towel and put on the robe and slippers. I give my hair a quick dry using the blow dryer and brush it straight. I have to remind myself not to be too long. Leah needs to get in here and we have to get back to the hotel. I apply some of the creams to my face and body before opening the door.

"Long much?" Leah asks, her tone sarcastic. She is wearing nothing but the towel Devon gave her earlier.

"Once you go in there, you are not going to want to come out. Where are your clothes?" I ask.

"A maid came by asking for them. She said she'd dry them for us. Thanks for locking the door because I had to drop my drawers in front of her." Leah holds up a piece of paper. "Anyway, I have the passport numbers. I'm gonna hop in the shower while you bring this to Devon."

"Sure. As soon as our clothes come back."

She leans into me, her hands on her hips. "That could be an hour. You are beyond covered up. That robe hides everything."

I look down. She's right. The robe falls at my calves and wraps around my body, snuggly up to my neck. "Fine." I say, taking the paper from her hands.

Exiting back into the corridor, I follow the way we came in, peering into rooms looking for Devon.

I search all of the areas on the lower level we're on with no sight of him. In the large seating area there's a staircase. I grab the black banister and walk up the steps.

The second floor is what I can only assume is the main living area. A grander living room is up here, similar in style to the one downstairs with more seating and a wall of windows leading to an outdoor deck with an outdoor dining area. I turn to the opposite direction and walk over the indoor dining room.

Devon is in neither of these spaces so I continue on, passing a gourmet kitchen that rivals anything I've seen on TV.

I blow out a breath and try not to think about how awkward it is to be walking around a stranger's boat wearing nothing but a robe.

Yes, not wearing underwear in someone else's home is super weird.

I call out Devon's name but he doesn't answer. In fact, no one does.

Where are all the people who work on the boat?

I follow a wide hallway, peering into more rooms, trying not to look like I'm spying. I really am just trying to find Devon. There's an office, two other staterooms, and a butler's pantry.

Man, if someone sees me back here, they'll think I'm trying to steal stuff.

I am about to turn around and head back downstairs when something catches my eye from a doorway left partially open. I backtrack and head toward the room at the end of the hall. I push open the door and am taken aback.

The room has a ceiling twice as high as the others. It sits at the front of the boat, with floor to ceiling windows, looking over the water. The view alone would make anyone stop and stare.

Except for me.

In front of the windows is the object that caught my attention.

A cello.

Okay, most people wouldn't stop and stare at a string instrument but they're not me. The cello is part of the violin family. The range of the instruments are similar but the tone quality and physical size distinguish them from one another. The violin is played under the chin, but the cello is played while seated and placed between the legs. With its lower octave sound, I always thought of it as the violin's sexy and sensual lover. Don't judge. It's just the music geek in me.

The violin was my passion for fifteen years. In grade school we were encouraged to play an instrument. My teacher played the violin for us and I asked to try it. After a few lessons, I was hooked.

While most people think of the violin as being purely classical, I took my love for it one step further, playing jazz, rock, and with the use of an amp, heavy metal rock. I was accepted at a young age to the Pittsburgh Music Academy and my mother drove me two hours, three times a week so I could have the best musical education money can buy. We didn't have a lot of money, but my parents knew it was my calling. My dream was to create a musical genre for the pop scene that no one had ever heard of. The sound was fresh, fun, and bold.

I was good. I was damn good because I loved it. But one accident, a broken hand and a crushed nerve left me unable to pick up a bow. If I curl my palm to a certain degree, and hold it just a second too long, pain shoots so far up my arm I want to scream.

Turning away from the cello, I walk to a far corner of the room where there is a large grand piano. It's black, sleek and I know without checking it's perfectly tuned. No one who owns an instrument as fine as this leaves it untuned. I take a seat and lift the lid to the keys. The ivory feels so smooth under my fingers.

Just being this close to one makes me feel jittery and excited. I'm like a drug addict falling off the wagon—this is my line of cocaine.

My mom has been trying to make me play something, anything. She doesn't care if it's the drums, the sax . . . a trombone. She just wants me to play. Said it would be good for me. But I couldn't.

Now, sitting here, in this foreign room, alone with this beast of dark musical power, I have an intense desire to put my hands down and . . .

Play.

Slowly at first, I let my fingers push down on the keys. I close my eyes and my hands dance. I play a melody that pops in my head. It's not one I know, it's one that is just playing. The piano is not my instrument. If I ever played, and it was so very rare, it was like this. Just a little melody from inside my head.

Using both hands, I play a few chords and let them harmonize with one another. The sound is nice and I'm slightly surprised by that. I feel my lips tip up and my head falls to the side as the music takes over me.

It's unexpected how good it feels to play. My fingers move faster and my hands travel up and down the length of the piano, playing sequences I haven't heard in so long.

The wooden case surrounding the soundboard and metal strings vibrates and hums with each stroke of my fingers. The percussion resonates in my heart until the pain in my chest settles back in, causing me to slow down. I remove my hands from the keys and let my head fall forward.

This felt good but it's not for me. It will never make me feel whole again.

Letting the air puff out from my lips, I swallow, then lift my head to rise and go back to finding Devon.

But when I look up, I startle.

Standing in the center of the room is a man. He is tall and commanding. His face is serious and tense by the look of his square jaw and stern brows. A straight nose and full lips are accented by light hair and bronzed skin. His body is well built, broad at the top and narrow at the waist.

And if there's one thing I notice it's his piercing gaze.

So piercing because of golden eyes.

You know how yesterday I said the view of Capri was the most beautiful sight I had ever seen in my life?

I take that back.

He is the most beautiful thing I have ever, without a doubt, seen in my entire life.

chapter FOUR

"What are you doing?" Those full lips let out a sound that's deep, thick, manly, and frightening as all hell.

I freeze for a second before remembering what I came in here to do. Staggering my words, I try to form a coherent sentence. "I'm sorry. I was looking for Devon." I grab the paper off the top of the piano and hold it up. "I am supposed to bring this to him."

"Well, he's not in here, is he?" Golden Eyes looks right through me. Even referring to him like that in my head makes him sound like a character out of a James Bond movie.

He is intense and way too annoyed with my being here. He is wearing black shorts, a white polo, and boat shoes. I'm assuming he is one of the crew. Surely he must understand how overwhelming this boat can be to a newcomer.

"I was looking for him when I saw the cello . . . I just had to see it, and then I saw the piano, and I . . . I just had to play." I am rambling like a ninny. What is wrong with me?

It's the eyes. They are definitely setting me off-kilter.

"You play the cello?" he asks.

"Yes . . . no. Well, not any more. It's a long, awful story. And the piano was just calling me. I can't explain it."

"You play beautifully," he says, his voice deep and melodic. Ugh, that sounds so ridiculous, even in my head.

I stop to think about what he just said. I don't play beautifully. I suck at the piano. Clearly this guy needs to be schooled in music if he thought that was good.

"Thank you." Even though he has no idea what he's talking about, it's best to be polite.

I rise from the bench and become very aware of my attire when his gaze skims my robe. I swear I see his pupils dilate and I suddenly feel very, very naked.

"Can you tell me where your boss is?" I ask, trying to break the unwanted stare.

His head pops up. "My boss?"

"Devon. I don't know his last name. My sister and I fell into the water and I lost my bag. He was kind enough to bring us back here and let us change. I think someone is drying our clothes too."

The man looks at me perplexed. "Let me get this straight. My boss—Devon, you say—rescued you and brought you back here to change?"

Clearly this guy is not going to bring me to his boss until I explain the whole story. "My bag fell in the water and it's gone. We lost our passports, money, credit cards, everything."

"We?"

"My sister Leah and I. She's downstairs."

He is just staring—hot-molten-lava-of-lust staring—and it makes the hair on the back of my neck stand up. His right arm is bent at the elbow and he is massaging his wrist with his left hand.

"Devon said he knew someone at the consulate and could help with the passports." I hold the paper out to him, again, and try not to make direct eye contact for fear I'll go into cardiac arrest. "These are our passport numbers. If you could just give them to him I'll go back downstairs and wait in the room."

Golden Eyes takes a few steps closer. His hand brushes mine when he takes the paper; I swear I actually gasp when his skin touches mine.

Why am I acting like this? I must have really hit my head hard when I fell into the water earlier.

He takes the paper but doesn't open it.

He's just staring.

And I can't help but stare right back.

Mi sono persa.

I am lost.

Someone walking into the room interrupts the moment. I look over to see Devon enter wearing the clean polo shirt he put on earlier but has changed into a pair of black pants. "Asher, excuse me, I—"

"Ah, Mr. Smith. I've been looking for you." Golden Eyes turns to face Devon.

Devon halts on his way in and looks at the scene in front of him. He must be wondering why I am standing in this room, where apparently I'm not supposed to be, in nothing but a robe, with one of his crew.

Golden Eyes turns to face me, and offers a hand, "I'm Asher," he says, with a tone of uncertainty. "I work for Mr. Smith."

It's an odd time for an introduction, but I'll take it. I hold out my hand and shake his, feeling the warmth of his smooth, yet manly hand. "Emma."

Devon looks back and forth between the two of us. "I'm sorry, I think I've missed something."

"Not at all, sir. I was just making the rounds and found this beautiful woman in your music room," Asher says, leaning into Devon. "Your very private music room where no one is allowed."

I open my mouth, feeling awful for intruding. "I am sorry about that. I was just looking for you and I got caught up. After everything you did for us today, I can't believe I was so rude." My voice is set to a pleading.

Devon waits a long moment before answering. Turning his attention to Asher he says, "May I have a word with you?"

"Yes, sir," Asher says with a cocky smile. It's odd for the level of tension that is currently festering. The two men leave me standing in the music room, still behind the piano trying to figure out what to do. I pretty much have only two options. Stay or go.

I feel like an idiot. I have to get out of here. The look on Asher's face was of dissonance and I do not want to face him again. Once he tells Devon, or Mr. Smith or whatever it is I'm supposed to call him, about how I was sneaking around his yacht, Leah and I will be asked to leave.

Opting for option two, I open the door and exit into the hallway, relieved not to see Devon or Asher anywhere. I walk down the hallway and head through the main areas, down the stairs and walk my way down the hallway to the room where Leah is.

I'm not in the room ten seconds before Leah is on me.

"Where the hell have you been?"

"You don't want to know. Are our clothes dry?" I ask, making my way around her and over to the phone.

"Not yet. What's up with you?" Leah's hair is dry and styled in the perfect way she always has it. From the smell of her she sampled some of the lotions and potions as lavishly as I did.

Sitting down on the bed, I hold up the phone to dial our hotel to see if they can arrange a transport from the boat. "I think I majorly overstepped my boundaries."

"What did you do?" she asks in a high-pitched voice.

I shrug my shoulders, embarrassed. My voice is sheepish. "Played his piano."

"Either that's a euphemism for something I desperately want to hear about, or . . ." She pauses, "Emma, did you really play a piano?"

I shrug again and slowly put down the phone.

Leah moves over to the bed and takes a seat beside me. "That's really good to hear."

The look in her eyes is one of relief. It makes me feel terrible to see it there. Relief should be a good thing but it's a reminder of the worry I've seen on her face before—and on everyone in my family, to be exact.

I wave my hands in front of me, wiping the air to change the tone. "Change of subject. This guy walked in on me. He was beyond pissed I was even in there, let alone playing on what had to be the world's most beautiful Steinway. I mean, it was ebony and had to have been a model D—" The look on Leah's face lets me know I've totally lost her. "Anyway, apparently it's Devon's private room that no one is supposed to be in."

"No shit," Leah says.

"Yes. And of course the guy was totally intimidating and I was a total mess."

"Was he hot?" she asks.

I lean back. "Excuse me?"

"He was hot," she concludes, nodding her head and pointing her finger at me. "You have your I-just-saw-a-hot-guy face on right now. How hot was he?"

I push her away from me and she falls back on the bed. "Shut it. He was not hot."

"Liar." She says with a laugh.

I look down at my slipper. "Fine. He was . . . cute."

Leah shoots up from her spot on the bed. "I knew it!"

With both hands, I run my fingers through my hair, pushing it away from my face. "Not the point. Devon is totally mad right now and probably isn't going to help us."

Leah calms down and takes in the gravity of what I'm saying. "God, that sucks. But the guy was super hot, right?"

"You have a one-track mind."

She gives me a full-teeth, wicked smile and I push her back onto the bed. She continues to prod me with uncomfortable questions about what the guy looked like and I answer them, grateful she doesn't want to discuss how I was playing the piano.

Her current fit of giggles is interrupted by a knock at the door. We both sit up straight and look over at the source of the knocking. We play one quick and silent round of rock, paper, scissors to decide who should get it. I lose.

I open the door and am taken back by the large figure standing in the doorway holding our folded, dried clothes. Devon.

"Your clothes are dry," he says, handing the garments to me. They're still warm and have that fresh dryer smell. "Your passports will be ready for you tomorrow. I'll have one of the crew pick them up for you. Were you planning on leaving before then?"

I swallow back my surprise that he is still helping us. "Um, no. We'll be here through the end of the week."

Devon nods and hands the garments to me. I take them.

He pauses for a second in the doorway, seeming unsure as what to do next. My free hand is on the door, anxious to close it and get back to getting the hell out of here.

Devon's hand hovers over his pocket for a moment before reaching in and pulling out an envelope.

"This is for you."

Confused, I release my hand from the door and reach out to take the envelope. "For me? I can't imagine what . . ."

Christ on crutches.

My thumb pushes open the top fold of the paper as my eyes skim through the inside of the envelope. There has to be a hundred different bills in here, all of various amounts. Off the top of my head I would say Devon just handed me an envelope filled with five thousand euro.

No sooner is the money in my hand than I am forcing it back into Devon's.

"Absolutely not. I can not accept money from you." Sure, he has tons of it, but to just throw it at me like a two-bit hooker? Well, maybe that's a little of an exaggeration. I didn't sleep with him. Unless he thinks . . . "You must have the wrong idea. Thank you for the help with the passports"—I hold up the clothes in my arm—"thank you for your dryer, but my sister and I would like to head back to shore, please."

I hope my words aren't rude. He seems like a nice guy—but shoving money at us? Something doesn't seem right.

Devon nods to both Leah and me from the threshold. "Mateo, our deck hand will escort you back to shore. My presence is needed elsewhere. Good luck, ladies." We thank him again for his hospitality, which he accepts, and then close the door as he leaves us so we can change.

With my back to the door, I lean against it and throw Leah her clothes. "Get dressed quick. We are getting off this boat as soon as possible."

chapter FIVE

Waking up in our hotel bed this morning was pure bliss. Leah let me sleep in and didn't try to throw me out in search of our next adventure.

It's probably because we have no money.

Gah.

Yesterday wasn't a dream.

You know that moment, the morning after a horrible event, when you wake up and for a split second you wonder if everything that happened the day before was all just a horrible dream? Well, that was me ten seconds ago.

Now, I'm slamming my face into the pillow at the realization that I dropped my purse into the Mediterranean.

I roll over and let my arms splay out on the bed, taking in our current predicament. Our passports will be delivered sometime today, so Leah and I will be able to return home from our honeymoon, or sisters sabbatical, or whatever you want to call this. Leah was able to FaceTime with Adam using her iPad so her knight in shining armor is taking care of wiring us cash. How that is getting to us, I have no idea.

Last night wasn't a complete bust. Since our hotel room is hooked up to a credit card, we ordered room service and a bottle of wine. The crazy thing was, while I was expecting Leah to ream into me for losing our things, she didn't. It's like she's afraid I'm going to break. Instead, she went on and on about how we fell in the water and she filled me in on all the details I missed.

Apparently, when I let go of Leah's hand, I fell backward into the water and smacked my head on the small wooden boat we were supposed to board. My falling caused Leah, who was already leaning over to try and catch me, to fall over too. She said she was back on our boat rather quickly, and when she turned around to help me out, I wasn't there.

Her face went so pale as she told the story I had to reach over and grab her hand. She said she started screaming that her sister was drowning and no one did anything. She was just about to jump in the water herself when a man, Devon, came up for air, with me in tow, tugging me back to a boat that was away from her.

Leah didn't even see Devon dive into the water. She said he must have done it as soon as I fell in. That also means he was under the water for a long time looking for me.

I remember hitting my head. Or shall I say, I remember the pain. First, the pain was in my hand from when I grabbed on to Leah. Then I felt like I was kicked in the cranium.

The water was murky so I didn't know if I was blacking out or just having a hard time seeing through the haze in the water. When Devon put his arms around me, I was floating lifelessly. He made it seem so easy, the way he grabbed me and lifted me up and out of that water. That breath of air I took, breaking the surface, was long, deep and so desperately needed. I must have been on some adrenalin rush because, until then, I didn't even know I couldn't breathe.

Leah kept on telling me how I was the strongest person she ever met. In return, I kept on drinking.

Luckily, today's hangover is nonexistent, thanks to Leah letting me sleep it off.

I lift myself up and look around the room. The curtains to the glass door are pushed open, which means Leah must have gone out for a walk. Looking at the space at the foot of the door I see Leah's shoes she wore yesterday and the slippers I wore home. Shoeless Emma chose to wear them instead of hobbling on one Top-Sider.

Shame. I loved those shoes.

Leah is still not back when I exit the bathroom, freshly showered and wearing a pair of navy shorts and a red tank top. I pull my hair back in a ponytail and am sliding on a pair of flip flops when Leah comes back into the room.

"Good, you're dressed!" she says, wearing a denim shirtdress, holding a newspaper and a coffee cup in her hands. "I went down for breakfast and picked this up for you."

I take the coffee and paper from her and take a sip. "Thank you. At least we know we can have three squares here at the hotel if the money doesn't come through in time."

"It's about five in the morning, Ohio time, so I don't expect to hear from Adam until this evening."

I pinch my mouth to the side of my face. "Looks like there's not much we can do but walk around."

"Oh, to the contrary my dear sister." She says, walking over the mirror, "We're finishing our boat tour today."

"How?" I ask into my coffee cup.

"Devon sent a note to the hotel this morning. They gave it to me when I was in the lobby. We're expected at the marina at noon." Checking her makeup, she applies some fresh lip gloss.

I point the newspaper at her like it's a sword. "Absolutely not."

Her shoulders fall and she turns to me with her head tilted to the side. "And why is that?"

"Seriously? I made a huge fool out of myself. He was pissed yesterday and, if you ask me, we have taken way too much from the man already. Come to think of it, isn't it a little creepy that he did all these things for us? I mean, what does he want in return? He wants something in return, Leah. I bet he's expecting something and I, my friend, am not giving it to him." I cross my arms in front of my body, careful not to drop my coffee cup.

Leah looks back at me; her body hasn't moved since I started my little rant. Pale blue eyes narrow at me as she stands there, quiet which is, as you know, so not like Leah.

She waits a minute and then straightens her body and lays it into me in a calm and very controlled voice. "Do you want to talk serious, Emma? The man dove off a boat to dive down, God knows how far, to save you from drowning. He also went out of his way to use a personal contact to get us passports. Passports! He was an absolute gentleman to us on that boat. In fact, he wouldn't even enter the room."

She noticed that, too, huh?

Leah continues. "You say he was pissed at you in the music room but he was nothing but friendly to us when we left. It sounds more like that other guy you saw was pissed. Yet out of everyone, you know who has the right to *really* be pissed?"

I look at her, shaking my head.

Leah points to herself. "Me. I should. But I'm not. The reason I'm not is because the universe wants us to have a good time. It's like someone somewhere knows exactly why we're here and they want us to have the trip of the century. We have a guardian angel and he is making sure we're okay."

I really like the idea of our guardian angel.

"Ems, yesterday was awesome. We fell into the sea. We were on a crazy sick yacht. When we go home, we are going to have the best story to tell. And now this man, who has a big heart and a hell of a lot of money, has invited us to finish our tour. He didn't even say he would be there. The note only said that a boat would be waiting for us at the marina. So put on a smile and grab that godforsaken fanny pack, because we are going on that boat!"

Damn—little sister knows how to prove a point.

Looks like we're going on a boat ride.

Safe to say I'll be leaving the fanny pack at home.

When I finish my coffee we walk down the stone steps to the marina. This time, we go into each of the shops and look around at the various items for sale. It's for the best we don't have any money because we would spend way too much buying tourist items for our family. Even though we aren't buying anything, Leah thinks it will be fun to get silly and try on the various T-shirts, scarves, and fedoras that are on display.

It is a hot day, the sun beating down, warming the skin. Tourists are wearing big floppy hats and sunglasses. I kick myself for leaving mine in the room.

Leah and I make it the dock of the marina promptly at twelve o'clock and follow the instructions on the note as to where we should meet our boat.

Even if we didn't have instructions we would have been able to figure out where we needed to go quickly. Amongst the older sailboats and motorboats is a very modern speedboat of black and silver, standing out like a supermodel in an old-age home. There is no ignoring the sleekness, newness, and absolute beauty of the boat. It looks like a bullet with its long, curved bow and is accented with see-through black glass and chrome.

The boat Devon drove yesterday was really nice but this piece of nautical transportation is down right sexy.

Sexy.

Sexy.

Sexy.

And I am no longer talking about the boat.

chapter SIX

Leah must have the same reaction because she gasps out loud, and grabs my arm. We both halt as a man appears, climbing up from the inside cabin. He has on a black crew-neck shirt and light gray shorts. His blond hair is perfectly styled back, accenting the prominent cheekbones and square jaw of his face.

His arms flex out as he reaches around the captain's chair and checks the instruments on the dashboard. His back muscles come into full view through the thin material of his shirt and I get an eyeful of something I hadn't seen yesterday. A perfectly defined ass.

He turns around just in time to see Leah and I gawking at him. My only saving grace is he wearing dark sunglasses that cover those golden eyes.

Leah turns her back to the boat and stands so close to me her shoulder rubs against mine. Leaning into my ear she asks, "Is that the guy you met yesterday?"

I nod my head yes.

"The one who was mad you were in the music room?"

I nod my head yes, again.

"And yesterday was the first time you ever saw him?"

I nod my head yes, again, even though it's a ridiculous question.

The bow of her mouth puckers out and she looks down as if trying to work something out. She opens her mouth and then closes it again before looking at me. It's for the briefest of moments, yet it feels like she's studying me for an eternity.

"Okay, then." With a nod, Leah turns around and faces the boat, pulling my hand up to the stern. "Hello! I'm Leah."

Asher steps forward and meets us by the back of the boat. He gives Leah a polite nod and then turns his face toward me. I can feel his gaze drilling me through those damned glasses.

"Emma, pleasure to see you again." His full lips are curved up on the side.

Leah looks at me, and then Asher, before giving me a nudge on my lower back. "After you, sis."

My body jerks slightly forward. Asher holds out a hand and I take it as I cautiously move my feet from the stone dock to the boat. I do not want any sort of mishap as I had yesterday.

His large hand holds onto mine, steady, as I climb on board. Sensing my unease, Asher pulls me toward him until I am flush to his front and wraps a hand around my waist. My body reacts in a non-lady like way to the hardness of his chest. I back away quickly and take a seat on the white cushion of the seating area of the boat.

When I am safely in place, Asher turns back to the stern and offers a hand to Leah. She puts out her hand and then quickly retrieves it before grabbing her stomach.

"Oh no." She grumbles, bending over slightly.

I swivel my body around in my seat. "What's the matter?"

"I feel sick. I can't go." Her hand rubs her tummy and her cheeks sallow in.

"Let's go back to the hotel." I rise from my seat but Leah puts her hand up in the air.

"*No!*" She exclaims, then retrieves her sickly composure. "No, please. You enjoy the ride. Devon went through a lot of trouble and I'd hate to waste it." She turns to Asher, "Please, take care of my sister."

If the sun weren't glaring in my direction, I could swear she winked at him.

Asher smiles at Leah and I think my heart just leapt out of my chest. Damn, the man has a great smile.

Before I have a chance to catch my thoughts and become a rational human being, Asher has the boat started and we are driving away from the dock. I turn to face Leah—she's waving a bon voyage from the dock and grinning from ear to ear.

I stare back at her as the denim devil gets smaller and smaller.

There is no way she knew Asher was going to be here. One look at him and she goes from needing to be on her next adventure to throwing me to the wolves.

Or in this case a golden god.

What is up with that? I mean, seriously, what is wrong with her? For three days she guilt trips me into doing whatever she wants. I have to get out of bed because I'm ruining her honeymoon. I have to go on Devon's yacht because I lost our passports. Today, I'm on this boat ride because we have no money and it's all my fault.

For someone who is so worried about me, she certainly has no respect for what I want to do.

Sitting here is definitely not where I want to be. Leah wanted to be here. But why isn't she here? Because of the supernatural being driving the boat. She thinks it's what I need. Like meeting a guy and getting some action on vacation is going to change the course of my year.

Well, it's not. Nothing is going to change what's been done.

Not even the gorgeousness of his taut physique staring me in the face.

Like I'd even. I was with the same guy for four years. I can count on my hand the amount of boyfriends I've had and I'd still have room for more. I don't do random hookups and certainly not with men in foreign countries.

"You can sit up here if you'd like," Asher calls out over the sound of the engine. The boat isn't going very fast, since we're close to the marina, but it's loud enough he has to speak up and out over it.

An uneasy feeling settles over my stomach. I am not ready to be charming and conversational. With my sister, it's easy. She knows everything about me. But with a stranger, it's uncomfortable.

The last time I had a conversation with Asher I was a blubbering mess. Not because of his hotness—that sort of thing doesn't make me all wobbly like it does some girls. No, I hated being caught in my most vulnerable state.

I stand up and carefully move over to the first mate seat on Asher's left. I am relieved when I make it the short distance without going overboard.

There is a large space between us as the door to the cabin below is in the middle. I slide up the seat and settle in for the ride. There is less wind in this seat, as the black glass surrounding the area blocks the breeze, yet I know when we really start to move I'm going to be very happy I wore my hair up today.

I look over at Asher. His face is set sternly. There is no glimpse of the smile he gave Leah. I bet he's pissed he has to spend the afternoon with me. I know he's only here because his boss told him to take us out.

With his eyes on the water and not on me, I get a good look at him. For someone with a masculine face, his profile makes him look kind. Soft skin over a square jaw that could chisel granite. High, wide cheekbones are offset by a tiny bit of stubble that makes them a touch rugged. Sensual lips are slightly pursed, but there's no denying their volume.

He bites his lip, not in a sexy way. Actually, I've never found lip biting to be sexy. I straighten my back and look ahead at the water.

It's hard to imagine a man as attractive as Asher would have a free afternoon to take me around on a boat. Then again, this is his job. I can only imagine that someone with his looks, traveling around the world on a yacht, would get a lot of tail. He's probably dreaming about where else he can be right now.

I open my mouth to tell him to take us back.

"You like speed?" he asks, before I'm able to get a word out.

"Excuse me?"

"Speed. Do you like speed?" He repeats, his eyes still focused on the water ahead.

Speed. Going fast. Driving erratically. Hitting things. Bodies flown. Hands crushed. Lives lost. Dreams expired.

No. The answer is no.

I like control. I like slow. I like safe.

"*No!*" I yell, grabbing onto the handlebar to my left and swallow hard. "The speed you're going is just fine."

By the look of Asher's jowls sticking out from the side of his face that was, clearly, the wrong answer. He raises his chin and turns the wheel of the boat, keeping the same speed as before.

He continues to drive, following the perimeter of the island past the limestone and sandstone rock that make up the island. The water in front of us is a gorgeous turquoise color. It must be the way the sun is reflecting off the sea because it is so much bluer than it was yesterday.

I inhale the smell of salt permeating the air. If I were to play a concerto it would be the Ernest Bloch, so full of heart and triumph. I hear the crescendo with each crashing wave and spray of white foam as my gaze travels up to three dramatic towering rock formations off the coast. Standing erect, the rocks rise out of the sea as if sculpted by wind and sea. I've seen the image on brochures. They must have significance to the island.

"What are those?" I ask, pointing at the rock formation.

Asher shrugs his shoulder and turns his wheel to the right, away from the rocks and toward the island. "I don't know."

Figures.

Just then, his cell phone rings and he looks at the screen, briefly, before answering it. It's a rude thing to do—talk on the phone with company—but he hasn't struck me as the courteous kind yet.

"Yeah." He answers. "What do you mean she didn't get on the plane?" His voice rises over the low roaring engine. "Then charter one."

Hopefully he doesn't talk to Devon like that, otherwise his ass should be fired. Without saying good-bye, he ends the call and tosses the phone into a compartment near his seat.

I cross my arms and sit back in my seat. This is the most ridiculous boating experience I've ever been on, and I'm counting yesterday's disaster. Devon must have a serious flaw in his judgment of character.

Asher drives the boat closer to the island but there is no shore or docking area in sight. Instead, there is a large opening in the rocks, peeking out from the bottom and half submerged in the ocean. It is similar to the one we saw yesterday at the Blue Grotto, but much larger.

Lowering the speed, he guides the boat inside the cave and then turns off the engine. The boat is too big to go inside the grotto so we are drifting in an alcove of rock that provides shade from the sun. The water here is a transparent aqua, which means it must be pretty shallow.

There is no one else in sight. No other boats or tourists groups. No sightseers on foot either, though I can't imagine you'd be able to walk here from the island. It looks like this is one of those rare and special places you can only access from the water.

Asher hits a button on the console and there is a rumbling heard from beneath as he lowers an anchor. He raises the sunglasses off his eyes and onto his head as he swings around his chair and walks over to the seating area in the back of the boat. Bending over, he lifts the cushion of one of the bench seats and reaches down. I'm admiring the way his forearm muscles twitch when he raises a cooler out of the compartment and puts the cushion back in place.

He places the cooler on the floor and opens the top, rifling through the items inside and takes out two bottles of Pellegrino and two oranges.

Palming the two oranges in one hand, he holds out a bottle of Pellegrino with the other, pointing it toward me in invitation. I nod my head and stand, my legs wobbly. I take a few steps toward him; grab the water bottle and head back to my chair.

"I don't bite." I can detect the sarcasm in his baritone.

Sure you don't. I turn back around and see one brow is tilted up. Other than that his expression is unreadable.

"Want one?" He offers me one of the oranges.

Deciding not to be a completely ungrateful brat, I accept the orange and take a seat on the bench to the right of him, setting my water next to my hip and curl my left leg under me. Focusing all of my attention on the orange, I pierce the skin with my nail and slide my finger down the side until the inside of the orange is peering back at me from beneath the thick rind.

The hairs on my neck stand the way they do when you know you're being watched. And from the proximity of the man sitting to my left, it's not difficult to feel his intense gaze.

I turn my head and meet him eye for eye. In this lighting his eyes are the color of honey wheat, but intense nonetheless. My head flinches back to observe my orange and I find myself biting my lip this time.

Curling my finger over a stray hair that came loose, I hook it back behind my ear and take the opportunity to look over at those unwavering eyes. Feeling incredibly self-conscious, I turn my head to admire the surroundings. "What is this place?"

"I don't know."

My mouth opens and I try to hold my tongue, but of course, I can't. "You are the worst tour guide ever."

Asher leans into my left shoulder and his body heat makes my already warm skin burn. He smells of sea and soap; I could drink him in. "I have a secret."

I raise my eyebrows in interest.

"I'm not a tour guide." He says before leaning back in his seat and opening his Pellegrino. The opening of the bottle perches on his mouth as his lips wrap around it to take a sip.

Blinking back any erotic thought that might come to my mind I gather my wits. "So what are you? I mean, what do you do for Devon . . . Mr. Smith? Are you like his assistant?"

Lowering the bottle, he tilts his head, looking back at me with an odd expression. "What if I told you I was his bodyguard?"

I let out a laugh and immediately correct myself. That was rude of me. I cough back my smile and am met with an unamused Asher. I let out one of those throat gurgles you do when you need to find your voice and swallow. "I'd say that due to the size of him, I doubt Mr. Smith needs a bodyguard."

Asher stares back at me for a second before shrugging his right shoulder and nodding into the air. He lifts the bottle to his mouth again and I watch as his Adam's apple bobs with each gulp.

I let out another breath of air and fiddle with my orange again letting my thumb graze under the sliced skin and peeling back a strand.

"So what do you do for him?"

Asher crosses his leg over his knee. "A little of everything. Mostly, I make sure people don't wander into rooms they don't belong."

My stomach drops and I swallow back the awful feeling creeping up my windpipe. I already apologized for that. There's no reason for him to be such a jerk about it. "Why is the room off-limits?"

His jaw moves from side to side and I'm glad he doesn't have his sunglasses on or else I'd miss the way his eyes dance around for a second before he answers. "It's a place for reflection. A private retreat. No one is supposed to be in there."

My mouth smashes together and I tap and pluck my fingers on the skin of the fruit the way I would on the strings of an instrument. It's what I do when I have something on my mind. I play a song in my head while I work out whatever it is that's plaguing me, which right now is how a music room as grand as that could belong to Devon.

"What are you thinking so seriously about?" he asks, staring at my fingers moving about.

"I just didn't take him as a musician."

"Why is that?"

I think back to yesterday, when Devon saved me from drowning. His hands, they're big and bulky. Callused and course. They're the kind that save people. They don't seem like they tickle the ivories, if you know what I mean.

"It's in his hands," I offer.

"What about your hands?" Asher asks, not fazed by my comment. "Are they the hands of a musician?"

I look down at my palm and shake my head. "No. They're not."

"You were playing yesterday."

"Yeah." I laugh. "You said I played beautifully. If you knew anything about music, you'd know what was coming out of that piano was far from beautiful."

My body jerks about as I talk. My nerves shooting through me like a bolt of lightening.

"I didn't say the music was beautiful. I said you *played* beautifully."

Asher leans up from his seat and pushes into my personal space, making me feel all sorts of uncomfortable for all the wrong reasons. "When you play, you are beautiful. It's as if the melody possesses you and takes you on a journey. I was in awe just watching you." His words come across as authentic and honest, his eyes burning with meaning. I part my lips, yet have nothing to say.

Asher, on the other hand, fills in the silence. "That said, the melody itself was dismal. It doesn't take a savant to know you are not a musician."

My eyes shoot wide open and I balk back at him. Fine, he is right about it being dismal but how rude can you be?

"I'll have you know I graduated from Carnegie Mellon. I, sir, am a classically trained musician." My voice is loud and rough. I don't know why I even said the words. I'm sure he doesn't even know what Carnegie Mellon is.

"You? Well you certainly didn't train to be a pianist." He's baiting me.

"What does it matter to you?"

"I'm interested." His voice contradicts his words.

"It doesn't matter."

"It matters to me."

"That's ridiculous." I bite back.

"What do you play, Emma?" he asks sternly, his tone loud and commanding.

"I don't play anymore."

"Just say it."

"The violin!" I shout. I don't know why I get so dramatic. But this guy just gets under my skin. "I *played* the violin." My voice lowers a few octaves.

The air is tight with tension and the only sounds are the waves crashing around us. I go back to peeling my orange, one I have no desire of actually eating, and peel off an entire portion of the outside layer.

"I know. I googled you," he says, laughing at his own joke. It's infuriating. "Why don't you play anymore?"

Man, he just doesn't let up.

"I don't talk about that with anyone."

"Why not?"

I stand up and walk to the side of the boat, away from Asher, his intense regard and his probing questions. They sound harmless but every mention of music and every furrow of his brow makes me want to shut down and curl into my metaphorical fetal position.

"Just stop asking." I shoot him a stern look. It's the first time I've been able to hold steady eye contact with him. He's so intimidating I have a hard time doing so.

The boat bounces in the water as a small wake comes in. We each ride the tide, waiting for the other to say something. Asher is looking out, his eyes zoned in on a piece of granite that hangs down from the top of the rocky archway. It looks like a teardrop of glitter hanging down from the face of a goddess of stone. Yes, I've decided the island is a woman.

"You're from Pittsburgh." Asher's statement is just that. A statement, not a question.

"Two hours outside, originally. Moved to the city a few years ago." Pittsburgh has been my second home for fifteen years. Seven years ago I made it my permanent residence when I got my first apartment just off campus and stayed as I pursued my Master of Music. It was the best seven years of my life.

Asher leans forward and rests his elbows on his knees. Shaking his head, he lets out a smile. "Klavon's still there?"

I lift my head at the mention of the historic ice cream shop in the strip district. "Yeah, it's still there. You've been to Pittsburgh?"

He slowly nods his head and a hazy look passes over his face. "I was born there."

"Maybe we ran into each other before. I practically grew up there."

"I left when I was ten and never went back," he says in a dark undertone. His body slightly shakes with the thought and pulls back with a grin. "Besides I am much older than you. If we'd run into each other I would have been in a world of trouble."

Appraising the man in front of me, handsome, fit, and nicely dressed, I would guess he's older by a few years but not that much. "You're not that much older than me."

"You forget, I am in possession of your passport information. I know exactly how old you are."

I roll my eyes. "Geez, talk about an invasion of privacy."

"Wanna hear something cool?" he asks, and my ears perk up. "We have the same birthday."

"January twenty-third?" I ask even though he just said he knew we have the same birthday.

"January twenty-third."

That's interesting, I guess. What are the odds? Well, I know what the odds are. It's one out of three hundred and sixty five. But what are the odds I would travel to Italy and meet a gorgeous man who takes me on a boat ride to a sea cave and has the same birthday as me? My guess is one in a gazillion.

"Why did you leave Pittsburgh?" I ask, suddenly interested in his story.

Rising from his seat, Asher walks toward me. His long legs only require three steps to reach me. I stand up straight from where I am leaning on the side of the boat. The top of my head stands just under his chin. He leans forward and grabs the orange out of my hand, brushing his fingers with mine. Ripping off the rest of the peel, Asher breaks it in half and hands the other half back to me.

"I don't talk about that with anyone," he answers with a wink, popping a piece of the orange in his mouth.

I put my hand on my hip and shift my weight to the side. "Are you just saying that because I said it earlier?"

Asher leans against the other side of the boat, directly across from me. "No. I don't like to talk about certain aspects of my past. There are things that no one needs to know and, quite frankly, I'd be happy never to speak of them again." His answer is honest and concise, and, boy, do I understand.

"Your family is probably completely different than mine. All they want to do is talk. Talk about things that happened. Talk about feelings. Talk about the future. They want to make sure I'm okay, when their constant pressure is making me so not okay I want to crawl out of my skin."

"Why don't you tell them to stop?" He asks this like it's the simplest suggestion in the world.

"My family . . ." Where do I begin? "They're kind and sweet. My mom is the type of woman who wears cat sweaters where there's a kitten wrapped in a ball of yarn with a saying that says, 'Hang in there.' And my dad, he's this really cuddly guy who teaches history and reads James Joyce novels. I mean, who reads *Dubliner's* anymore? And he makes taffy. Like, a lot of taffy. But he doesn't eat it. He makes it because he thinks we love it, but no one has the heart to tell them we don't like it either!" My hands have taken on Leah's Italian like way of talking, and I have to rein them in.

"You're pretty funny, Emma Paige." Asher crosses his arms and the creases around his eyes form as he gives me a real smile. It's luminous and beautiful, showcasing two divots on the side of his face. They're not dimples but they're definitely only seen when he lets out a big smile.

"Nice to see my pain is entertaining."

"I don't mean it like that. It sounds nice to have people around you who care." As soon as the words are out of his mouth, his stance changes and the light in his eyes falters.

"They do care, too much. But I don't want to be taken care of, ever. They raised a strong, independent woman and, lately, all they do is hover like I'm going to break. I'm not angry with them for the way they act. It's the opposite. I feel awful for causing them to worry. They have their own lives to focus on. I can take care of myself."

Asher leans his hands on the edge of the boat and cocks his head to the side as if working something out in his head. I just gave him a mouthful. More than I even told my shrink, and that's not saying a lot.

"Sorry for blabbering."

"You apologize a lot."

"Sorry?" I dip my head and cringe to myself even as I say it.

He smiles again and uncrosses his arms. "For someone who doesn't like to talk, you seem to have an easy time talking here."

He's right. Maybe it's the confines of the cave. They make me feel like I'm in another universe. Maybe it's the fact that we're on a boat and far removed from the mainland. Or . . .

"Maybe it's because I know I'm never going to see you again." This time it's my turn to be honest and concise.

Asher nods, the perfect arch of his brow a little straighter; his lips pucker in. Placing his hands in his pockets, he leans back on his heels and looks back at me.

"So, Emma, what would you like to do? I've offered my services to you and so far I've passed a rock formation I couldn't tell you the name of and brought you into a cave I only discovered during an outing of my own last week."

"Do you bring a lot of girls here?" I mean for it to come out sarcastic but I know it sounds anything but.

"You're the first." Those divots make an appearance again.

A tingle shoots up my back and my eyes instantly fall to the side. I wipe my palms on the sides on my shorts and look at the rock surrounding us. Asher steps next to me.

The sides of our bodies touch and it's not affecting me at all.

Nope. Not one bit.

"I was thinking about this place last night. I wanted to take you here."

My head shoots up to look at him, almost causing me whiplash. "Take *me* here?"

"Yes." Those golden eyes bear down on mine. Damn, I wish I had pretty eyes too. When I look into these I am positively mesmerized.

"What about my sister?" My words almost a whisper.

"I was hoping she'd stay home, but I was willing to take her with us."

"Why?"

His brows cave in. "Why would I care if your sister came?"

No. I know why someone would want to take Leah. She's funny and pretty and spontaneous. The question is— "Why *me*?"

Asher lowers his chin and holds my gaze in place, as if to make sure I absorb every word he says. "I wanted to get to know you. People intrigue me and when I am intrigued I want to know more. Watching you play yesterday. It made me want to know the woman behind the keys."

My lips part on the inhale and I grab hold of the railing to steady myself. I am so not worth getting to know. It wasn't that long ago I was thrown out of bed by my sister, urging me to take a shower and end my months-long sleep. That's all I'd been doing. Sleeping and crying and going to therapy. I want to get better. I want my hand to work. I want to play again. But my last scan showed too much scar tissue and a nerve whose damage is irreparable.

The woman behind the keys is a shell of who she used to be. For a brief moment I felt that power I craved. I played the music I love. But it's lost on me now. And this woman he sees is not . . . me.

"We should go. I don't want to leave my sister alone all day." I walk around Asher and take my seat.

He stands for a moment, the muscles of his back rising and falling ever so slightly. The awesome thing about Asher is he doesn't press the issue or ask questions. He just nods and does as he's told. Maybe Devon did know what he was doing when he hired him.

And maybe he just doesn't want to be stuck with me a moment longer.

The rumble of the anchor being drawn up echoes in the cavern and Asher backs the boat up slowly until we are back in the bright sunshine. Turning the boat in the direction we were heading earlier, he raises the speed on the boat and drives again.

I'm surprised we're still heading in the opposite direction of where we came. "I said I wanted to go back."

Ignoring my request, Asher lowers his sunglasses over his eyes and pushes the throttle faster. My body jolts backwards for a second with the increase in speed, I have to reach my hands out in front of me to brace myself on the dashboard.

I take back what I said earlier. This guy doesn't know how to follow orders.

"Slow down."

His body stands tall, unaffected by the increased speed. I, on the other hand, am an unstable mess.

"I said, slow down!"

He drops the throttle down another level and the horsepower kicks up a notch, sending my ass into the seat behind me. Do these things come with seatbelts?

I'm trying to breathe but the wind in front of me fills my chest and I think I'm going to have a panic attack. Asher, on the other hand, is stoic and calm, acting as if he's taking a Sunday drive.

I raise my voice to him. "I want you to slow down, now!"

The engine is now growling a loud thunder. Chancing a look behind me, I see the island getting smaller as we head into the open waters. This is not the direction I want to go and not the speed I want us to drive at.

"Sometimes you don't always get what you want." His deep voice echoes over the boom of the ocean.

I turn my head back to face him and see him for who he is. Asher may be Devon's hand but he's not a servant. He's not a slave or a submissive. This is a man who does whatever the hell he wants and gives no apology. He doesn't need someone to worry about him because he can take care of himself. Asher is in control.

I have no control. Everything in my life right now is way too slow. And it doesn't matter how safe you are, you can still get hurt. I don't know why but I find myself saying, "Faster."

He looks over at me. "Are you sure?"

I nod. "Go as fast as you want."

It was the right answer because I am rewarded that Asher smile. It's so worth it.

Almost. He pulls the throttle as far down as it can go and my body hits the back of the seat. I have to grab onto the metal bar to my left and brace myself on the wall portion in front of me. A large lump forms in my throat and I think I'm going to be sick. My legs are shaking and I have to look down to block the fear of what could happen from my brain.

I start to count, in measures and downbeats, but my head can't wrap around the chords in my head.

"Emma!" he calls out with an outstretched hand. "Come here."

I shake my head no and he slows the speed. My heart settles back in my breastbone from its previous position in my stomach. I start to breathe normally again. My chest is heaving up and down, my fingers gripping the sides of the chair.

The boat is still moving but at a much slower speed. With one hand on the wheel, Asher reaches over to me and grabs the hand I have resting on the arm of the chair, closest to him, and pulls me toward him.

Like a rag doll I float over to him, dragged by his impressive strength until I am gently lodged in the space in between him and the helm. Asher encloses his body around mine, my body nestled in between his strong thighs, my back pressed against his solid torso.

My breath hitches when his arms swing around each side of my body, leaning down to place his hands over mine. He raises them and places my left hand on the wheel in front of us, and the other on the throttle to the right. His chin rests just above my head making me feel like I'm wrapped in a security blanket of rock hard silk.

Asher's mouth grazes down the side of my head until its nestled just above my ear. "Ready?"

I swallow and try to tame my breathing, which is still erratic but for completely different reasons than it was earlier. All I can do is nod my head.

His hand gently squeezes mine and it lowers the throttle a notch. My body leans back into his with the pushback and I'm rewarded with the feel of his rumbling chest against my back. Sensing I'm okay, Asher guides my hand down the throttle, pushing into another gear, until we are back to the increased speed we were at earlier.

My spine stiffens at the pace, and he must feel it because he releases his left hand from over mine at the helm and snakes it around my waist, holding me tight to him.

Okay, so now, I cannot focus on anything except his hand that is settled on my lower belly.

And it feels good. Very good.

Molto buona.

Our hands move the throttle down one more notch and our bodies have become so melded we are practically one.

Asher releases the throttle and puts his right hand on the wheel and drives us over the current, taking slight turns when he feels I'm ready. I know he knows I'm ready because his left hand is holding me so tightly he can practically feel my pulse.

The feel of him is starting to become second nature; I relax a bit and take in the action in front of me. Maybe it's the feel of Asher around me, or perhaps it's the fact this boat is made to drive this fast. It's a virtual tank. Whatever the reason, I am starting to actually enjoy the ride.

The speed is exhilarating.

Asher takes a hard turn and my heart nearly leaps out my throat in fear. But when we've straightened back out, I laugh out loud and ask him to do it again. He does it again, and again. Water sprays around us and we get a little wet. This causes me to laugh louder as I wipe the droplets away from my face.

The island of Capri is a distant pebble in the distance and I'm okay with it. We glide across the water and the speed we are driving isn't causing me anxiety. I would tell Asher he can release me but, the truth is, I really like having his arm around me. I'd never tell him that and I will never get an opportunity like this again. For now, I'm just going to ride the waves.

I don't know how much time passes when he turns the wheel and starts pointing us back toward the island. As our approach grows closer, he lowers the speed and I try to hide my disappointment when my blanket of Asher is removed as he takes the seat behind him. I am about to move over to my seat but he grabs my waist again and pulls me back into him so I'm cushioned in between his legs. When I am snuggly in place, he lowers his hand so it's resting on my hip.

"You drive. I'll be right here to make sure you don't run us into ground."

Normally, I would be apprehensive to do something like drive a boat. I don't like to do anything out of my comfort zone. But with him behind me, I feel confidant we'll be okay.

We circle the island, continuing west and then north, completing the grand tour we were set out on. I tilt my head back every now and then to ask Asher which direction I should drive or if I am too close to a rock. He guides my hands gently and helps me keep the boat on a safe path and steady in the water.

We pass the Blue Grotto and the line of boats of tourists waiting to go in. I thankfully decline Asher's offer to see what's inside. Not only would I feel bad going without Leah but I cannot risk another episode like I had yesterday.

By the time we are heading back east, completing our circle of the island, I am so at ease at the helm I don't look back to ask Asher for help.

We pass Devon's boat and I, once again, marvel at how impressive it is. From this direction I can see the front of the boat where the two-story glass room I know so well sits. It must be amazing to have your own sanctuary of music to go to whenever you want. I'd love to be able to stand in front of that glass window, looking out at the sunset over the sea and play the melodies of love and drama and laughter and tears. I've played in symphonies and concert halls, but to play to the sunset, now that would be amazing.

With my head arched all the way to the left as I look at the yacht, I catch Asher watching me and I turn my head back to the waterway in front of me. He releases his hold on my hip and I instantly miss the warmth.

It's why I shouldn't be surprised my spirits fall as we approach the Grande Marina. Our tour is ending and we have to dock. I move away from Asher and take a seat in the chair to his left and watch him skillfully pull the boat to a stone landing.

When we are close enough, he leans his body overboard to secure a rope to the spindles in the ground and I check out the way his shirt rides up with the arch of his back. His body swings back around toward me so I stand at attention and hide the fact I was just checking him out.

Asher brushes his hands against each other. "It was nice meeting you, Miss Paige." His voice is formal and dismissive. He still has on his sunglasses but I can tell he is purposefully not making eye contact with me. I don't know if he's in worker mode or if I have done something to offend him.

"I had a great time," I say.

"It was no problem. Have a good day."

The curtness in his voice tells me my presence is no longer wanted. I move to the back of the boat. My hand on the railing, I start to make my decent to the dock but I stop and turn around.

"Did I do something wrong?"

His arm swings around to rub the back of his neck, his other resting on his hip. With his head down, he pauses a moment and then rises to ask me a question. "Were you disappointed when I showed up this morning and not Devon?"

The question catches me off guard. The truth is, I was disappointed this morning. When I saw him I was reminded of the scene I caused yesterday. If I could, I would have turned around and gone straight to the hotel because he unnerved me.

He still does but for a different reason than he did yesterday.

I slant my head to the side, confused. “Why would it have mattered?”

Asher’s scrutiny over my response causes me to gawk back at him and wait for a reply. Those stern eyes are set in as if they’re looking for an answer in mine.

A beat . . . two beats . . . three. He doesn’t answer.

So I do the only thing I know how to do lately. I retreat.

chapter SEVEN

Walking back to the hotel, I can't stop wondering what went wrong. One minute I was driving, enjoying the view and the next—

Ooof.

"Excuse me." I say as I carelessly walk into a woman. My overanalyzing is getting the best of me.

I step back, giving her room to pass through the lobby doors of the hotel. Looking down I notice a gorgeous pair of Prada shoes with a heel elevated off the ground four inches higher than my rubber boat flats.

The Prada heels aren't moving so I look up. In front of me is a tall woman with hair dark as a crow's wearing an oversized hat and large round sunglasses hiding, what I presume from her exposed features, is a glamorous face. The dark lenses of the glass are facing me, looking directly at me, so I stare back at them, only seeing my confused expression in the reflection.

Since she has no desire to move, I bow my body down and shrug past her through the entrance. She is still standing there as I make my way through the lobby and out the opposite doors toward my suite.

Closing the door to the hotel room, I am immediately bombarded by sixty-four inches of blonde excitement.

"Details!" Leah exclaims, leaping across the room, the stray hairs from her messy bun falling around her face. She's wearing a red bikini and the air smells of sunscreen and cherry lip balm. She must have just gotten back because her skin is still damp from the pool. "I want to know everything. Where did you go? Did he flirt with you? Did he take his shirt off? It was hot. Please tell me he took his shirt off. You've been gone for a really long time. I'm hoping you have a major story to tell. You didn't get all weird on him, did you?"

That last question really gets to me.

Before I even think about answering a single question, I have a major bone to pick with her. "You ditched me!"

Leah holds up a finger in defense. "I did you a favor."

"How so?"

"You don't think it's a total coincidence the hot guy you ran into yesterday is the one who showed up to take us on a boat tour?"

I move around her and over to the wardrobe. "I think he was doing what his boss told him to do."

Leah spins around to face me. "He has eyes for you, and can we please talk about how freaking hot he is? I mean, he's a total McConaughey. Like, *How to Lose a Guy in 10 Days* McConaughey. Not *Dallas Buyers Club*. That was not his finest hour."

I take a T-shirt out and slam the closet door. "He was playing an AIDS patient, Leah. I don't think he was going for buff and brawny."

She follows me into the bathroom where I go to change out of my damp tank top. "Speaking of Brawny, did our boy today have the 'Strength to get things done'?" She uses air quotes when referencing the paper towel slogan.

Where do I begin when it comes to my day with Asher? It started off all right. I mean, I didn't want to be there and I didn't want to sit next to him and I didn't want to talk. Okay, so I was a complete bitch.

But then it was all right. He made me feel comfortable and he was easy to talk to. There was that moment when he said he wanted to get to know me, and my entire world stopped for just a second, until I flaked on him. For the life of me, I cannot imagine why he wanted to keep the tour going. Not that he was any good as a tour guide. Actually, he sucked.

Something changed in me today. My fear of speed for one. Six months ago I thought I'd never get into a moving vehicle again. I overcame that fear out of necessity, only allowing the driver to go a safe speed, dictated by me. Today, I was racing across the ocean with no protection other than Asher's steel grasp. I shouldn't be surprised. My fear is new and I was probably going to let it go sooner or later. I'm sure it's no big deal.

What is a big deal was how Asher treated me when we returned. He was dismissive and cold. It was as if he hadn't had his arm wrapped around me. Nice to know I made as big an impression on him as he did on me.

Not.

"It was boring. We drove in circles for a few hours and he didn't speak to me at all."

Leah follows me into the bedroom. Her hands fall to her hips as she chews on her lip. She looks like she's been deflated. "Oh, well, that sucks. I'm sorry you had to spend the day like that."

I let my hair out of my ponytail and shake out the tightness of it. I'm wrapping it back up in a messy bun when I see that look in Leah's eyes.

"It's fine. I'm not gonna get all sad because I had a crap tour," I say taking a seat on the bed. She looks up at me, trying to decide if I'm lying. "Besides, it was pretty nice to be able to look at a hot guy for a few hours." I throw in a smile for good measure.

Leah relaxes and nods her head. "He was totally hot. Did he take off the sunglasses? What color are his eyes?"

"They're like a warm honey." I clamp my mouth shut as soon as the words come.

Leah's face lights up in a magnanimous smile. She is just about to squeal something but is interrupted by the chime of her iPad.

We both look down at the device, which is perched on the end table next to us. Our mom's face lights up the screen and the word PAM flashes at the top. Leah enjoys referring to Mom by her first name.

I make a face at the thought of having to talk to her, but Leah lifts the iPad and swipes on the screen anyway. "Hi, Pam!"

"Hello, sweetie. How are my girls doing?" Mom's voice echoes from the speaker. She and Leah are on FaceTime but Leah has the screen faced in her direction.

I'm surprised mom isn't calling in a panic because her daughters are stranded in Italy. Using a series of eyestrain and head tilts, I ask Leah if Mom knows what happened yesterday. She gives me a slight shake "No" and goes back to talking to the screen.

"We're good. In fact, we're having the time of our lives. We went on a boat tour yesterday and today we spent some time by the water getting some sun." Leah continues to go on and on about the hotel we're staying in and the gorgeous pool she sat by today. I have to give the girl credit, she doesn't lie once.

Bend the truth? Sure.

Lie? Absolutely not.

Mom and Leah have a lively conversation. Every once in a while, Leah gets carried away in her conversation, and Mom makes comments like, "You're so fresh" and "Behave."

The two of them have a comfortable relationship. They can get silly with each other. Actually, that's just Leah. It's in her nature to draw you in and make you feel as comfortable as possible.

"How's Emma? Is she there with you?" Mom asks.

I shake my head dramatically but Leah's flashes a huge smile and says, "She's right here."

I pinch my lips together, scowling at Leah but my face quickly turns into a polite smile when the screen is turned in my direction.

Mom is sitting there wearing a T-shirt with an orange calico cat on it that says, “Every life should have 9 cats.” It’s early in Ohio so she must be getting ready to go out in the garden.

“Hi, Mom.”

“Hi, baby. How are you feeling?” she asks, her voice turning down an octave from when she was talking to Leah.

I run my nails along my neck and scratch down the sides. “I’m good. Just as Leah said, having a great time.”

Mom moves closer to the screen as if she can see me better if she rests her retinas against the glass. “Leah said you went out to a club. Did you have fun?”

“I did.”

“You’re getting out and seeing the sites?”

“We are.”

“Are you eating?” Her eyes skim my face.

“I am.” Leah’s staring at me from the other side of the screen. She doesn’t understand how I can answer in two-word answers. She is the world’s biggest chatterbox.

“Is it beautiful?” Mom asks and I find myself smiling out of natural instinct. Capri is the most magnificent place. We’ve only been here for three days yet I can commit to memory every sparkle of the sun on the copper landscape and every crash of a wave against the granite rock. It is as if I were meant to be here. I just feels right.

“More so than I’ll ever be able to describe.”

Mom’s eyes crinkle as her cheeks rise up. “That’s good to hear, baby.” She shifts in her seat and then leans forward again. “I’m glad you’re together. It’s your brother’s birthday soon. He’d be so happy you two are in such a beautiful place.” Mom’s eyes tear up at the mention of Luke and I have to turn my head to the side and take in a deep breath.

Luke.

We don't talk about Luke. At least, I don't. What is there to say? If it wasn't for me and my stupid relationship and my stupid desire to get out then he would still be here.

I can't stand to see the sadness in my mom's eyes, nor can I handle her seeing me break down. I turn the iPad away from me and point it back toward Leah whose mouth is wide open. Her face is giving me a what-the-fuck expression.

Rising from the bed, I leave Leah to talk to my mom while I head out of the room. I open the sliding door, step out on the portico and walk through it to the grassy area looking over the Marina Grande.

The sun is still out but the sky is taking an orange-ish color, as the sun is in the early stages of its decent. Plopping down on the grass, I pull my legs in to my chest and rest my chin on my knees.

I am so far away from home. So far away from the troubles that leave me feeling broken and afraid. It doesn't matter how far away you are from your problems, they live with you, deep inside your soul. You cannot escape.

My throat heaves out and I bellow from deep inside my gut. I know I am a bitch. No one needs to explain it to me. My poor mother lost a son and instead of thinking about how sad she must be that her baby boy's birthday is in two days and he isn't here to see it, I am so caught up in my own selfish head. I can't comfort her because I don't even know how to process it all.

Luke was my baby as well. I was only four years old when Mom and Dad brought him home, but I remember it vividly. He was wearing a soft blue layette with white ruffle trim.

The first time they placed Luke in my arms I was nervous. He was so small and delicate. The adults kept on chanting things like "Watch his head" and "Hold on tight." He had light red hair and these dark eyes like mine and

Mom's. When they looked up at me for the first time I was in love.

When Luke was old enough to sleep in his own bed he would go in properly at night, just as Mom and Dad told him to. But every night, like clockwork, he would crawl into my bed when the adults were asleep. He said he was afraid of the dark, but I think he just wanted to be close to me. When Mom and Dad found us snuggled together in the morning they never said a word.

When Mom started driving me to Pittsburgh for music lessons, Luke would come for the ride. He had to endure four hours in a car and more hanging with my mom in a lobby, waiting for me to finish my lesson. Leah kicked and screamed when she had to go, so Mom made arrangements for her to stay with a friend on those days. Luke was different. He came because it was important to Mom and me.

I went to college two hours away from home at the time Luke started high school. My formative years were much different from his. I was a music geek who spent my free time playing the violin. Luke lived the life. He was on the varsity football team and held the keg parties in the woods. I looked forward to our weekly phone calls during which he described every escapade of the week. Sometimes he asked advice about problems with girls or a fight with a friend. I tried to give him solid advice and I'd like to think he took it.

The last year and a half, we spoke less as he partied it up at Ohio State and I settled into my career. Still, once a week we were on the phone. The bond was still there and still strong.

I can't talk to my mom about Luke because I am still trying to figure out how such an awful thing happened.

I raise my head from my chin and wipe away the tears that are soaking my face. Leah comes around to look at me.

As soon as she sees my red, splotchy face, she falls to her knees.

"Oh, my God, Emma. Are you okay?" She holds her hand out to me and puts it on my back, rubbing up and down in comfort.

When my palms are full of moisture, I use the backs of my hands to continue wiping my face.

"I'm fine. I . . . I'm just not ready. Okay?" I look up at Leah, who is nodding.

"Sure. We don't have to go there right now. I just—" Leah moves her hand in broader circles on my back and takes a seat next to me. "I thought you were doing better. You are doing better. You know that, right?"

I sniffle and try to breathe while I pull myself together. "I know I am. I just can't talk about him yet."

Leah pulls me into her side and rests her head on top of mine. She breathes out a sigh and sits with me, looking out onto the world in front of us. "We all lost Luke. We are all grieving. You are not alone in this," she says. If I were her, I'd hate me. "You went through a lot, Emma. You lost your music and your brother in one night. We are all giving you time to heal. But at some point, you're going to have to let someone in."

I turn and face her. Leah was a mess at Luke's funeral. She cried and grieved like everyone else. Even though she was sad, she did manage to give an awesome eulogy. She told funny stories and reminded people about the incredible life he lived. Luke would have loved it.

Looking at Leah now, I see a woman who is concerned for the well-being of her sister. I don't want her looking at me like that.

"Was Adam able to send us money?" I ask.

Leah lets go of my back and brushes her hands on her knees. She knows how to take a hint. "Yeah. He did. And the passports arrived today. As promised." She rises and holds out her hand. "Why don't you and I go out and have a really expensive dinner and drink our weight in wine?"

I get up from my spot. "I'll settle on a reasonably priced *prix fixe* dinner and a glass of wine. I think I lost enough of our money this week. No need to go for broke."

Leah turns to head into the room. "Killjoy," she says, but then turns toward me and walks backward. "But I get to pick out our clothes."

I agree and that seems to bring Leah back into her natural state: absolutely crazy.

chapter EIGHT

Last night, Leah and I ventured into Anacapri. It's part of the island of Capri but on the opposite side of where we are staying. We had to walk to the Piazetta to catch a bus. My heart was in my throat as the bus wound up the steep mountain with little guardrail protecting us from driving off the cliff.

We made it there in record time, and caught the last chairlift to the top of Mount Solaro, the highest and most panoramic point on the island. It was on Leah's list of places to visit. From up there we could see the Bay of Naples and the Amalfi Coast. Since we'd lost our phones, we stopped at a store to buy a disposable camera. We were both surprised they still sold those.

In town, we visited the shops. Leah and I both bought silk scarves and added them to the dresses Leah picked out for us to wear. Leah wrapped her scarf around her neck, and I tied mine around my head, making a headband.

It was nice being a tourist with my sister. We ate a great—and reasonably priced—dinner, then settled into a cafe where we had a cappuccino and dessert. We stopped to listen to a band play in the street and by the time we settled into bed last night, I almost forgot about the crazy day I'd had.

Almost.

Today, we are at a beach club on the Marina Piccola, on the south side of the island. I say beach club, because that is what it's called, yet it's a far cry from what I was expecting. We walk along narrow stone steps, following signs for the place we chose to spend our afternoon in the sun. We approach a stone structure of three levels leading down to the water. Each level has lounge chairs on it, facing the water. We walk down to the level on the water. We came to use the beach, so we want to be on the beach.

The beach, however, is not the white sand beaches we are used to back in the States. Instead of sand, the beach is made of small rocks hot from the sun, so we keep our flip-flops on as we walk to our lounge chairs. There is a cafe inside and music playing over a speaker. A family of four is to our left and a couple who seem to be on their honeymoon are to our right. I'm surprised there aren't more people enjoying the sun.

From my chair, I can see the rock formation I passed with Asher yesterday, which, I now know, is the Faraglioni. Three spurs of rock formed by erosion of ocean waves. In fact, every time I look up, I see the rocks and try not to think of Asher.

Lathering on the sunblock, I take in the sunshine. After a while, Leah gets us a few cocktails and waters and when those are done we decide to go for a swim. We tentatively walk into the water, trying to keep our feet steady on the rocky ground. My feet actually hurt from the pebbles digging in my skin. The family to our left is all wearing water shoes. Smart.

After a few hours of enjoying the beach club, we head back to town. Instead of taking the bus, Leah wants to follow the map and walk back, cutting through the mountain. I tried to warn her it was farther than it looks but, Leah being Leah wants to have an adventure and "do like the locals do."

Trust me, there is no way the locals endure this torture. If I say we climbed a thousand stairs, I might be underestimating the climb. Leah whines on the way up and I remind her how great her butt will look after this exercise. It seems to make her happy enough to keep on going.

When we reach the top, we treat ourselves to gelato.

Between last night's trek to Anacapri and today's climb up the mountain, we are both ready to head back to the hotel. A nap is in order before we can even think about where to go for dinner.

Leah and I enter the hotel and pass through the lobby, walking to our room. In front of our door is a large package. From the distance it looks like a bouquet of flowers. When we get closer we see that it's really . . . shoes.

In a large wicker basket is an array of shoes, each on its own stick, assembled in a display to look like a flower arrangement. In between each shoe is tissue paper and the entire thing is wrapped in cellophane.

Leah picks up the basket while I take out my room key and open the door. When we're in the room, Leah places the basket on the table of the seating area and removes the card on the front.

"It's for you," she says, handing me the envelope.

"Me?" I take the envelope from her and look at my name written on the front. I open the envelope and slide the card out.

So you don't

lose your footing.

I look over at the bouquet that Leah is unwrapping. Inside are a dozen shoes. These aren't any shoes. There are six pairs of Sperry Top-Siders in the basket. The same shoe I lost when I fell in the water. I left the other on Devon's boat and wore slippers home.

I look back down on the card and read the next line.

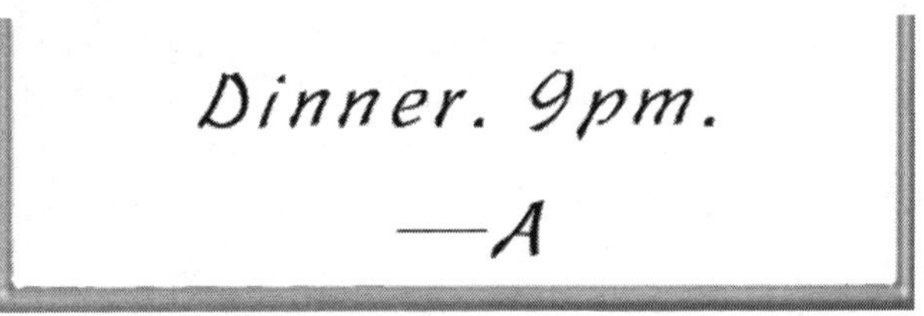

Leah rips the card from my hand and reads it. "For someone who didn't talk to the guy, you certainly made an impression."

I wave her off and look at the shoes. It's an odd gift. Who buys someone six pairs of shoes? There is a gold pair, a silver, red, navy, white and green. All in my size. I don't know how much Asher gets paid but he spent a pretty penny.

But why?

I take the card from Leah and read the note again. It's actually pretty funny. If I were in a different headspace I would appreciate the cleverness of the gift.

"Looks like you have dinner plans tonight." Leah says with complete excitement.

"No way. I am not going to dinner with a stranger." The card feels like a lead weight in my hand.

"Yes, you are. This is awesome. He sent you shoes! That's better than jewelry!" Leah starts taking the shoes off the sticks and pairing them together on the couch. "I'm picking your outfit!"

"No, you're not. I am not leaving you to go out. This is our vacation, remember? Our sister's sabbatical." I take the shoes and place them back in the basket.

"You're going. Besides, I am so tired from all the walking today. I'll be more than happy to drink a bottle of wine on the patio and talk to Adam." She leans down and grabs the navy Sperry's and walks them over to the closet. "I know just the thing for you to wear!"

"I don't think you're listening, I'm not going."

Leah opens my closet and pulls out my favorite yellow racer-back tank dress. "Emma, yesterday you were sobbing on the grass. Today, a beautiful man wants to take you out to dinner. Let me ask you, do you want to be the girl who cries in her hands or do you want to be the girl who has fun?"

Her question takes me completely by surprise. Is that who I am? The girl who cries? It's not who I *was*. I was the mature one. I took care of our family. I didn't need taking care of.

I take the dress from her hands and walk into the bathroom. "You're doing my hair!" I shout before slamming the door in her face.

The note said, "Dinner. 9pm." There was no location. Hell, there wasn't even a question in there. It's as if I don't have a choice whether I want to go to dinner or not.

I'm wearing the dress Leah pulled out. It's tight and hits a few inches above my knees. The racer back makes it difficult to wear a proper bra so I put on a strapless one that's thin and doesn't show through the fabric. The front is a scoop neck and shows ample cleavage but nothing pornstar-esque. Leah insisted I wear the navy-blue Sperrys. It's not the shoe I'd normally wear with a bright yellow but it works. The dress is cotton and casual. Sexy without looking like I'm trying too hard.

My hair is blown out with a soft bend at the ends. Leah wanted to do my makeup but I did it myself, subtle and natural-looking. As the clock strikes nine, I find myself fiddling with the gold "E" I wear around my neck. If someone writes something like "Dinner. 9pm," you know they must be punctual.

"Am I supposed to wait here?"

Leah thinks for a second, then says, "Wait in the lobby. It's less first date-ish."

I agree and head out the door. My stomach is in knots. Is this a first date? It's weird if it is because there won't be a second. We're in Italy, for Christ's sake. I don't even know where he lives. I'll go back to Cedar Ridge and he'll go back to . . . wherever it is he came from.

This is stupid. I feel stupid. I want to turn around and go back to the room. I should.

I turn on my heels and start heading back. Then what? Leah will just push me out the door again. And do I really want to be the girl who cries?

I do another one-eighty and head for the lobby. The clock behind the desk reads 9:05. Should I stand in the middle of the room? Have a seat? Ugh! I don't want to look like I'm waiting. I walk over to the man behind the desk and ask him if we have any messages. This way if Asher walks in, I won't look like I'm desperately waiting for him to arrive.

Which I'm not, for the record.

"Your name?" the man asks.

"Emma Paige." I look over at the door. The anticipation is killing me.

"Paige?" A look of realization crosses his face. "A gentleman was here. I have no Paige. I told him you no stay here. I look in the computer and see you with Reingold. I tell him I'll call. He leave."

Asher was here and left already? Where did he go? I walk out the front door and look outside but he is nowhere to be seen. I can't believe he is standing me up when he's the one who asked to go to dinner. No. He demanded dinner. I didn't have a choice in the matter.

I walk to the street, looking both ways. If he came in a car, it's long gone. Where would he even get a car? No, he had to have walked and if he came from the boat he's headed back to the marina.

I make my way toward the stone steps Leah and I walked up on the first day we got here, carrying our suitcases to the hotel. The stairs lead to the marina and is most likely the way he went. Taking two at a time, I skip down the steps until I see his six-foot frame, walking down the path in a slow and purposeful manner.

"Where are you going?" My feet stop at the step I'm on when I see him. He's about twenty steps below me.

Asher stops his descent and slowly turns around. The sun has already set, so it's hard to make out his expression in the evening light. From his posture, it looks like he's mad.

"Who's Adam?" His voice is thick with inquisition.

Okay. That is the last thing I expected out of his mouth. "Why do you care about Adam?"

Asher doesn't move and neither do I. We have a stand still on the steps while I try to figure out how he even knows about Adam. And, seriously, why does he care?

"I gave your name to the man at the hotel. He said you were staying in Adam Reingold's room." Asher crosses his arms in front of his chest. "Are you married?"

My brows lower over my eyes lids while I try to figure out this guy. "If I were, do you think I'd be all dressed up, ready for you to take me to dinner?"

Asher doesn't miss a beat before answering. "Yes."

His answer leaves me speechless but only for a second. "No. I'm not married."

"Boyfriend?"

"Nope."

"Kids?"

"No. But would it matter?"

"Only if you lied about having them."

I feel like I'm on trial. I guess it's normal to ask someone you're about to go to dinner with if they're already taken. Maybe I should reciprocate. I cross my arms over my chest. "What about you?"

Asher cocks his head to the side. "What about me?"

"Married?"

He balks as if the idea is ludicrous. "No."

"Kids?"

"No."

"Boyfriend?" I ask in attempt to lighten the mood.

At this, Asher lets out a laugh and releases his arms. "Never."

I walk down the stairs until I am two steps above him, making me slightly taller than him. The perfect height to appraise. Leah says he's hot but that's not the word. Asher is the most perfectly created person I've even seen. His smooth skin is evident even in the darkness of the night, and the perfect structure of his face is outlined in the moonlight.

"You confuse the hell out of me." It's true. I thought he was mean but then he was nice. I thought he wanted to take me out and now he's running away.

Asher looks into my eyes and I stand here, awaiting his response. Usually I'm not so brazen with men. I'm not shy. I just don't have the time for games. I should go back to the room and take Leah out to dinner. But first, I need answers.

"What is it you want from me?"

"I'm trying to figure out if I can trust you." His words are light, like a whisper.

"Trust me?" I let out a slight laugh. "You don't even know me. And I don't know you. How am *I* supposed to trust *you*?"

Asher lets out a deep breath. "That's why you intrigue me."

If I had a nickel for every time this guy baffled me I'd have . . . a quarter. Yeah, not so dramatic when I put it that way.

I take a step back and up, away from him. “Here’s the deal. I had a crap year. Like, a total crap year, so I don’t have any room for games. I got all dressed up and I’m going out to dinner tonight, with or without you. And since I’m never going to see you again it really doesn’t matter to me either way.”

Asher places his hands in his pockets and leans back on his heels. His mouth widens in a smile. “Since you put it that way, it looks like I’m taking you out to dinner.”

“Now that we have that straightened out, where are we going?” I take my three steps down and walk past him on the staircase. Asher follows.

I spin my head around; he’s glancing at his watch. “Are you starving or do you want to walk a little?”

Leah and I did eat and drink a lot today on our escapade. We also did a lot of walking but I’m not that hungry, yet. “I can stand to walk.”

Asher and I reach the bottom of the stairs and are at a street. If we keep going, we’ll land at the Marina. Instead, we make a right and start walking through the streets.

The light down here is brighter than on the stairs. I look over at Asher and see he’s wearing khaki pants, a black-button down with the sleeves rolled up, and loafers. His blond hair is glistening in the lamplight and his honey eyes look dark. He’s about a half foot taller than me, and his posture is perfect, more so than any guy I ever met. The fit frame of his body combined with the way he walks, as if with purpose, makes his stature intimidating. If it wasn’t for that smile I would be a nervous wreck. But then he spreads those gorgeous full lips and I’m at ease.

“Are you going to tell me who Adam is?” he asks.

I glance up at him as we walk side by side. “Adam is Leah’s fiancé. They were supposed to be here on their honeymoon but the wedding was called off. That’s why the room is in his name. I came in his place.”

"He must have done something deplorable for her to call off the wedding."

Deplorable? Who uses words like that? Never mind.

"Adam is the world's kindest man. He would never do anything deplorable or whatever fancy word you want to use."

"Then it must have been Leah. She cheated." His jaw tightens with the word.

I stop walking and it takes a few steps for Asher to realize I'm behind him. When he turns around, I am standing with my hands on my hips and a scowl on my face. "Why do you assume one of them did something awful. Do you always assume the worst in people?"

Asher blinks a few times and tilts his head slightly, his eyes darting out to the side as he thinks. "Yes. I do." His eyes stop roaming and settle on mine. "Why else would they call off a wedding?"

I should have just let him believe one of them cheated. Now I have to answer him. Ugh. "Something tragic happened in our family. It isn't the best time to host a wedding." I just took a cue from Leah's school of "Lies while only telling the truth."

"Is this one of those things you don't talk about?" His question surprises me. He was really listening to me yesterday.

"Yes," I reply, releasing my hands from my hips.

With a slight nod of his head, Asher shows me he understands and then lifts his chin in the direction we were originally going. He turns around and continues walking. My Sperrys move on the pavement and find my spot next to him.

We walk for a few minutes in surprisingly comfortable silence. I follow him around a bend.

There was something he said to me yesterday I haven't been able to stop thinking about. "How did you know about the way I play the piano? I mean, was that just a line you use on girls or did you really see something?"

"I play too." He puts his hand on my back and leads me up a narrow staircase going back up the hill. "My mother taught out of our home."

"You must be pretty good."

Asher turns to me and winks. "I'm very good."

"Was that back in Pittsburgh?" My question causes him to stop this time. I turn around on the stair and face him. "If that's an off-limits topic, I understand."

Asher lets out a breath, his eyes skimming my face, working something out in his head. "I'll tell you what. For every thing I tell you that's off limits, you have to tell me something." Even as he says the words I see the hesitation in his eyes. They must match my own. Yes, he's a stranger. I'll never see him again after this trip. But there are some things I'm not ready to talk about.

Leah says I should let someone in. I just can't go all the way with my feelings. Who knows where my emotions will land. I don't need to have a meltdown in front of my European hookup.

Oh, dear God, am I really thinking about him that way? He hasn't even kissed me. Will he kiss me? This is a date. Oh, crap, I didn't think any of this through.

Suddenly, my other issues don't seem so big compared to the six-foot golden god in front of me.

Maybe if I open up a little I'll scare him away. This way I won't have to worry about the "what ifs" and "maybes" of tonight.

"Why do you want to know so much about me?"

"I honestly have no idea." His tone is deep and smooth.

"I need something." I match his tone, soft and pleading.

Asher takes a step closer to me; he is a step lower, and we're eye to eye. From this distance I may just fall into his gaze like Alice fell into the rabbit hole.

“When I saw you in the music room”—he swallows, the tone turns serious—“I was moved for the first time in so long. I don’t know why. I wish I did. There is something about you and I’m waiting for you to do something to make me realize you’re just like everyone else.”

This time it my turn to swallow . . . hard. “But I am like everyone else.”

“Not in my world.” He grabs my waist and I gasp.

“Why were you so mean to me yesterday? When I left the boat?” I barely get the words out because my mind is too focused on his hand on my rib.

“Why did you tell me to take you back to your sister yesterday after I said how intrigued I am by you? I think we’re both trying to work through our issues.” His mouth is dangerously close to mine.

Asher’s other hand snakes up around my torso and I think I might faint. My breathing starts to pick up.

“Why are you nervous?” he asks, his lips barely brushing mine.

“I don’t know if I’m ready for this.”

Asher’s mouth moves past my lips and kisses my jaw. I let out a large breath I didn’t know I was holding. His lips then graze the skin on my neck, just under my ear, before pulling back and releasing my waist.

He walks passed me. I take the moment to collect myself, placing a hand to my lips. My mouth is wet from anticipation. My jaw tingles where his lips just touched the skin. I wasn’t ready for a kiss but that was more intoxicating than any type of kiss I have ever experienced.

When I turn around to follow him I see he’s standing on the stairs, holding out a hand. I grab it and am surprised by the smoothness of it.

Asher is looking down at our conjoined hands. He has a look of satisfaction on his face. He likes it too.

I am definitely going down the rabbit hole.

"Okay. A story for a story. I'll share if you share. But you have to go first."

Asher's hand holds mine gently as we walk on. Parker and I were never hand-holders. It wasn't something he ever enjoyed. I didn't either. The feeling of being tethered to someone while strolling a mall seemed ridiculous. But, this, right here, walking with Asher . . . It just feels . . . it feels so . . . I don't know.

"When I was a kid, my mom taught piano lessons in our living room," he says. The words start off slow, as if he doesn't know where to start. Maybe he just doesn't tell the story often. "We had this really tiny apartment. There wasn't any room for a piano, nor did we have the money to buy one." He frowns a bit. "For a while, she had this keyboard she used. She seemed content with it. One year, my dad found a piano in salvage. The people selling it said it didn't work. The keys were broken and the strings were snapped. When we brought it home, my mom didn't care that the thing couldn't hold a tune."

Asher's face lights up with the memory. "You know how people fix old cars? My dad and I fixed that piano. The first time she played a chord, she cried. When was the last time someone gave you a gift so monumental you cried?"

I shrug. "I can't remember."

"Me neither. I don't think it was just the piano. It was the fact we created it for her. We had so little back then that actions were more important than things."

"That's a beautiful memory. That doesn't seem like something worth keeping to yourself."

"I don't talk about my family. Ever."

"Why not?"

Asher stops and tsk-tsks at me. "My turn."

"Your turn for what?"

"Why don't you play the violin anymore?"

I release my hand from his and wrap it around my injured one. I haven't thought about it all day. It seems like every time I want to forget, I'm drawn back to the reality that is my life.

"Emma, your hand?"

"What about it?" I bite back at him. How does he know something is wrong with my hand?

"You're clenching onto it like it might fall off," he says. I look down and see my knuckles are white. I release the grip and flex it out, feeling the pinched nerve. "How did you hurt it?"

Asher takes my right hand in his, placing his left underneath it like it's a wounded dove. With his right, he skims my palm with his thumb, rubbing gentle circles over the scar I bear.

"Six months ago. I was in an accident. A car accident. My hand was crushed. Surgery wasn't enough. I can't handle the bow for long without screaming in pain." I pull my hand away from his.

"Maybe you need a better doctor. I can—" Asher is offering something he knows nothing about.

"It's irreversible. It's over." I cut him off. "I inquired. Went to the best doctors. Sought the best therapists. The hand is shot. My career is over." I step back from him and continue our walk.

Asher follows me, his long strides catching up with me quickly. "What will you do now?"

"Oh, you know the saying. Those who can't do, teach." Bitterness is oozing out my pours. I hate the fact I'll spend the rest of my life teaching music when I wanted to be the one playing.

Asher grabs my arm, jolting me from my step forward and pulls me back. "There is nothing wrong with teaching."

My chest slams against his when I land. I look up into him. His brow is creased. Crap, this guy just told me his mother was a music teacher. Of course, he'd be insulted.

"It's nothing against teaching. It's a noble profession. You don't understand what this is like for me. I love playing the violin. No, I *live* to play. I gave up my entire life up until the accident so I could be the best. I was on my way to *being* the best. Do you know what its like to have something you love ripped away from you? To have your dreams crushed in a single night?" My eyes well up with tears, but I fight them back. I breathe to regain my focus on the present. I cannot lose myself right now.

But I do because Asher leans in and kisses me. His mouth crashes against mine, parting my lips in two, invading my personal space. Those luscious lips wrap around mine, pulling them in, tight.

I don't move. I can't move. I stand here, stunned, waiting for him to back away. Instead, his tongue slides in and moves against my own, causing my body to jolt with heat and excitement. His kiss goes deeper when his lips move, sucking on mine and going back for more. I haven't had a first kiss in over four years. And even that one wasn't as powerful as this. This kiss is filled with need, desire, and complete yearning.

Asher wraps both hands around my head and takes me in further. I can't help it. I lose myself into him and kiss him back with every bit of anger I've been holding onto the past six months. Every emotion, every feeling I have been holding is let out in the form of passion.

My fingers brush his sides and grip him, pulling him in closer. His groin lines up with my belly and a need for everything *Asher* consumes me.

When he pulls away, I am left lost. My lips still perched for more kisses, but he is backing away.

My hooded eyes slowly open to see a grinning Asher. "What did you do that for?"

"You needed to be kissed." His thumbs graze my cheek. His skin smells of soap and sea, again.

My daze is slightly lifted. "I told you I wasn't ready."

"I was." He says, leaning in for another kiss. "Now, let me feed you."

Asher slides his hand around my back and leads me toward the Piazetta Umberto I. We had been walking and talking for so long, I hadn't realized we were in the city center.

We get a table at a cafe in the piazza, overlooking the square. Asher takes the liberty of ordering. Normally, I would be annoyed by this, but I'm still focused on that kiss. I can't even be bothered with ordering something as trivial as food.

Asher keeps the conversation light. We talk about things like our interests in music and our favorite television shows. He tells me a story about this barber he goes to who has a great Italian accent. He tries to do an impression I think he's botching on purpose for sake of making the story funny. I also learn that he and Devon met in Pittsburgh. They grew up in the same neighborhood and reconnected five years ago. Apparently, he and Devon were thick as thieves as kids. Once, they were caught stealing candy—York Peppermint Patties, which turns out to be both of our favorite candy—and had to work at the shop for a month to make up for being caught. He smiles broadly when he recalls all the candy they snuck when they were working off their debt for stealing the first piece. He said it was the best punishment in the world. He doesn't mention how Devon made his money and I don't ask. I'm not interested in Devon. I am so into Asher.

He asks me about my childhood in Ohio. I tell him stories of Leah and I, mostly. Since we are only a year apart, we were always together, putting on plays for our family and singing into hairbrushes while watching MTV. I don't leave out Luke completely. I just can't talk about him. So I don't.

Taking a bite of calamari, Asher asks me more about my parents and I explain that, yes, my mom is really into cats.

"We've had no fewer than three cats at a time my entire life." I answer. The Campari drinks he selected are awesome. I try to keep to sips; I don't want to be the drunken girl tonight.

Asher puts down his fork. "How many does she have now?"

I swallow my Compari and think for a second. "Ben, Eddie, Woodie, and Dallas. Four. She currently has four."

"Those are interesting names for cats."

"They're named after Matthew McConaughey characters." I answer like it's a normal response. Asher cocks an eyebrow so I explain. "Ben Barry from *How to Lose a Guy in 10 Days*, Steve Edison from *The Wedding Planner*, David Wooderson from *Dazed and Confused*, and Dallas, she's a girl, from *Magic Mike*. Even the girl cats get named after him."

Asher lets out a deep, boisterous laugh. It's the first time I've heard him laugh like this and I'm mesmerized by it. For someone who looked so intense two days ago, this look is magnetic and personable. I wish I'd met this version of him first.

"Your mom has a thing for Matthew McConaughey?" He leans forward, completely into our conversation.

"No. That's Leah. She names all the cats. She's kind of obsessed. She owns a bar back home named after him."

"You're kidding."

"Nope. Although, most of the locals don't know she's the actual owner. She is really young to have such a successful bar and says it's better for business if they think she's just the bartender. This way she can know what is really going down inside the bar."

"She's a very smart businesswoman."

I like that he appreciates Leah's entrepreneurial expertise.

"What about you?" he asks. "Ever think of starting your own business? Maybe open up your own music school?"

I shake my head and look down. "No. I'll teach for a while. That's all. Besides, I don't love teaching as much as someone should if they were to open up a business like that."

"What do you love then? If you can't play, there has to be something about music you love enough to pursue?"

"I love creating music. I was working on this new sound. I can hear it in my head and I know what it's supposed to sound like. But, without being able to play, I can't get the notes out."

"Of course you can. There are computers and even keyboards with—"

"Not the same." I stare him down to let him know the conversation is off-limits. I know there are other ways to create music. I just need to play in order to feel it. I can't create it if I can't feel it. He'll never understand.

"Did you have any pets?" I ask.

"No. I always wanted a dog."

"Why didn't you ever get one?"

"Too poor as a kid. Too rich growing up. I guess there's no happy medium." The waiter comes to our table to clear away our plates. Asher asks for the check and pays it, leaving more than enough cash on the table. In fact, I think he just left a fifty-euro tip.

"You don't have to impress me like that."

His head looks up while he places his wallet in his back pocket. "Like what?"

I gesture to the tip on the table. "That's a lot of money. Don't leave it just because I'm here. I'm not into that sort of thing."

"What sort of thing would that be?"

"Money."

He lets out appreciative laugh and shakes his head. "I know. You didn't take the money."

I look down at the cash on the table. Of course I didn't take it. It's right there.

"The money Devon offered you. You didn't take it. I know," he says, rising from his seat. He holds out a hand and I take it, brushing off my startled expression on how Devon told him about the money he offered me when we were on the boat.

I glance up at the clock tower in the piazza and see it's eleven in the evening. Asher leads me through town. Leah was right. Italians like to eat late. Some of the shops are still opened as well. We pass a few and I am reminded about the gift he gave me earlier.

"Thank you for the shoes," I say, way too late for a proper thank-you.

Asher glances down at my navy blue shoes and his eyes skim slowly up my body, stopping for a moment at my bust and landing on my eyes.

"I noticed them earlier. Thank you for wearing them."

I kick my toes up and show them off. "They're my favorite. I was so upset when I lost my shoe the other day. I'm pretty upset at you for buying them. It was too much."

Asher's eyes soften and he smiles shyly. He has this look on his face that is so hard to read. "I wanted to do something nice for you. I was a jerk yesterday."

"I was a jerk first. That doesn't mean I'm going to start buying you gifts." I hit him on the shoulder playfully and am rewarded with his hand snaking around my waist again. I really like it there. "Do you always wear loafers? You were wearing them yesterday too. Do you ever wear sneakers?"

"Only to the gym."

"What about flip-flops?"

"I've never worn a pair of flip-flops."

"Never?"

He shakes his head. “My grandfather never allowed me. When I was ten I went to live with him. He had these strict rules about what he expected from me. Dress code was one of them. I was allowed to wear loafers and boat shoes. Sneakers were for working out. Even my slippers had to look like loafers.”

I don’t know what kind of man his grandfather was but Asher is clearly deprived of a staple foot fashion. Even I spent a good part of my life wearing high heels and black shoes appropriate for the symphony, but when I was offstage, those puppies were off and the flip-flops were on.

“Come with me.” I grab his hand and lead him down the street until we find a store that sells what I’m looking for. “I’m buying you a pair of flip flops.”

Asher put up a fight in the store. Not because he was opposed to buying the shoes. He was just opposed to *me* buying the shoes. Since he bought me six pairs on his modest—whatever he does—salary, I convinced him to let me pay.

“So what do you think?” Asher and I are walking along the south side of the island overlooking the Marina Piccola.

Asher looks down at his feet, his loafers in his left hand; his right hand is holding mine. “I hate them.”

I let out a loud laugh. “What do you mean, you hate them?”

Asher’s forehead crinkles. His words are cautious like he’s going to hurt my feelings. “I really hate them. This thing in between my toes is so uncomfortable and my foot is constantly separating from the bottom of the shoe. Is that supposed to happen?”

I place my hand over my mouth to stifle another giggle and look over at him. “Yes, that’s supposed to happen.”

"Maybe Grandfather wasn't so crazy." He's acting like an alien coming to earth, witnessing everything for the first time.

"You can take them off," I say.

"No." His body turns toward me and pulls me back in. "I'll keep them."

We walk side by side for an eternity. We talk some more and I learn Asher is a really smart man. You wouldn't think he's been working for someone else. I guess his grandfather held him back in that way. I try not to pry too much. I know if I do, he'll try to pry into my life and right now I'm happy with what I am revealing about myself.

That is, until he asks me this question.

"I know you said you're single but is there someone back home you're dating?" He tries to keep the question light but I can tell he has major trust issues. Between his trust issues and my control issues, we're a recipe for disaster.

My relationship with Parker is not an off-limits conversation. That is something I've had no problem talking about. It's what happened right after that sends me into a cesspool of guilt and agony.

"I was dating someone. I thought he was the one, but I was wrong."

"How long ago was that?"

"Six months ago." I say, watching Asher piece another portion of the puzzle together.

"You have had a crap year."

He has no idea.

We make it back to my hotel with Asher telling me about his motorcycle. I tell him I've never been on one before and he offers to take me for a ride sometime. That would be nice but we both know it's impossible, even though neither of us mentions it.

I look up at the moon, which is so large and bright, I feel like Jimmy Stewart trying to lasso it closer.

"This place is magical." Every day since I've stepped off that boat I've become more amazed at not just the beauty of the island but its power. It's as if the moon is casting a spell of enchantment over it so only the good can prevail and all terrible things are kept at bay. "I could spend eternity here."

When I lower my gaze from the moon, Asher is looking at me with a mix of interest and desire. He takes a step closer and threads his fingers through my hair, grazing his thumbs along by cheeks and jawline. "Can I see you tomorrow?"

I lick my lips in anticipation for the kiss I know is coming. "I can't. I have Leah. I can't leave her. It's our honeymoon." I say with a smile.

"Bring her with us. I want to see you again." Asher lowers his lips to mine. This time his kiss is soft and purposeful. Not like the frantic one we shared before.

"Yes." I breathe when he releases us from the kiss. I don't want him to go. If I had my own room I'd invite him in.

Oh, God, look at me. A few hours ago I was unsure I could handle a kiss. Now I'm ready to drop my pants.

It's him. He's like a drug to me. A very lethal drug.

Watching him walk away down the path toward the marina, I remind myself that is exactly what will happen. In four days, Leah and I have to leave. And then my European romance will be over.

Oh, fuck it. I've already had a crap year. It can't get worse, right?

I gently open the door, careful not to waken Leah. It shouldn't surprise me; she's sitting in the dark, waiting for me.

"You little harlot!" Her voice is extra high.

"Were you spying on me?" I turn and flip on the light switch. Leah is wearing her silk shorts pajamas and has Adam's surveillance binoculars in her hand.

"They have night vision. I was just on the veranda watching you and hottie McHottness hooking up!" She leaps onto the bed and starts jumping up and down.

I'm not going to lie; it's the exact reaction my heart had when he first kissed me. I jump on the bed with her and start bouncing up and down. It's against my usual persona but fuck that sad girl. I used to be happy and silly. Today was a good day. No, today was a great day and I want to enjoy it a little longer.

Leah plops down on the bed Indian style and pulls me down to sit next to her. My dress rides up but not enough that Leah would care. Part of me wants to tell Leah everything about tonight. I want to replay every touch, every smile, every word—but I can't. Asher is as private a person as I am. To tell her anything would violate a bond we formed tonight. Even if it was just for tonight.

"I'm glad to see you happy."

"Thanks. It feels good," I say, surprising myself.

"Adam is all kinds of pissed at me," she says, her mouth cocked to the side.

I laugh at the thought of Adam being upset with Leah until the look on her face lets me know she's serious. "Wait. Why is Adam mad at you?"

"He called and I was so excited about your date I told him the whole story. I told him about the yacht the other day and your boat tour yesterday and now your date tonight. He. Was. Pissed." Leah seems as surprised by the notion as I am.

"When you asked him to wire money you didn't tell him the whole story?" I ask.

"No. I left out the part about us following a giant to his massive boat. Thought it was wiser for all parties. I got excited about you going out that I thought he'd appreciate the story. Instead he lectured me on how careless we were. It got ugly." Leah shakes her body, like a shiver. "Ahh, bad karma, bad thoughts. Forget that nonsense. He'll be fine tomorrow. Because, you're fine. Right?" Her brows rise.

I give her a wide smile. "Yes, very fine. And I'm seeing him again tomorrow. Actually, we are both seeing him. He invited us somewhere, unless, of course, you don't want to go." My offer is two-sided. It's genuine because Leah means the world to me. But deep down I will be crushed if she says no. I really want to see Asher again but tomorrow is Luke's birthday and we girls should be together.

"You're seeing him again?" Her voice heightens in surprise.

"You don't think it's a good idea? I can cancel—"

"No," she says quickly. "That's awesome. It'll be awesome. I'm coming, too, so what could go wrong?" She hops off the bed, planning her outfit for tomorrow's excursion and I thank God for her love of adventure. I'm going to need her on this one.

chapter NINE

I can't believe Leah is sick. Like, honest-to-goodness sick. This morning she woke up with some sort of food poisoning slash stomach bug slash I don't know what.

At first, I thought this was her way of getting me alone with Asher again. Last night, she was crazy excited about what he might have planned for us. She loves surprises. And she didn't seem to mind that we'd be spending Luke's birthday with a stranger and she didn't seem too concerned with what Adam might say about our hanging out with him.

Then when she woke up she started grumbling about how she doesn't feel good. But this is Leah we're talking about: she has lied in the past about being sick.

I now know she is not lying. She is locked inside the bathroom and the sounds coming from that room are far from human.

"Go without me. There is no reason why you should be locked up in this room all day too." Her words are strained and breathy.

"What if something happens to you while I'm gone? You don't sound so good in there," I say to her through the bathroom door. She has been in there with the door locked for the past twenty minutes.

I hear the sound of a toilet flush and then the running water of the sink. I step back when I hear the click of the door being unlocked. Leah opens it. Her hair is a disheveled mess and her eyes are bloodshot.

"I feel much better. I promise you I'm not going to die while you're out today." She is padding her way to the bed. Leah is most definitely out of it. She would never make a death comment around me on an ordinary day.

Pulling down the comforter, Leah climbs in and falls back against the pillow. "Go spend the day with your boy. I'll park myself by the pool later on."

I'm already dressed in white shorts and a canary-colored V-neck, fitted T-shirt; my gold shoes from Asher garnishing my feet. "I feel terrible your vacation is ruined. I'm not leaving you alone to lay in this bed."

"Oh, yes you are. You are so going out there and enjoying yourself. I'll feel awful if you stay here and miss out on a gorgeous afternoon because of my sick ass." She grabs the pillow next to her and stuffs it under the one already under her head. She sits up a little, elevated. "I'll be in and out of that bathroom all day. You do not want to be here for that."

I stand by her bed as I try to decide what I should do. I hate when people give you an option like this. Leah says go but will she secretly resent me for leaving her alone? Will she throw it in my face later on that I ditched her when she was sick in Italy? Probably not. Leah's not like that. But still.

"Oh, for the love of all things holy. Go, Emma. If not for me, do it for McConaughey." Leah says. I cock a brow at her and she adds, "You gotta keep on livin'."

I leave Leah with everything she needs for a day of being sick. Her iPad is plugged in and next to her on the bed. She has the hotel phone on the end table in case of an emergency. A glass of water and a trashcan are by her side, as well as the remote, a bottle of soda, and her binoculars. I didn't really see the use for the spyware, but she wanted them near by.

Leah promised she would contact the front desk if she felt dizzy. I stop by the concierge and place a room service order for her. Even if she didn't eat, I knew someone would be there to check up on her.

After making arrangements for my sister, I head toward the lobby in anticipation for another day spent with Asher.

As I walk through I spot the woman I bumped into two days ago. She is seated in a large wingback chair, reading a magazine. Her large hat covers her face as bright red nails flip the pages. I look down at my casual outfit and wonder if I should be wearing more day-dresses like the pretty striped one she is wearing. It is a mix of colors, most of them primary and dark.

I shrug my shoulders and walk out the lobby doors and down the stairs toward the marina.

Asher told me to meet him by the Marina. Growing up, I never went on boats. Once or twice we went fishing with my uncle on the lake, and there was that family cruise to the Bahamas. But other than that, I may have been on five boats my entire life. It's fascinating I've been on six since we landed in Italy and I have no idea what we're doing today.

I'm carrying the note Asher left at the hotel. I really like that he leaves hand written notes. With the age of cell phones and emails, there is no use for the old paper and pen method. Then again, I don't have a phone with me anymore as it's at the bottom of the ocean. So, this morning, the concierge handed me a note from Asher with the location I should meet him. I was also surprised it came with a yellow rose with red tips.

I'm walking along the steps to the Marina Grande, my rose in my hand and the card in the other. The sun is hot today and it's not even noon. I am just about to step onto the final stair when a body rounds the corner and almost slams into me. I take a step back and, just when I'm about to be upset, I find myself breaking out into a huge grin.

"I thought I was meeting you at the boat?" I ask, but my words are swallowed up when Asher snakes his hand around my neck and pulls me into a kiss. I don't know what to do with my hands, but my mouth knows exactly where it needs to be.

When Asher finally pulls away he gives me a kiss on the nose. "I couldn't wait any longer."

If I had a mirror I'm sure I'd see dimples on my face.

Asher takes the note card from my hand, slides it into his back pocket and grabs my free hand. He guides me along the marina and I check out my date for the day. Leah would say he looks edible and I would agree. It's not so much what he's wearing but the way he wears it. His navy shorts showcase his strong legs and the polo he has on accentuates the broad shoulders and narrow waist.

"You're wearing flip flops!" I say, completely surprised. "I thought you hated them."

Asher flashes me a grin. "I'm doing a lot of things these days I thought I'd never do."

We walk over to the dock area where the same boat Asher had the other day is waiting.

"Does Devon mind you taking his boats out all the time? Won't you get in trouble?" I ask as I climb onto the boat. I turn around and Asher is looking at me like I have an orangutan sitting on my head. "What?"

He walks forward and kisses my lips. "Nothing. You're cute." Asher must catch my eye roll because he adds, "Don't tell me you're one of those girls who hates to be called cute?"

I cringe at the word. Saying a girl is cute is like saying she's your little sister or some small thing that needs care. I much prefer being called bold, accomplished, or successful. Not cute.

I scrunch my nose at Asher and shake my head letting him know I am not a fan of the word *cute*.

He laughs. "You're not helping your case."

I lean my weight onto one foot and give him a stare-down. Asher stops laughing. His tongue skims his lip as he places his arms around my waist and pulls me back into him.

"I take it back. You're not cute." His eyes looking directly into mine. "You're talented. You're feisty. You're mesmerizing. You're captivating. And you are the most beautiful woman I have ever seen in my entire life."

Yeah, those words will do.

With a soft kiss on my neck, he releases me, leaving me breathless and brimming. I set my rose down and watch him untie the boat from the dock. His shirt is clinging to him, showcasing the deep curvature of his muscles and the two divots at the bottom of his back.

I am staring at the perfection that is Asher when he turns around and stops, looking startled. "Wait. Where's your sister?"

"She's not coming."

It must be the thing he wanted to hear because Asher gives me a smile the size of Ohio.

"Lucky boy," he says, walking past me to start the engine while the boat drifts from the dock.

I take my place, standing in front of the chair I sat in last time. We're not going fast at all so I choose to stand up and hold on to the panel in front of me. I love being on the island of Capri but not as much as I love looking at it. I know we have "mountains majesty" back home but this place is just surreal.

Asher grabs my arm and pulls me into the spot between his legs and drives holding on to me. This isn't a lesson in driving like it was the other day. This time, it's out of pure need to be next to me. I settle in as the boat skips over waves and sea spray mists around us.

The waves and wind in our ears make it hard to hear anything. That's okay. I don't need to hear anything. I have the intense feeling of Asher behind me, the smell of the sea and the sounds of ocean. I use the hymn of the motor humming and the sound of it muffling with each crash down on a wave as a down beat in my head. Soon a chord plays over that and I hear the sounds of my violin. The chords build up and I hear them playing out an amplifier, and then another violin joins in and then another until there is an electronic symphony in my head. It is exactly the sound I was working on before the accident.

Before I couldn't play anymore.

Before I couldn't feel anymore.

I'm torn between feelings of excitement for my breakthrough, or fright for what it could mean, when the boat starts to slow down. So caught up in my own head, I didn't realize Asher had released me.

I crane my head back to look at him. His gaze is fixed ahead. His face is pensive, lost in thought. I don't know when the mood changed. I look around at my surroundings and see water on all sides of us, the island lost in the distance.

Asher turns off the engine. This should be about the time I wonder if the hot guy I met on vacation is really a murderer who dumps bodies in the middle of the ocean. If that's the case, I should have a weapon and, unfortunately, all I have is a rose.

I remain standing by the controls while Asher walks down to the lower cabin. He stays down there for a few minutes and comes back with a cardboard box and places it on the floor at the back of the boat.

The boat is moving up and down, riding waves from the current of a large ship that passed us. By the time the boat settles down to a calming bob in the water, Asher is standing at the back of the boat, staring out in the sea.

With his hands placed on his hips and his head bowed, Asher breathes deeply. I maintain my spot by the controls and watch him. We stand in silence for a long time. I'm not sure how long, because I'm not wearing a watch, but it feels like a long time.

Finally, Asher turns around and lifts the cardboard box off the floor and opens the top. From inside, he takes out another box. This one is a black cube. It's a thicker material than the cardboard and from the way Asher is handling it, I can tell its contents are important. He holds the black box in his hands for a moment, staring at it and not saying a word. His expression is solemn and distant.

Asher breathes in deeply and when his head lifts and sees me still standing by the controls, his expression softens.

"This is my grandfather."

His grandfather? *In a box?* This is so not how I saw the day playing out.

"Nice to meet you?" I say to the box with an awkward wave.

Asher lowers his gaze back to the box and lets out a sigh. "This is weird."

I shake my head in agreement. "This is weird."

We both share a grim look, which causes me to snort and him to laugh, and a tiny bit of the tension is lifted off the boat.

When Asher told me stories about his grandfather, I hadn't realized the man was dead. And by dead I mean cremated in a box ten feet from where I'm standing.

When Asher was ten, he was sent to live with his grandfather, who was difficult to please. That must have been a nightmare. Being ripped from your warm and loving home? That's just cruel.

I didn't press for more of the story last night and I won't today. Obviously, this is something Asher is trying to work through. I don't have my own shit together, let alone have a say in how someone I just met should handle his emotions.

"I've been holding onto this thing for a year. First, it just sat in my apartment collecting dust. My grandfather, he was a control freak. He planned everything about his life. Hell, he even planned his own funeral. But the one thing he never did was tell me what to do with the fucking ashes."

Asher is looking down at the box, observing it like its the first time. His eyes skim over it a few times before he lifts the top.

"For six months I've been sailing around the world trying to find the right place to leave him. Nowhere back home seemed right." Asher frowns. "Isn't that strange? I couldn't think of a single place to scatter the ashes back home?"

Confusion and desperation sound in his voice. I search for the right words to comfort him.

"It sounds like you were trying to find the most perfect place," I say, and then dare to go further. "Or maybe, you just weren't ready to let him go."

Asher slowly shakes his head but doesn't answer. He walks over to the back of the boat and opens the door to the small diving port and takes a step down closer to the water. Kneeling down, he balances the box on his knee and opens the plastic bag inside containing the ashes.

I walk over to where he is and take a knee down beside him. "You don't have to do this if you're not ready."

He swings his body toward mine and those molten caramel eyes look so soft. "I didn't know where to put him because my contempt is so deep I didn't care where he went. Then yesterday, you spoke about how magical this place is. You said you could live here forever, and I just knew. This is where I should put him."

Last night I made a comment about an island and he decided he was going to scatter the ashes here and I had to come along for the ride. Hell, he even invited my sister.

"Have you always been this impulsive?"

Asher's lips widens in a closed-mouth smile. "Every second of every damn day."

I know I should be alarmed by his actions but I totally get them. I understand what it's like to put your emotions on hold. Avoidance has been my companion for the last six months. Asher's been dating the emotional devil for a year.

Actually, something tells me they've been together for years.

He takes the box with its opened plastic bag inside and holds it upside down over the water. Gray ashes drift out of the box, hitting the water and drifting off with the breeze. Either his grandfather was a small man or there aren't as many ashes from a cremated body as I assumed there would be.

When the box is empty, he gives the bottom a final pat before setting it down on the floor beside him. Our legs are getting wet with the current that splashes up.

The two of us sit here for a while, watching the ashes drift away from us. A pile seems to stay close to the boat, not wanting to leave but after a while as the boat drifts away, the ashes gain some distance.

I won't tell him that I've already said about fifty prayers in my head. I say most of them for the man the ashes belong to. I say a few more for Luke. He would have been twenty-one years old today. I bite back my tears and let out a breath to control the feelings falling from my eyes. Hopefully Asher just thinks I'm emotional because of the experience he is sharing with me.

"What would you have done if Leah came?"

"This wasn't as monumental a moment as you think. I didn't care who was here. I just wanted you."

He has to stop saying things like that. It makes my heart beat twice as fast and my head spin in twenty different directions of anxiety.

"Why would you want me here?" I ask and then sidestep my words a bit. "I mean, I'm not weirded out or anything."

Asher doesn't miss a beat before looking straight into my eyes and explaining with deep conviction, "I'm drawn to you. When I want something, I take it. You already caught on how impulsive I am. It's just the way I operate."

I envy him. Everything about my life had been planned out. Now I don't know what to do. I want to be impulsive and free too. Maybe losing control is the only way to really gain it.

I look at the surroundings. Asher didn't drop anchor so we are drifting out, the ashes now far in the distance. We are surrounded by nothing but the open ocean with the mainland in the distance.

My hands rub along the top of my thighs, and I catch Asher's eyes as they follow the action. He rises on his knees, those intense eyes bearing down on me. I know he is going to kiss me and for a second I think about leaning forward. But, instead, out of sheer loss of control of my own nature, I spring up on my toes and dive into the water.

Cold Mediterranean water cools my warm skin. My body is submerged under and I break away, diving further down before swimming up to the surface.

My arms rise to push my hair smooth against my scalp. Looking up, I see the sun shining above me, beating down in approval. My body spreads out onto of the water, my arms and legs out like I'm making a snow angel. Instead, today, I'm an ocean angel looking up at the heavens.

This is for you, little brother.

Weightless, I bob and weave with the waves, a spatter of water covering my face but I'm not concerned. I don't have any real cares at the moment. Everything feels so buoyant and it feels wonderful.

A splash awakens me from my date with the sun. Asher saddles up beside me and takes a place with me. We're like two starfish in the middle of the ocean.

If anyone passes us they'll think we're out of control.

Because we are.

chapter TEN

Wrapped in a large towel, I swaddle myself and settle onto the sun pad at the bow of the boat. With the sun at its peak, our clothes will be dry in no time.

Asher's may dry faster than mine. His shirt will, at least, because it is hanging from the railing of the boat, drying in the breeze and sunshine. In return he is wearing his shorts and nothing else.

Well-defined pecks with the perfect sprinkle of chest hair . . . Yeah.

A lean, taut stomach with two, four . . . Yeah.

Gorgeous thighs whose definition are made out by the wet shorts currently sticking to him. Oh yeah.

A loud sound from deep inside Asher's throat catches my attention and I immediately avert my eyes north of the border. When I look back at him, he shakes his head and smiles, liking that he caught me gawking.

He kneels down to the sun pad, then lays his body next to mine, facing me. "Its ninety degrees out here. Lose the towel." His hand grabs the lining and pulls the towel away from my body,

I grab hold of it. "No way. I'm wet and cold and have all kinds of lady parts that aren't acting very ladylike." Not only is my shirt getting increasingly tight but when I put on white shorts this morning I wasn't planning on taking a swim in them.

He rolls his beautiful blond head back and laughs out loud. "It's okay for you to check out my man parts but I can't see yours?"

My lips purse. "My parts are more . . . sacred."

"That they are. But you'll dry off faster without the towel." He peels the towel off my shoulder and lets it fall to the side. "I promise. I won't check out your—okay, I lied. I just checked them out."

My arms jerks up and hit him in the arm. "You're such a fool."

"Watch it, woman. You have a serious hook. Nice to see that hand of yours is still useful for something."

I look down at my hand and notice it didn't hurt. That doesn't mean it will ever heal. It just means it may not be as fragile as I have been treating it.

Asher leans down and grabs my injured hand in his, rubbing his fingers along the scar. "I'd like to know more about the accident."

"I'd like to know more about your grandfather," I counter. So far, Asher hasn't told me anything worth sharing my secrets for.

Asher's brows curve in. "There isn't much to tell. He's dead."

"When did he die?"

"Last summer. He had a massive heart attack. Died before I made it to the hospital."

His eyes stay down, his voice void of the emotion one would expect to bear when losing a loved one. Even though he seems to have no feeling toward the man, it still seems important to share my condolences.

"I'm very sorry for your loss."

The jaw on his chiseled face tightens as he works out a thought in his head. Asher closes his eyes tight and holds it for a few beats. A heavy sigh releases and when those eyes open, they're honey.

"Are you for real, Emma Paige? Can I trust you? I've searched for a reason to believe otherwise. I've done my research and I can't find anything that leads me to believe you aren't anything but perfect."

A red flag goes up in my head. He did research on me? What kind of research? I know in the age of Facebook and Google, you can pretty much find out anything about anyone but I've never done that. Never needed to. And in this case, I didn't even have an urge to.

But with the red flag is a white flag waiving so dramatically my body does a double take as I try to contain my excitement.

This man thinks I'm perfect. Yes, me. The broken mess with a broken hand and a broken dream and a broken soul.

I lean up on my knees and gain some space from Asher. "If you knew the half of it you wouldn't think I'm perfect. You want to know if I'm real? Well, I need *you* to tell me something real. And don't say that you're impulsive and you're drawn to me. Because right now I can't believe how someone as amazing as you is here with me. It doesn't make sense and it makes me feel so insecure you won't believe."

Asher rises to his knees as well and meets me eye to eye. "I make *you* feel insecure?"

I nod my head slowly. He looks to the side, clenching his jaw. I think he's going to tell me he wants to head back but he opens his mouth and says, "My mother's name was Juliette Asher and my father was Alejandro Gutierrez. I haven't said those names out loud in twenty-two years."

My mouth falls open slightly. I haven't said Luke's name in six months but I'd hope twenty-years from now I'd be able to tell stories about him.

Asher looks back to me and continues. "My father was a mechanic with no family to speak of or two cents to rub together. Not to mention Latin, something my Scottish grandfather would never have allowed. But my mom, she was in love with my dad. She gave up her family and everything that came along with it. We lived in a poor section of Pittsburgh while my parents tried to figure out how to make ends meet. My mother was educated but she didn't know how to do anything other than play music. She was bred to be a rich man's wife, not a money-maker."

"And my dad, he was a hardworking man. He had a criminal record so work was hard to come by. We didn't have much but I never went without."

Asher' s hand takes mine and skims over the scar again, keeping his focus on the imperfection while he tells his story.

"When they died, I didn't have any other family. My grandfather took me in under one condition: I was never to speak of my parents again. It was the first time I ever met him. He didn't show love the way my parents did. I learned early on that if I pleased him, his pride in me was as good as love. I let him breed me into who he was. Work consumed me. Family was not an option. According to him, who can have one when they are going to leave you anyway."

My own jaw tightens as I try to control the burn in my throat that comes before a good cry. I breathe in calming breaths. "Asher, you know that's not true. Family is what you lean on when times get hard. I know you don't remember that but your parents seemed like the kind of people who would be there for you no matter what."

His cheeks hollow but with a deep rumble he lets out a puff of air and shakes his head. "I know. I just have a hard time remembering sometimes."

Is that what he's doing out here? Working for Devon? Trying to figure out who he is?

He must think I'm such an ass. I've been complaining about my overbearing parents, yet here he is trying to remember his own for the caring people they were. Probably exactly like mine are.

And to not have spoken about them, said their names out loud in so long. Well, that's just sad. It's a sadness I am swimming in, myself, and if I don't fight the current I'll drown. I can't let that happen.

"Luke." I whisper the name.

Asher's eyes pop open not understanding why I am whispering another man's name. I mentioned my brother vaguely yesterday but not his name. Just the casual mention of having a brother.

My heart is beating a million miles a minute. My lip trembles slightly. I try to keep it together. "Luke. I had a brother named Luke. Today is his birthday. At least, today would have been his birthday."

Understanding crosses Asher's face. His posture straightens as he leans forward and takes my face in his hands. "Emma, you don't have to—"

"He was impulsive like you. Always down to go to the next party or jump off a cliff or drive across country with his friends just because he had a free week from school. Luke was really smart too. He wanted to be an architect. I like to think he would have made a great one."

I take a deep, cleansing breath and continue. "Last winter, Luke was home for the holidays. Just after the New Year, my boyfriend, Parker, broke up with me. Luke was pissed. He said he never liked the douchebag anyway. His cure for a broken heart was to go out. So I let him take me."

My eyes flutter closed at the memory. "I had ten too many shots of Fireball. Luke didn't drink. When it was time to leave, I didn't want to go home so we went for a drive."

Images of snow covered roads and the inside of Luke's car as he blared Kings of Leon from his radio flash in my mind. I didn't comprehend how fast we were going and I certainly didn't do anything to make him stop. I'll never forget the look of his face as he tried to regain control of the car. Clawing, grabbing, desperate for control. He was frightened.

"When I woke up in a hospital room the next day, they told me my brother died at the scene. Said it was a miracle I was alive. I had major injuries but most healed. My hand, unfortunately, was crushed. The next day the doctors told me it would never work again. They said I was lucky they were able to salvage it at all. I told them they might as well have severed it."

Asher's thumbs rub the spot just under my eyes, catching the tears that are falling. I lift my gaze to his and see they are slightly red-rimmed as well.

I look into his eyes and say the thing that has been driving a knife through my heart for six months. "I killed my brother. If I hadn't asked him to go for a drive he would be alive. Don't you see I'm broken? I'm not perfect."

Asher's mouth finds my forehead and gives me a gentle kiss before pulling me into his chest. I like the way my body fits against his but I can't go daydreaming about what could be. I am damaged and he can't fix me.

"You are, by far, the most amazing person I have ever known," he says into my hair.

I lean back and blink at him. Hasn't he heard a word I said?

"How can you say that?"

Asher pushes my shoulders back and leans down slightly, putting me face-to-face with him. "Emma, in three days you had your heart broken, lost your brother, and your ability to play music. And you're still here to tell the tale. I don't know many people who would make it through a month, let alone six."

He is giving me far too much credit. He doesn't know what my family had to endure all this time. The doctors, the meds, the anxiety and worry over what I might do. The truth is, I barely made it through.

I look down at my hand and see that awful scar that takes up half my hand. "I hate this stupid scar. Not for how it looks. I hate how it reminds me of everything I lost. Everything I'll never get back."

Asher takes my hand and raises it to his lips, placing delicate kisses along every inch of the scar. My body pulsates at the feeling of his mouth on my most vulnerable piece of flesh.

"I want to try something with you but I need you to trust me. Do you trust me, Emma?" he asks and I look back at him, unsure of the truthful answer. I've already told him my darkest secret. Why not go further into the rabbit hole with him?

I nod my head yes. Numb to the fact I just bared my soul and he still wants to spend time with me.

I seem to have a problem saying no to Asher Gutierrez.

chapter ELEVEN

We arrive at the yacht; Asher pulls up to the dock on the starboard side. We get off and Mateo hops on to park the speedboat. Asher grabs my hand and leads me past the pool area and through the sliding glass doors I entered days ago. I follow him through the living area, past the bar and up the stairs. I get nervous as we round the corner to what I believe to be Devon's private areas. The staterooms and the office are back here. I know Asher is impulsive but I hope he doesn't do anything to get himself in trouble.

Or me for that matter. I'd hate to piss off the man who went through so much trouble to help me and my sister.

I follow his pull down the hall to the door at the far end. I know this door very well and my heart starts racing when Asher opens it.

The grand two-story music room is just as impressive as it was the first time I saw it. The piano still sits to the side looking all polished and pristine. I hope Asher doesn't expect me to play again because I don't think I'd be able to after his appraisal of my performance last time.

Asher closes the door behind us and flicks on the light switch, setting them to dim. The sun is hidden from our view out the window. On the horizon, dusk awaits.

I turn toward Asher. "We shouldn't be in here. This area is private. I don't want you to get in trouble."

Asher grins and places his fingers in my hair, pushing the ashy strands behind my ear. "No one is here. It's just you and me."

"No Devon?" My voice is shaky, like learning my boyfriend's parents are out of town for the weekend. No supervision. No rules.

"No Devon. We're free in here. It's our sacred space." Warm lips brush my cheek as he grabs my hand and whirls me around toward the cello. "I want to play with you. Together." He walks around a seat and stands just behind it. "I know that wound on your hand runs deeper than the superficial scar."

I stop just next to the cello and really think about that. I've been on one date and countless boats with the man. I think it's clear I trust him in the physical sense. In the emotional sense, I don't trust myself.

"Asher, I don't think I can—"

"Shh." He guides my body down onto the chair and slides another stool behind mine, so close the two are touching. He presses his body behind mine, his legs straddling my hips. "Close your eyes."

I want to explain to him the cello and the violin are different instruments. I want to explain they're the same instrument. I want to explain my injury prevents me from playing any bow and I want to tell him to stop whatever he is about to try.

But I can't.

Because his entire body is wrapped around me and all I can do is feel his heat.

I close my eyes and breathe in. His scent of sea and soap eradicate my senses and the velvet skin of his forearms along with his strong thighs outside my own feel like a warm blanket on a blistery cold night.

Asher glides his right hand underneath mine and lifts it in the air, palm to knuckles. "Hold onto me just like this," his voice whispers in my ear.

I nod and then jump a little with the feel of the weight of the cello resting against my kneecaps. "Open your legs."

I do so and allow him to place the cello in between my thighs, resting on my left knee. He spreads his even wider to accommodate the heavy instrument in between us.

He lifts my left hand and places it on the strings of the cello. My fingers instinctively find a chord even though the strings are placed further apart than I'm used to. With my hands in place, Asher weaves his free left arm around my waist and pulls me in tight.

"Are you ready?" He rests his head beside my neck. His lips warm on my skin. I know he can feel my quiver at the feel of him. All my attention is focused on him and not the instrument in front of me.

"Ready for what?" I say with a swallow.

I feel his mouth turn up against my neck. "To feel."

With his words, Asher raises his right hand, which mine is laying on top of, and grabs hold of the bow. My hand gently forms around his in response. His elbow up in the air, his palm poised for performance, Asher dips the bow across the strings eliciting a glorious sound. He guides our hands back and dips back across the strings again, creating more familiar sounds.

His hand is gripped around the bow, taking the control I cannot obtain without screaming in pain. With my hand wrapped around his massive one I am able to imitate the feeling of playing.

Tension in my spine stiffens. It feels unnatural to be playing in this position. My elbow props up on his with each glide and I pretend not to notice when his forearm casually brushes against my breast with each stroke.

Instead of focusing on the unnatural, I keep my eyes closed and try to feel the movements. My fingers shift chords and his hand dips to let the bow strike the strings in a new direction. I allow my head to fall back against his shoulder and breathe in the sounds we are creating and suddenly my arm doesn't feel like following anymore.

With a tightened grip on his, my hand glides free and takes control of the movements, this time telling his where to go. I weave and thread the bow across the strings, my movements faster and with more purpose.

My back leans forwards and I grab the neck of the instrument and play chords up and down, pulling the massive wood with me to create a musical force I haven't felt in months.

The sounds keep playing and the song is magnificent. It's not one I know, but something that is pouring through me. With every pump of his muscles against my body I play harder and with every feel of his breath against my very tender skin, I play louder. Faster and with more control than I've felt in a long time, I play that instrument until the sound is so vibrating throughout the space I'm afraid I'll shatter the windows.

I open my eyes and take in the site of the ocean in front of us. I play to the crash. I play to the white tops. I play to the rumbling of the waters beneath us.

Even before the accident, my heart and soul have never felt so liberated. You can't truly learn of the bliss and joy of something until its been taken away from you.

In this moment I am feeling exhilaration.

In this moment I am feeling rapture.

In this moment I am . . . Feeling.

Asher chances releasing me and grabs hold of the cello and plays a few chords with me. Together we play the instrument. Our bodies mold together as one. If anyone were to walk in on us, they would think we are performing some sort of impressionist dance. A modern movement of lust and love and passion. That is what this song is instilling in us.

Passion.

Our breathing is tense and erratic. His heart is beating against my back, striking it like a ten-pound percussion. Our bodies are entwined so deeply with each other I feel like we are one.

When Asher puts his hand back around my waist he slows his hand control under mine and brings us to a slower tempo. We play this way until our bodies are calmed and we're aware of how sweaty our palms are.

Our movements sashay and sway together in a dance of lovers and together we bring the song to a close.

When the humming has stopped, Asher leans over, placing the cello back in its stand and rests the bow next to it. I release my hand from his and rest the other on his knee.

I close my eyes and lean my head on his shoulder and breathe out the greatest breath of a lifetime.

"Thank you."

His broad chest against my back is rising and falling in tantric rhythm to my own heavily beating heart. My own movements are steady, yet as intense as his. That's why my skin hums with electricity as his hand comes circling around my waist and his palm lands on the inside of my thigh.

"I've never felt someone playing before. You ignite with a fervor and rage and ardor and devotion. I am infatuated."

Warm, heated breaths play on the soft skin of my throat and I constrict when his warm mouth crosses the nape so gently it feels like a breeze tickling my skin. His tongue darts out and licks the sensitive skin sending shivers down my body and into the very core.

I curve my back into him and let the warmth envelope me. Leaning my neck further to the side, I offer him more of me, asking to be taken.

And he does. French kisses dance up and down my neck, making my body feel alive—and I didn't even know I was dead.

"Emma." My name off his lips is the sexiest thing I've ever heard. I know he's asking if I'm okay with where his hand is. Asher is a man who takes what he wants. And my heart beats a thousand strums for the fact he wants to know if I'm okay with what his intentions are.

I don't know what I'm okay with. I know I'm scared. I know I'm turned on. I know I don't want to cry and I know I want to feel alive.

So in quite the most impulsive moment of my life, I place my hand over Asher's hand and move it further up my legs so it's resting under the white shorts.

As his palm presses deeper into my thigh, his fingers caress the flesh and make their way up and down, playing me like chords of an instrument.

And I so want to be played.

I want to be the music.

I turn my head toward him and connect with golden eyes, so intense and full of passion. I take his mouth into mine and kiss him so intensely I think I might combust.

Two hands are now on my thighs, working them up and down until I am in a frenzy. My breasts push through my bra and my skin feels as hot and brightly colored as the tank top they're trying to be free of.

I let out a gasp when one of Asher's very delicate fingers slip further inside my shorts and brushes along the outside of my thong.

"You are so sensitive," he says, his mouth in a smile I can feel against my skin.

I am throbbing and need to be touched. Even in this lustful haze I can understand how insane it is that I want him so much. I am not an overtly sexual person. Parker and I were in a loving relationship but I never craved him. Not like this. This is primal.

At this moment I can only think of how alive I feel.

In this room.

With this man.

Asher's fingers work me over my panties, drawing dangerous circles sending me into a crescendo of pleasure. He kisses my shoulder and continues to rub me. When my body is on the brink of an orgasm I swing my head back around and kiss him, feeling his tongue in my mouth as my body falls apart, collapsing into him with an orgasm so intense I could stop breathing.

My head falls to his chest, reveling in the best sexual experience of my life and his fingers didn't even touch my skin. If he can do this to me with our clothes on, I can't imagine what can be done with them off.

I don't know Asher very well, but I want to get to know him further. He is so easy to talk to. He doesn't push me like everyone else, yet he makes me want to tell him things.

Most importantly, he gave me the greatest gift anyone could ever give. He made me feel music again.

I slowly rise from my seat and do something so bold and daring, so unlike me, yet so absolutely right for this very moment.

I strip.

My fingers deftly work the button of my shorts, allowing to slowly fall off my hips and down my legs, getting turned on as Asher's eyes turn black with lust. A smile crosses my lips as I watch his gaze travel down my legs and back up in complete appreciation for what I am doing.

I cross my hand across my body and lift my shirt over my head, leaving me in nothing but my lace bra and matching thong.

Asher's breath hitches. His teeth bite down on his lower lip and skim the plum of his mouth.

Remember how I said I didn't find lip-biting sexy?

Turns out, I lied.

"Baby, I like where this is going but I need you to know this is not why I brought you here." His words are sincere but his tone and the incredible bulge in his pants lets me know he wants me to keep going.

"Just call me impulsive," I say and I'm rewarded with a crooked smile that turns smoldering when I hook my thumbs under my panties and lower them until they hit the floor. When my bra comes off, I swear the room gets ten degrees hotter.

So, here I am, stark naked in the music room, standing in front of the most beautiful man I have ever seen in my life who happens to be sitting in front of a massive window overlooking the Mediterranean. In my wildest dreams I never would have envisioned this moment taking place.

But I'm here.

And I'm nervous.

Nervous because he is not saying anything. He is staring at me. His eyes let me know he likes what he sees but his lack of expression right now is making me want to shut down and run from the room.

I have one orgasmic musical experience and suddenly I think I'm a porn star. What is wrong with me? How could I think—

"You're perfect."

His words catch me so off guard, I have to think for a second if I heard them right.

"Come here." Asher says and puts his hand out in front of him.

I take a step forward and grab his hand. He closes his legs and places his hand on my hip, guiding me over him, until I am straddling him.

Our hips join and I can feel his need for me rubbing against me. I look down at the source of his arousal and have to take a moment to gather my wits.

"Emma, look at me." Asher wraps his hands in my hair, guiding my face up so we are staring at each other. His thumbs caress my cheeks. There is something about his touch that makes me feel protected.

"I've never done anything like this before," I say.

Asher offers a kind smile. "I can tell."

I shrug away from him but he pulls my head back. "Don't be embarrassed. I like that you're nervous. It makes you real."

I can almost laugh. "A real lunatic." I look at him and relax as his hands rub up and down my spine. "I've known you for moments—yet I want you more than I have ever wanted anyone else. Isn't that crazy?"

Asher doesn't match my expression. Instead, he looks on as serious as ever. "It's insane."

My eyes shoot up. Is he regretting this moment? Because if he is, I think I might just curl up and die.

"Don't do that," he says.

"Do what?"

"Search for a reason to leave. I've been doing the same thing for four days. Trying to find a reason why I should leave you alone. And I can't. I feel so connected to you. And I know you feel it too. Hell, I barely touched you and you fell apart in my hands. There is a fire between us, Emma, and I know we're going to get burned but I want to walk into it anyway. This is crazy and insane and, by God, it has me so fucking scared I don't know if I should kiss you or walk away from you."

"Kiss me," I say, leaning into him, taking his lips back in mine. He seems hesitant at first but then his mouth opens up further, drinking me in as he did before.

We are a mess of emotions.

Two broken people trying to be put back together.

And one we become.

Asher's hands lower under my bottom and grabs on tight as he stands and lifts us from the chair. My legs grip tighter to his waist and my arms cling on to his neck to keep from falling as we move through the room. He must know how to navigate the space in the dark because his mouth is still on mine and his movements are sure and aimed for a very specific destination.

He loosens one hand to open the door to the music room. Not caring if anyone is in the hallway, he walks us down the corridor and turns to another door, opening it and shoving it closed with his foot after we enter.

My back is lowered onto a plush bed of fine linens. The weight of me sinks into the fabric. It feels divine. Not as divine as the hands of the man who is still holding me, kissing me, and taking me with his mouth in mine.

Asher breaks the kiss and kneels over me. Hooded eyes skim my body. Instead of feeling embarrassed I take the empowerment I get under his stare and lift my back up off the bed and help him undress.

First, I peel off his shirt and get an intimate view of the perfectly sculpted chest I was admiring earlier.

My hands rub over the hard muscle and weave in the soft hairs of his stomach that lead a trail to the edge of his boxer briefs sticking out of his shorts.

Next, I unhook his belt and leave it hanging loosely from the hooks. My fingers, steady and controlled, undo the top button of his shorts and then glide the zipper down.

With a hiss through his teeth and his stomach constricting, I lower his shorts until they're hanging loosely by his bent knees. I reach my hand inside and pull his massive erection from his boxers, feeling the weight of it in my hand and rubbing my palm up and down his length, circling my thumb around the tip.

"Baby, that feels so good. You feel so good." His moans send me into erotic bliss. I lean forward and lick the very sensitive head, swirling my tongue around in circles and then glide up the vein until Asher's head falls back.

"Emma . . ."

I lick and roll and dance with him, taking him to the back of my throat and listening to the beautiful sounds his throat makes with every ounce of pleasure I am giving him.

Warm hands snake around my head. His fingers weave into my hair, guiding my head up. For as worked up as he is, Asher leans down, and brings his legs down between mine until he is settled above me, between my legs, hovering over me and kisses me with a steadied passion that is more determined and purposeful than anything he has exhibited in the short time I've known him.

"I need to be inside of you." His voice is hushed, his breathing hard. "I don't think I'll be able to breathe until I'm buried deep inside you."

My body is burning with want and lust for this man. The taste of him in my mouth and the feel of him between my thighs is too much. My core is begging to be taken by him, in every way. And if he doesn't tame the throbbing between my legs I might just flip him over and straddle him on my own.

I have nothing to offer in the form of words so I give him my permission by pushing his clothes off as far as I can reach them. My palm flat against his gorgeous ass, pulling him toward me.

"I need to hear you say it." He says, not budging his body from hovering over my body. I want him lower. On me. In me. I want him closer but he's holding back.

"Say what?" I ask, looking up into those eyes that have turned my heart citrine.

"Tell me you need me. I want to hear you say the words." His chiseled face, softens with emotion.

His eyes are asking me for something very more than just sex.

They're asking me to fix him.

To let him fix me.

They're asking me to love him.

My throat tightens and my mouth waters. From the tips of my toes to the pad of my fingers. My skin is on fire and igniting brighter with every extra inch of skin of his that touches mine. Together, we are a raging fever. The only antidote is to quell the desire burning between us.

"I need you, Asher. I need you to make me feel. I need you to make me burn. I need you to burn with me."

"It's you," he says as his lips come crashing back down on mine. In a heartbeat his clothes are off and he is opening a foil packet I didn't see him grab. He slides the condom down his shaft and positions just outside of me.

With soft kisses and strong hands, Asher holds me still as he enters me. My back instantly bows and arches into him. If I thought the feel of him outside of my clothing was intense, the feeling of him inside me is immeasurable.

Moving in me, he hits every nerve ending inside my body. I didn't even know it could feel this good with out a mechanical toy. It's as if he was made especially for me, to fit inside and milk me from the inside out with pure perfection.

His body rolls in and out of me; rubbing his groin against mine to give friction to my very swollen clit. I'm being loved from the inside and the outside. It won't take long for me to . . . my God . . . my hands grip the sheets . . . my toes curl in . . . I feel so much.

My body starts to spasm, arching off the bed closer to him, needing more. I start pumping my own hips with him.

Asher's buries his head in my neck, biting my skin. "I love the feel of you. Keep doing that."

My body moves with his. My core is soaking wet and I'm still climbing.

Asher bends his back and leans his head down to take a nipple in his mouth. My body spasms more with pleasure and my orgasm is driven home when he adjusts his hips and pushes inside me so deep and hard I think I might be having an exorcism.

Screams and cries are coming from the room and they're all from me. Asher pulls me in tight and kisses me hard, sucking on my tongue and biting on my lip as he finds his own pleasure, coming hard inside me. I can feel him pulsing from inside.

Our bodies are a mix of sweat and heat. I feel sticky but I don't want to move. I want to be glued to this moment forever.

And I think he does too. Brushing the hair off my forehead, Asher rubs my temples and smoothes my hair with his hand. Gorgeous honey eyes skim my face. I reach up with my own hand and let my fingers trace the outline of his jaw, rubbing the light scruff.

Our skin remains tethered to each other as our hearts find a mutual beat and our breaths take on a synchronized rhythm.

My left leg lifts off the sheet and wraps around his thighs, pulling him in closer. He arches his hips in and kisses me, rolling onto his side, taking me with him, my leg still wrapped around him.

We lay and kiss on our sides until our lips are numb and then we kiss some more. I feel like I am complete for the first time in forever.

Asher tilts his back to look at me as his fingers lightly brush the long strands of my hair. "Have you ever heard of Sirens' Rock?"

I lightly shake my head.

"It is here, in the bay, at the center of the marina. The ancients believe it to be the place where the sirens seduced Odysseus with a song," he says, his voice slightly above a whisper. "It's *you.* My temptress who lured me in with a song."

Leaning down, Asher takes my lips again and holds on to them, ever so still, and I savour ever last breath he breathes into me.

"What is your favorite dessert?" Asher breaks our kiss and rubs our noses together.

It's a silly question but one I don't mind answering. "Ice cream. You?"

"Cheesecake. But only the New York kind. I'd like to take you to this shop near my house. You'll love it. In fact, I may bring it home and eat it off of you." His lips find my neck and start to nibble.

My heart sighs with the thought. "Where is your home?"

He leans back and looks at me as if I already know the answer. "New York. Manhattan. I thought you knew that."

I laugh into his chest. "I know nothing about you. Like, what kind of cologne do you wear? Because you always smell delicious." I drink in my very sexy maritime man.

Asher's body stiffens. "I don't wear cologne. I used to, but someone ruined it for me."

My head shoots up. First, I can't believe that he smells this amazing on his own. It's sinful and totally unfair. Second, who ruined cologne for him? A woman? A lover?

He gives me a look I'm starting to know well. "Not today. Someday I'll share that secret but this, right here, this is too perfect to taint with the past."

I nod in understanding. This moment is too pristine.

"Favorite color?" I ask.

"Black. I'm guessing yours is yellow."

I scoff. "Black is not a color and how did you know I love yellow?"

"I'm very observant. You wore it two days in a row. Two days you knew you were going to see me, might I add." His cocky smile is annoying yet totally kissable.

"It just so happens to look best on me." I curl further into him. "What did you want to be when you were a kid?"

"I wanted to play the cello."

"Looks like we have something in common."

"We have a lot in common. I've never met someone so similar to me before."

"Like our birthdays."

"Yes, like our birthdays. And Emma . . ." Asher rolls us so he is on his back. I let out a yelp as he pulls me with him until I am straddling his hips. The growing erection beneath lets me know he's ready for round two.

"Yes?" I say, cocking my brow, letting him I'm on to his wicked agenda.

"I don't want to talk anymore." Asher's hands take my hips and guide me into position.

"Sounds good to me." And it does. So we make love again.

This time we are rough and reckless and completely free.

chapter TWELVE

The sun is in the beginning stages of setting when I walk up the steps toward the hotel. I asked Asher to leave me at the marina. If he walked me up, I feared we'd never make it inside. My body is so addicted to him at this moment, I'd never leave.

Asher didn't take well to being told what to do but I promised I'd leave word with the front desk when I arrived and he could check in with them.

I have a bizarre feeling he's following me anyway to make sure I get back to the room safely but I keep going forward, making sure I stand my ground. He can't be near me or else I'll jump him again and today is too special a day. I need to be with my sister.

When I make it into the room, Leah is on the bed, looking sick but much better than she was hours ago.

"How are you feeling?" I ask with concern, even though I want to scream with excitement from the amazing afternoon I had.

Leah's face is forlorn. If she weren't so sick I'd think she was upset. "Why is your hair wet?"

My hand tangles a lock of hair. It's still damp from the shower I took with Asher. Shower sex is definitely better with him than it was with Parker. Hell, everything is better with him than it was with Parker.

"Oh my God, you slept with him," she says with minimal excitement. The Leah I know would be on me right now desperate for every dirty detail. But this version of her is more subdued.

I fight back a blush. "We showered because we went swimming in the ocean."

Leah's eyes widen. "You said *we*. You showered *with* him? You, like, got crazy nasty dirty with him?"

There's the Leah I know.

"Stop it." I wave her off. "We . . . he . . . you see . . ." Oh what the hell. "Leah, I just had the most amazing, mind-blowing sex of my life. It was wicked, and sinful and soulful and powerful, and I think I'm in love with him."

Holy shit. What is wrong with me? What the hell is wrong with me?

It sounds bat-shit crazy to me and I'm the one thinking it.

No, I'm the one knowing it.

Leah's mouth is puckered, her eyes narrow. "Asher?"

I nod my head in affirmation.

Leah's next words come out methodical. "Did Asher happen to tell you his whole name?"

"Asher Gutierrez. Why?"

Leah looks back at me, frozen in a trance. I take a step forward and put my hand on her shoulder. "Leah, are you okay? You look like you're going to be sick."

She places a hand over her mouth and nods before darting off the bed for the bathroom. I chase after her, grabbing her hair, and she hurls into the toilet. Poor Leah. I was spending the day in the arms of a gorgeous man and she was puking her guts up.

I rub her back until she has her stomach under control and guide her to the sink so she can brush her teeth. When she is steady on her feet, she walks back to the bed, me in tow, and climbs in, curling her knees into her chest.

Walking over to the bed, I take a seat next to her. "Can I get you anything? I feel terrible you've been sick all day. Do you want to see a doctor?"

Leah's crystal blue eyes look up at me, rimmed with worry. She shakes her head, "No, I'm fine. I haven't gotten sick in a few hours." She notions toward the bathroom, "That wasn't from being sick. I threw up from nerves."

My body is on alert. Confusion etches my brain. What in the world would make Leah so upset she'd get sick over it? "What are you talking about?"

"I'm so worried about you. I don't know if this will set you back. You've made so much progress. And yesterday, you were so happy," she says, her eyes looking everywhere but at me.

"What happened, Leah?" She's scaring me.

She rolls her head and then lifts a magazine from the ground. It's an American magazine, one I easily recognize, as well as the face on the cover.

"This came under the door this morning." Leah holds the magazine out two feet in front of her as if it is going to catch on fire. "I didn't pay any mind to it at first but when I finally got a good look, I called Adam."

I take the magazine and look down at the golden eyes gracing the pages.

"Why is Asher—"

Leah takes the iPad that was sitting on top of the bed and places it on her lap.

"Adam was mad. I told you. He couldn't believe that we went on that yacht. So he did some investigating." Leah punches her code in her iPad. "Devon doesn't own the yacht, Emma. He doesn't even come up on a Google search."

I cross my arms in front of me and balk at her. "So what?"

Leah inhales deep. "The boat belongs to Alexander Asher."

My face scrunches up in annoyance. "Who's Alexander Asher?"

Oh, wait.

Asher.

Asher?

Leah turns the iPad to face me. On the screen is a picture of Asher, my Asher, dressed in a gorgeous suit. His hair is styled perfectly, slicked back but a little spiky at the top. On each side of him is a gorgeous woman, both of whom I recognize from a certain lingerie catalogue. On the top of the screen the headline reads, "Billionaire Playboy At It Again."

I drop the magazine on the ground and grab the iPad from Leah and skim the article. Leah leans over and places a hand on my arm. "He's a womanizer, Ems. There's article after article of this guy and every woman under the sun. He's known for being an elusive cad and leaving women wanting more. I wanted you to have an international fling but I know this means more for you. I'm so sorry I steered you in the wrong direction. I never would have pushed you toward someone like him."

My head darts up at that comment. Not someone like him? Like who? Like Asher? There has to be an explanation. "I don't understand. Are you telling me Asher's been playing me?"

"I don't know what I'm telling you. All I know is that he has been manipulating you the entire time. Pretending he's someone else. Why would he lie about being rich, Emma? According to Adam, he was lying to get in your pants and when it's over you wouldn't know how to find him because you never knew who he really was. I want you to have fun—but not with someone like this. Not with someone who is going to make a fool of you. You've been through too much. I screwed up. I'm so sorry."

I drop the iPad on the bed and shrug my arm away from her. Here I am again. Poor Emma. Damaged and broken, needing to be looked after. Because apparently I can't even have a proper one-night stand without it being a major catastrophe.

A one-night stand? A one-day stand? Whatever.

I rise to my feet and pace about the room. Asher isn't Asher. Well, he's Asher but that's his last name. Why would he lie to me? Why would he let me believe the boat was his and that he worked for Devon? He lied. Didn't he?

I backtrack to every conversation trying to remember if he actually lied or if I just believed Devon owned the boat and Asher worked for him. No, he told me he was Devon's bodyguard, right?

Think, Emma, think.

His parents were poor and then they died. He went to live with his grandfather who doesn't let him wear flip-flops. He didn't own a dog because he was too poor growing up, too rich as an adult.

How can I be such an idiot?

He plays the cello and the piano. The music room is his. That's why he was never worried about Devon.

I'm not an idiot, I'm a moron.

My hands fall over my head at the thought of him playing me like that. Did he want me to believe he was the lowly boathand?

I bet his parents aren't even dead. He was never poor growing up. He's a rich asshole who made up a depressing story about his broken life so I'd fall like a ton of bricks. And I did.

I fell.

And I felt.

This time it's my turn to be sick.

I run into the bathroom and throw up. I opened up to him. Told him my secrets, my fears. For months I've been too numb to talk about anything. Not Parker, not the accident, not my hand, and certainly not Luke. In three days I talked about all of it.

Did I open up to my very expensive psychiatrist? NO.

Did I open up to my caring family who have done nothing but dote on me while I was sick in the head? NO.

Did I open up to a psychopath con artist who creates false lives to lure women into his web of lies?

Hurl.

"Don't do this. I didn't mean to make you upset." Leah's hand rubs my back this time. "I shouldn't have said anything. We're leaving here soon. It won't make a difference who your Italian hookup was. Emma, please, don't make yourself sick over this."

Leah's voice is a plea. A sad one. One I've heard before.

I lift my head and wipe my mouth, taking the same routine Leah did before. After my teeth are brushed I walk over to the bed and cross my legs. The iPad is still on the bed but I push it to the side, thankful the screen is black.

I promised myself I wouldn't be this girl. The girl who makes everyone worry. I'm not her anymore. I can go fast now. I can say Luke's name. And I can feel the music again.

The night Parker dumped me, Luke said something I'll never forget. "Never let a man believe he broke you, because a diamond can not be destroyed." I agreed with him. It's probably why I was able to get over Parker so easily. It is also why I'll be able to forget Asher.

Leah is sitting next to me, waiting for me to say something, make a move. Today is Luke's birthday. We planned on celebrating it together and that is exactly what we'll do. I'll worry about this Alexander Asher nonsense tomorrow. Today is about me and Leah.

"Get dressed. We're going out."

I toss and turn all night.

Leah and I went out to dinner but took it easy on the alcohol. Her stomach was still too sensitive and my heart was too fragile. We didn't talk about Asher. Instead we spoke about Luke. Leah was so happy to be able to mention him around me and tell stories without my falling apart.

Hearing her talk about him reminded me how close the two of them were too. I was a fool to think his death only affected me.

When we get back to the room, Leah collapses on the bed, exhausted from a day of being sick. My mind is revving a million thoughts a second. I can't sleep and I don't even try. Instead, I hop on Leah's iPad and google Alexander Asher.

Just as she said, there he is. Looking gorgeous. But instead of the guy I've grown to know, on the screen is a man of intimidating power. Every article is of businesses he's developed, bought, or flipped. He went to Columbia University, confirmation he's as brilliant as I knew he was. He owns three restaurants, a tech start-up, a media house . . .

And that doesn't count the business he inherited when his grandfather passed away. That's at least one portion of the story he is telling the truth about. His grandfather was Edward Asher, a Scottish billionaire and real estate developer who was a big deal in New York City.

I try looking up Asher's parents, but nothing comes up. There are a few mentions of his mother. She was a very talented young woman, performing at Julliard and winning awards for her piano playing. But after the age of twenty, she vanishes. It's as if she doesn't exist.

One article mentions Asher's career highlights and a charitable concert event he was funding. Of the four pages long article, it merely mentions his family, stating his mother died in a car accident and his grandfather took him in. The article makes his grandfather seem like a really good guy. Not the monster Asher alluded to.

I look over to the ground beneath the bed and see the magazine sitting on the floor. *New York Magazine.* On the cover is Alexander Asher standing on top of a tall building in Manhattan above the city he controls. The headline reads: *Asher. The new face of an empire.* I don't even have the heart to open it up.

Something doesn't feel right. Why would he lie to me? He is guarded and complex. He wanted to know if he could trust me. I thought I gave him every reason to believe I was trustworthy. I thought *I* had his trust.

I guess I didn't have enough of it to have him tell me the truth.

I pop up from my spot of the sofa and walk to the window. The sun is coming up. My body is too antsy to sit back and wait for word from him. I need to see him now. If this is all a misunderstanding, then I need to hear it from him. And if he is a player, then I need him to tell me to my face.

Opening the sliding glass door, I peer out into the marina. Even if I have to hire a boat to take me to him, I will. Walking back to the room, I go into Leah's suitcase and take out the binoculars. Walking them back outside, I raise them to my eyes and look for his boat.

It's not there.

It has to be.

I follow the water to the furthest point west, looking for the massive yacht. I don't see it there nor do I see it anywhere to the east.

My heart drops to my stomach.

He left?

Clad in only pajamas bottoms and a tank top, I sprint across the grass and through the lobby of the building. When I reach the street, I take the stone steps, three, four at a time, nearly breaking an ankle flying down the narrow walkway.

When I reach the bottom, I jog the street, barefoot, until I'm at the marina. The binoculars find their way to may face again as I look out for his boat.

It's still not there.

He left?

He left?

He left.

He's gone.

Alexander Asher, international playboy, used me, abused me, and deserted me.

I am such a fool.

PART II
MANHATTAN, NY

chapter THIRTEEN

The slamming of brakes and a prolonged, ultra loud horn honk causes me to jerk and spill my evening latte on the pavement. It happens to me every time. A cab and a sedan have nearly collided and two men are screaming at each other from their respective windows. No one gets out of their vehicles though. They just flip each other off and go their merry way.

It's an occurrence I have almost gotten jaded to. That and the slouched being hanging outside my building's door.

"Hey, Mattie. Locked out again?" I ask, whipping my keys out of my coat pocket and leaning over my neighbor.

Mattie opens his eyes and is taken aback to see me hovering over him. "Oh, hey, Emma. Yeah, keys are probably sitting on my counter."

My forgetful neighbor rises to his feet and takes a step behind me as I push open the door. This is the third time in the two months I've lived here he has locked himself out. That I know of, at least.

We met just like this. The first time, I was petrified to let him in. I didn't know if he was homeless or some psycho trying to break into my building. Granted, we don't live in a lavish high-rise uptown. That would be the type of building someone would want to rob. Instead, ours is a modest prewar on Mott Street. The rent is cheap and the building is clean, even if the floors are slightly slanted.

It didn't take too much convincing to realize he was harmless. Mattie is an undergrad from Boston, enrolled at NYU. For a genius, he sure is forgetful.

"Thanks for letting me in. Have a good night," he says, passing me in the hall and heading up the stairs.

"Any requests?" I ask, unlocking my apartment door.

Mattie stops on the step and thinks for a moment. "Something soothing. I had a wicked day."

I give him an affirmative smile and head into my apartment.

Closing the door behind me, I flick on the light and immediately walk over to the window facing the street. Living on the first floor means I have to utilize heavy-duty blackout curtains to keep the passersby from gazing in through the curved security bars.

When I first saw the apartment, I was hesitant about living on the first floor. But after considering the twenty other apartments I'd seen that weren't nearly as nice, I decided the luxury on the inside was better than its level off the ground.

Perhaps *luxury* is the wrong word. Stepping into my home, you are in the living room where I have a sofa, TV and bookcase. To the back left is a small galley kitchen, so tiny it can't house standard-size appliances. So I have a two-burner stove, a modest-sized refrigerator, and a half sink. No dishwasher, of course.

The kitchen is separated from the living room by a half wall that creates an island. In the living room, my coffee table doubles as a dining table and my bookcase as extra storage. I have a secretary desk that was once my grandmother's in the space where one would put a dining table. Beside it is a wing backed chair and a floor lamp that composes my reading nook.

Behind the kitchen wall is a bathroom with a shower, stall, and pedestal sink. The plumbing is ancient and echoes throughout the building whenever someone flushes.

The real luxury to the space is the bedroom. It's not big or even nice, really. The luxury is the fact that it exists. In my price range it was hard to find an actual one-bedroom. Every apartment I saw was a studio and I really wanted a sleeping space separate from my living space.

Studio apartments are fine but when I'm paying nearly double the rent to live in New York as I was in Pittsburgh, it makes it hard to downsize completely.

Despite the spatial limitations, I have made a great space for myself here. I wasn't supposed to paint but I did it anyway. I didn't want to start the next phase of my life staring at white walls. Instead, I painted the living room a fun purple, and I bought a turquoise sofa that cost more than my rent. The living room was inspired by the nineties television show *Friends*. They are the epitome of what a girl from Ohio thinks living in Manhattan is about. Some would say *Sex and the City* or even *Girls*, but not me. I am a *Friends* gal all the way.

I even put a picture frame around the peephole on my front door.

Walking over to my speakers, I synch my iPhone and select an allegro by Joshua Bell. Mattie mentioned a few weeks ago he could hear my music through the floorboards. When I profusely apologized, he commented on how it actually helps him study. So now I take requests and let some of my favorite melodies drift upstairs.

Moving into the kitchen, I open the refrigerator and take out the makings for a dinner salad. When that is made, I take my bowl, a glass of wine, and a stack of papers to review and cuddle up on the couch. I'm content, having gotten myself into a nice routine. I like my home.

A lot has happened in my life over the last nine months. I'm still living in the year from hell. It's been nine months since I lost my brother. Nine months since I crushed my hand. And nine months since that douche with a flute left.

But it's better.

Don't assume I'm leaping off balconies and singing in the street. I still haven't picked up or played an instrument since those two times in Italy.

A time I try not to think of.

What *is* better is that I am taking control of the situation. No more lying in bed wallowing. It's time I try to make something out of this mess that is my life. The first step was getting a new apartment in a new city. Next, was finding a new job. After that—I have no idea.

Looking over at the coffee table I see a white envelope peering up at me. I put my salad bowl down and reach over for it. Inside is an invitation to the wedding of Leah Marie Paige and Adam Geoffrey Reingold.

A smile crosses my face. Those two crazy kids are finally getting married. Since they called off their summer wedding, everyone wondered when they would set a date again. Looks like a Christmas wedding is in order.

I can't help but think back on that July trip with mixed emotions. When I arrived, I was half broken, on the mend from having my dreams torn apart and the devastation of losing Luke. I was going through the motions of life but I wasn't living.

Then I met a man. An intense, complex, emotion extracting, sinful man who made me feel more in four days than I had in six months.

And then he played me like a fiddle.

Stupid fiddle.

I explained all of this to my shrink when I returned to Cedar Ridge. I booked a three-hour appointment and unloaded. Every feeling, every emotion and every ache that has burnt me since that fateful night in January, was put out there.

She didn't seem impressed I had finally decided to open up. Instead, Dr. Schueler said my rendezvous in Italy set back all the progress we made with my PTSD. She wrote out a stack full of prescriptions and sent me on my merry way.

I, in turn, went home, tore them up and packed my bags.

It doesn't take a world-renowned psychiatrist to see I needed out of Cedar Ridge. There were too many memories. I need to be far away from there and Pittsburgh and the reminders of all that was lost over the course of a weekend.

Maybe it wasn't Asher that made me heal the way I did.

Maybe it was Capri.

Whatever it was, I needed to get away. At least for the time being.

My parents begged me to stay, but they know their headstrong little girl better than to expect her to listen. I was determined.

Shortly before I left for Italy, I sent my résumé out to various schools in the area looking for a teaching job. Since my hand is shot, I'd only be able to teach courses like Music Theory and Introduction to Music. It wasn't what I wanted to do but it was better than living in my pajamas.

When I returned, I received an offer not to teach, but help run a music program in New York.

Having been enrolled in prestigious music schools my entire life, it seemed logical to put my knowledge to good use. Sure, it's a lot of administration work but it's perfect for my type-A personality. The program I am working on is brand new and just what I need to distract me for a year or two until I decide what my next plan of action is.

My cell phone rings from the side table next to the sofa. I lean over and grab it, seeing a pretty blonde with a bob and pale blue eyes looking back at me. I hit the green icon and say hello.

"How's my little Carrie Bradshaw doing?" Leah pipes on the other end of the phone.

"I prefer Rachel Green. And for your information, I am curled up on the chesterfield, drinking a nice Pinot and listening to the soulful sounds of Joshua Bell." I take a sip of my wine and twist my face a bit. I said it was a nice Pinot, not a great one.

"First, you are so a Monica. Second, the couch is awesome but you need to stop referring to it as 'the chesterfield.' It makes you sound like Grandma. Next, I'm jealous, and last . . . what was the last thing you said?"

I laugh into my sleeve. "Joshua Bell," I remind her.

"Oh, yeah. Boring! Throw on some pop music and dance around in your underwear. That's what I do."

If Leah could see me she'd be privy to an eye roll. I know she dances around in her underwear. I grew up with her and witnessed it many times.

"I got the wedding invitation. Do I have to RSVP? You know I'm going."

"Of course you're going. My maid of honor has to be there. That's actually why I'm calling. I decided I want my bachelorette party to be in, drum roll please," Leah's hands can be heard slapping a table on her end of the phone in a drum roll pattern. When they come to a halt, she shouts in her best game show voice, "New York City!"

My legs swing around from under me and hit the floor. "You're coming here?" My voice squeaks in excitement. "When?"

"In a few weeks. Halloween gets crazy around here and of course there's Thanks Conaughey weekend so that leaves the middle of the month as the best time." Leah's mouth crunches around a potato chip, the sound easily recognizable through the phone.

My toes dance at the thought of seeing Leah. I haven't seen anyone in my family since I moved to New York. Even when I lived in Pittsburgh we saw each other at least once a month. "I will have to start researching the best places to go. I haven't gone out since I've been here—"

"Ems," her curt voice cuts me off, "you've lived out there for two months. What do you mean you haven't gone out?"

This—coming from my social butterfly of a sister—is expected. She thrives on going out and meeting new people. It's in her nature. Not mine.

When I first got to New York, I had two weeks to find an apartment before my new job began. I stayed in a hotel, spending way too much of my savings to do so, before I found a place to live. And for the last six weeks I've been working my ass off getting the Juliette Academy ready for opening day.

The Juliette Academy is a free after-school music school for children in New York City. It is offered to everyone, regardless of economic status. You are accepted through a lottery. All you need to enroll is a New York City address and the willingness to learn.

I love the school's name. Juliette sounds like a mini-Julliard. It's a cute play on the name of the famous school uptown where some of the greatest musicians have trained.

A lot of inner-city kids submitted an application for entry. I wish I could give the spots to only those kids but the lottery is open to everyone. Our first run is two hundred and fifty kids, each receiving a lesson once a week. If they progress, they can apply for grants or pay out of pocket for more lessons.

Running a program isn't what I had planned for my life. In fact, if I weren't at the place in my life I was this summer, I never would have taken it. But I needed out and New York was a perfect escape.

I've kept myself busy hiring the final round of teachers and working on a curriculum for them to follow. My job description also requires me to make sure every applicant is in the proper class for their age and skill level as well as make sure they have the proper equipment. Ordering two hundred and fifty instruments with the budget I had was difficult but it got done.

And then, of course, it was getting said two hundred and fifty kids in the right classrooms with the right teachers with the right equipment—

Yeah, I've been so engrossed in getting the program up and running I haven't had time to go out.

I explain this to Leah but she doesn't seem to be buying it.

"I'm surprised you haven't tracked down the dirtbag and banged down his door already." Leah's tone gets feisty whenever she refers to Asher. "When you first took the job in New York I thought it was because he lived there. Like you needed to be near him or something. But every time I call you you're at home or at work."

"That's because that's all I have time for. And seriously, what am I going to do? Knock on his door and say, 'How dare you let me have sex with you?' He didn't promise me anything, Leah. It was just a fling. It was exactly what you wanted it to be."

"I didn't want you to get hurt."

"I didn't get hurt." My lie repeating itself as it has for the past three months.

Leah lets out a *hmpf* sound. "Well, you did say it was the most mind-numbing sex of your life. The least he can do is offer you round two."

If she were in front of me I'd punch her in the arm. "You dirty skank!"

Her laugh is so loud I have to pull the phone away from my ear. "I'm kidding. Not really. Well, kind of. But seriously, you need to get laid. Aren't there any nice boys around?"

"No boys. Just Frank and a few guys at the academy. And Mattie who lives upstairs. He's way too young. I don't even think he can drink legally."

"Oh . . . Do Mattie. Do Mattie!" she chants.

I shake my head at the thought. "Good night, Leah."

"'Night, sis. I'll text you the days the girls and I are coming to town. Love you!"

I hang up with Leah and finish my salad, tuning the pages on the class list for next week.

I look over the pages but my mind is only thinking of one thing.

Asher.

I could kick myself for letting my mind go there.

Leah and I stayed on Capri for three more days after he left. Three days I hoped he would return and clear up the misunderstanding. But there was no misunderstanding. He lied to me about who he was, got me in bed, and then disappeared.

For a split second I thought I was falling in love with him. Isn't that tragic? After knowing him a short time I let myself think he was worth giving my heart to. I blame the sex. Yes, it was really good sex.

Clearly it was the kind of sex that makes you think only illogical thoughts.

Gah! I stand up and shake off all thoughts Alexander Asher. I need a cold shower and a good night's sleep.

I turn up the stereo slightly and decide Mattie and I need something with more edge. I blast One Republic because while Mattie had a wicked day it looks like I'm gonna have a wicked night.

chapter FOURTEEN

For a girl who grew up in the Midwest and spent the last few years in Pittsburgh, moving to Manhattan was quite a change, though I'd like to say I've been catching on rather easily. Since I've moved to New York I've learned: avenue blocks are longer than street blocks, there are separate downtown and uptown train entrances (a lesson I learned the hard way, after swiping my trusty Metro Card), cabs with the number lit up are empty and available, cart food is delicious, five dollars for a domestic beer is completely reasonable and an empty subway car during rush hour is not a good thing. I'll let you use your imagination as to why (I also learned that one the hard way).

The city has an energy unparalleled to any other. Even in the fall, a time of melancholy when the leaves are making their way to the ground, I find myself breathing in the new life the city has given me. Sure, I haven't taken advantage of the nightlife and I only know a handful of people, but just walking through the streets, looking at the architecture, seeing the people and hearing the sounds of the hustle and bustle gives me the charge I need to put one step in front of the other.

I chose my neighborhood because it's a short walk to the Juliette Academy. The school is housed in a landmark building on the corner of Suffolk and Rivington, in the Lower East Side. The Gothic Revival architecture of the building has lancet windows and spiral-like finials that make it look like a nineteenth-century church.

I wasn't home from Italy two weeks when Frank contacted me, letting me know the school was opening the first week in October and looking for an Assistant Director of Music Performance. I couldn't believe they wanted me. I mean, the pay isn't that great. But, an assistant director role? That's huge, especially for someone with zero teaching or managerial experience.

Frank and I know each other from the music circuit. He heard about my accident and knew I was in need of a career change. He said he would deal with the benefactors and finance managers. That works for me because accounting, spreadsheets, marketing . . . that is all way over my head.

It's not lost on me this job is a blessing. I don't have many job skills and teaching is something I did not want to do. For starters, it's difficult to teach someone control of a bow when I can't hold one myself for more than a few seconds. We'll also try to put aside it's incredibly depressing. If I can't play, why do I want to teach someone else how to play?

Yes, it is selfish. I know. I'm working on that.

I push open the heavy wooden stairwell door and exit onto the fourth-floor hallway. My office is a tiny seven-by-seven–foot space housed inside one of the four classrooms on this level. It has white plaster walls, linoleum floors, a desk, a chair, and a filing cabinet. I decorated the walls with music note decals I bought off the Internet. Treble- and bass-clef bars line the wall you face when you walk in. Behind my desk is another decal that says, "Music is not what I do, it's who I am." I have no idea whose quote that is, but he or she should be revered.

To get to my office, you have to walk through one of the music rooms. Frank says it's part of the charm of working in a historic Manhattan building.

The classroom attached to my office belongs to Crystal, who is teaching cello.

Go figure.

She also has a bad habit of leaving her instrument in my office so she doesn't have to lug it to and from work. I can't deny I loathe that it sits in the corner of the room looking at me all judgmental.

At least it's better than bunking with Lisa. She's the violin teacher.

Crystal is a sweet twentysomething like me who trained at the Fiorello LaGuardia High School of the Performing Arts and then furthered her studies in Rochester. Unlike me, she is a professional cellist who books regular gigs with a wedding orchestra. Teaching is a great way to supplement her income and keep herself familiar with new techniques and trends.

Lisa is older than us, with a husband and two kids. She teaches at a local public school during the day and then at the Juliette Academy in the afternoons. Her patience and experience with the younger children is something I'd like to emulate someday.

For now, I'm happy to stand in the back with a clipboard.

It's only been a few weeks, but the two have been nice to talk to as preparations to open the school were underway. They don't seem bothered by the fact I'm their boss or that I don't go out, ever. I'm not against it. As I said, I've been busy.

Especially on days like today.

Today, the Juliette Academy will open its doors for the first time. There'll be a ribbon-cutting ceremony in the morning, followed by the influx of fifty new students enrolled in the after-school program. Tomorrow, we'll welcome fifty more and the next day and the next. By the end of the week, we'll have welcomed all two hundred and fifty students to a world of music and wonder. I'm actually a little nervous.

"Hey, hey, hey there, Ohio. Are you ready for the big day?"

I look up from my notes to see Crystal walking in with her massive tote bag in hand. She's wearing plaid capris with a fitted, white button down top and black blazer, accessorized with a chunky necklace and high heels with a strap that wraps around the ankle.

"Nothing to prepare. This is the Frank show. I've respectfully asked to be excused from the media circus that is taking place today." I motion my pen over to her cello that's been judging me from the corner. "You shouldn't leave that here overnight. The school is not responsible if it's stolen off of school premises."

Crystal shakes out long, loose curls with her hand, letting them fall over her shoulders. Her hair is a deep brown that looks almost burgundy in certain lighting. In the sunlight, it has a Julianne Moore-esque tint to it. Her eyes are hazel green and she has the most flawless skin I've ever seen.

"Eh, let 'em steal it. It's my old piece."

Her words are like a knife to the stomach. If she only knew what I would pay to be able to play again . . .

I brush off the thought. "I'll have to have you sign a document dissolving the school from retribution should it go missing."

Sensing the seriousness of the situation, Crystal changes her stance. "Yeah, yes, sure. Whatever needs to be done." She removes her coat and places it on the hook behind the door. "Are you okay? You seem a little on edge."

Am I okay? What does okay even mean? Well, if I'm gonna be a smarty-pants about the whole thing, it's from the Dutch phrase *Oll Korrect*, meaning "all correct."

But I've come to find okay to stand as an acronym for "otherwise known."

So today I'm okay.

Otherwise known as, I can't stop thinking about a certain man who captured my soul and hasn't given it back.

Otherwise known as, trying to find a new place for myself in this world since the one I thought I had has vanished.

Otherwise known as, will there ever be a day when people stop asking me if I'm okay?

"Yeah, I'm okay. Just making sure everything is set for today." I offer her a kind smile and go back to reviewing my notes.

"You?" She asks in a flabbergasted manner. "You're the most organized person I've ever met. You've got everything covered. Let's go out for a drink tonight. Celebrate!" Crystal says, reminding me a lot of Leah, just a bit more refined.

"Thanks, but I have work to catch up on," I say, hoping she can't read through my fib.

Crystal eyes me cautiously but shrugs as she usually does, shaking out her hair again. "Sure. Well, maybe next time. I'm gonna go freshen up before we go down. Meet you back here in fifteen?"

I nod my head and go back to my work. The city has given me a newfound energy and purpose, yet I still find myself withdrawing at times.

At noon, Crystal and I make our way downstairs and take a spot in the middle of Rivington, where a large crowd has gathered for the ribbon-cutting ceremony. The street has been blocked off for the event. NYPD are stationed at both ends of the street where barricades have been placed for the next hour preventing cars from coming down the one-way street.

A small stage is set up to the right of the front door with a podium and microphone. A woman is currently doing a mic check as the mayor—who I was impressed would be here—is talking to Frank off the side of the stage.

Crystal and I spot a dazed-looking Lisa and flag her over to where we are standing. When she sees us, her eyes light up and she side steps her way through the crowd. Her hair is in a messy bun and she's wearing a large oversized sweater over leggings and Converse sneakers, clutching a cup of deli coffee in her hands. Everyone was told to dress nice today. For Lisa, this is nicely dressed.

"I can't believe I took a day off work for this. There are so many other things I'd rather be doing right now," she says, sliding in between me and Crystal.

"Like practicing for an audition I have tomorrow," Crystal says.

"Or creating an agenda for a spring concert," I add.

"Or having sexy times with the husband," Lisa chimes in. Crystal and I roll our heads in her direction. "What?" she says, shrugging. "Two kids, remember? Some day you'll understand."

Crystal and I just shake our heads and laugh. At least Lisa has someone to go home to at night. Crystal and I are still hopelessly single, though not for the lack of Crystal's efforts. She is constantly on Tinder and Match, swiping left and right. I think working all those weddings every weekend makes her wistful. I just hope she doesn't choose someone based on what society thinks she should do by a certain age. No woman should ever settle.

"Hey, Emma, I saw I have eight kids in my Introduction to the Violin class. That's too many," Lisa says, her lips perched on her paper cup.

"I know," I say apologetically. "I couldn't deny the little guys. I mean, a seven-year-old who wants to play the violin? That's amazing. What did you want me to do, tell them they had to take the drums?"

Lisa's head tilts forward and gives me her deadpan stare. "I need a co-teacher. It's impossible to teach that many kids, that age, with no musical experience, at once." She ticks off the challenges using her three fingers.

"I asked Frank. There's no funding for another teacher. Sorry."

She gives me an exasperated look, her free hand flying out in a dramatic gesture. "You're a classically trained violinist. Why can't you teach them with me?"

Damn Frank for boasting about my has-been career. I hate this. I hate that I can't even teach a child to hold a bow. I hate that everyone knows I'm incompetent in my craft. I rub my hand and try to figure out a way to avoid the conversation.

Crystal senses my unease. "Emma is way too busy setting up the program. If she had the time to teach she'd be doing so. Maybe she can get you an intern or something."

Lisa nods and tells Crystal that's a good idea. I, in turn, thank her with my eyes.

News reporters, students, teachers, parents, and local political representatives have all arrived for the special occasion. It's a beautiful October day so a spot in the afternoon sun is greatly appreciated.

Cameramen point their cameras at a podium situated a few feet from the front of the building. First, a woman from the Children's League makes a short speech and introduces the mayor. Everyone claps and listens as he deems the Juliette Academy a great asset to the city of New York.

More people have appeared in the crowd, many seem to be nosey passersby looking to see what the commotion is. My back gets slightly jostled and I have to steady myself on the pavement.

Calm down people. It's just a school opening. Not a Jay-Z sighting.

"Oh, my God, he's here," Crystal breathes out in a loud whisper, moving closer to me and Lisa.

I hip check the guy to the side of me and let him know two can play this game. "Who's here?" I ask Crystal, missing part of her statement.

"—No one has seen him for months. He just disappeared one day," Crystal continues, her breath hitching a bit.

"Eh, I don't see the appeal. At all." Lisa rolls her eyes.

I get shoved again and am about to tell the person to shove it when the mayor says something that causes my jaw to drop, my stomach to lurch, and my heart to nearly explode.

"Alexander Asher."

The crowd erupts in applause. I look up at the podium.

Asher.

He's here.

He's walking up to the podium.

He's shaking the mayor's hand.

I gasp at the sight of him.

I stand, frozen. The last time I saw him, his arms were wrapped around me and he was begging me not to go.

The man next to me pushes so hard into my side, I fall forward onto a woman in front of me, causing her to yelp. My hands hit the pavement to prevent myself from a complete fall. I rub the tiny pebbles, from the blacktop that has indented into my palms, on my pants as Lisa pulls me up by my shoulders, erecting me into position.

"Thanks." My voice is shaking as I push my wayward hair off my face. The woman in front of me gives me a nasty look as I offer my hushed apologies. The man next to me is now far in front of the crowd. I hope body checking me was worth it.

It's at this moment I notice the crowd is eerily quiet, all looking up waiting for the man at the podium to speak.

I look up myself and see why he's not speaking.

He's staring.

At me.

Golden eyes hit me like a Mack truck and I instinctively grab hold of my stomach to keep it from falling apart. I stand here like a deer in headlights just waiting to get run over.

His mouth opens slightly, the sides tentatively curve up before they clench down. His lips purse as molars rub together, a look of pure disgust on his face. It all happens in a flash. The look he gives me, the change in his expression and then he turns his attention back to the mayor, offering him a full, boisterous smile.

I've thought about what it would be like to see him again. I daydreamed about what I'd do. I've imagined everything from kicking him in the balls to screaming to pretending I don't know who he is.

What I wasn't planning on was him being angry to see me and for me to be so utterly devastated by the look he'd give me.

I stand and wait for Asher to make his speech. When he does, I try to listen but my mind is a scrambled mess.

"The Asher Foundation has been a cause near and dear to my heart for some time now. Over the years, with the help of the great city of New York, we have raised millions of dollars for children's charities. Today is the culmination of our efforts."

Looking about the crowd as he speaks, his tone is jovial and kind yet his hands are on each side of the podium, holding on with white knuckles as if to ground himself from being swept away from the current.

"Where do you think he's been?" Lisa whispers in Crystal's ear.

I know exactly where he's been. Cruising the Mediterranean with an urn full of ashes and a bed full of women.

"I don't know but he looks amazing." Crystal sighs all too appreciatively for my taste. I can't believe these two know who my Asher is.

My Asher.

Ugh. I have to get out of this city.

When his speech is done, Asher and the mayor shake hands and pose for a photograph. They then make their way off the stage and talk to a media outlet that is positioned to the side ready to interview them.

No sooner is the ceremony over, I am pushing past the crowd toward the front door of the school. I need to get inside and away from him. Why is he here? Why am I so confused about how I feel about him being here?

I should be mad. I should be angry. Instead, I am so damn muddled I need to get my head on straight.

I am almost at the door when a strong hand grabs hold of me and pulls me in the opposite direction. I lurch back and am swung around to come face-to-face with eyes so dark they've lost their golden touch.

"What are you doing here?" Asher's voice is harsh; that full mouth is in a hard line. Using his body as a shield, he pushes me into the corner where our building meets the one next to it.

I blink in disbelief. Pulling my arm back, I try to get loose but he tugs harder.

"I work here." My face contorts as I try to get away from him. Anyone looking at us would think we are just talking rather closely. He is keeping his hold on me hidden.

"Since when?" His voice is hushed but angry nonetheless. I can't help but notice he no longer smells of sea and salt.

"Two months ago. I got a call offering me a job and I took it. If I knew you had anything to do with it I wouldn't have accepted." I give my body a final yank and release myself from his grasp.

Asher's eyes narrow on mine, becoming beady and accusatory. "I promise you I had nothing to do with you being here. Who would do this?" he asks, massaging the back of his neck with his hand.

Rubbing my arm, which is now tender from his abrasive hold, I lean back and look to my right. I'm about to tell him how I know Frank when I see a familiar giant in a black suit standing near an SUV on the corner, just behind the barricade.

Devon's hands are clasped in front of his body, standing at attention. The two of us make eye contact and I am offered a kind smile and a shrug in apology.

Asher follows my gaze and lands on the not-so-innocent giant.

Without a word, he turns from me and makes his way toward Devon. I use the opportunity to rush inside and get my head together.

By seven o'clock my head is a flurry of new faces I will soon come to recognize and a sea of kind words from the many parents who walked through the door with their children in tow.

Since the media was here, I strolled the halls with them, showing the various classrooms and the teachers conducting lessons. Whenever someone asked for a quote on camera, I politely pointed them toward Frank.

I sat in on a violin lesson given by Lisa to seven students, a guitar introduction with one of our teachers, and the twelve teenagers who are dreaming of being the next Taylor Swift or Ed Sheeran or whoever their current idol is.

It's been a hectic day I've been looking forward to it for six weeks. Problem is, I wasn't expecting it to start the way it did.

With everyone gone for the day, I take a seat in one of the chairs in the corner of Crystal's empty classroom. My small office doesn't have a window so I come in here to enjoy the view. The sun is setting as I sit idly in the corner going through the schedule for tomorrow when the door swings open.

The sound of leather Oxford loafers echo in the empty room causing my head to rise and take in the figure walking in.

I swallow, hard, at the sight of him.

Six feet tall and absolutely stunning.

Asher walks into the room, each step controlled, commanding, and with purpose. He is wearing a black suit that frames his broad shoulders perfectly and is tailored to showcase his lean, narrow torso. His white shirt and silver-gray tie make him look like a man in charge. And he is. Because right now I couldn't lead a moth to a flame if I tried.

His skin is still golden from his many months in the Mediterranean sun. Those gorgeous highlights are brushed back, accentuating the masculine structure of his face. And those eyes? Gone are the honey wheat, kind eyes. These here are so dark, I fear the Asher I know isn't there anymore.

Maybe he never really existed.

I take a deep breath and steady myself in my seat. I am suddenly very nervous. Very much like the first time we met.

He takes in the classroom. His hands deep in his pockets as he looks over the decorations on the walls and the various seats and stands that are in place for the students to learn. The tick of his jaw is tight but his brows are closed, sloping at the ends; his lips are pursed as if he's trying to put the pieces of a puzzle together.

It's uncomfortable watching someone from a dark corner in the room. Part of me wonders if he even knows I'm here. He doesn't say a word, nor does he look at me.

Still I can't open my mouth to say anything.

"You're not teaching?" he asks and I startle at the question.

Okay, so he does know I'm here.

I clear my throat and look for the right words. "No. I still can't play." My hand flexes out of habit, and I feel the burn in my palm, up through my fingers.

Asher's attention turns to me. He doesn't look angry like he did earlier. Instead he looks . . . God, I wish I knew what he was thinking. I gather my papers off my lap and grab my bag off the floor.

"Why didn't you come find me?"

I halt putting my papers in my bag. My eyes scrunch together in confusion. "What?"

Asher is standing on the far side of the room. His feet are spread wide apart, his arms now crossed in front of his body. His chin rises and he stands as if prepared for a duel. "You've been here for two months. Why didn't you track me down?"

I shake my head in disgust at his bold attempt to assume I'd even want to see him. "Why would I look for you in New York when you didn't have the decency to stay for me in Capri?" The hair on the back of my neck stands up, as nervous energy takes over. I'm unprepared for this conversation.

Studying the pattern of the hardwood floor, I wait for him to answer me. Silence fills the air and I have the need to fill it. With a shaky hand I swing my tote over my shoulder and start to move. "Guess I was just another one of your playthings, Asher . . . or Alexander. Whatever the hell your name is."

My feet are mid-stride when he steps in my direction, coming to a stop in front of me. "You would know all about that. Some actress you turned out to be." His hands rise in front of his body, palms up. For as jittery as I am feeling at this moment, he is exuding complete control. "Don't play dumb. You knew who I was the entire time."

My mouth opens in a huff and I breathe out an expletive. "I know nothing about you. Just some pathetic made up stories." I brush past him with my shoulder and make my way toward the exit.

"You had me followed." My feet come to a screeching halt. *What the hell is he talking about?* "My boat was pinged, my information gathered."

I turn my head to the side, peering over my shoulder, and look at him out the corner of my eye.

Asher takes a step toward me, his presence close yet so far away. I wish my body wasn't so aware of him, sensitive to him, even if it is screaming with fury and pain. My heart is pounding out of my chest, and it's not only because of anger or hurt—and that makes me angry and hurt all over again.

"Why was Adam Reingold researching me?" It's not a polite question. It's filled with accusation and judgment.

Adam was worried his future wife and sister-in-law were being taken advantage of. He feared we'd be hurt while gallivanting with some billionaire on his yacht. He cared for our safety.

Is it so difficult for someone like Asher to assume a person cared so much about his loved ones he went out of his way to keep them safe? Does he always think someone has an ulterior motive? Are we all untrustworthy?

After everything I shared with him. In seventy-two hours I laid my soul bare to him, gave my body to him. In return, he's accusing me of something so heinous, it's as if the moments we shared meant nothing.

He takes a step closer. His jaw is clenched, his arms flexed in agitation. He's mad. I can see that. But I can also see something else in those golden eyes.

He's scared.

Of what, I have no idea and I'm not going to stick around to find out.

With my back to him, I cast my words over my shoulder; he doesn't deserve my full attention.

"You've been looking for a reason to walk away from me since the moment we met. Let me make this easy for you."

I turn my head back around and walk out of the room and out of the building, my feet not stopping until I'm back, grounded on the pavement outside.

chapter FIFTEEN

Despite what Leah thinks, I do not, have not, and will not google Alexander Asher. Call it sheer will, call it strength, or call it the fear of falling off the wagon . . . whatever it is, after that one night in Capri, I refused to look him up.

I learned all I needed to know about him that night. He is insanely wealthy, from a family dynasty that spans generations, and he's known as a playboy and ultimate bachelor.

What I didn't read anywhere was his connection to the Juliette Academy. I could kick myself.

Let me see if I actually can.

Standing in my kitchen, I'm literally bending my knee and kicking myself in the ass over not even attempting to see a correlation between Asher and the Juliette Academy. He said his mom's name was Juliette. And here I was thinking it was a pun on the school Julliard.

Argh.

My butt hurts now.

I walk over to the kitchen drawer, take out my tension ball and do some hand aerobics per my occupational therapist's instructions. Leaving Ohio meant stopping my therapy sessions. Even though I don't have someone telling me what to do, I make a point to spend ten minutes, two times a day doing my exercises.

Eating with my left hand is fine. Writing is a project. Thank God for computers or else everyone would have to read my chicken scratch.

I have this special pen that's supposed to help me write but I don't care for it. It has the same shape of a hole puncher laying on its side. The two arms sit by my thumb and middle finger while my pointer rests on the pen. I use it sometimes but it's uncomfortable. My dad made his own design using a pen inserted through a rubber ball, fashioned so my hand doesn't have to squeeze tight around it. I don't use that one either. It reminds me of when Asher had me rest my hand over his to play the cello.

I blow air out my lips, causing them to vibrate.

He thinks I knew who he was when we met—some gold-digging whore pretending to not know who he was in order to win his millions. Or billions: apparently he inherited the world.

Asher may not have said all those things but I can read the writing on the wall. The guy has serious trust issues. But for him to insinuate that I wanted anything to do with his money is unfathomable.

It's as if he was goading me all those days in Capri. He could have just said his name was Alexander. Instead, he said it was Asher—the name known for gluttonous wealth and power. At least to everyone but me. I'm from a small town in Ohio and have been living in Pittsburgh. Sorry, Alexander Asher, but the whole world doesn't know who you are. Narcissistic jerk!

What am I doing here? Maybe Leah's right. A part of me was intrigued by New York because I knew it's where he is from. There is that small part of me that wanted to see him and, now that I have, I hate him more than I did the last time I saw him.

Maybe it's time to go home.

I pick up the phone and call my parents. I need a reality check, fast. My mom picks up on the first ring.

"Emma? Emma? Are you okay? Did you get mugged?" I can picture her grabbing hold of the cross she wears, tugging it until the chain makes an indent in the back of her neck.

I let out a sigh at my very loving yet overly concerned mother. "Yes, mom. I'm okay."

"Why are you calling? You never call. You can come home any time, honey. Daddy and I have your room ready. We won't change it like we did when you went to college."

I sink into the chesterfield. I'll give it to the end of the week.

"Thank you, Miss Emma. See you next week."

"See you next Friday, Madison." I wave off the little girl who started flute lessons today. Fourteen and full of life, Madison is a girl whose parents can probably afford lessons on their own, but deserves to be here like everyone else.

Standing at the door, I watch as Madison and her mom walk to the corner. Her mom was a sweet woman who asked for a tour of the facility. Part of me is hoping the family will make a donation to the school. I cross my fingers and watch as the two get into a cab.

"Can I have a word?"

I turn my head to see Frank standing on the stairwell.

"Sure." I say, wrapping my cardigan around me. The afternoon chill is coming in through the open door. I close it and walk over to Frank.

"Good first week?"

"Yeah." I let out a breath that's half laugh, half sigh of relief. "We had thirty no-shows, sixteen kids placed in the wrong class, forty-seven missing guitars that UPS claims are in Jersey City, and Crystal just got a gig for the winter playing Friday night weddings, which means she needs to give up her end-of-the-week class."

"Sounds like a great first week to me!" Frank laughs and I find it refreshing. The thirty kids who didn't show up have another week to claim their spot or else they lose it. The sixteen kids were properly placed in the right classes and those instruments better be here Monday morning or else I'm taking the ferry to New Jersey and bringing them here myself.

As for the teaching position I have to fill . . . "I placed a few calls yesterday to the candidates we passed on to see if they're still available. It's not easy finding a cello teacher for an after-school music program that pays as little as we do."

"Don't worry. I took care of it." Frank says, his feet next to mine as the two of us ascend the stairwell.

"Oh, thank God."

Frank shakes his head and smiles out the corner of his mouth. "I'm not usually called God, so a simple *Thanks Frank* will do."

"Thanks, Frank," I say, and he laughs again. I head up the stairs, Frank right behind me. "Whatever can I do to repay you?"

"Glad you asked." Frank opens his padfolio and takes out a few papers and holds them out toward me. "I'd like you to make a speech at the fund-raiser next month?"

The fund-raiser. I didn't forget about it. I just wasn't planning on going. Before the school opened, a party had been planned. I can't really call it a party. It's a soiree at the Waldorf Astoria in honor of the Juliette Academy. I was planning on going until I realized Alexander Asher was attached to the school and most likely would be there. Seeing him at a party with a gorgeous woman draped around his arm? It's the exact reason I won't google him. I don't think I can deal.

I hold up my hand and ignore the papers. "I'm not going." My voice is matter-of-fact.

"What do you mean you're not going? You're part of the reason these doors even opened. Before you came we were a mess. You got our schedules in order, the instruments placed properly and hired the best teachers.

Emma, your knowledge and passion for this school is why we are here. We had the funding but you had the heart."

I reach the third floor landing and turn around to look at Frank. I had no idea he felt that way. It actually makes me want to tear up. I don't, of course, but I feel like I should.

"Um, thank you, Frank. That is really—it's really kind of you to say." I swallow. How do I reply to that? *Thanks for the kind words but I'm still not going because Alexander Asher is a cad?* "I have prior arrangements." Liar.

Frank's face looks forlorn. "That's unfortunate. I was really hoping you'd do this."

My shoulders fall with lament. I hate letting people down. I've been doing a lot of that this year. First with all the worrying I put my family through. Now with Frank.

Insert dramatic sigh of defeat. "I'll see what I can do. What kind of speech did you have in mind?" Frank hands me some notes he has. I listen as he tells me what he'd like me to say.

Just one pass over his copy and I know it is in need of major changes.

Taking the papers in hand, I bid Frank good-bye as he exits on the third floor and I continue my walk upstairs. If there is a new cello instructor, I will have to sit in on the class. I've been sitting in on many classes, seeing what is working and what does not. Next week, I'll have a one-on-one meeting with all the teachers and go over the points I have for each of them.

My feet carry me up the stairs to the fourth floor. I swing open the heavy wooden door and am instantly hit with the melody of a cello, obviously Crystal's. The rooms are soundproof so the door to her classroom must be open.

I take a few steps toward Crystal's room and see the door is, in fact, open. There are people standing in the entrance, longingly looking toward the front of the classroom, entranced in the melody that is being played.

Tapping someone on the shoulder, I ask if I can squeeze in past him. He moves to the left so I can walk into the room, but there are more people than I thought standing in here, coupled with the chairs filled with students and their instruments. I hope this isn't against fire code.

Dancing through the people to get to my office, I get to the middle of the crowd and am surprised to see Crystal standing in the back. She catches my puzzled expression and looks back at me as if asking "What?" I look back at her in confusion. If she's not playing, than who is?

Then I see what everyone is staring at. Asher. He is wearing dress pants and a button-down shirt. The sleeves are rolled up. The tie and suit jacket rest on a folding chair beside him.

His strong thighs are wrapped around the cello. The neck of the instrument is in his left hand as his right strokes the strings with a bow. And it's not just the beautiful man who is playing the instrument that causes you to stop and stare. It's the way he plays.

His eyes are hooded, feeling every note his delicate hands are eliciting from the heavy wooden instrument. His body is strong yet moves ever so slightly in a beautiful dance with the instrument.

A wave of chills run up my spine, and my body ignites in a force of electricity I've come to expect whenever I'm in the same room as him. I'm sure others feel it too. He is magnetic and intoxicating—the most sinful sight the eyes have ever indulged.

Yet for me it is more than what my eyes are seeing. It's what my body is feeling—because unlike the people around me, I know what it's like to be in between that man and the instrument he is playing.

My eyes are fixated on Asher and, damn it, I hate that he makes me react this way.

His fingers work the strings of the fingerboard and the neck settled further into his shoulder as he takes the song into a wolf tone. With each pluck of his fingers, the strings vibrate, moving the air around it.

Instinctually, my body moves with his and again we are one with the song.

Loud beats.

Resonating sounds.

Bowed and plucked.

Like the strings of my heart.

Asher dives deeper into his performance and if I weren't paying close attention I would have missed the startle of his muscles, the jolt in his shoulders at the very second he realizes I am standing right here.

His face rises and I am hit with intense emotion. Every feeling he has at this moment is being projected to the back of the room with a look of remorse so powerful I feel like I've had the wind knocked out of me.

He continues to play. He continues to feel. And he continues to keep his hold on me. The connection is too powerful, too much for my damaged heart. I can't let him pull me in further. I've been down that rabbit hole and almost didn't make it back up.

I excuse myself from the crowd around me, pushing past the ones in the doorway and make my way into the hallway. The air in here is too stuffy; I can't find my breath. Running, my feet charge down the hallway and through the heavy doors to the stairwell, leaping down the four flights and through the lobby. I leave the building as quickly as possible forgetting my coat and regretting it as soon as the afternoon chill hits my bones.

And my bag? I left my damn bag upstairs!

My palm begins to itch at the thought of my bag being so far away from me. My hand rises to my head and I yank down on my hair, contemplating whether I should head back upstairs for it or stay as far away from that room as possible until I can get my emotions back in check.

I pull my sweater in tighter and hunch my shoulders into my body taking quick steps hoping to get home as quickly as possible. I'll have to ask Crystal to drop my bag off on her way home.

"Emma." My name is shouted from a space in front of the building. It's not a voice I immediately recognize but I turn around anyway. I may not recognize the voice but the face is familiar. Devon is dressed in black dress pants and matching button down, gesturing over to me. "Do you need a ride?"

I shake my head. "No. I'm just a few blocks."

He walks over to a black SUV and opens the back passenger door as any chauffer would do. "I have time for a few blocks."

If the man hadn't been anything but a complete gentleman to me this summer I would say, "Screw you." I find it hard to believe he had anything to do with what happened then. And, let's face it, the man saved my life. I don't have the privilege of being a bitch to him.

I walk back toward the building and up to Devon. Placing my hand on the top of the proffered door, I push it closed. Devon is taken aback by the action. He is about to open his mouth in argument but is surprised when I push past him and place my hand on the front passenger door handle and open it.

"I'll let you drive but I won't let you chauffeur me around."

Devon lets loose a small grin as he closes the door behind me. He walks around the car, climbs in, and starts the car.

"Make a left at the light."

"I know where you live, Emma." The hoarseness of his voice brings me back to the moment he rescued me in the water and told me to hold on.

"Keeping tabs on me?"

Devon eyes are focused straight ahead. "Only to make sure you're okay."

God, for someone with his stature of discipline and chivalry, he certainly found himself in less than gentlemanly company working for Alexander Asher. "Why did you let me believe it was your boat? Why did you pretend to be . . . him?"

"You came to that conclusion on your own." His tone is calm and soothing. He's right. I know Leah and I came to that assumption by ourselves. I want to be mad at him but I know better. He was the one who helped us get our passports and get home. I can never thank him enough for that.

This gentle giant doesn't belong with a conniving predator like Asher. Which makes me wonder something that has been plaguing my mind for the past week. "You made the call to Frank, didn't you? You are the reason I got the job."

Devon doesn't say a word. I take that as confirmation.

I throw my hands up in agitation. "Why? I don't understand why you would purposefully get me to the school of the man who used me. You have no idea what happened in Capri. If you did, you would never have wanted me here."

My adrenaline is at an all-time high; I could leap out the roof of the car. Devon, on the other hand, is stoic, unfazed by my drama.

"You know what happened in Capri yet you still came to New York." He steers the car in front of my apartment on Mott Street. Putting the car in park, he leans back and turns to speak to me. "What he did to you was awful, and I'd be lying if I didn't say I've watched him do worse."

A taste of bile rises in my throat. I close my eyes to calm down the surge of feelings I have been riding in the last fifteen minutes. "Then why did you bring me here?"

He doesn't miss a beat. "Because you're different."

I look up at the ceiling. What a mind-fuck. I bang my head against the back of the seat. "That is the stupidest thing I ever heard."

"He tends to . . . make decisions based on the people around him. The wrong person getting too close to him can be dangerous. You're good for him, even though he tries to convince himself you're not."

"Well, I've never seen someone more unhappy to see me than when he looks at me." I shake my head. "How did he not know I worked here?"

Devon looks at me with a crooked smile. "How did you not know he founded the school?"

My mouth falls open. Is he accusing me of knowing Asher was here? Does he think I'm a gold-digging whore like Asher does? Is he insinuating—

"What I mean is, it's not a coincidence neither of you knew each other was here."

I sit back and take in his words. It is at this moment I am realizing that while I thought I had control over my life these last few months I was actually being played like a pawn in a game of chess. Lord knows who Devon thinks he's playing this game against. "I don't understand. And, why are you telling me this, anyway?"

"What do you mean? I didn't tell you anything," Devon says, pushing the unlock button on the car, letting me know my time is up. He reaches into the inside pocket of his suit jacket and pulls out an envelope. It's the familiar rectangular white envelope you get at the bank. This one has a Chase symbol on it. "I've been instructed to give this to you."

I bang my head one more time against the headrest and unbuckle my seat belt, turning my back on Devon and the obnoxious white envelope. As I'm getting out of the car I hear his voice in the background.

"Didn't think so."

I slam the car door and watch the SUV drive away. This time, it's my turn to buzz Mattie for entrance into our building.

chapter SIXTEEN

When you're trying to pick up the pieces of your broken life, it's hard to sweep up the mess when someone keeps throwing shards of glass at your feet. That's how I feel knowing Asher is back in my life.

A year ago, I would have locked myself in my room and poured my feelings into my music. Now I have to find a new healthy outlet for my feelings. In my new Manhattan life that includes walking to Washington Square Park.

Every Sunday since I moved here, it has become my haven. As I walk into the park, I brush my hand along the marble of the Washington Arch, a thirty-foot–tall monument in honor of our first president. It is one of the most recognized landmarks in the city, as it resembles the Arc de Triomphe in Paris. If I were to pick a song for this place it would be "*La Vie en Rose*."

While the park has lush grass areas, I prefer to sit with my iPod on a bench in the grand stone circle at the foot of the park and watch the spray shoot out from the large fountain in the center.

From the men who play chess on the stone table, or a gentleman who does charcoal sketches from his spot under a shaded tree, the park is always filled. Parents come with their children to play in the playground or dip their feet in the fountain in the warmer months. Today, it is chilly but not freezing. I lean back and let the autumn sun warm me. I scroll through my music and select Edith Piaf.

When I lived in Pittsburgh, I had a favorite park I loved to visit. Same in Cedar Ridge. Growing up, Luke used to be my weekend park buddy. He'd play on the jungle gym while I listened to my music and wrote in my journal. As he got older, he started bringing his bike and then his skateboard. He was my tagalong, and I loved it. I wasn't the type of older sister who complained about her little brother following her around. Leah did enough of that for the both of us.

By the time I was fourteen, I was responsible enough that my parents would let me take my violin to the park to practice. I'm pretty sure it was more because they couldn't stand the sound of it being played loudly in the confines of our small house. Luke would skate around while I worked on my bowing technique. A couple times I caught Luke putting a hat at my feet as if asking for tips for my playing. I'd just kick the hat out of the way and laugh.

It is a memory I am reminded of every weekend when I sit on this bench. Around now, a young girl, about early twenties will show up with her violin, stand by the fountain and play her instrument in exchange for tips.

On cue, she arrives.

Walking through the archway, her brown hair is in a ponytail and her head is down. She is wearing a checkered jacket, jeans, and sneakers. In her hand is her violin case.

I watch as she takes her usual spot near a bench and bends down to place the black case on the ground. She lifts the violin with her left hand and picks up the bow with the right. It's now that she finally raises her head and takes a look around, observing the crowd around her. It is a fascinating thing to watch. She seems almost timid until she has that powerful piece of maple in her hand. Then she becomes fierce.

Her violin box is open at her feet. A dollar bill and some change are already laying in it. When she lifts the bow to the strings, I turn my music off and my heart skips a beat in anticipation of her playing. It's the tenth time I've watched her and every time I am incredibly moved. While I can tell she needs training, she has great technique. The brand of her violin is for an intermediate, which leads me to believe she doesn't have money for an upgrade. She's probably had it from when she was a student. At her level, she should be using a Schneider or Gunter Lobe, which are better for advanced players. Those run anywhere from two to five thousand dollars.

You don't even want to know how much I spent on my Laura Vigato. Let's just say it was enough to have purchased a Hyundai.

Listening to her play, I close my eyes and enjoy the song. Since I've moved to New York my mother has been asking if I've seen the Philharmonic play at Lincoln Center. My answer is consistently no. I'm not ready to see my peers doing something that I am supposed to be doing.

Yet for some reason, I can work at the school with no problem and I can come to the park and listen to this girl play without feeling despair.

I've thought about this a lot over the last few weeks. I know what most people would think if I told them this. They'd say, "Of course you don't mind listening to people whose skill level are beneath you." That's not it. I don't see the children at the school or this girl in the park as being inadequate or beneath me. Sure, I'm higher in skill level but I should be upset she can play and I can't. I'm not. Instead, I find myself looking forward to seeing her walk beneath the arch and playing for the crowd. I shrug my shoulders and go back to listening to the young woman.

I eat my packed lunch of a turkey sandwich and water and do a fair portion of the *New York Times* crossword. I've never completed one without asking for help but am determined to someday.

When I see the violinist is ready to pack up, I rush up to her case and place a twenty-dollar bill inside. The first time I did so she looked surprised. Now, she just smiles and politely thanks me. She's probably wondering why there is a weird lady who stares at her every Sunday while eating a sandwich and tips her very well. If she only knew how I envied her.

I look at my watch and see a few hours have passed; the sun will start to set soon. Autumn in New York is beautiful in the sunshine but when the sun starts to settle down, the temperatures drop considerably.

Gathering my garbage and belongings, I rise and walk over to the trash. As I'm placing my brown paper bag in the garbage pail, I notice an SUV lurking in the street just beyond the trees.

For a second, I think it's the same one Devon drove me in the other day and then I remember something: I live in New York. There are black SUVs everywhere.

Looks like me, the chesterfield, and our good friend Pinot need to have a get-together tonight.

It turns out Asher is teaching at the school every Friday. Don't you think Frank would have mentioned that in the hallway? A simple, "Hey, Ems, Alexander Asher, the billionaire whose foundation is funding this little school of ours, will be teaching the cello every Friday in the classroom attached to your office" would have been nice.

I also did a little digging on something Devon touched on in the car. How did I not hear the words *Asher Foundation* once in the last two months? According to Frank, he and everyone on the board with him signed a confidentiality agreement. They weren't allowed to mention the foundation's involvement until the opening.

Well, that makes sense, I guess.

What the hell do I know? What I do know is I have a problem with my Friday colleague. I would avoid him but after a long chat with Leah I decided against it.

The conversation went a little like this:

"I knew that fucker was going to make his way back into your life."

"Don't worry. I just have to avoid him once a week."

"No way, Ems. To quote the great McConaughey, "You've got blood in your body. Lay it on the line!"

"Um, what?"

"Lay it on the line until the final whistle blows. And if you do that, if you do that, we cannot lose—"

"Leah?"

"—we may be behind on the scoreboard at the end of the game but if you play like that we cannot be defeated!"

"We are Marshall?"

"We. Are. Fucking. Marshall. Emma. You are playing on the same field. Don't let him push you to the sidelines. Take the ball and ram it down his throat!"

I couldn't deny she made a valid point. As theatrical as it may have been.

"To quote the film How to Lose a Guy in 10 Days, 'You're like a crack-enhanced Kathie Lee'." That got a good laugh out of her.

With a weekend to process the situation, and a mini-marathon of McConaughey films, as recommended by Leah, I arrive at school with a new attitude.

I can do this.

My first order of business is to tell Frank I am going to the fund-raiser and I'd love to make a speech.

My second is to make this school one of the most sought-after music programs in the country.

I have a feeling I'm getting a reputation as a control freak. Okay, I know I have a reputation because Crystal told me. I don't care. If this school is going to be a success, it needs to be run a certain way. The students need to be trained on par with any other acclaimed music academy. It doesn't matter that it's a free program. We are either the best or we don't perform at all.

Don't think I am going to shy away from Fridays. No sir. If Alexander Asher wants to teach in my school than he is going to get the same treatment as everyone else.

As Friday rolls around, I find my confidence is at full peak. Walking to the back of the classroom, I pull a folding chair to the corner and take a seat. The afternoon students are arriving, their cases in tow. Watching these kids walk into the room reminds me how incredible this place really is. Not only is this school providing music lessons for free but they also gave out instruments to the students pro bono. The amount of money that went into this is astounding.

I take out my iPad and Bluetooth keyboard, preparing to take notes. If it weren't for this little device, I don't know how I'd get any work done.

The students continue to enter, each taking their places. With each new face, my heart races a tiny bit more. I bite down and look straight at my computer screen, appearing to be very busy. When he enters, I want to seem all business.

Hopefully my outsides are appearing that way because my insides are racing at *prestissimo* tempo.

Consider that racehorse fast.

My eyes momentarily close when my stomach drops a beat. That's how I know he has entered. Keeping my jaw clenched and my attention fixed, I try to ignore how he stops in the doorway for a fraction when he sees me, before carrying on like he hasn't a care.

Keenly aware of my excellent peripheral vision, I watch him sit down and open his cello case. When he is engrossed in the task, I glance up and take a look at him. He's once again wearing a suit. That makes three encounters in a row I've seen him in formal attire. His hair is combed back, his entire appearance structured. I miss his shorts and crew-neck shirts, his wind-blown hair and sun-kissed skin.

When he rises, his gaze meets mine, briefly, without a hint of acknowledgment, before greeting the class. He takes a place in the center of the room, addressing the students who are formed in a circle around him. "Today, we are going to learn to listen. The key to playing great music is to be able to listen to great music. I want you to develop your own musical voice. Find what gives you the most satisfaction. When you hear it, when you *feel it*, you'll be able to play it." Asher's words remind me of my own inability and those brief moments a few months ago when I felt the music again.

He hands each student a notebook made of brown leather-like material, asking them to take notes and starts the lesson by placing Bluetooth speakers on a table and synching his iPod to them. I assume he's going to play something classical. Instead, he completely shocks me when I hear heavy metal.

The song is one I recognize easily. The students look up with mild curiosity. You start to feel old when you meet people who have never heard Metallica.

"'Enter Sandman' moves at a tempo of 123 beats per minute. Listen to the E minor chord at the top." The class, me included, listen to the sound of the guitar playing. "Now, hear the buildup of the beats. It hits you fast and then never lets up. The riff continues throughout the song."

It's hard not to be sucked in. The tune is quite catchy for a song about a child's nightmares and the destruction of the perfect family.

The students bob and move their heads, some closing their eyes trying to listen for the rhythm. Asher is entranced as well, lost in the song, almost too familiar. Its heavy undertones of a child being frightened by the dark remind me of the story he told me about being an orphan. That is, if his version of the truth was, in actuality, the truth.

Ignoring the memory, I go back to watching the class as they soak in the song. When it is over, he talks to the students about the rhythm and together they describe their emotions when hearing it. In my head, I do my own assessment. I felt a gust of energy. I could have taken a run or charged the field. The faster the song got, the harder the beats hit my chest and I felt a rush.

When the discussion is over, Asher turns to his iPod and plays them the same song by a band using only four cellos. The students are mesmerized that the song they were just listening to was recreated using only the instruments they are learning to master.

By the end of the sixty-minute class, with the room sectioned off into groups of four, Asher has the students playing the main riff. It's incredible. So incredible, I stopped taking notes because I was so caught up in the lesson.

When I saw him play the cello last week, I knew he was skilled. What I was not aware of was how good he was with the students. Some, I am learning, have known Asher for years. Imagine my surprise to find out he's been teaching underprivileged kids in Harlem for the last five years.

His rapport with his old students is apparent in the way they address each other with respect and familiarity. His newer students are given the same attention. If he was telling the truth about his mother being a music teacher, teaching out of their home, than he gets his grace from her.

When the students gather their belongings, I watch as they thank Asher and tell him they'll see him next week. I gather up my tote bag and am walking back toward my office when his deep voice calls out from behind me.

"How'd I do, boss?"

How did he do? Amazing. He was kind and interesting and a truly exceptional teacher.

I won't tell him that. Instead, I turn my cheek letting my voice travel over my shoulder. "You should have submitted a lesson plan for approval." And then I walk into my office and close the door.

I stay in my office until I am positive Asher has left the building. When the coast is clear, I rise from my desk and walk into Crystal's classroom.

Halfway through the door, I stop short at the sight of an exotic-looking woman standing in the middle of the room.

I fall back and straighten myself, trying to emulate the composure of the woman standing in front of me. She is tall, with jet-black hair and matching eyes, wearing a blood-red wrap-around dress. Her shoulders are back, and she has a stance so fierce I want to ask how she does it.

Her irises enlarge when she sees me. "You."

"May I help you?" I say, straightening out my cardigan.

She offers me a wicked smile and assesses me in a way that makes me uncomfortable. "*You* work here?"

I hold out my hand in greeting. "I'm Emma Paige, the assistant director." There are many beautiful women in New York so it shouldn't surprise me there is something familiar about her. "Have we met?"

She doesn't shake my hand. Instead, she looks me up and down with a knowing look. "I'm looking for Alexander Asher."

Of course she is. I narrow my eyes at her. "May I ask what this is about?" I may not like the man but, apparently, he is somewhat important to this city. She could be a deranged fan or a scorned ex-girlfriend. On second thought, maybe I should send her his way.

"His office told me I'd find him here . . . teaching." She says the word *teaching* in mockery.

With my shoulders pushed back, I answer her as honestly as I can. "His class ended thirty minutes ago."

The dark-haired woman looks at me again the way a feline looks at catnip the moment before it pounces. Her eyes linger on the scar on my right hand.

I turn in my injured hand, hiding the scar. Something about the way she is looking at it—at me—makes me feel like she knows more about me than I'd like. Though I know it's impossible.

"Did Asher bring you on board or did you make your way here on your own?"

It is not any of her business but I feel compelled to let this woman know I am not at the beck and call of Alexander Asher.

"Frank Leon contacted me." I pause a beat and then add, "How do you know Mr. Asher?"

The tip of her tongue is riding along the underside of her teeth. "Interesting. Hundreds of people applied and you get a phone call."

The hairs on the back of my neck stand straight. "I'm sorry but I didn't get your name."

"If Asher comes back, tell him Malory Dean was here." Her heels click on the hardwood floors as she walks to the doorway.

"I will," I say, even though it's a complete lie.

chapter SEVENTEEN

Over the next three Fridays, I sit in my office and listen in on three more of Asher's sessions. He continues his lesson on listening to the music. They listened to "Rolling in the Deep" by Adele, a popular song about giving your heart to someone and having it "played, to the beat" and the week after it was "Apologize" by One Republic. The man has a tone for the melodramatic.

Today, they're listing to "Wonderwall" by Oasis and I'm bemused he chose a song about a man needing saving.

I don't tell anyone Asher's class is my favorite and while there are other things I should be doing, I find a way to make sure I'm in my office so I can mock participate from the small space in the back.

When Asher's classes are done, he hangs back for a few minutes, doing God knows what. I sit in my office practically holding my breath listening to the stillness of the adjacent room until he decides to pack up and head back to wherever it is he comes from. If I were a dreamer I'd hope he were standing there, conjuring up the courage to walk into my office and apologize, even profess his love to me. But I am a realist and I know what happens when you start dreaming: you get your heart broken. The reality is he never enters my office and I'm grateful for that. Feigning indifference is exhausting enough without having to be in direct contact with him.

Today, after Asher's class is complete and he has left the vicinity, I make my way down to the first floor to accept a shipment we are expecting.

When the shipment arrives, I open every box and make sure they are all filled with the exact books I requested and the precise quantity is here. When I am satisfied with the delivery, I tell the man from UPS he can leave and I bring the boxes into the supply room, myself, to ensure they are where they are supposed to be.

I lock the door to the supply closet and walk the hallway back toward the stairwell when I hear my name said from inside one of the offices. No one is calling my name. Instead, it's being said in conversation.

"We played Heinz Hall together. They gave her a solo that would have blown you away. It was incredible."

That is Frank. If I didn't know his voice, I know he is the only person here who played in the Pittsburgh symphony with me. It is against my better judgment and everything I stand for but for some reason I feel compelled to stop, step closer, and listen in.

"I saw a few clips on YouTube. She was very good." Asher's distinct masculine voice echoes through the wall. Why isn't he back on his merry way to his dark fortress ruling the city? And "very good"? I was magnificent! The term *good* shouldn't even be an adjective allowed to describe how well I played. "How is she doing as assistant director?"

"She is possibly the one person who cares about this place more than you do," Frank replies and is followed by silence. Damn Asher really knows how to take his dramatic pauses. He's the kind of person who makes you want to say something just to fill in the void. "I'm glad you informed me of her accident."

"That wasn't me."

"Well, I'm glad your office told me. I had no idea." Frank's tone takes a nosedive into the melodramatic. "Talent like Emma Paige should not be wasted. She's remarkably brave to have gone through what she has."

I fight an urge to kick the wall.

"What was she like? Before the accident, I mean?"

Frank chortles. "You mean because she's so serious? You think it has something to do with the accident?"

I assume Asher is nodding his head, since I can't see or hear his response.

"What was Emma Paige like a year ago?" Frank asks himself out loud. His seat creaks back and forth and that's the only sound I hear from a few seconds.

"Fire." He finally states. "She was fire, like a bolt of lightening striking down on the stage. Emma was fierce and she had this confidence about her that as soon as she walked out on stage, you knew you were going to hear magic.

"She wasn't cocky though. No, she was kind and shared the accolades. It made it hard for the rest of us to hate her." Frank laughs at his own joke and then his tone comes back down. "Emma was . . . is . . . very special. You'd be hard-pressed to find someone as genuine as her. Don't let the frown fool you.

He continues. "I spoke to her a few times about playing again. Apparently it would take a miracle to get her to lift a bow. Praise be the person who gets her to try." Frank's words are followed by more silence and I'd kill to see the expression on Asher's face. "Well . . . needless to say, she's doing an outstanding job."

Asher lets out a loud breath accompanied the sound of his chair rubbing against the floor as if he leaned back in his seat. "Let's hope so."

I push off the wall I've been glued to and make my way down the hall and back up to my office. My teeth are rubbing together fiercely.

Let's hope so.

Let's hope I don't ram his cello up his—you know where I'm going with this. Alexander Asher is making the douche with a flute look like Romeo.

I swing open the heavy stairwell door like it weighs as much as a feather and huff my way into Lisa's classroom.

She'd asked if I would swing by her beginner's class; she still hasn't gotten an intern and it's starting to cause her problems. Eight kids, all between the ages of seven and nine. It's even younger than I was when I started to play.

By the time I get to the room, the students are all in their seats. It's the fifth lesson for them, so they know where to go. Lisa begins by showing each child how to hold the instrument properly. Walking from child to child, she rests the violin on the collarbone, explaining the left hand and the shoulder should support the weight while the head stabilizes the violin on the collarbone.

It's an awkward posture for a child to hold.

By the time Lisa has gotten to child eight, the first four kids are already losing their proper hold. I can see why she asked for assistance. She instructs them to grab the bow with the right hand and starts to talk about up strokes and down strokes.

I see a young boy struggling with the instrument, squirming in his seat like he has ants in his pants. Walking around to his spot in the room, I take a chair and sidle up next to him.

"Hi," I whisper.

The young boy just stares at me. His eyes big and brown, darker than mine. I look down at my paper and his seating placement to find out his name. "Are you Charlie?"

Charlie nods. His face is set in a frown.

"My name is Emma. Do you mind if I help you?" My voice is soft, so as not to disrupt the rest of the class. When Charlie nods that it's okay, I place my hands on the violin, resting it properly on his neck. "Relax your neck. You're very tense. You'll hurt yourself this way. Rest your head right here." I pat down and he rests his head a bit. "Very good, Now, place your left hand right here." I move his hand in place, noting it's very stiff. "If you hold your bow up in your right hand, it will help relieve the tension in your left. Does that make sense?"

Charlie nods but I don't think he entirely gets it. He's still very young. In time, the instrument will seem like second nature to him. Until then, it will take practice.

He takes the bow, placing his thumb on the base and the other four fingers to rest at the top.

"Good job, buddy." His finger placement is great except for the pinkie. "Don't hook your pinkie like that." I think for a moment, trying to make this lesson relatable to a seven-year-old. "Do you like Peter Pan?"

"Like Jake and the Neverland Pirates?"

Who the hell is that? I look up to Lisa, who is assisting another child. She gives me an assuring nod that this Jake is, in fact ,just like Peter Pan. She would know, she has two children of her own.

"You see this guy?" I pinch Charlie's pinkie with my thumb and pointer finger. "This is Captain No-Hook. Can you say that?"

Charlie lets out a laugh. "Captain No-Hook."

A smile crosses my face. "Yeah, Captain No-Hook. Don't let this guy hook your instrument."

"Does that mean I'm a pirate?" His eyes light up with the question.

I nod and continue to smile. "Yes. Now don't let Captain No-Hook hook your violin."

Charlie looks at his fingers carefully and tries very hard to keep them in place. To my surprise, he does it correctly. I just taught him how to properly hold an instrument. I look over at Lisa who is nodding and smiling. My face blushes a bit. Yeah, teaching is pretty cool.

I stand to see if any of the other kids need help when a commanding figure in the doorway catches my attention. I almost trip over a backpack when I catch the intense stare of the one person I don't need seeing me right now.

Asher.

He is looking through the partially opened doorway, his brows creased and his head tilted ever so slightly. His lips are pursed but not the way he does when he's mad. This time, he looks thoughtful.

He's different. Something about him has changed and I'm afraid to find out what it is.

I lower my chin and go back to helping the students. After a few minutes I risk a look back at the doorway to find it empty. I don't know exactly how I feel about that.

chapter EIGHTEEN

If my mom knew what I was about to do she'd freak out.

If my dad knew what I was about to do he'd cry.

I kinda feel like doing both right now.

It's a warm October day, warmer than the past few weeks. My park is filled with people who are getting their last bit of sunshine until the cold weather settles in.

I'm here later than I usually am. I like to get to my park before the girl with the wrong violin shows up. Today, however, I paced in front of the chesterfield, staring at my Laura Vigato violin propped up on the cushion, wondering if I should go through with it.

When I left Cedar Ridge in August to come to New York, my mom tried to shove the violin in my arms. I had enough bags to lug through the airport but I reluctantly took it just to make her happy. It has been sitting on a shelf in my bookcase collecting dust since. Except for this morning when it sat on my couch staring at me as if saying, "Make a move. I dare you."

"Well, I'll tell you, Miss Violin, what kind of move I'm going to make," I said, pointing to the wooden instrument on my sofa while walking back and forth in front of it, "I'm going to . . . I'm . . . shit!" I exclaimed and then grabbed the violin off the couch, placed it back in the case, and hauled ass out of the apartment before I could change my mind.

So here I am, at Washington Square Park, staring at the brown-haired girl with her ponytail, playing beautiful music. Squaring my shoulder I walk up to her and hold out my hand.

"Here."

She stops playing at my brash assault on her space and takes a step back as if I am about to attack her.

"Here. Take it." I say, practically throwing the violin case at her.

She looks back at me with hesitation and shakes her head a little before looking around to see if someone is going to save her from the crazy lady practically throwing a violin case at her.

Okay, she is not going to make this easy. I put the case down on the ground, open it up and lift the violin out of it. The beautiful fir-wood still shines and glistens in the sun.

"I'm giving this to you." I show her the violin and while her eyes beam when she sees the gorgeous carved fillets of the Vigato, her body falls further back.

My cheeks puff out with air as I think of another way to approach this. I rest the violin at my side and instead of holding out the instrument again, I offer her a hand.

"My name is Emma."

She looks at my hand for a second before placing her violin and bow in her left hand together and offering me her right in return.

"Allyce." She says, shaking my hand quickly and then motioning to a place behind where I'm standing. "I've noticed you on the bench over there. Why do you always give me so much money? Most people just drop a dollar or two."

"You look like you could use it." As soon as I say it I see her body go on the defense. "I don't mean it like that. I mean, you could use a new violin. That is for an intermediate player." I hold up the Vigato again. "This is for a professional. It's has quite a few miles on it but it's a better grade for you. You'll play better." I offer the instrument to her again.

A breeze passes through the park and I watch as the hair in her ponytail dances in the wind. She eyes the violin

I am holding and then looks at me, questioning my judgment and her own.

"Why would you give that to me? Is it stolen? Am I being set up or something?"

"No. I just have no use for it anymore." I hold up my hand and show her the scar. "I've been put out of commission indefinitely and she needs a new home."

Allyce doesn't question my referencing of the violin as *she*. She places her old violin on the ground and takes the Vigato.

"She's beautiful." She studies the hour-glass shape of the Italian-made instrument. She then places it up to her chin and checks for comfort. They look like a perfect fit. "I'm sorry to hear about your hand. Must have been rough. Why would you want to give her up to a complete stranger?"

Looking down at the pavement, I think about that for a moment. The truth is, I have no idea. In fact, this is the third most impulsive thing I've done this year, and perhaps in my entire life.

The first was asking Luke to drive fast. The second was stripping naked in front of a god with a cello. Those two events left me feeling empty. But this? Well, if it makes me feel empty again I can live with that. For some reason, I don't think it will.

"I don't know. I just know it will get better use with you. Selling it feels wrong. I can't imagine her going to the wrong person. You two just look right together."

Allyce takes my answer and seems to understand it in an odd way. She places the bow to the strings and starts playing. As soon as the bow hits the strings I feel burn in my eyes and a feeling of loss takes over me. Before I start to lose it, I turn around and start to walk away.

My feet are just a few feet from Allyce when she stops playing. "Wait." She says and starts to walk toward me. "What do you do now? I mean, now that you can't play?"

I turn back around toward Allyce. “I work at the Juliette Academy. It’s a free music school over on—”

“I’ve heard of it. Wait right here.” She says before walking back to her spot and gathering up her old violin that was wrong for her. She puts it back in its case and walks it over to me. “Here. Pay it forward.”

“No. Thank you but you don’t have to do that—”

“Actually, I do. I believe in karma. Giving you an old violin for a new one is the least I can do.”

I nod my head and with pure reluctance accept it. “Thank you.”

Allyce nods her chin and steps back, walking to her place by the bench. “Any requests?”

“La Vie En Rose.”

With a smile, she lifts the violin to her chin and starts to play. The beginning chords vibrate so beautifully. I can’t stand to listen so I take the old violin and walk out of the park. My heart rate is not as rapid as I thought it would be. My anxiety levels are manageable. This was a good thing to do. It was right. My mouth is widening on my face. I actually feel okay.

Near the exit I see a black SUV and today I don’t think it’s a coincidence. My smile instantly fades.

I stomp over to the car and as soon as I reach it, I grab the handle and open the back door. I nearly jump out of my skin when, instead of finding an empty backseat, my entire field of vision is filled with Alexander Asher.

As the door opens, his body jerks back in surprise. He must not have expected me to approach the vehicle, let alone open the door. His mouth is open and his eyes are wide; a shocked expression mirroring my own.

Okay, I’m surprised, too. I assumed Devon was the driver but I’m not prepared to see him here. I was just going to launch the case into the seat and slam the door or something.

“Here.” Hands shaking, I shove the case onto his lap. His hands rise as he stares at the violin resting on his thighs. “It’s a gift for the school.” I step back and am about to close the door when I add, “And stop following me.”

I make a point to slam the door as hard as I can and walk away.

Yeah, so you know how a minute ago I was pretty calm and cool? Well, not anymore.

Karma is a bitch.

chapter NINETEEN

A ninja turtle, four Elsas, and an astronaut knock on your door. What do you do? You give them candy.

I'm glad Mattie gave me a heads up on the amount of kids that would be knocking on the door tonight.

I put orange Halloween lights in my apartment window and have been standing at the building's door with a giant bowl greeting the trick-or-treaters. I got tired of walking back and forth from my apartment so I thought it was better to just stand post at the front of the building.

"Happy Halloween!" the kids chant as they walk away. Another group approaches and we start all over. This time there are only two Elsas, a Cinderella, and a Darth Vader.

"If I ever have kids they are never allowed to dress like Elsa." Mattie startles me when he creeps up behind me.

I place my hand over my heart and catch my breath. "Geez, give a girl a warning." Looking down, the trick-or-treaters are staring up at me with their open trick or treat bags.

Mattie snakes an arm around me and grabs a Reese's Pieces from the bowl. "Damn, woman, you give out good candy. I thought you couldn't give out anything with nuts to kids anymore?"

"What do you know about kids? You're still one yourself?" I scoff.

Mattie hold up his hand showing his middle, ring, and pinky fingers. "Three sisters. Seven, ten, and fifteen. All from my dad's second marriage and trust me, they live in a nut-free world."

He pops the Reese's in his mouth and moans as if he just tasted the most tender piece of filet mignon. He swallows and points a finger at me. "And don't call me a kid. I'm the same age as you."

I give him a laugh. "No. You're in school. I run a school. You're a boy. I'm a girl. In maturity years that's like a decade."

Mattie puts an arm on my shoulder and pats it lightly, "Yes, mam."

I offer a wry smile at his sarcastic remark. When he steps in front of me I appraise his costume for tonight. "*Beetlejuice*?"

"Robin Thicke. You should see my girl's costume. She's a goat."

The look on my face is filled with confusion because I have absolutely no idea what he is talking about. Mattie lets out a belly laugh that carries him to the corner and out of sight.

I back away to close my door when something catches my eye. A light reflects off a piece of chrome from across the street and I step forward to look again. There is a shiny motorcycle parked on the opposite side of the street. Standing beside it is a piece of gold, brighter than the setting sun.

That gold is a man, and one I would never in a million years have pictured standing on my street corner.

I tilt my head and look back at him wondering why in the world Alexander Asher is here. He's wearing black jeans and a black leather jacket. It's a look so different from the two I've seen on him. Far more relaxed than the suit and tie, yet more intense than in Carpi. His hair is styled back but with a messier look, which must be from wearing a helmet.

I look down at my own attire. I'm wearing jeans and an orange V-neck sweater in honor of the holiday.

There is no reason I can think of for why he would be here. We haven't spoken a word to each other in weeks, aside from when I caught him spying on me at the park.

When I got home, I sat in the chesterfield contemplating what the hell it meant. I came up with nothing.

And now I'm completely confused as to why he's standing across the street looking at me. With no clue as to what it is he wants, I turn around and go back to my apartment, leaving the front door to the building open and the door to my apartment slightly ajar.

I take a spot in the kitchen and turn down the volume on my speakers and wonder if he'll follow me inside. Do I want him to come in?

Kind of.

Damn it!

I'm picking at the polish on my nails when I hear footsteps and the sound of the front door of the building closing. Those footsteps get louder as they draw near and I know he's coming in. My door slowly opens as Asher pushes it with the pads of his fingers. I watch as his eyes dart around the room taking in the space.

He turns his head to the living room and the bookcase along the wall. Something on the shelf catches his eye so he walks in, taking slow, tentative steps into the room. He has on boots, which is better than the loafers. They're heavy and make a low thud as he walks.

Stopping in front of the bookcase, he picks up a picture of Luke and me, taken on his eighteenth birthday. Luke's red hair is shaggy and an absolute mess. It was right before he started wearing it short to "appease the ladies." I am wearing a grin from ear to ear, hugging his torso and looking in to the camera with eyes so bright, I haven't seen them in my reflection in months. Asher picks up the photo and examines it, probably looking at the girl in it like she's a complete stranger. The corner of his mouth tilts up and then he puts the photo back in its place. He looks at a few more photos I have, including one of my parents and another of Leah and Adam at their engagement party and my sweaters that are folded on display on some shelves of the bookcase, before walking over to the couch and rifles through the magazines I have on the end table.

Taking in the artwork, the sparse furnishings and the reading nook, he looks to be examining my home. It takes him all of three minutes. When he has made a full three-sixty around the room, he looks over at me in the kitchen, standing here like a frightened turkey.

"This is where you live?" he asks.

I blink a few times, assessing the question. My eyes shift from side to side in confusion. When I don't give him an answer, he looks down the hall and zeros in on the door to my bedroom.

"Don't even think of going back there." My words are sharp. Bad enough he's standing here judging my home. There is no way I am allowing him to invade my bedroom.

Asher looks to his left and smirks. "Emma, your room is no more than ten feet from where I'm standing. You're not hiding anything back there." He is looking around the place like it's beneath him. "I can walk across this entire apartment in ten steps."

I fold my arms across my chest. "What do you want from me?"

He doesn't answer. Instead, those gorgeous golden gems travel up and down my body, as if it's the first time he's really noticed me since we reconnected. His chest rises and Adams apple juts out with a swallow.

"You look good." His voice is sincere and not condescending but it's the way he's standing, so dominant, that makes me wary of his intentions.

"Thank you?" I want to kick myself for answering in such a way.

His eyes bear down on mine, the two of us in an intense standoff of silence. He looks like he is going to say something . . . profound? Instead, he closes his mouth and walks over to the window in the front and investigates the lock. The window frame has been painted over, quite possibly fifty times in as many years, so the metal latch is painted shut. I watch as Asher tries to raise the window but to no avail.

"You shouldn't be on the ground floor." He motions to the iron bars on the outside of the window. "Those need to be updated."

My mouth is agape at his rudeness. "Did you come here to criticize where I live?"

Asher closes the curtains to make sure they provide enough privacy. He nods his head in approval and then opens them again.

I tap my foot in annoyance as he walks over to the front door and fiddles with the lock. I let out a loud huff. He must hear it because he turns around and faces me. I make a face as to say, "Satisfied?"

Asher walks toward me, his presence filling up the room, stopping on the opposite side of the small island of the kitchen. As he approaches, I can smell the leather of his jacket. Its not the same as salt and sea, but it'll do.

We stand in silence; I vow I will not be the first to break it. He came here. He has to be the one to say something.

His chin tilts to the side as his ear leans in to hear the faint sound coming from my speaker. Before I can stop him, he reaches over and raises the volume and his brow rises in interest. The cello version of "Wonderwall" by Oasis is playing, confirmation for him that I have been listening in to his lessons.

I fold my arms across my chest, my foot resumes tapping, an act he finds amusing as the corner of his mouth curls up ever so slightly and than vanishes instantly.

"Who's the guy?" He asks with a nod of his head toward the door. He's referring to Mattie.

"None of your business."

His square jaw protrudes with the clench of his jowls. I look away from him, gathering my bearings. I should let him think Mattie is someone to me. Make him suffer thinking I'm with someone else.

Who am I kidding? He doesn't care.

I turn my head back to Asher, who is smoldering. It's as if he thinks this is some kind of game.

A game I have no intention of playing.

"He's my neighbor," I say, clipping my words through my teeth. "And what does it matter to you? You already had me. Conquest accomplished. Wasn't that the goal?" My throat burns as the words come out. I intended to say them to hurt him. Instead, they're killing me.

His eyes are ablaze with indignation. I don't think this is what he came here for but this is certainly where it's going. "What exactly do you think my goal was?"

I bite back any emotion attempting to rise from me as I continue. I managed three weeks of decorum around him. I managed to be in the same building and not say a word when the hurt was sitting on my chest like a lead weight.

Turns out I can't fight it anymore.

"Find a girl, trick her into pretending you're some brooding boathand who needs saving, fuck her, and leave. Wasn't that the goal . . . Alexander?"

Asher pushes off the island and runs his hand along the back of his neck. He paces a few steps and then turns back to me. His chest rises and falls with deep, hard breaths.

"I never once lied to you. I tell it like it is, I do what I want but I never manipulate the truth." He moves toward me, severe and snappish. "Don't act so innocent. You have no idea what I have been though. I had no idea what your intentions—"

"My intentions?" I cut him off. This time, it's my turn to push away from the island. "What exactly do you think I was doing in Italy? Tell me!" Outrage and resentment rise in my chest.

Asher looks back at me, his breath heavy, his words controlled. "You knew exactly what you were doing." His voice is filled with accusation but his eyes—his eyes are filled with something else.

I turn away from him for fear if I look at him for one more second I'll fall down the rabbit hole. I fought too hard to be brought back down. I rose from the bed. I lifted the fork to my mouth. I got on a plane and came here to make a new start for my new life.

I am the diamond. I cannot be broken.

"Why are you doing this?" I turn back to him, lifting my arms in exasperation. "You know everything about me. You see this." I hold up my hand revealing the scar that brandishes my skin. "This is me. On January second, my boyfriend, who I thought I loved, broke up with me. He tore my heart apart. So my brother—my sweet, funny, wonderful brother—took me out. I asked him—no, I begged him to drive. I pleaded with him to take the pain away with the rush of an engine and that cost him his life. And this"—I hold up my hand higher, closer to his face—"this is all I have left!"

I pull my arms away and clench the tarnished skin in my other hand. "But you know this. You know this because you looked me up. No one as untrusting as you would have gone near me without knowing everything. You know I lived to play the violin. You know what I was doing in Capri. And you know every single word I said to you on that island was true."

"Emma—"

"Don't." I shake my head. "Don't say anything except the one thing I need you to say."

"What do you want me to say?"

"Say it!"

"Say what?"

My heart squeezes tight as I march toward him. "That you were wrong! I want you to—"

"I was wrong!" He speaks so loudly the room vibrates. "I was wrong. I knew I was wrong the next day."

I let out a loud breath, expelling the weight that was sitting in my ribs. My heart continues to race and now my mind is playing catch-up.

Did he just—?

Is he admitting that he—?

"Then why didn't you come back for me?"

"I don't know!" Asher spins around. His back widens as his arms rise and his hands run through his hair, pulling it at the ends. "I don't know. I just . . . That night when security called, saying Adam Reingold was looking into me, researching me—I was furious. We pulled up anchor and got out of there. I wanted, *needed* to believe you were like everyone else."

"I don't want your money if that's what you're accusing me of." I practically spit the words at him. "I don't want anything from you. I liked you when I thought you had nothing."

My words force him to turn around and face me. The look on his face is one of defeat and disappointment. "I know."

His sullen posture and red-rimmed eyes take the bitterness away. He's hurting too. "I don't understand. When you first saw me at the school you were so mad. You have been so mad."

With my words, Asher is quickly moving toward me. When he reaches me, he places both hands gently on my arms. "I am mad. Hell, I'm fucking furious. I don't want you here. And, no, it's not because I don't want you. I have been fighting the urge to come find you. To go to you and apologize. I came close."

His forehead leans toward mine, his eyes full of something so sincere, I could swear I am standing on a stairwell in Capri. "But every time I thought about it, I couldn't. I'm scared, Emma. I'm scared of what might happen if you turn out to be the woman I feared you were."

My eyes close and I try to process everything he's saying. Asher wants me. He's always wanted me. He knew he was wrong.

"How do you know I'm not that kind of woman? What's changed?"

He rubs the back of his neck slightly, his head tilting to the side. "Everything. Nothing."

Those eyes have turned to honey and the look of the man I fell for is back, right here in front of me, saying all the words I've wanted to hear.

There is one major problem. He still left and never came back. He lied in Italy and he is lying now. His words sound right but they're all wrong.

They're empty. Like his heart.

I step back from him, attempting to distance myself from his hold on my body and my heart. "I know why you left me. Even that next morning when I stood on the marina, looking for you, wondering why you left. I knew." My fists clench tight and I feel the searing pain rising from my hand all the way up my arm. I use that pain as power. I use that pain as a reminder. I use that pain to feel. "You're a coward and a user. I trusted you. By God, I let you into my heart when I had shut everyone else out. I gave you a piece of me that was so sacred it can't be given back. You take and take but you never give."

When the pain of the words matches the pain of my hand, I release the clench and hold my hand up high to my chest, cradling it with care. Asher reaches for me again, his eyes carnal as he takes a step forward and grabs the injured hand with his and puts it up to his heart. "Emma—"

"I'm fine." I try to pull my hand back but he pulls it toward him. His other hand inches up and rests on the side of my face, his fingers tangle in my hair. My chin rises but my eyes keep their concentration on the zipper of his jacket and the heavy rise and fall of his chest.

“No, you’re not. Neither of us are.” Asher’s thumb grazes my lip and I let out a sigh at the feel of his touch. I recall the taste of his lips and the feel of his hands as they work their way along my body.

My body may want him but my heart is in pieces.

“I need you to leave.”

His body jolts against mine. “What?”

“Leave.”

My cheek feels an instant chill as his hand releases me. The pain in my right hand still burns but when he releases it, it feels like its being crushed by four thousand pounds of metal again.

I hug my body tight and look up at him. His jaw is hollowed and his face is clenched. “Emma, I—I don’t know how to tell you. I’m trying to show you how I feel. I’m not good at this.”

I sniff back a tear and breathe deep into my gut. “You need to leave.”

My eyes clench shut and I hold them still, waiting for him to move. When I open them it is just in time to see him back away, rubbing the back of his neck. He looks around the room one more time before gaining his full composure. Right before my eyes I watch as the Asher Gutierrez I met in Italy becomes the Alexander Asher I know he really is. The man who uses and takes. He didn’t get what he wanted so he is walking out the door.

I walk over to the window and watch him cross the street and climb on his motorcycle. He revs the engine and then just sits there idling, looking at my front door as if waiting for me to come out.

I must be a glutton for punishment because, for a brief moment, I consider going outside and going with him. Absolutely not. I have pride.

He’s forgetting he accused me of dishonesty and trickery. I can’t forget the way he made me feel, standing with my bare feet looking at a sea void of his presence. He left me. He disappeared.

And what did I do?

I followed him to New York.

"When you first took the job in New York I thought it was because he lived there. Like you needed to be near him or something." Leah's words echo in my head. I lean down and let out a low scream at the fact she was absolutely right. I didn't know if he would be here. I didn't know if I would ever see him again. But I have to stop lying to myself and own up to the fact I wanted to see him. And he's here, looking devastatingly gorgeous and saying the right words and he wants me to follow him.

"There is a fire between us, Emma, and I know we're gonna get burned."

I walk over to the front door and slam it shut.

chapter TWENTY

Gasping.

Gasping.

Breathing is too hard.

I need to count.

Beats.

One, two, three, four . . .

One, two . . .

Gasp.

One . . . Two . . . Three . . . Four.

Breathe.

Breathing.

It's pitch black and the clock confirms it's the middle of the night. My shirt is plastered to my back. Sweat is trickling down my chest, starting at my forehead. I wipe my hand across my head, brushing the hairs stuck to my skin away from my face.

I had a dream. We were in the car driving fast. So fast. This time, instead of asking Luke to drive fast, I was begging him to stop. My voice shouting over the radio, pleading with him to save his life.

He wouldn't listen. His foot like a lead weight pushed down on the accelerator and all of a sudden there was a bolt of lightening. Everything went white and then there was a fire. Raging fire. Burning. We crashed and we were burning. When I stepped back to see if Luke was okay, his face had changed, morphed into someone else.

It was Asher.

I like to be the first one in the building every day. I do a check of every room, make sure the chairs are in place and stands are at the correct height for the first class. I assess the decorations on the walls and make sure they are relevant to the month's theme. In a small room on the second floor, we keep an inventory of unused instruments. I double-check it every morning making sure nothing has been stolen.

When I have fully assessed the building, I make my way to my office. The building is mostly quiet. Classes don't start until two and end around seven. That's when the building is really alive.

Until then, I have to occupy my time, focusing on what needs to be done to enhance the program, move us forward, be the best.

Especially today.

After yesterday's visit and last night's dream I'm afraid I am losing my control.

I open the heavy stairwell door; there's a jazz quartet playing down the hall. Last week, Frank and I started allowing people to rent the classrooms as rehearsal space. It is a great way to bring in extra revenue for the school.

We started making a schedule to start performance classes for mixed instruments on Saturdays in the spring. Next year we'll host recitals in the performance room on the first floor. Until then, we just have to keep the school afloat and on track so we can grow.

I have applications for bands and performers who would like to utilize our space in the meantime. I have to review those this week. I open the door to Crystal's classroom and see it is occupied.

"Hey, I didn't know you'd be here so early. I—" My words stop mid-sentence when I see Crystal is not alone.

She is standing in the middle of the room talking to Asher. He's not wearing the suit and tie he's been sporting around here for the last month. Today, he has on gray corduroys and a gold V-neck sweater. And those stupid loafers.

Crystal watches me enter and greets me merrily. "Good morning. Mr. Asher is here to discuss taking over more of my classes."

My head twists in Asher's direction. "I'm sorry, what?"

Asher places both hands in his pockets and leans back on his heels. "I have some free time, so I'd like to take over the advanced cello sessions."

"Don't you work?" My words startle Crystal. She doesn't know Asher and I have a history and is visibly shocked I would talk to the head of the Asher empire this way.

"Nope," he states simply, bouncing on his heels.

I turn to face Crystal. "You need this job to supplement your income. You can't just give up four of your classes."

She bites down on her forefinger and glances over at Asher like the cat that ate the canary. I volley back and forth between the two of them trying to decide what they're not telling me.

Asher sees Crystal's apprehension and answers for the two of them. "I'm paying her to take over her classes."

My mouth falls open. "You can't do that."

With two slow strides, Asher walks toward me, saddling up next to me so our sides are touching, shoulder to bicep. He leans down and says directly into my ear, "I can and I will."

Manipulator. He's a liar, a coward, a taker, and now I can add manipulator to the long list of adjectives I have for Alexander Asher. I walk into my office and throw my bag on the floor. When I throw my phone on the desk, I notice a brown paper wrapped package with a twine string sitting beside it.

Tilting my head to the side, I look at it, wondering who would have left me a gift. I roll the tote strap off my shoulder and place the bag on my desk chair. Reaching over, I grab the package and pull the twine. When the string is undone, the paper opens quickly. Inside, is a brown, leather bound, journal with a leather tie and lined pages. I lift the book up and open the front to find a handwritten note.

Hope you're taking notes.

—A

I stare at the signature. He knows I'm listening in on the class. I feel like my territory has been invaded. Now, not only do I have Crystal's cello mocking me from the corner of my office but I have a six-foot-tall cello-wielding god sharing a room with me.

What should I do?

Just keep on keepin' on.

Oh, fuck you, McConaughey.

I know Leah said I have to "play on the same playing field" and all that nonsense, but right now I need space from Asher. I sit in on all of Lisa's violin classes, offering my services. At first, she is surprised and a tiny bit apprehensive, wondering why the sudden change. But then she welcomes the help, especially with the little ones.

In between one of the classes, I head up to my office, planning to grab my bag before Asher arrives to teach his class.

Walking into the room, I notice the notebook he bought me, sitting on my desk. It has been moved, sitting on top of a stack of files. It has also been tampered with. I step closer and notice there is a blue flower tucked into the book. When I pick up the notebook, it falls open; I take up the flower, holding the petals to my nose. It's a blue rose, manmade and impure.

Knowing Asher, the flower has a specific meaning. I lift my phone out of my pocket and type "Blue rose meaning" into the search engine.

Blue: The unattainable; the impossible.

I roll my eyes and place the flower on the desk. With the notebook still in my hand I look down at the opened page.

You think you're broken
but maybe it's me who needs
to be saved.

There's a loud thud in the adjoining classroom, and I realize the students are all walking in. I'm about to leave when I hear one of them greet Asher. It's too late to make my escape and, in all honesty, my interest is piqued, so I take a seat at my office desk and listen in on the lesson.

Asher begins the class, not by playing a song from his iPod, but by playing a song on the cello by himself. It takes me a second to recognize the song. He's playing "Stay" by Rihanna. I look down at the words on the page in front of me. He proceeded to write out the words to the song.

The lyrics telling the story of a girl who falls for a man, disillusioned by falling that she ignores the signs that are telling her he's all wrong. She is asking for something real and all he can do is take her away to his fantasy world.

At least that's the way I interpret them.

When he gave me this notebook, he told me to take notes. Looks like he's the one taking them for me. When Asher is done playing, he gives his lesson and, like always, it's fascinating. I am so transfixed by his words, the sixty minutes pass by quickly.

Sitting in my office, I listen as one by one the students pack up and head out the door, thanking Asher for an awesome class. It was their first with him and, thanks to Crystal, not his last. He bids them farewell and says he'll see them next week.

When they are all out of the room, I listen to see if he has left too when I hear his footsteps walking across the room. I don't know if he is walking back here or waiting to see if I'll come out.

Whatever it is he has in mind, I have my own agenda. I lean my foot over and slam the door shut.

Using my very wobbly left hand, I flip to a clean page in the notebook and scribble the words to a song by the Veronicas.

When I'm done writing, my hand has a cramp but I'm satisfied with the message.

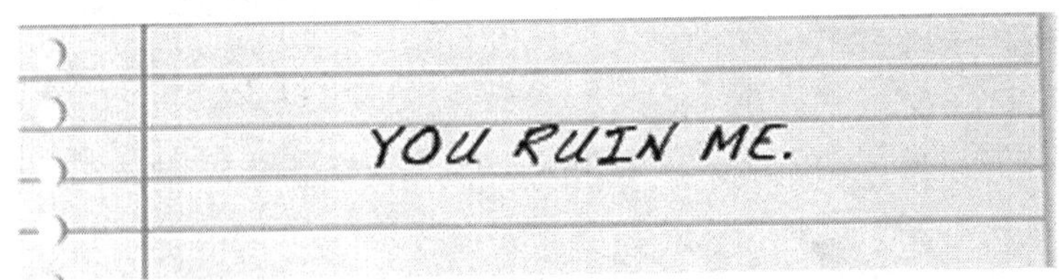

Thud, thud, thud.

The telltale sign of wheels rolling can be heard. I lean over and see Asher pushing a piano into the classroom. When I got to work this morning, the notebook was still on my desk, closed, with another rose.

Light pink: *Sympathy.*

I refused to open the notebook all day. I don't need to know what ridiculous message he has in store for me.

But, what the hell does he plan to do with the piano?

I sit back, my ears perched high like a canine on the defense. I listen as Asher says he wants to play a little something for the class. My stomach flops down when I hear the chords of "You Ruin Me" by the Veronicas. His deft fingers hit the keys perfectly. The ivory hums with the push and touch of every note of the song I dedicated to him.

My eyes close and the hairs of my spine stand up straight as the haunting melody resonates in the air. It hits my heart and touches my soul. My eyes well up from behind, the water threatening to fall—but I bite it back. My lips tremble, fighting emotion.

He is, literally, playing me like a symphony.

When the song is complete, I take deep cleansing breaths, bringing myself back to the moment. I lean over and grab the notebook. Inside, I see Asher has written back the lyrics to the song I wrote to him, matching me word for word.

The class is still in session when I lean my foot over and slam the door.

I know, I'm a glutton for punishment. I should be somewhere else right now instead of in my office waiting for another class to start.

In the other room, Asher hands out sheet music and has the students play a song I have never heard before. I hear the familiar voice of Mike, who teaches guitar.

What in the world is Mike doing in the cello class?

I look over at the notebook, a peach flower peaking out of the pages.

Sincerity.

The song of a guitar strum causes me to peek into the room. Mike is sitting at the front, on a stool, strumming the chords to a simple melody. Asher is seated beside him, the cello in place. I watch for a second as Asher starts to play. If I had more self-control in this situation, I'd keep myself from opening the notebook.

I don't, so I open it and see the song is called "Save Me From Myself."

Your strength amazes me
even after everything
I put you through.

I listen to the entire lesson. When it's over, I know he's standing alone in the room, waiting for a response. I slam the door, anyway.

Is he really bringing an organ in here?

I peer into the room, watching Asher and one of the maintenance crew push the one and only organ we have in the building into our classroom. It's old, it's made of wood, it's on casters, and it has to weigh a thousand pounds. I don't know that for a fact but I did see it come in on delivery day and it did not look pretty. The delivery process, I mean. The organ is gorgeous.

Fifteen minutes later that organ ignites and I open my book to see Asher is pulling out the big guns: ColdPlay.

And today's flower? Deep burgundy: *Unconscious beauty*.

Looking, ever so discreetly into the room, I see someone else playing the organ and Asher is in front of him on the cello.

The words are a diatribe of my life just months ago. I lost it all. Could it be worse? No. Losing Luke was the most horrific tragedy I ever encountered and ever want to endure in my life. I wouldn't wish that pain on anyone.

I know the song like I know my Social Security number. It's quite possibly my favorite. It's why I have to catch my breath just before I hear the notes that play to the words:

I will . . . Fix You.

I risk looking back into the classroom again. Asher is behind the cello, playing that beautiful instrument with passion and vigor, his eyes fixated on my doorframe. When he sees me, his head lifts in surprise.

Standing by the door, I watch for a few moments as Asher continues to play, his body in entrancing movement, eyes on me and filled with passion. He wants me to save him. He wants to fix me. The problem is, I can't save him and he shouldn't be the one to fix me. I am fixing myself.

I lower my head and look at the floor as my hand finds the knob and I slowly close the door.

The lessons and note-taking back and forth between Asher and me have been going on for two weeks. The song messages go from sweet and caring to soulful and mind-numbing to downright angry.

The angry ones are from me.

Yeah, I even threw a little Alanis "You Oughta Know" in there. It's the scorned woman's mantra.

He reciprocated with a little Maroon 5 and on a particular Tuesday when he was feeling particularly brave, Sir Mix-A-Lot's, "Baby Got Back." That made me laugh.

It may seem romantic to some but it's killing me.

I'm a wreck.

Every day, I enter my office to the sight of the notebook and a new flower. I hate how I look forward to seeing it there and am anxious to see what the pages have written in them. I hate how I fear it won't be there and what I'd feel if he gave up. I haven't slept in two weeks, fighting the feelings I have. He is tearing at my heartstrings.

He is also slowly creeping into my life in ways he probably doesn't even realize. Like how the other day I accidentally opened the door while he was walking in, causing him to spill his coffee on his tie. Instead of being mad, he just let out this adorable grin and said, "You'd never believe how many of these I ruin on a daily basis." I laughed a little before realizing I'm supposed to be mad at him. Or how he saw me having trouble opening a package because I needed to use both hands so he walked into my office, opened the package for me and then left, without a word. I should have thanked him, but of course, I didn't.

Last week, he brought in this giant tub of York Peppermint patties and left them in the classroom. I sneak one only when I know he's not in the building.

And then there's how I always see him watching me assist Lisa's class. Not for the entire session, but at least once a class I feel those golden eyes on me and I pretend I am not affected at all by him watching me teach. When I do chance a look up, it's always the same. A mixture of intrigue and appreciation. I hate that look.

Today, there is silence in the room next to mine. It's odd because Asher should be having a class about now. I peek into the room and see it is, in fact, empty. On the white board there's a note stating the lecture was moved to the first floor performance space.

I turn around and look back toward my office. The notebook with today's rose is nestled sweetly inside. It's a yellow rose with red tips. I walk back to the desk, grab the book and walk it out of the room.

My feet move down the hallway, taking me down the stairwell, two at a time, curious about what awaits me downstairs. My hair flips as I round the stair landing and go down another flight. I hear music pouring through the walls.

I'm not the only one interested in what is happening in the performance room. Almost everyone who works in the building or who attends a class tonight is making their way down as well. They must hear the music coming through the doors or word has spread throughout the building that something special is going on.

I pull the heavy door open and walk through it. My pace quickens and then slows as I approach the performance room. I make my way through the people, slipping inside. And I see something I've never seen before.

An orchestra. A real life orchestra is in our building. The room was built to host concerts by the students, the capacity maxing out at two hundred and fifty. The orchestra on the stage is easily made up of fifty people, many performing from the rows as there's not enough room on the stage.

The first violin section is in the walkway to the left of the stage, the cellos are on the right. The second violins and the violas are on the floor in the front. In the back of the stage are the harp, horns, percussion, trumpets, and basses set from left to right. In front of them are the clarinets, flutes, bassoons, and oboes.

The people playing the soft chords aren't students. They're adults. Classically trained adults. This is when it hits me. He brought the New York Philharmonic with him.

They're playing a soft hum of a tune, a prelude if you will. I'm able to make my way to the front of the room, taking in the sight before me.

In the center of the stage is a black grand piano similar to the one I played on the yacht in the middle of the Mediterranean. The one I was playing when the most beautiful man walked in and caught me in my most vulnerable state.

And that beautiful man is on the stage, seated at the piano in the middle of a real life orchestra about to play a song . . . for me.

His fingers start to play the notes and the string section around him picks up as well, causing my soul to soar before they all quiet down to a low hum as Asher continues to play.

I open the notebook and look down at the words he has written.

Halos casts down beyond the glass
In the darkness is where I stand
She is a beacon summoning me to shore
My siren. My light.

All around me, people are mesmerized not just by the orchestra and the song they are playing, but by the man in the center. The man in the center who is staring at no one else but me. Honey wheat eyes and staring down at me, his fingers playing the chords from memory.

Her eyes are closed. The water is calm.
From my soul it's a raging sea.
I've traveled alone for so long
Forgetting what it was I was looking for.

My stomach drops and my breaths become deep to still my nerves. With every glide across the ivory keys and pump of the pedal, I feel my resolve for Asher wavering. I wanted him to give and for two weeks he *has* been giving me words and meaning. And today he is giving me that honey-wheat soulful gaze I once fell in love with—and it is destroying me. I stare down at the words on the pages.

Flames rise on this dark soul.
And the angel is staring back at me.
A kiss. A moment. Entwined hands. A beating heart.
The planks light up in flames.
I go down with the sinking ship.

This is a song about someone leaving. It can't be to me, because I never left him. To the contrary. He left me. This song isn't about me.

It's about him.

Like a mirage she is gone.
And I coast alone.
No soul. No hope.
No beacon to call me home.

Scanning the page, I run my fingers over the words, over the smoothness of the page. There is no song title. There is no author. It's a song I've never heard of before yet I feel like I know it by heart.

He said I should be taking notes and I am. But what if I'm taking the wrong notes? Songs can be interpreted in so many ways. What if I'm reading this all wrong?

When the song is over, the crowd erupts in applause. People shout admiration for Asher's playing and some of the students ask him to play something else. He obliges and asks them if they have any requests.

I take this as my cue to leave and let him wow his audience. I suppose that really was what this was all about. A lesson for the students.

I turn around and make my way through the crowd that has subsided. I walk through the lobby and am on my way back up the stairs when the stairwell door opens and Asher calls my name.

"Emma."

I stop and turn around, looking at the man who went from ruining me to asking me to save him to making me want to fall in love with him. I know I should say something about the performance but I don't know what to say. Instead I clutch the notebook to my side and stare at him, giving him the control because right now, I don't know what I should do.

"I never got a chance to ask you. What happened to the shoes?"

I stare at him for a second before realizing he's talking about the bouquet of Top-Siders he bought me. I consider lying, more for the fact I don't want to appear crazy, then decide against it. "I burned them."

Asher tilts his head, his face contorted as he tries to decide if I'm lying.

I answer him matter-of-factly. "Leah and I had a bonfire when we got back to Ohio. We doused them in limoncello and lit them up."

His lips curl up on both sides as he shakes his head. "Well, that seems like a perfectly good waste of limoncello."

I laugh at his response and let my shoulders release the tension I was carrying so tightly. I'm a wreck. He ruined me. But by God he owns me.

chapter TWENTY-ONE

"I'm getting marrriieeedddd!"

Leah squeals from her place on a white bed in the middle of a Manhattan male strip club that caters to celebrations just like this. Instead of tables, there are several white beds big enough for ten girls to sit in and enjoy the show on display.

After the last few weeks—hell, the last few months—I've been having, Leah's bachelorette party is a welcome reprieve.

"Your sister is crazy!" Crystal screams in my ear over the loud music. A man wearing a piece of dental floss and what can only be described as a banana hammock has Leah's friend Suzanne in the air, wrapped around his waist as he simulates thrusting into her. Leah is throwing money at the stripper to give all her friends a lap dance.

It's all in good fun. Leah is fully clothed in jeans and a silky halter-top. She has on her favorite black Stetson with a veil we taped to the inside. She wanted a *Magic Mike*–themed bachelorette party so Crystal and Lisa helped me orchestrate tonight's event.

And from the looks of it, Leah approves.

Despite her outward persona, Leah likes to look but she'd never touch. She says Adam is enough for her. Instead, she'll spend a week's salary making sure each of her friends – Jessica, Suzanne and Kimberly - who traveled with her from Cedar Ridge has the time of her life.

"She's a class act, that one," I say to Crystal, then back up when I see the naked man is heading my way.

I place my hands up in the air and push the man away from me. "Oh no. No way, no way, no way!" My efforts are in vain as Leah and her friends Suzanne, Kimberly, and Jessica push the stripper toward me.

"Oh, come on, do it for your sister!" Crystal places her hand on my back and pushes me forward into the arms of a very oily, very sweaty man. He is attractive—dark hair and dark eyes. He looks like Eric Bana. Earlier he was dressed in a doctor's costume and did a performance on stage where he cured one of the bachelorettes by stripping and then dry humping her up and down the stage.

I look over to Lisa for help but she just shakes her head from the corner.

The doctor-slash-stripper has his hands around my waist and I squeal when he slides them around to grab my ass lifting me up so my legs dangle as he whirls me around and slams me onto the bed Leah and her friends are sitting on.

"I'm going to kill you!" I say, with a laugh, when I catch Leah's eye.

She howls and waves her hands in the air. "Enjoy it Emma!"

I start to smile and laugh at her happiness when the stripper, who was standing on the ground in front of me, leaps from the floor, up in the air and lands on the bed with his knees on each side of my waist and he is straddling me.

Oh, dear God. I hope he doesn't . . .

Yeah, he is.

The stripper dances and moves up my body, gyrating his pelvis. I raise my hands to cover my face, blocking out the sight of what he's doing and the awful smell of stale oil and stinky boy that he is dripping all over me.

The girls love every minute of it. Lisa is the only one who looks slightly uncomfortable for my sake. I'm starting to question my judgment of asking my work friends to come out.

I turn my head to the side to avoid the banana hammock from coming anywhere near my face. The stripper sits straight up and I am instantly relieved, thinking the show is over, when he does a mock push-up over my body and then pretends he is penetrating me.

"Okay, that's enough!"

I push my hand out and shove him away. Rising from the bed, I push past him, ignoring his fake hurt look—puppy-dog eyes, a stuck-out lower lip, and hands over his heart. When Leah pushes a twenty into his G-string, all is forgotten and he moves on to his next victim.

"You're a good sport." Lisa pats me on the back and hands me a drink. It's pink, girly and just what I need.

"Yeah, that wasn't so bad, was it?" Crystal asks, helping me readjust my halter-top. "Aren't you glad I told you to wear pants!"

I take a sip of my Cosmo and release the straw. "Thank God. I would have died if he did that while I was wearing a skirt!"

"Now that you got that over with, let's dance!" Crystal beams and the three of us dance to the Calvin Harris song playing. It's nice having Crystal and Lisa here. Turns out they were in need of a girl's night.

Looks like I did too.

My life was always about music and perfecting my craft. I did go to a few keggers and house parties in high school. But not all the time. More often than not, I had a competition or recital to go to. Then in college I met Parker, who shared my passion. Instead of getting rip-roaring drunk, we went to dinner, art galleries, and the theater. My time in Pittsburgh was about culture. It was what Parker and I wanted to do.

I can't say I never had fun. When I was back home, I was at the bar with Leah. Before she opened McConaughey's, she worked there as a bartender when it went by another name. Amstel Light was my drink of choice and I sang along to the silly karaoke tunes.

My Pittsburgh life and my Cedar Ridge life were complete opposites. When I was home I could let go. Leah and Luke were always getting me to do crazy stuff with them. But when I went back to Pittsburgh, I morphed back into the polished violist. It seems the longer I stayed in Pittsburgh, the more I lost the fun me.

My arms rise above my head as I dance, getting a little closer to Crystal and moving to the rhythm of the music. The beat is traveling from my fingertips down through my hips and into my toes. When you dance, you not only hear the music but you feel it. Maybe it's the pink elixir working through me but I am feeling it—and it feels great.

The other girls, including Leah, join Crystal, Lisa, and me on the dance floor and the seven of us dance, forming a circle. We dance for a few more songs, twirling each other, some girls rubbing up against another in an attempt to be sexy and others just dance and enjoy the company. Exhausted, we all take a spot on the bed.

"This is the best night, ever!" Leah says, swaying slightly with her words. She has easily drunk double the amount I have. She turns to Crystal, her finger losing traction in the air, "You are awesome! I'm so glad Emma found you!"

Crystal puts her arm around me, "I love Emma. She's amazing!"

"That," Leah says with a hiccup, "is very true. My sister is amazing!" Her words rise in a high pitch at the word *amazing*.

Lisa and I exchange a look at my sister's obvious intoxication. She's not in the danger zone, just yet. I'll make sure she doesn't get too smashed. Right now, she's giddy drunk.

"What is it like living in Manhattan? Is it like *Sex and the City*?" Jessica asks.

"Yeah, do you, like, hook up with guys all the time?" Kimberly directs her question to Crystal and me. She learned earlier that Lisa is married.

Crystal and I both scrunch our noses at her question. "No."

"Emma does not do one-night stands. She's a good girl," Leah says, leaning to the side before catching her weight and righting herself.

I take a big sip of my drink, trying not to think about the last time I was with a man.

"Except for the asshole," Leah adds and I nearly spit my drink out.

"Leah." My tone is reprimanding. When I told her Crystal and Lisa were coming tonight I asked her not to mention Asher. No one at the school has any idea what happened this summer. Perhaps Leah is tipsier than I thought. I'm giving her a serious scowl, telepathically reminding her of our conversation.

"What asshole?" Lisa's interest is piqued.

Shit.

"No one." I shoot the Ohio girls a similar look to the one I am giving Leah, but no one seems to be getting the hint.

Suzanne leans forward, not noticing that her necklace I dangling into her drink. "The one who spent their entire trip pretending to be a ship captain and bedded her in every port along the Amalfi coast."

Huh?

"That's not exactly what happened—"

"Oh, are you talking about the guy from Italy?" Kimberly joins in as I offer Leah a death stare. "Emma, you are so lucky he didn't turn out to be some crazy person and dump you in the ocean."

"Could you please not—"

"Or given you a disease," Suzanne adds. "You know how those sailors are."

I throw my head into my palm at the realization my blabbermouth sister told all of Cedar Ridge about my Italian rendezvous. At least they don't have their facts straight.

"Are you kidding me? I saw his photo. I would have fucked him up and down the coast and then some. Use me, please, Mr. Asher!" No sooner are the words out of Jessica's mouth than my head pops up, my eyes dart out of my head, and my stomach drops so low I may never be able to retrieve it.

"Asher?" Crystal asks and Lisa immediately follows with a similar look of confusion.

My head slowly rotates toward the girls and I'm met with looks of exasperation. "They don't know what they're talking about."

Leah raises her hand. At first, I think she's about to vomit and I'm quickly realizing she is . . . with words. "I should have known better when I saw him going at it. It was so damn hot. I was like, damn, there's a man who knows how to work a woman. That's what my sister needs!" Leah says, pointing her finger out into the open air like she's making a monumental statement.

I have no idea what she is talking about. But Leah continues her tirade. "He had a body like Abercrombie but, like, way nicer. He was Kama Sutra all over that boat."

Her words are sloppy but I've heard her say them before. She told me this about someone once. My body goes rigid as I think about what Leah is saying.

Or is it what she's not saying that has me worried?

When we were in Italy, we saw a man and a woman having sex on Asher's boat. Leah watched them long after I went to sleep. When I thought the boat was Devon's, I assumed he was also the man we saw having sex on the boat. Leah said it wasn't.

"Are you saying the man you saw having sex on the yacht, the day we arrived in Italy—Leah, did you know that was Asher?" I ask, even though I should be shutting this conversation down. My words are very controlled for being a mix of nerves and hurt.

"Of course not, of course not." Leah waves me off. "Neither of us knew who he was. We'd never heard of him."

I sink back into my seat, relieved my sister hadn't handed me over willingly to someone she knew was lying.

"But when I saw him in person, I knew the guy giving us a tour was the same one giving some bow-chica-wow-wow," Leah says with a thrusting motion, then continues, with the finger pointing in the air like she's making a declaration. "And I said to myself, 'Self, there is a hot as hell man here who only has eyes for your sister. And she's been so sad. She needs something to help her forget how sad she is. Even if it's just a flirt or maybe a little something else . . . she needs to feel beautiful. And this guy . . . this guy is going to do it for her.' But did he fix her? Noooooo. He used her. And, therefore, he will forever be known as the Asshole." Leah falls back into her cushion.

The Ohio girls are all shaking their heads, pissed for me that I was used. It's not until Kimberly looks at me with pity in her eyes that I nearly lose it.

"You're telling me that instead of warning me that he could be a player, you made it so I was trapped with him?"

"Uh-huh," Leah says, her eyes starting to slope down a bit.

"And when he asked me on a date, you didn't think it was important to tell me about the connection? You didn't think I might get used or, more importantly, get my heart broken?"

"Emm-hmmm" is all Leah can muster.

Now I understand why Leah was so upset when we learned who Asher really was. She wasn't upset for me. She was upset at herself.

I don't know if I actually believe what is happening right now. I have a right to be royally pissed, right? I'm not overreacting. Am I?

I turn to my New York girls and assess their reactions. Lisa looks like she's in shock, and Crystal is stoic when she says, "I think it's time we put your sister to bed."

Crystal helps me wrangle Leah and her friends into two cabs. Since we seem to be the most sober and know our way around town, we split up. I hail a cab with Leah and Jessica. Crystal hops in another with Kimberly and Suzanne. Lisa has to get home so she says good-bye and whispers in my ear she has no desire to share any of my story with anyone. She never cared much for Alexander Asher anyway, even if he did create the school she works at.

According to Lisa, "It's all publicity bullshit, if you ask me."

Crystal's cab pulls up to my apartment just behind mine and she helps me escort the girls into my small apartment. The sleeping arrangements aren't ideal but they're free for the girls so no one is complaining.

I half carry Leah to my room, her weight hanging from my shoulder like a thousand pounds, as she whispers words to me about how much she loves me, how she had the best bachelorette party ever, and, of course, reminding me that she's getting "marrriieeedddd."

With Leah snug under the covers, I turn her to the side and place a trash bin next to the bed in case she gets sick. I close the bedroom door and make sure the other girls are comfortable. Suzanne is passed out on the chesterfield, while Kimberly and Jessica are raiding my cabinet for late-night munchies. A blow-up mattress is next to the couch for them to pass out when they've finished loading up on empty calories.

Slowly, blowing the air out of my lungs, I assess the damage. Not to my apartment. To my reputation.

When the air is completely out of my lips, I brave a look at Crystal, who is standing by the door with her hand on the doorknob. She is waiting for my full attention before she speaks.

"Listen, I don't want to tell you how you should feel but from meeting your sister, I know with all my heart she was only trying to help you."

I give her a look of understanding. As pissed as I am—and this is going to take a long time to get over—I know Leah wouldn't have done anything to hurt me.

"And Asher? I don't know what happened between the two of you but you were obviously hurt bad by it." Her green eyes are downcast. "I've been hurt before too. But I still believe in a happily ever after. Don't give up hope, okay?"

I nod my head. I don't necessarily agree with her yet I understand where she's coming from.

Crystal opens the door and is about to step out when she turns around. "You don't like to talk about your private life and I get it. But from the looks of things, you need a friend in New York. A real friend. I won't tell anyone what I heard. Neither will Lisa. She told you that. Let us be here for you."

I always had friends. I never shied away from that. I have simply not wanted to talk to any of the ones I had because they reminded me of what I lost. And since I've come to New York I haven't given myself an opportunity to really open up for fear of what might come out.

I give her a hug in appreciation for being a great person. "Thank you, Crystal. Maybe we'll go out for a coffee this week."

She smiles as she lets go of our hold. "I'd like that."

I'd like that too. I close the door and head off to bed. I already know tomorrow is going to be a bad day.

chapter TWENTY-TWO

The familiar sound of my bedroom door creaking alerts me that Leah is up. It's almost two in the afternoon and, while I am still pissed at her, I did check on her twice to make sure she was breathing.

When I was satisfied she was alive, I retreated back to my spot at my kitchen island and continued to stew.

Leah's footsteps are heavy, dragging what I assume is a weighted hangover. I listen as she walks slowly down the short hallway. When she rounds the wall and comes into my line of sight from the kitchen, I take in her unsightly appearance. She's wearing a pair of pajama pants and a matching sleep shirt. I figure she put them on after waking up, as I stripped her down to her skivvies last night before putting her to bed.

Her hair is a mess of tangles and fly-a-ways, and her eyes are smudged with black liner. Pale skin and chapped lips. Leah looks, in a word, awful.

"Here," I say, holding out a brown bag to her.

Leah takes the bag from my hand and peers inside. "You got me a bagel?" Her words are a mixture of grateful yet surprised. She should be. I'm still really upset about last night.

"Emma, I—"

"Sit down, eat, then we'll talk." I motion for her to take a seat on the lone stool I have at the island. I'm bossing her around like I should. I take the coffee I bought her a few hours ago and put it in the microwave. While the coffee warms up, I watch Leah eat her bagel.

"Where are the girls?" she asks in between small bites.

"Sightseeing. They tried to wake you a few times but you wouldn't budge."

Her eyes fold over as she rubs the temples of her forehead. "I drank way too much last night."

I give her a curt nod and slide the coffee to her.

"I feel like this is my last meal before the electric chair."

"It is." I cross my arms across my body, standing over her while she's perched on the stool.

Leah puts her bagel down on the plate and pushes it away. "Okay, let's have it. I can't eat with you standing over me all righteous. What do you want me to say?"

"Just to be clear, you are well aware of why I am so rightfully pissed at you, correct?"

Leah nods her head. Her words are of mild exasperation. "Yes, Emma. I was drunk and stupid, not comatose. I know why you're upset."

My arms fly up, out and around my body. "What the hell were you thinking, Leah?"

Placing her hands on top of her head, Leah looks down and shakes her head. "I'm not going to sit here and have you yell at me like a child."

I march around the island, my finger pointing at her like a weapon. "A child would have more common sense."

Leah's head shoots up, her eyes ablaze with a look I've never seen on her before. My usually sweet and bubbly sister who goes out of her way to make people feel like they're part of the party is looking at me like I'm the enemy. "Don't you dare talk to me like that. After everything I've done for you. Don't you dare!"

I stare back at her dumbfounded. "Excuse me?"

Leah stands up and walks past me, making a lap around the room and finally coming to a stand behind the chesterfield, using it as a shield.

"Don't talk to me like I'm in the wrong here, Emma. Don't accuse me of doing something to hurt you when I was only trying to help."

"Help me? Leah, do you realize how much you hurt me?"

Leah's mouth falls open, her face heaving as the breaths come pouring out. "Do you hear yourself? Do you honestly think I set out to hurt you?" Her eyes well up with tears ready to fall any second. She takes a second to breathe in order to regain composure. "You selfish bitch."

Her words stab me in the chest and I bleed out. It's not just the words that hurt, it's the way she says them. My sister has never spoken to me like this before.

Leah takes a look behind her and sees the picture of Luke on the bookcase. As she stares at it, her tears start to fall, big and heavy and true.

When she turns back to me, her hand goes to her chest as she points dramatically at herself. Her pale blue eyes surrounded by red.

"I lost him too. Luke was my brother too. I cried. I mourned. But I got up. I didn't do it because I had Adam. I had to be strong for you, Emma. Because no matter how much I lost, how much any of us lost, it wasn't more than what you were going through. Everyone put their lives on pause for you."

Leah wipes her face with her hands and down her neck, looking up at the ceiling. "I called off my wedding. I brought you on my honeymoon. I have been trying to help you." She looks back at me, her face red and splotchy. "You were dead too. Don't you get it? We didn't just lose Luke. We lost you too."

I catch my breath. My spine is so stiff I'm afraid to move. She's not telling me anything I don't know. She's just saying it in a way that has finally gotten my attention.

Leah lets out a loud sigh and places her hand on her hip. "And the Asher thing . . . God, I don't know. I guess I saw him on that boat and I just thought, I don't know, Emma. Honest to God, I really don't know what I thought would happen. When we went to Capri you were doing better but you weren't the same. Asher put the light back into your eyes. I was so grateful. I had my sister back. For two days you were the old Emma. I mean—yeah, I hate Alexander Asher and what he did to you but if I'm being completely honest, he *helped* you. Look at you! You're living in New York, you're running a school, you're around music again. I don't know exactly what happened between the two of you but I'm glad it happened."

Leah takes a step toward me, wiping her tears with her shirtsleeve. "You're always looking for someone to blame. It's Parker's fault you hurt your hand. It's my fault you got screwed over by Asher and you think it's your fault Luke is dead. Emma, it was no one's fault. Sometime things happen in life and no one is to blame. If you keep on looking for a finger to point at the sadness in the past you'll forget to enjoy the happy times in the now."

I open my mouth to say something but I don't know what to say. I still want to be mad at her. I am mad. But how can I be?

Leah is right. I have been the selfish one. This whole time I've been preoccupied by feeling sorry for myself and annoyed at the thought of others worrying about me, yet I never stopped and really focused on what they were going through.

We all lost Luke.

It's at this moment, the front door opens as Kimberly, Jessica, and Suzanne come in carrying shopping bags. Their loud laughter echoes through my tiny apartment. The three don't notice the tension between Leah and I in our living room standoff. When they see Leah's face they assume she looks like hell from being hung over.

I leave the girls to pack their belongings. They have a flight back to Ohio in a few hours. While they chat about their day, I retreat back to my room and think about everything Leah said. My only interruption is when Leah knocks on my door to ask if I want to go with the girls for something to eat. I decline.

When they return, it's to grab their bags and hail a cab to the airport. I walk them to the curb and wait until a taxi approaches. The girls thank me for an awesome weekend and hop into the car.

Leah has to go around the car to get into the passenger side. Before she does, she idles on the sidewalk, standing next to me.

"So, we still good?" she asks, uncertainty in her voice. "You're still coming to the wedding, right?"

Still coming to the wedding? "Oh, my God, Leah, of course," I say, pulling her into a hug. "Nothing would keep me away."

She lets out a sigh of relief and smiles. "Good. I'll call you tomorrow?"

I nod my head and help her into the front. We still have a lot to talk about. Things aren't completely right between us but she's my sister. No matter how bitter or bad things may seem, I'd rather be mad at her than not have her at all.

I played hooky from work today. In fact, I've stayed home for the last three days. It is out of character but I just couldn't bring myself to go.

Leah has given me a lot to think about. On Monday, I woke up feeling sorry for myself. Mad at what I have done to my family. I stayed in bed all day and didn't get up.

That afternoon, Crystal texted to see if I was okay. She mentioned Asher was looking for me. I told her I was ill and would be out for a few days.

That night, I heard the roar of an engine and the ring of my doorbell. I didn't answer it. When I opened my apartment door the next morning I noticed a purple rose taped to my front door. Purple: *Enchantment*. I wonder what my song would have been.

On Tuesday, I sat on the chesterfield and thought about the last ten months of my life. Leah is right. A lot did change after I met Asher. As much as I hate what he did, he helped me overcome some of my fears. My fear of speed, my fear of playing music and most importantly, he made me feel. Even if that feeling became anger in the end, it was pure emotion running through me.

That night, I ignored the knock on the door and cursed Mattie for being the one who is probably letting Asher into the building. When I heard the engine roar off in the distance, I open the door to see another rose taped to it. Fuchsia: *Appreciation*.

Yesterday, I spent my third and final day locked in the house looking through every photo album I own. I looked at pictures of Leah, Luke, and I through the years. I opened scrapbooks my mom created for me of every recital program, newspaper clipping, and accomplishment I every enjoyed. I surprised myself at how nice it felt to look at everything I accomplished. Instead of looking through my memories for contempt of what I lost, I looked on with feelings of joy and a renewed vow to be great again. Maybe not in music, but in something else. I accomplished so much and I'm only twenty-five. Imagine what I can do in twenty-five more years?

Last night's rose was red.

Today is Thanksgiving. I didn't go home for the holiday. The banquet for the Juliette Academy is this weekend and the quick turnaround for holiday travel is too much. Plus, Leah and Adam's wedding is in two weeks. I'll be home for that.

Instead of eating my mom's turkey and dad's famous stuffing, I am spending the day doing something I have been wanting to do since arriving in New York. I am going to explore the city.

All by myself, dressed up and ready for my date of one, I hop on the subway and trek uptown to Lincoln Center to see Yo-Yo Ma perform with the New York Philharmonic. Since I only needed one, I was easily able to get a ticket to the almost sold-out show online.

Walking through Lincoln Center, I feel the old giddiness I used to get as a kid going to see a performance. I walk through the elegant buildings, taking in the sights. I've been here before with my parents and once for a competition, but tonight it feels different.

It is just as amazing as I dreamed. I have listened to Yo-Yo Ma's music and seen him play on YouTube, but never live.

When the performance is over I walk across the street and grab dinner at Café Fiorello. While eating, I scroll through my phone and order more tickets for this weekend. Tomorrow, I am going to the opera. Saturday, I am going to see a Broadway matinee and then the ballet. And on Sunday I am going to watch Allyce play my violin in the park. I call my parents for the holiday and spend an exorbitant amount of time telling my mom about the concert and the school and the city . . .

By the time the waiter comes with my check, I have a weekend of the arts fully booked and my mom and I are laughing and talking, she is completely neglecting her holiday company.

And when I get home I have a beautiful bouquet of mixed wild flowers waiting for me outside my door. Once I am securely inside my apartment I hear the familiar sound of a motorcycle rumble down the street. I may have a new sense of purpose but my feelings for Alexander Asher have not changed.

What they are, exactly, is up for debate.

chapter TWENTY-THREE

My stiletto heel sinks in the lush carpeting of the Starlight Roof at the Waldorf-Astoria. This is my first New York City event and so far it is as visually stunning as anything I could have dreamed up.

The landmark hotel banquet room has a gilded ceiling of art deco design, illuminated by Austrian crystal chandeliers. In front of a wall of windows is a thirteen-piece band on a stage, surrounded by banquet tables. In the middle is a dance floor of black and white design.

Six hundred guests came out for tonight's occasion, all dressed in elegance.

I look over at Crystal in her black, one-shoulder gown with beading along the bodice. Her curls are pinned up, her beautiful porcelain skin glows. Lisa is here with her husband. She is wearing a navy cocktail dress with a matching wrap. Her husband looks handsome in a tuxedo, even if he doesn't appear to be happy to be wearing one

I am wearing a strapless, dark purple chiffon dress I borrowed from Crystal. I was very happy to see it fit, though not as well as it would Crystal's hourglass figure. I paired the dress with metallic gold shoes and a necklace that used to be my grandmother's.

Crystal and I spent the afternoon getting our hair done. I opted to keep my blonde tresses down but I did let the stylist at the Louis Licari salon talk me into getting highlights. After two hours of foils and glaze, I was nervous to see the transformation. I had never done anything to my hair, aside from dipping it in Kool-Aid when I was thirteen, streaking a few strands red.

Noting my hesitation, Crystal insisted I not look until everything was done. I felt like one of those women on the *Today Show* who get makeovers that make them look like a completely different person. One look in the mirror and I was impressed with the transformation. My hair is still the same length, with slight shaping and a few angles. The strands, however, are much lighter and brighter. I look sunnier, somehow. I even let them do my makeup. They didn't overdo it. They made me look just right.

Lisa's husband hands me a glass of champagne and I take it, giving a cheers to the girls.

Frank appears from behind and asks if I can be taken away as he has people he'd like to introduce me to. I walk around the room with Frank, greeting the guests who are here to, hopefully, donate money to our little school. Some faces I recognize and many more I am meeting for the first time.

The band plays on and I look over to see Lisa and her husband twirling around the dance floor having a good time. Crystal is at the bar talking with a gentleman I have never seen before and I hope they are hitting it off. She deserves to meet a nice guy.

I continue to look around the room when my eyes stop at the entrance and a man who is so beautiful it takes my breath away.

Alexander Asher walks into the room looking fierce and determined. All six feet of him are standing tall, and he's positively gorgeous in a black-on-black tuxedo fitted at the waist, showcasing the incredible body underneath. A white shirt and black bow tie outline his masculine neck and square jaw, while his golden highlights twinkle in the mood lighting of the room and his bronzed skin looks like silk. Strong thighs, broad shoulders and a chest that was created by God to model a double-breasted suit . . . oh, my.

The band is currently playing a Brian Setzer tune, but I can only hear Beethoven's Eroica playing in my head. It's a structurally rigorous composition of great emotional depth, just like the man who inspired the song to play in my head.

He looks around the room, taking in the event. A man approaches him and shakes his hand. While they talk, Asher's eyes continue to roam. Another man comes up to him and he carries on a conversation with him, as well. In between words, his eyes still look about the gala . . . searching . . . for something.

It is when those golden eyes find mine and the full, luscious lips curve up slightly that I realize what he was looking for.

Me.

Asher courteously excuses himself from the men he is chatting with and walks toward where I'm standing with my feet frozen on the black and white tiles on the floor. I wait for him like I am the bull's-eye about to be struck by an arrow. When he approaches, he stands in front of me looking directly into my eyes. Taking a moment, he gives me an adorable half grin and extends his hand.

"Hello. My name is Alexander."

I place my palm in his and quiver at the memory of what it feels like to have these hands on my body.

"Emma Paige," I say, shyly. I laugh inwardly at our little exchange.

Asher releases our hands, our palms skimming as they pass, our fingers lingering just a little too long. He raises his left hand lacing his fingers through my hair and curls a strand behind my ear. "You changed your hair."

I nod and blush at the fact he noticed. My head wants to fall into his hand but I keep it upright.

"You look beautiful," he says, his voice smooth like caramel.

I accept his compliment and offer him one in return. "You look very handsome, yourself."

And, by God, he does.

"I've missed you."

I wasn't expecting him to say that, so I don't know what to say in return. We are a ball of electricity, the two of us, standing here in the middle of a crowded reception surrounded by hundreds of people yet feeling like we are the only two in the room. He looks down at me and takes a small step forward and speaks in my ear, his words almost a whisper. "Dance with me."

My hand instantly finds his as I allow him to walk me over to the dance floor. The band is playing a slow melody, the lead singer now crooning to an Adele ballad. His right arm snakes around my waist and pulls me in tightly. His left hand encloses my right, delicately, as if he might reinjure it if he's too rough.

He pulls our hands into his chest. His eyes on me as we dance.

I follow his lead, dancing slowly, but with rhythm and purpose. Being this close to him again, it triggers every feeling I have for him. From the moment I fell in love with him in Italy to the day he shattered me into a million pieces.

Walking hand in hand through the streets of Capri I got to know him. On a boat in the middle of the ocean I let him into my heart. Playing the strings of a cello I fell so deep for him I have been trying to claw my way back to the top ever since.

Looking up at him, flecks of brown dance in his honey-wheat eyes. My tongue absentmindedly skims my lower lip and his pupils dilate.

"I have been dreaming of this."

I blink back at him, unsure of his meaning. "You dream of dancing with me?"

"I dream of holding you."

His strong hand places pressure on my back, pulling me in tighter so we are virtually melded together. His other hand raises mine and his lips skim my scar. He is so beautiful and his words are equally as gorgeous . . . but they are just words. And he is just a man.

"Asher—"

"Alexander."

"What are you doing?"

"Dancing."

I push away from him but he pulls me in, holding my tight. My voice takes on a serious tone, low and questioning. "No. What are you doing with me? The roses and the songs are perfect. The man who you are pretending to be, right now, is perfect. But you are not perfect. Why are you acting this way?"

Asher stops moving, our bodies halt, and he loosens his hold on me, although we're still touching. His jaw squares, sharper on the sides. "Emma, I'm trying to tell you that I want you. I want what we started in Italy. I don't know how to make you see that I'm sorry."

"Then show me," I say. "Prove to me something more than the lyrics of someone else's song and roses of a different color. I fell for a guy on a boat who spoke honestly and deeply; who showed me how to be free. Did he ever exist or was he made up?"

Asher's brow furrows in as he takes in my words. I use the opportunity to free myself from his arms and step back. The band is ending their song and the people clap.

My eyes still on Asher, I speak the one thing I have been asking from him from the very beginning. "I need something real."

The cool disdain of Asher's body language shows me he is wary of what I am asking. I want to know who the real Alexander Asher is but I don't think he's willing to let me in. I want to know more about the man I met months ago. Instead, I am face-to-face with a man who is a hardened imposter.

Our moment is broken when Frank takes the mic and asks everyone to find their seats. We stand on the dance floor a beat too long as I wait for Asher to give me something, anything. When it is clear he has nothing to offer I walk away, leaving him there. When I've gotten to my seat at the table, Crystal and Lisa are instantly on me, asking questions about dancing with Asher.

I ignore them, because I must look over the speech I worked on with Frank. It's heavy on statistics and a diatribe on how learning an instrument teaches skill, purpose, and raises the IQ. It's interesting and it's insightful. It's also boring as hell but it's what the two of us worked on together and what the Juliette Academy needs these people to hear.

When Frank calls my name, the crowd offers a polite applause. I rise to my feet and try not to trip as I walk to the podium. My hands are shaking from nerves. I haven't given a speech in front of a crowd this size before.

I climb the step to the podium, holding the speech in my hand. I unfold the paper with my jittery hands and offer the crowd a smile before I begin. I start by thanking everyone for coming and explaining what an honor it is to be a part of the Juliette Academy. Light clapping is heard throughout the room.

I am halfway through the first part of my speech when I look to a table on the right hand side of the dance floor and see Alexander looking at me.

He introduced himself to me. It was a moment that seemed so ordinary but was it? That was him being real. Giving me something real. It was small, but it was there, and I passed right by it.

I look down at the paper in my hands. These words are as generic as the ones I accused Alexander of saying to me. There is no heart and no soul. They are just figures, numbers, and information. They are not real. And by real, I mean, they're not true to me. They are not why I am here, not why I started to play music in the first place, and not why this little school in the heart of Manhattan has meant so much to me in a short amount of time.

When I look back at the crowd, I realize I must look silly. I've stopped talking mid-speech, and everyone is staring at me, waiting for me to speak.

Feel, Emma.

Be real.

Burn.

"I was ten years old the first time I saw someone play the violin," I say, my words unsure at first as I'm going off-book, but I continue anyway. "I'm sure I'd heard a violin before but I had never seen someone play. As I watched the woman play, I was moved by the look of her. She wasn't just playing a song. She was feeling the music. I wanted to feel what she was feeling too.

"For fifteen years the violin was my life. I studied it, pursued it. It wasn't just my career. It was my life." I look down at my scar and flex my hand feeling that sting that reminds me why I am here today. "Earlier this year I lost my brother in a horrific car accident, and my world was over. I couldn't feel anything. I also lost my ability to play that day and I have the scar to prove it.

"Then I met a man and I fell madly in-love with him. He taught me how to feel the music again. And when that love was lost, it was music that got me through the pain.

"You see, teaching someone how to play an instrument is all in the mechanics. You can show a child how to push down on the key of a piano or bang on the head of a drum. But feeling the music? That comes from the heart.

"Most of the kids we teach, they won't ever play professionally. Many will give up before they get to college. But if we can instill the love of song into every child that walks through our doors we are giving them a greater gift. We are teaching them how to feel. We are showing them how to connect. And we are making them better human beings for it.

"I lost everything, yet I still have something. I have passion. I have the beat in my soul to carry on and the strings in my heart to play it forward. The Juliette Academy is more than a building on Rivington. It is a place of love.

"Isn't that why we're here today? It's not to get dressed up or drink and dance. There are children out there who have lost more than I have. Many will grow up and realize we live in a cruel, harsh world. Yet if we can give them an ounce of the passion and feeling and love we have to offer . . . well, we may be able to save them." I smile at the thought. "And we may, just may, be able to save ourselves."

The audience around me begins to clap and a few people rise to their feet and then a few more and a couple more. Soon, the entire room is on its feet, applauding for me. I say a quick thanks and depart the podium quickly. On my way to my table, I glance over at Asher's table and notice that he's not there.

I guess I should be used to him disappearing on me.

chapter TWENTY-FOUR

My taxi pulls up to the curb of my Mott Street apartment. The night was long and my feet are hurting. After my speech, we enjoyed a delicious dinner and then we danced until the event was over. I decided dancing with Crystal and Lisa was the best way to keep from having to answer their questions about Asher.

Asher—who, by the way, never came back. I saw Frank looking for him a few times and I can't deny I glanced around, but to no avail. He did what he does best. He left.

I pay the cabbie and get out of the cab. I see the familiar figure of a man, huddled in the doorway, and I worry about poor Mattie, who must be freezing in the early December chill. It isn't as cold as some of my Ohio nights, but it's not the kind you want to be locked out of your apartment on.

But when he raises his head, I see it is not who I thought it was.

Asher stands up, brushing the gravel off his pant legs. He is still wearing his tuxedo. His bow tie is undone and hanging around his neck. Other than that, he still looks as perfect as he did when I last saw him a few hours ago.

I stop in my place by the curb and approach him tentatively. "What are you doing here?"

Asher's eyes are sullen and leaden with emotion. He takes a deep breath and when he lets it out I start to hold my own. "My name is Alexander Gutierrez. My mother was Juliette Asher and my father was John Gutierrez—"

"You don't have to—"

"No, Emma, I do. You asked for something real." He holds out his hands to the side, open as in offering. "This is me. This is real."

"Okay." I pull my coat in, protecting myself from the evening chill. "Go on."

Asher takes a beat to start, as if the weight of his words are hard to lift off his tongue. His red-rimmed eyes look deep into mine and I know what he is about to say is going to be potent with meaning.

"When I was ten years old, my parents took me to a hockey game. The roads were a mess. We had no business being out that night but they wanted to take me for my birthday. It was the first game I'd ever been to. It was also my last. Our car rolled off an embankment. My parents, they were both crushed on the impact. We were in the middle of nowhere and we didn't have cell phones. There was no one to call for help.

My hand rises to my mouth as I let out a gasp. I don't say a word, though. I let him speak.

"I watched my parents die in that car. My father died first. My mother tried to fight but she eventually lost. I sat in the back seat for five hours, staring at them, hoping they'd wake up but they never did."

Asher takes a step toward me, his eyes wide and red, the beautiful gold gone. In its place is sheer sorrow. "My grandfather hated my father. When I came to live with him, he told me I was no longer my father's son. I was an Asher now. He didn't even call me by my first name because it was my father's name as well. Instead, he called me Sunny. Said it was my hair."

I can imagine Asher as a towheaded little boy. Although the images on my head are one of a carefree boy, not someone who lost the love of his parents and was shipped off to live with his tyrant of a grandfather he'd never met.

"Edward Asher was a good man. He didn't know love but he knew how to teach. He trained me to lead. And I have. I am the CEO of Asher Industries, a business he built from the ground up. A legacy he left me when he died last year. I spent the better part of this year traveling around Europe trying to find a place to bury him. When I did, I came home and took over the life I was groomed to live.

"I play the cello and the piano. My mother taught lessons out of our home. She was classically trained before she gave it all up to live with the man she loved. A poor man, but a good man. The reason music is so important to me, the reason the school is the only thing in this world I am proud of is because it is my one connection to them.

"I've broken two bones in my life, I hate pickles, and I think soup is completely overrated. I prefer movies to television, Thai is my favorite kind of takeout, I'd rather go to a museum than a ball game, and I only read autobiographies. I don't know how to do laundry but I can make a great spaghetti Bolognese."

Asher takes another step closer to me, his breath smokes out in the cold. I look up at him and take in the honesty of his words and actions.

"I have been in love twice in my life. Once to a girl who loved me for all the wrong reasons. Another to someone I loved for all the wrong reasons."

My eyes well up with tears and I swallow them back, taking deep breaths to keep my emotions at bay. He takes one final step closer to me, his body pressed up against mine. His arms lay outside my arms, holding me gently yet with purpose.

"Right now I am falling for a woman who seized my soul with the play of a piano and arrested my heart with a walk until dawn. And she made me fall for her with the words of lyrics we may not have written but they're still ours." His voice is low and breathy. "Do you remember what you said right before I kissed you the first time?"

I thinks back to the day but I can't recall. I look up at him for the answer.

"You said no one knew what it was like to lose everything, to have it all ripped out from beneath you."

Asher's body comes dangerously close to mine, too close because I can feel the pain of his words radiating off his body. "*I* know, Emma. I know what that's like. That is why I had to kiss you and I have wanted to kiss you every day since. Hell, my lips haven't touched another since because I can only think of you."

"I find that hard to believe—"

"Believe it."

Asher rests his palms on my head as his ice-cold fingers lace through my hair. My cheeks burn at his touch and my heart sears with his words.

"The me you saw in Capri, that was the real me. You're the first person in twenty years to call me by my name, my real name. I gave myself up to you a long time ago.

"I want to be with you for all the right reasons, Emma. And despite all the wrong reasons there are for you to be with me, I'm asking you to. This is me. This is real."

Tears pool down my cheeks and I smile at the words he is saying. There are more reasons why I should stay away from him than there are reasons I should be with him. He is broken and scared but he is real and absolutely perfect.

With reckless abandon, I lean into his touch and kiss him with every ounce of love and passion I have in my body. His cold lips give way to his warm mouth and I sink into his heat. My hands wrap around his body and pull him in tight as his tongue skims mine and his lips grab hold of my own, desperate with need.

Our mouths move as one, kissing and licking. The cold air is no longer an issue, as our bodies are hot from arousal. I whirl us around toward the front door of the building. Our bodies still connected, he tightens his hold on my face, refusing to break the connection. I remove my hands from him to rustle through my bag, searching for my keys. I give up for a second when his kiss gets impossibly deep, which then reminds me why I so desperately want to take this party of two inside.

Keys in hand, I reach over and blindly navigate the metal into the lock and open the door. Asher spins us around and uses his back to push open the door and pulls me into the hallway. When we are inside, he slams my body up against the wall. He releases the buttons to open my coat and weaving his arms around my waist, pulling my body up against his. When his groin connects with mine I gasp and start fumbling for the keys again.

I release my mouth from his kiss and look down at the keys to find the one that will unlock my front door. My arm has to bend at an awkward angel as I try to unlock it. When he begins to gently suck on my neck I almost drop the key ring.

Finally, the key is in the lock and we hear the telltale click.

"Thank, Christ. I need you inside . . . now." His words are hot and harsh on my neck.

Asher kicks the front door closed and pushes my coat off my shoulders. His hands lace through my hair again as I back up and guide him toward the couch.

I pull back from Asher, and look back into those golden eyes. His fingers are frozen to the touch. Taking his two hands in my own, I lift them to my lips and gently blow hot breaths onto them to warm them. His breath hitches with each blow, so I do it a few more times for good measure.

When I am sure his fingers are nice and warm, I lift my hands up to touch him in a way I've been dying to for months. My palms skim over his strong, broad shoulders, passing over the blades along with the tuxedo jacket. I watch it fall to the floor.

With sultry fingers, I unbutton his shirt. With each one that comes undone, a hint of the velvety, bronzed skin of his taut stomach peeks out; I have to lean forward and run my tongue over it. Delicious.

Asher hisses as my palms join my tongue and his shirt, too, makes its way to the floor. Next, I unbutton the top button of his pants and slowly lower the zipper.

My heart is beating fast and my core begins to throb. I know how powerful it feels to have him inside me and I am thirsty for that feeling again.

My hand skims the elastic of his boxer briefs and his stomach pulls in at the touch. Thick, hard want is pushing through the fabric of his pants so I do what I can to relieve it.

I reach in and grab him.

"Baby, that feels so good. You, touching me . . . it's . . . everything." His are words breathy and filled with immediate need. I pump my hand up and down the hard shaft and let my thumb roll over the sensitive tip. My mouth finds his again, our kisses hot and wet. He pulls me in and holds me tight as I continue to touch and caress him.

Asher's hands reach around the back of my dress and slowly pull down the zipper. When it hits my lower back, the dress opens up and starts to fall down my body, pooling at my ankles. Standing in a strapless bra and nothing else, I lean closer and let his shaft touch the burning skin of my belly.

"No underwear?" he murmurs in between kisses.

"Panty lines."

"Lucky boy," he says with a laugh and it reminds me of a time he said it before when we were on a speedboat in Capri. He flicks the clasp of my strapless bra leaving me completely naked and positively burning with lust and need to have him deep inside me.

Pushing him back onto the chesterfield, I stand above him, looking down at the man who knows my sins and my faults, yet wants to be with me just as I am.

His body takes over most of the sofa, with his muscular thighs parted and his beautiful chest rising and falling in anticipation. Reaching into his pocket, he pulls out his wallet, takes out a gold packet and places it on the cushion beside him. He then raises his hips and strips down. He is marvelous, magnificent really, and straining for me.

Asher takes my hand and guides me over him so I am straddling him with my knees on each side of his hips. He opens the foil packet and I watch as he unravels it down, over his thick, hard shaft.

When he is fully protected, his hands find their rightful place, on each side of my face; his so full of lust, of love, it takes my breath away.

"This is it for me. No more running." His thumb skims over my lip and traces the outline of my mouth. His eyes glaze over. "I need to know you're in this with me."

My lips purse up and kiss his finger as it passes over my pout. I grab hold of his hand and kiss the inside of his palm and then pull it down into my chest over my heart.

"I'm here. I'm always here. I never left."

Our mouths find each other again and I raise my body over his. My fingers splay through the hairs of his chest and my head falls into the curve of his right hand. Asher's left hand drifts down my neck and gently caresses my back.

Our lips break apart as I slowly lower myself over Asher. We take a moment to adjust to the incredible feeling of, once again, being buried deep inside each other. I love the stretch and pull as my body welcomes him.

I gasp when he hits the most pleasurable spot of my being.

Those strong hands find a spot on each side of my waist and guide my body up and down in a powerful rhythm. With each pulse, he pushes up on his hips, allowing my throbbing core to rub against him.

We move as one but with each wave of pleasure I find my back arching further away from him, my hair falling down my back and my breathing louder, my moans deeper.

Asher leans forward and takes a nipple in his mouth. He nips and pulls, tugs and sucks on my breasts. I am near convulsing as he moves to the other and bites down, hard.

I lean forward and take his mouth in mine, massaging my tongue against his. Sweat trickles on the skin of my back as I work his body harder and faster.

Our arms hold tight onto one another and our kisses are deeper. Our bodies are so tightly drawn together I hope they never separate. I feel the buildup inside my body. If I stop I may lose it so I continue to pump and grind and build and burn until I explode.

Heaven and hell and everything in between open up as I writhe around him, coming hard and breathless. I don't stop moving, trying to make this ride last forever.

"That's my beautiful girl. Come for me, baby. Stay with me. Say you're mine."

Through heavy breaths and hooded eyes, I continue to move against him and utter the words against his lips, "I'm yours."

He breathes out a cry and I know it's his turn so I ride him gently to the end and let him find his release.

Our arms still around each other, our lips still attached, we breathe in each other's air, coming down from our erotic experience.

Looking into his eyes, I see my beautiful Asher. My sweet Alexander. The man I fell down the rabbit hole for.

He leans back to look at me. His mouth curls up and he smiles so big and bright—that gorgeous illuminated smile I missed so much is back.

"I need you, Emma."

"I'm yours."

With my words, he leans forward and kisses me again and I hope he never, ever stops.

chapter TWENTY-FIVE

Alexander and I finally make it back to my bedroom. He looks around at the pale yellow walls and remarks about my favorite color. I love that he remembered.

He is walking around my room in his black boxer briefs eating a bowl of Captain Crunch cereal. Apparently, he worked up an appetite.

I throw on an old T-shirt and panties, crawl onto my full-size bed and sit Indian style. Asher looks down at the size of it and I know exactly what he's thinking.

"I need a bigger bed. I'll go out tomorrow and buy a new one."

He takes another bite of cereal and a small bit of milk pools at the side of his mouth. Using the back of his hand, he wipes it away and looks back at me. His brow wrinkles. "Why would you buy a new bed?"

I tilt my head at him, my hair falling down my shoulder. "It's too small for the two of us."

He takes another bite of his cereal and swallows. "Yeah, but we won't be sleeping in it." His tone is matter-of-fact.

Okay, so I get how he thinks we'll be having massive amounts of sex on the bed but I hope he knows he has to sleep over. I'm not one of those girls he can sleep with and then leave before the sun comes up. If he thinks that's going to happen then he's not nearly as serious as I thought and everything he said is just—

"Why won't we be sleeping in it?" My words come out tentative and soft.

He shrugs his shoulders, indifferently. "Because we'll be sleeping in my bed."

Oh.

When he sees my face, which I'm sure is confused, he puts the bowl down on my dresser and walks toward me. Stopping at the foot of the bed, he looks down at me, his hands at his side. "You're not living here anymore, Emma."

My brows shoot up at him. "What?"

Alexander climbs on the bed, up to the place next to me, stretching out along the top of the comforter. His feet hit the very edge and his arm curls up around the pillow and leans his hand on his head, propping it up. "You're moving in with me."

My heart stops for a beat and I have to remind myself to breathe. This is an unexpected turn of events. "I am not moving in with you."

"Yes, you are. My girl is not sleeping in a ground floor apartment in downtown Manhattan every night by herself. It's bad enough I've been following you home every night just to make sure you're home safely. I want you with me, in my bed, every night."

"You've been following me?" I ask and he nods as if it's the most normal thing in the world. I push the hair back from my face and down my scalp and look down at the floral design in my comforter.

Move in with him? It's so very sudden. I thought he liked me, and then I thought he hated me. Now, he's falling for me and this is all within just a couple of months. I like my apartment. I'm proud of the life I've made here and the woman I'm becoming inside these walls. I never planned on staying here forever but to move out now, and for him?

"This is you being impulsive. I want this to work but we have to take it one day at a time. What do I do if in a month you realize you're bored of me and want out? Then what? Not only will I be crushed and devastated but I'll be homeless. I'm not taking that chance."

Alexander's mouth falls. He sits up and rises to his knees taking a position directly in front of me. He lowers his face so it's even with my own.

I am still looking down at the large hibiscus flower on my comforter and playing my fingers along my thigh, trying to focus on anything but his brooding face. He does brooding well.

"Emma, look at me," he commands.

Reluctantly, I lift my gaze. He takes his hands in mine and skims his fingers along my scar.

"I want to get bored of you. I want you to get bored with me. I want the ordinary and the mundane. I want the exciting and the extraordinary. I will never want you out because you and I are one. Isn't that what you want?"

Damn him and his perfect words. I bite my lip and think of the predicament. He's promising forever after a few hours of reconciliation. He wants me to give him all of me when I'm not ready to hand it over. And, despite what he's saying now, I fear he will get up one day and decide he wants out. We haven't known each other long and his track record is far from impeccable. It's all moving fast and I need to gather the reins.

I want to be with him, though, more than anything in the world. "It would have been nice to be asked."

He smirks and lifts my hand to his mouth. "Emma Paige." Those plumb, beautiful lips kiss my knuckle. "Will you move in with me?"

I blush at his sweetness and give him a cocky smile. "No. I like my apartment."

His face falls but he doesn't relent. Instead, he looks around the room and resigns. "Well, it looks like I'm moving in here then."

My head rolls back with a laughter. When his body crawls up my body, I stop laughing and let him get very, very serious.

With me.

On me.
In me.

"Are you sniffing me?"

I am nestled into the crook of Alexander's neck. His arm is draped around me, holding me tight as his fingers play with the loose strands of my hair. It's sometime in the afternoon. We haven't left my apartment all day. Right now, we are lying in my bed, listening to music and enjoying each other.

My cheeks redden at being caught smelling my boyfriend.

Oh, God, that sounds so high school.

"Yes. In Italy you smelled of sea and soap. Now you just smell like soap." I burrow my head back into its special spot along the side of his neck and resume playing with the light hair of his stomach. He never wears cologne. I tried to broach the topic in Capri but he skirted the issue. If we're going to make it work he has to tell me everything.

"Who was she?"

His body stiffens beneath me. My head is so close to his pulse I can feel it elevate through his skin. Whoever she is, he's not entirely over her. He doesn't answer immediately so I push harder. "Was she the first or the second love?"

"The second." He lets out a long breath and his pulse begins to taper.

"What was her name?"

"Does it matter?"

I look up and lightly kiss his tightened jawbone and take my spot back into the crook of his neck. "It matters to me."

His breathing is deep yet controlled as if he's trying to calm himself. Who ever she is, whatever she did to him, has scarred him deeper than the wound on my hand.

"Her name was Kathryn."

Kathryn. That's a really pretty name. I was hoping she'd have an evil name like Onyx or Lex. Instead, she sounds like a member of the royal family.

"She loved the smell of my cologne. She never told me. I knew from the way she reacted so I used to spray it everywhere for her. When she left, I couldn't stand the smell of it anymore."

I remember his words from last night so vividly. It's not often the man you love tells you that you aren't his first, or his second, but his third love. I find myself reciting the words he said about her, "You loved her for all the wrong reasons."

His hand stops moving along my hairline. I can't see his face so I don't know what he's thinking. All I know is his pulse elevates just slightly whenever I make a mention of Kathryn. When he resumes playing with my hair, he also resumes talking.

"She'd already given her heart to someone else. She was married."

This time it is my turn to freeze. He was in love with a married woman? He was the other man in a relationship? Okay, I get it, he's not perfect. But cheating is a huge deal breaker. I am a very closed-minded person when it comes to the sanctity of marriage. When I eventually make that vow it will be forever.

I sit up on the bed and turn around to look at Alexander. He is exquisite and masculine, everything a woman would fantasize about. I get how a married woman, any woman, would want to be with him. But at what cost?

I feel my face morph into a look of disgust. The skin between my eyes tightens and my mouth turns down.

Alexander leaps off the bed and stands in my small room, his presence taking over most of the space. He runs his hands along the back of his neck and paces slightly beside the bed. "Don't do it, Emma. Don't judge me. You asked me to be real. Don't make me regret it."

I cough back an exasperated noise. "Sorry if I'm letting you down with my reactions but this is a lot to take in. Did you know she was married when you fell in love with her?"

"Yes. I didn't know she was a mother. That part hurt."

A mother? I look up and his face resonates hurt as if he's recalling the day he found out. The relationship they shared must have been powerful for her to forsake her family.

He releases his neck and looks down at me on the bed. His hand bangs on his chest in a dramatic gesture. "This is me, Emma. Yes, there were women before you. If I knew you existed I never would have been with any of them. I'm a grown man. You can't fault me for having a past. And you certainly can't fault me for thinking I was in love with someone. If that's how you are going to react then you might as well leave me right now. Why wait until later?"

His eyes are ablaze, widening with his words. I have never seen him be more serious about something in the five months I've known him. He is like Jekyll and Hyde with his emotions. One moment he's saying he wants everything with me, and the next he's ready to call it off. His trust issues are deeper than I thought, which makes me realize they're not trust issues . . . they're abandonment issues.

"You're right. I'm sorry. You're right. I just . . . this is difficult for me. I can't control your past and it's hard for me to deal with."

His body relaxes a bit with my words. We're both adults yet we have a lot of growing up to do when it comes to relationships.

"I'm a grown man. I have a past. You are going to have to learn how to deal."

I sit up on my knees and bring myself to his level. “And you’re going to have to learn how to trust I’m not going to leave you just because I don’t like a decision you made before you met me.”

Alexander nods his head and seems to accept my words. He has to learn how to trust that I won’t leave him. I pull him down back onto the bed and lie down with him, resuming our previous position. I had an easy, uncomplicated relationship with Parker for four years, and I’m glad it’s over. Here, I’ve had the most heartrending five months with a man so complex I may never truly break through.

And if it ends, I’ll be devastated.

chapter TWENTY-SIX

The past two weeks have been amazing. Alexander, as I have become accustomed to calling him, has spent every day at my apartment and we settle into a little routine. Since my shower is too small for the two of us, he showers first and then I hop in. It works for me because I discovered a little secret about Alexander Asher: he sings in the shower. Turns out he's a Bruno Mars fan. I found that very surprising.

Devon dropped off a small arsenal of suits and loafers. I placed them all in my small closet and wondered how we will make my small space work for the two of us. Alex goes to his fancy job uptown bright and early as I casually make my way into the school around the corner. Around three o'clock he arrives to teach his classes and then leaves at five to head back uptown.

When I get out of school at seven-thirty, he is outside the door waiting to walk me home.

He likes to eat out so we go to fancy dinners that are more than I am used to. I am no stranger to a five-star restaurant but a Michelin-grade private room on a Tuesday night is a lot, even for me.

Last night I asked him if we could go somewhere a little more laid back. When he asked what kinds of things we did back in Cedar Ridge, I said, "Bowling"—thinking he'd laugh at me. Instead, he obliged and as soon as we stepped into Lucky Strike, I knew why it was so easy for him to amend.

Lucky Strike is a bowling alley on crack. No, not crack. High-potency cocaine. The place looks like an exquisite nightclub with mood lighting, a DJ, a bar that rivals most high-end restaurants, and giant screens everywhere. He reserved a private room—yes, a private bowling alley room, just for us. We even had our own waitress. I just shook my head at the largess and vowed to figure out some way to get this guy to be a little more down to earth.

The sweet aspect of the night was that since I can only bowl lefty, he did too. He still beat me but at least it was on an even playing field. When we came back, he made his "famous" spaghetti Bolognese but was not thrilled when I took the leftovers upstairs to Mattie.

We still have a few kinks to work out in this relationship.

Gigantic kinks.

Right now, he is teaching in the room next to me. Today's lesson is on the song "All of Me" by John Legend. I have the lyrics in the notebook next to my desk and a beautiful coral rose to accompany it.

Passion.

I thumb through my notebook and look at the pages that have been filled in. Twenty-eight song lyrics from him nestled in the pages. Twenty-four are from me.

Pretty soon I'm going to need a new book.

I pick up a pen and start to think of what song I'd like to dedicate to him today when there is a knock on my door. I look up from my desk and see Lisa walking in.

"I thought I'd catch you in here," she says, looking back toward Alexander teaching in the next class. She closes the door behind her and crosses her arms in front of her.

I raise a brow at her disposition. "Can I help you with something?"

"What's going on with you and the Prince of Darkness?" she asks and I'm completely taken aback by her question.

"What do you mean?" I say indifferently.

Lisa places a hand on her hip and looks down at me. "I don't want to go all mother-hen on you but I'm worried. What's a sweet girl from the Midwest doing with a guy like him? He already left you once, Emma. I've tried to mind my own business but I have to speak my peace."

I lean back in my chair and cross my arms one in front of the other. "Is there something I should know about?"

"Just be careful, okay? That's all I ask."

I look over at my friend. She is a dedicated wife and a devoted mother. Lisa has no reason to scold me on my relationship unless it's out of true concern. She's not a jealous person or a gossip queen. If she says she's worried, I have reason to believe it's genuine.

Besides, her words are no different than the ones Leah reamed into me the other day when she found out Alexander and I are together. They went something like this.

"Can't say I didn't see this one coming."

"You did not."

"Oh, I did and that asshole owes you big time."

"What happened to all that talk about how he helped me? Doesn't that count for something?"

"He still left your ass in Italy, Emma. And don't think I haven't been stalking him on the Internet. He wasn't exactly mourning the loss of your love these last few months."

Those words stung a lot. "He had a right to leave," I say.

"Whatever. You're gonna do what you wanna do so, mazel tov."

"Leah, we're not Jewish."

"You really think he's for real this time?"

"I do." I sigh into the phone. "Give it to me."

"What?"

"The great McConaughey speech."

Leah didn't miss a beat. "The truth wills out and everybody sees. Once the strings are cut, all fall down."

"You've been watching 'True Detective' on Netflix again haven't you?"

"Just be careful."

So looking at Lisa, I understand her concern. Problem is I can't just hang up the phone on her like I can with Leah. I used to hate everyone asking if I was okay. Now getting told to *be careful* is becoming my new hated phrase.

"We're taking it slow. Don't worry about me. I know what I'm doing," I assure Lisa and she seems to accept that.

The door to my office opens and Alexander sticks his head in.

"Am I interrupting?" he asks, stepping inside as if he doesn't care if Lisa and I were in a private conversation or not. He grabs his suit jacket from behind my chair and leans in for a kiss. "I have a meeting in twenty minutes. Meet me uptown when you're done. I want to show you something." Shrugging on his jacket, he checks his pockets to make sure he has his wallet and phone. "Devon will pick you up and bring you to my office."

Alexander has never asked me to go to his office before. It's new territory for me. I'm interested to see where he spends his days but I don't need a chauffer. "I can take the subway."

"Devon will be outside at seven-thirty. That's final." He gives me a stern look making sure I understand. I return his sternness with a sarcastic salute from the forehead. He grins at the action and is just about to walk out the door when he adds, "Oh, and . . . you're spending the night at my place."

I shoo him away with my hand and pretend to ignore his bossiness. He laughs and then nods to Lisa as he walks out. When I look back at Lisa she is rolling her eyes.

"Yeah, looks like you're taking it really slow."

I snuck out of work a half hour early hoping to go home to pack a bag to appease Mr. Bossy and to, hopefully, avoid having to be chauffeured by Devon. I'm a New Yorker now. I can take the subway.

Of course, Devon was outside the academy waiting for me.

He knows me too well.

After we swing by my place for an overnight bag, I hop back in the car.

When we arrive at our destination, I thank Devon for the ride. He didn't give me a hard time when I insisted on the front seat, again, but he doesn't like me getting out without his opening my door. I assure him I am safely on the sidewalk and can escort myself into a building.

The Asher Building is located in midtown Manhattan. Standing on the concrete outside the giant turnstile doors, I lean back and look up at the impressive skyscraper of steel and glass. The heavy opening notes of Beethoven's Fifth play in my head. Despite what I know about Alexander Asher, when I think of him, I still picture the guy who jumped in the ocean with me. I smell sea and salt and feel wind in my hair.

What I don't see is the imperial tower standing in front of me.

Walking into the massive lobby I am overcome with realization at just how powerful the Asher name is. Quite possible because, directly in front of me is a security desk and on the wall behind it is the name ASHER set atop an omega symbol.

Again, an omega symbol just doesn't resonate. He's more like an A-note or a treble-clef.

The two-story lobby has floor-to-ceiling glass panels overlooking the street and steel bars that run vertically through the space. The walls are lined in black granite and behind the security desk is an elevator bank of six steel doors, one of them leading to the man who controls all of this.

All around me, people who work in the building are walking toward the exit, as it's the end of the long workday. Around their necks are lanyards with Asher ID badges along with their name and photo.

There isn't a directory or guide anywhere, so I walk through the grand lobby toward the security desk and ask where I can find Alexander Asher. The woman behind the desk looks at me like I'm insane and tells me unsolicited visitors are not welcome. It's at this moment, a man wearing a black suit, no smile and one of those rubber ear pieces like the CIA, taps her on the shoulder, and whispers in her ear. When the female guard looks at me again she eyes me differently and asks for my ID.

I reach into my bag and hand over my driver's license. She looks me up and down, then hands it back.

"Mr. Asher is expecting you. Right this way," the man in black says, but the female guard stops me to take my picture with a tiny camera on the desk before she allows me to go.

The man in black swipes his badge at the turnstyle leading to the elevator and the two of us pass as another guard takes a look at our credentials. My escort walks me to an elevator and hits the up button. We stand in silence waiting for it. I fiddle with my fingers and play a melody to pass the time.

When the elevator arrives, I step in and the man reaches inside and hits the button for floor forty-two, the highest number on the panel. He bids me a good night and lets the doors close, leaving me alone in the steel car.

I watch the numbers on the panel above the door rise and wonder what I am doing with a man who doesn't just work in a building in midtown Manhattan, he owns it.

Shaking my head I stretch out my hand and feel the burn. It's becoming a bad habit of mine again.

When the doors open, I exit to an office of dark mahogany and glass. There is a reception desk in the open waiting room but no one is behind it. The computer is off and the chair is pushed in as if the person has left for the day. Nice to know Mr. Asher isn't a total slave driver.

To the left of the reception desk is a set of double doors with a name plaque on the door that reads "Edward Asher." That must have been his grandfather's office. To my near right is a seating area of sleek black leather and my eyes immediately fixate on the massive fish tank that nearly takes up the entire wall.

Before I am able to walk over to it, I hear voices coming from the large double doors on the far back right, past the fish tank and to the side of the reception desk. One of the doors is slightly ajar and the voices behind it are loud enough they can be heard from the waiting area.

" . . . hanging out at that silly little school. You have decisions to make and you are neglecting them." It's a woman, her voice deep and throaty.

"Security has you on the red list. How did you get up here? I told you months ago it was over."

"Yes, I remember, in Italy when you tossed me off your boat like a two-bit hooker."

Italy???

"You came uninvited."

"Well, I was certainly welcomed while I was there."

"You didn't leave like you were supposed to. Why didn't you get on the goddamned plane?"

"I had business to take care of."

"My business, I'm sure."

I stop moving in fear I am not supposed to be eavesdropping on this conversation.

"You have decisions to make, Asher. You told me you were signing those papers. That envelope has been following you around for over a year."

"What does it matter to you?

"We were going to take on the world together. 'Fuck them all,' remember? That's what you told me. And then you just left. It took me months to track you down."

"I needed to get away."

"From me? You said I was the only one who knew what it was like to be unloved. You said I was the only one who really got it."

"I've changed."

"You think you're in love. Tell me, how has that gone for you in the past?"

"Get out!" His words are loud and booming, and I jump a little.

"You're making a mistake."

"I said, get out!" I hear him bang on something, possible a desk and my body flinches at the sound.

The office door opens completely and a woman exits, rubbing her hands against each other in frustration. As she walks out, she stops at the sight of me and I recognize those dark onyx eyes.

Her lips fix into a wicked yet disappointed smirk as she slowly nods her head in understanding. Alexander is quickly behind her; his body also stops at the sight of me. He has an infuriated look on his face and his hair is dishevelled as if he's been running his hands through it.

I push my shoulders back and look back at Malory Dean. She still looks as sexy as she did the first time I met her but tonight she has a determined look in her eye.

Taking three catlike steps toward me, she stops and looks down from her four-inch heels. "Emma Paige." She says my name like it's a revelation.

Alexander looks from her to me, uncertainty in his eyes. His footsteps are quick and heavy as he walks over to the elevator and hits the down button. "Leave." The abrupt word is directed toward Malory.

Still looking at me, Malory's already narrow eyes squint at me. The ping of the elevator causes her to lift her head. She looks over at Alexander, whose jaw is so tight I'm afraid his teeth are going to break. Malory walks toward the elevator but before she gets in she stops. Her eyes skirt towards me, again, for a second before zeroing in on Alexander. "Not everyone is willing to give it up as easily as you are."

She walks into the elevator and the doors close behind her, leaving me and Alexander alone in the waiting room. I have no idea what that exchange was about and I have an awful feeling I don't want to know.

Alexander walks over to me and I temporarily lose my balance when he takes my hand and pulls me through the double door and into his office. My feet find traction as they scurry behind him.

I have so many questions to ask him but my feelings are momentarily pushed aside as I take in the room we have just entered. This isn't a typical office. This is a command center.

The room takes up half the floor. Granted, the building gets narrower as you get to the top, but there is no denying the immensity of the room. It is divided into four sections. To the left is what looks like the main office area with a large desk in front of floor-to-ceiling windows. An equally massive chair sits behind it. The sky is dark tonight so I can see a stunning view of the city with the buildings lit up like Christmas.

To the right side of the room is a seating area with furniture of black and gray and closer to the entrance is a conference table. Directly in front of me is a bar, fully stocked and large enough to host a party. The room is accented with glass tables, a mahogany honeycomb ceiling and golden eyes that are staring at me, waiting to say . . . something.

"How do you know Malory?"

I have to bring myself back to the scene I just witnessed between him and the gorgeous woman with dark eyes and a wicked smile.

"She came by the school a few weeks ago looking for you. She was rude to me, and I was mad at you anyway, and I had no intention of delivering her message to you." I take a second to swallow even though my mouth feels dry. "You said she was with you in Italy. Is there something still going on between you two? Because I can't—"

"There is nothing going on between me and that woman," he says, taking me in his arms. "Long ago but not now. Not since I met you."

I want to know how long ago, but would it really matter if it was two months or two years? He told me he's been in love with two women in his life. I appreciate his honesty but I hate the idea of knowing there are two women in this world he loved, or perhaps still loves. "Is she one of the two?"

His eyes search mine trying to understand my question. "One of the two?"

I raise my brows waiting for him to answer me. His brows furrow a bit and then relax as he realizes what I'm asking. He takes in a breath and then slowly exhales. "No, Emma. She is not one of the two."

I take a deep breath of my own. He's been with other women before. I've been with other men. Well, I'm sure my number is a teeny tiny fraction compared to his.

"Does she work with you? Why was she here?" I ask, trying to make sense of the situation.

"She used to work for me but was fired. Our professional relationship ended a long time ago but I kept her around in my private life for," he looks around as if trying to find the most tactful word to use, "company."

Okay, maybe I don't always appreciate his honesty.

It makes me wonder how low his self-worth is that he would spend time with someone just for sex even though he clearly despises her.

With extreme pressure on my arms, he looks me square in the eye. "Emma, I don't want you anywhere near that woman. If you see her again I want you to call me immediately."

Why doesn't he want me near Malory? I'm pretty sure I've already heard the worst of it. What could she possibly say that he doesn't want me to hear?

He feels my resistance and pulls me toward him. Taking my head in his hands, he skims the hair on the right side of my head and curls it behind my ear.

"Don't go there. I know what you're thinking. I have nothing to hide. I meant it when I said this is it for me. No more running. I'm here. Are you here with me?"

I look into the beautiful brown flecks of his eyes, surrounded my warm honey and I melt.

"I am. I'm here. With you."

His shoulders relax and he kisses me softly on the lips. "Good, because I have something to show you."

I want the kiss to continue but he takes my hand and pulls me out of his office and over to the elevator.

"Where are we going?"

"Surprise." He leans in and kisses me again and before I know it the elevator has arrived and we get in. He hits the button for thirty-three and we make our descent.

"Are we going to your company floor?" I ask.

"My company?" He tilts his head, confused. "They're all my companies."

This time it's my turn to tilt my head and look confused.

Alexander explains. "This entire building is occupied by companies we own or are partial owners in. If we have stock in it, it's here."

I look over at the elevator panel of forty-two buttons. I was just coming to grips with the fact he owned the building, but not everything that occupies it. Minus the two-story lobby and his office floor that leaves thirty-nine floors of businesses. Alexander Asher runs thirty-nine companies. At least. That's assuming there is only one business per floor. When I heard it referred to as the "Asher Empire" I thought it was all in jest. I didn't realize there really was an empire to run.

The doors open when we arrive at the thirty-third floor. In front of us is a glass-panelled wall with the name Black Dog etched in the glass. There are still people occupying the space, working as if it were three in the afternoon, not eight-thirty at night. When the people see him, they immediately stop what they're doing, straighten up and give him a professional greeting.

I laugh inwardly at the thought they find him so intimidating. Lord knows I did the first time I met him but when he lets you in he can be pretty adorable, like that time he wore flip-flops for the first and last time.

"What are you smiling about?" He is holding open a door with one hand and pulling me inside a darkened room with the other.

As I pass through the doorway, I give him a kiss on the cheek. "Just you and your adorableness."

His smile reaches his eyes. "I've never been called adorable before."

Alexander flips on the lights and room comes alive. I flutter my eyelids to make sure I am seeing this correctly.

We are inside the booth of a recording studio. The black panels of the recording equipment with their various buttons and levers that I have no idea how to use are in front of us. A couple of computers are there as well with two large sofas on the opposite wall. In front of the equipment is a wall of glass looking into a large recording space that is currently empty except for lone band equipment and a few microphone stands.

"You own a recording studio?"

Alexander has a look of pride on his face. "Lifelong dream. I bought Black Dog earlier this year. We just moved them in this fall. Everything in here is new.

I look over at him incredulously. "Weren't you sailing the seven seas earlier this year? When did you have time to buy a record label?"

Alexander laughs. "You'd be surprised what you can do over the phone."

I roll my eyes and run my hand along the control panels. I was working on something in a studio like this before the accident. It was a new sound that I've been searching for since.

Two strong hands rest on my shoulder as Alexander walks up to me from behind me. "I was thinking we could run it together. You can make music again."

My body tightens at the idea. I pushed that dream aside. I was just coming to accept my new life without being in the spotlight, without feeling the song playing through my fingers.

"Alex—"

"I love when you say my name." His arms circle around my waist as he circles me around and pulls me into a kiss so powerful I forget what I am upset about. How could anything in this world bother me when I am in Alexander Asher's arms?

I run my hands through his hair, and tug at the ends. I am rewarded with a sigh.

"I was going to give you a tour of the studio but now I have a much better plan," he says in between kisses, and I laugh.

My back bows in his arms so I can face him. "I don't need a tour. I can't run this with you. We don't even know what this is yet." I motion to the space in between us.

His face falls and I'm momentarily hit with the feeling I've just said something wrong. "I'm in, Emma. I'm all in. I don't know what else to say or do to let you know this is real. Unless . . ." His voice falters off, his body loosens its grip around me. "If this isn't what you want, then you have to tell me now."

I told a room full of people I fell in love with him in Capri but I don't know if he heard me say it. Something is holding me back from saying it again. "This is what I want and it scares me. You asked me to move in with you. You're telling me we can run a recording studio together. You are the most impulsive man I've ever met. I have no control over you."

He starts laughing, really laughing and it catches me off guard. "Oh, baby, you have no idea how much control you have over me." He kisses me on the forehead and grabs my hand. "I'm taking you upstairs."

I sigh and fall into step with him.

When we are back in the elevator, Alexander places a card in the panel, hits a code and we start to rise. He places his chest against my back, wraps his arms around my waist and rests his chin on my head. Our eyes meet through the reflection of the steel elevator doors. I've never seen what we look like together.

Alexander stands behind me as beautiful and perfect as ever. His nose hits the top of my head and his mouth—that I have memorized how perfect it is—is buried in my hair. His gorgeous eyes, light and bright and full of soul, stare back at me with the most content look I have ever seen on his face. He is wearing a herringbone suit and tie, his brown leather loafers sneaking out from the sides of my feet as his legs stand far apart from one another.

Standing in front of him is me, plain Emma Paige with her fancy new highlights. I am wearing skinny jeans and pale pink button down top with my navy pea coat. My feet are clad in brown boots that stop just under my knees. My brown eyes are wearing an equal look of contentment.

Together, holding each other, we look like a couple in love. Well, I am at least. Damn, I am so unbelievably in love with Alexander Asher. I want this moment to last forever. I want to take a picture of our reflections in the steel and look at it . . . forever.

This is real for me. So real I am frightened at what will happen if I lose it again. I know I can't go through life always scared of losing. I lost Luke and I survived. I lost my music and I survived. I know if I lose Alexander I can survive it as well.

But, God, how I don't ever, ever want to know another day without Alexander Asher in my life.

When the elevator opens we are not in Asher's office like I thought we were going to be. Instead, we are in a vestibule. The walls are black granite with a modern metal light fixture hanging from the ceiling. At the opposite end of the vestibule are black double doors. Instead of a lock, there is a security panel on the door. Alexander walks up to it and hits another series of buttons. The door unlocks. Turning around, he reaches out from my hand and escorts me inside.

We walk into a two-story living room with floor-to-ceiling windows void of curtains or drapes. I suppose at this height you don't need privacy. A white marble fireplace surrounded by bookshelves is the focal point of the room; there's a giant mirror above the mantle reflecting the black walls, glass tables, and a gray couch, which is the only color in the room. That is, if you consider a gray a color.

No pictures on the wall, no knickknacks or personality anywhere. It's simple, clean, and completely barren of life.

I turn and ask where we are.

"This is my home."

His home? To the left is a dining room of, again, black and glass and beyond that is a kitchen of . . . you guessed it. Don't get me wrong, it's stunning. Pin lights in the ceiling make the shiny surfaces gleam so brightly you can see your reflection. Every fixture is high-end and even the throw rugs scream expensive.

Alexander takes my coat off and hangs it in a closet in the foyer area. When he comes back, he offers me a drink but I decline. Seeing my curiosity in his apartment, he gives me a tour.

Down a long hallway we pass two guest rooms, a home office, a state of the art gym and a music room equipped with a black grand piano, a cello, and chandelier made of chrome.

The hallway curves so we make a left and he walks me into the master bedroom. The room is similar in design to the rest of the place but feels more like him than other areas of the apartment. It's probably because I can visually see pieces of Alexander in here. From his cufflink box on a dresser to an autobiography on Steve Jobs on the nightstand, little bits of him are here and there.

There is a door in the room that I assume is the bathroom. Stepping inside I see a lavish latrine that pales in comparison to the one I saw on his yacht. When I walk back into the bedroom Alexander motions to another door. I open it and am inside a massive walk-in closet. Suits and more suits, oxfords, and a leather jacket. A black umbrella sitting in the corner, a small wardrobe of casual clothing and a separate space dedicated to ties, lots of them.

It looks like a Brooks Brothers showroom in here, although I assume his suits are all bespoke. Aside from the cheap flip-flops I purchased in Capri that are sitting on a shelf, all of his shoes are imported from Italy.

I must have a peculiar look on my face because Alexander is instantly on top of me. "Is something wrong?"

I open my mouth and then close it, trying to figure out what it is exactly that's bothering me. I'm not intimidated by the space. I'm not overly impressed by it, either. I'm just . . . intrigued? "Your closet is the size of my apartment."

Alexander looks around and then shrugs as if he hadn't realized that before.

"You have a panoramic view of Manhattan from your living room."

He nods in agreement, unsure of where I'm going with this.

"You have a California king-size bed."

His mouth cocks his mouth to the side but he still doesn't quite understand.

"You said you'd move in with me," I say, tentatively.

Alexander nods his head again, slowly, in agreement, his eyes squinting a little as if trying to read me.

My breath hitches as I try to comprehend it all. My voice is nearly a whisper. "You'd give all this up for me?"

A slow, sexy-as-hell smile takes over his face. "All in."

Holy shit, he really means it.

chapter TWENTY-SEVEN

"My flight gets in at seven. Can you meet me at the airport?" I am on the phone with Leah, making plans for the wedding. I get into town tomorrow night. Just in time for Leah and Adam's wedding on Saturday and then I'm staying for the Christmas holiday. Being that I missed Thanksgiving I know it would break my parents' hearts if I weren't there for Christmas. That and I haven't seen them since August.

The front door of my apartment opens and Alexander walks in; I gave him a key last week. It makes me smile to see he is so comfortable coming in and out of my apartment. He has a palace uptown yet he'd rather spend his nights slumming it with me downtown.

He is unraveling his tie, which, I see, has a huge stain on it. In the three weeks we've been quasi-living together, I've had to work my magic on getting the stains out of two of them.

Alexander places an overnight bag and a briefcase on the chesterfield and then takes off his overcoat, hanging it on the wall hook. He sees me on the phone so I place my hand over the receiver and mouth "Leah" to him.

Leah just started telling me a story about a fight her and her friend Jessica had over the bridesmaid dresses.

He raises his brows and tilts his head, and I know he is asking *Did you ask if I can come to the wedding yet?* I shake my head: *No.* He is not happy about it, but kisses me on the side of the head anyway.

"I have to take a shower," he whispers.

"Great, I ordered Thai," I whisper back, my hand still on the receiver. Leah is still rambling.

Alexander's face lights up knowing I ordered his favorite food. "My wallet is in my bag. I'm buying." His face is stern and I know he means business. I would fight him on it but since I treated him to dinner a few times over these last few weeks, my meager budget is running low.

Plus, Christmas is coming up. What do I buy the man who has everything?

Good question because even I can't figure it out.

"Are you there?" Leah asks from the other end.

I snap out of my self-thought and tend to our conversation. "Yes, I can't believe that bitch," I offer, assuming whatever their fight was over, it's best to take the bride's side.

"I know, right?" She huffs and then I can almost hear her shaking it off. "All right, enough of that. What are you doing tonight?"

"We ordered in. We'll probably watch a movie or something."

Leah is quiet for a second, but it only lasts for a second. "Does he, like, live with you now?"

Does Alexander live with me? He said he would. Everyday he brings over a bag of more clothes and never seems to bring any back uptown with him. All of his toiletries are in the bathroom and my kitchen is filled with enough health food to feed a commune. And cereal, he really likes cereal. The sugary kind.

I laugh to myself. He is such a contradiction. Alexander Asher is a guy who eats healthy throughout the day but loves high-sodium takeout, cheese cake, and sugary cereals at night. His eating habits reflect the two very different people that are Alexander Asher.

Alexander is a guy who loves music, plays the cello and the piano. He is soulful and desperate at times, needing connections and affection. He likes to play board games, dance and reads the funny pages when he thinks no one is looking.

Asher is serious and controlled. He works uptown and watches cable news and the stock market all day long. He drinks three thousand–dollar scotch, completes *New York Times* crosswords, gets his face professionally shaven by a master barber and controls an empire of two thousand employees.

The crazy thing is I love both sides of him. Even though I fell in love with the soulful version of him, I can't help but be mesmerized by the controlled side of the man. He is impressive in every aspect.

Oh, man, I have hit rock bottom of the damn rabbit hole.

"Okay, you are not even paying attention to me anymore." Leah is starting to sound irritated and rightly so. My head is so into Asher right now I can't think straight.

We hang up just as the doorbell rings. I rush over to Alexander's briefcase and unzip the bag. He only brings it with him when he has to bring files back and forth. His laptop has been sitting on my grandmother's secretary desk for weeks so he can plug in while he's here. Some of my favorite nights are when we're curled up on the couch together, he on his laptop and me skimming through my iPad.

When the bag is fully opened, the first thing I notice is a large manila envelope.

Malory made a comment about a manila envelope. I would be lying if I haven't been itching to know what she was talking about. I am so curious to know if this is the one she looked at. The one that made him so angry.

The bell rings again and I rush over to the door, wallet in hand. I pay the deliveryman and tip him well, closing the door and placing the white plastic bag on the kitchen counter.

I walk back to Alexander's briefcase and place his wallet back inside. The shower is still running. Would I be a bad girlfriend if I snooped a little? I would, God, I know I would, but he is so damn secretive. He told me to trust him. I do. But I want to be there for him in every way. If what is in the envelope is important then I want to know.

In the past, I have been known for my willpower. Hell, I went months without using the power of the Internet to look him up and here I am caving at the site of a yellow tab folded over.

I look behind me and see the bathroom door is still closed. Turning back to the bag, I pick up the manila envelope and open the top flap.

Inside is a thick stack of papers. I lift them up slightly. They are legal documents; the heading for a lawyer's office is at the top. I do a quick skim and see Edward Asher's name, the name Asher Industries and Alexander Gutierrez. There are a lot of legal writings and I start to feel really uncomfortable going through Alexander's stuff. If this is about him taking over his grandfather's business, I don't want anything to do with it.

I put the papers back in the envelope and then push it back into his bag. Good timing because I hear the shower water turn off. Making sure the envelope was exactly where it's supposed to be, I notice something else in the bag. It looks like a Christmas card that has been taken out of the envelope and haphazardly thrown inside his briefcase.

We haven't even put up a tree. I wouldn't know where we'd put it in this tiny apartment. I lift the card and walk it over to my door where I taped the holiday greetings from my parents and Leah and a few family members who have my New York address. This will be symbolic of Alexander living here. His first Christmas card in our new place.

I notice it's one of those picture Christmas cards where everyone is dressed up and look perfect in their professional family photo. Perfect isn't even the right word to describe them. The family of four are sitting on the bow of a boat wearing matching sweaters. It's pretty cheesy.

The father is a really good-looking man with dark hair and blue eyes. He is holding a little boy who looks just like him. Next to them is an equally gorgeous woman with brown hair and another little boy in her arms. The woman looks so happy and content surrounded by her perfect family.

I step back to take in the family. The Monroes. Even their names are perfect: Gabriel, Kathryn, Jackson, and Grayson.

Kathryn.

Kathryn?

You've got to be kidding me!

This is the second woman he ever loved. This is the woman who had an affair on her husband with Alexander.

This is *Kathryn*!

"What are you doing?"

I turn around to see a very annoyed Alexander standing in nothing but a towel and a scowl. His right hand is holding onto the white fabric, keeping it closed around his hip. His other hand is fiercely grabbing at the back of his neck.

I have so many questions; I don't know where to start. "Why do you have a picture of your ex and her family in your bag?"

He looks exasperated. "Were you looking through my things?"

My mouth falls open at his . . . absolutely correct assumption. "No," I lie. "I was getting your wallet like you asked and it was in there. I thought I'd add it to our Christmas cards over here on the door. Why would she send you a card, anyway? Are you two friends or something? Because that's weird, Alex, and I am not comfortable with that because it means you might be . . . Are you? Are you still in love with her?"

My heart drops at the thought and I want him to take me in his arms and tell me he's not but he doesn't move.

He's just standing there in the middle of my tiny apartment in his towel looking devastatingly handsome, yet his eyes are so sad and mad and confused. I don't know what he's thinking.

He takes a few breaths. He raises his free hand as if to explain. "I don't know why she sent it. I haven't spoken to her in two years. She sent me a card last year, too, and I lost it. I took off." He points to the object of our disagreement. "That is the reason I left. It's why I spent nearly seven months searching for an answer."

My eyes widen in surprise, fear, you name it. "An answer to what?"

"To everything," he says on a long exhale. "My grandfather died, I had those fucking ashes with me and his goddamn company to run. And then she sends me that. It was like a reminder of the life I couldn't have."

The words pierce me like a dagger. I don't know if I can form a coherent sentence but I manage to breathe out a few words I'm so scared to know the answer to. "You want a life with her?"

"No. I want—God I'm saying this all wrong. Emma, sit."

My arms cross in front of my chest like armor. "I'll stand, thank you." Finding out your boyfriend is still in love with another woman requires a standing position.

He takes a determined step toward me. Golden, warm honey-crisp eyes connect with mine, penetrating the shield I have up. "I'm not in love with her. I never was."

He breathes in deeply and exhales. "Emma, I don't want her but I want that." He points to the photo on the wall. "I want . . . a family."

He loved her for all the wrong reasons.

My weight shifts from one foot to the other. Wanting a family is not something to hide or be ashamed of. "I don't understand."

Alexander runs his hands through his hair. "The first girl I ever loved . . ." he starts, as if I could have forgotten there was a first girl. "She loved me only because I was an Asher. She wanted the money and the power, not me. I learned a long time ago that having what my parents had would never exist for me. No one would ever love me for me. It's the Edward Asher way. My grandfather believed that love is what ruined people. You could have business and you can have pleasure but you can never rely on someone."

She loved him for all the wrong reasons.

"And then Kathryn came around and she was different with me. She didn't care about the money and she wasn't impressed with the power. She was something I was searching for but she wasn't right for me. She didn't love me and I just loved the thought of her."

I see nothing but darkness because my eyes are closed so tight. Is it possible that no one in this world has ever loved this man as much as I do? He doesn't believe anyone could. I bet he never let anyone in long enough to see the real Alexander.

I loved him when I thought he had nothing. I hated him when I learned he had everything. Despite it all, I am soulfully in love with him but I don't know how to prove it.

"You're funny."

"Excuse me?"

I open my eyes and see a confused look on his face. "You're funny. You make me laugh. And you're a pretty good cook. I think you'd be better if you tried making more things at home. You're also kind to strangers and incredibly smart. That's probably the first thing I ever learned about you. How smart you are. It's really attractive."

One brow rises. "Attractive, huh?"

I look down at the ground and smile. "Among other things."

His lip curls into an almost-smile. "What else do you find attractive?"

I look up at him and scrunch my face using a sarcastic tone. "Your modesty." He shakes and I continue. "You have a terrible singing voice," I say and he looks up at me in surprise. I offer him a laugh and go on. "You can dance. You're also an amazing teacher. You have patience with kids and an incredible way of making your lessons interesting and fun. Your heart is so big and full of love and hope. What you did with the Juliette Academy, creating it from scratch, is remarkable."

I take a few steps toward him. "You have a great smile and when you let it out, it's like the whole world lights up too."

Alexander places his forehead against mine. "Thank you for that."

I lace my hands around his waist. "I mean it."

His eyes close and he breathes out as if his body is saying, *I so hope you do.* He takes his free hand and tugs a stray hair of mine behind my ear. He can't see what he's doing but he's done it so many times, it's muscle memory.

"What were you doing hanging that stupid card up anyway?"

"I thought I'd put up some Christmas cheer. I didn't get a tree this year. It's the first time I've never had a tree up."

"I haven't had one in years."

I push back from him and frown. "Your grandfather didn't let you put up a tree?"

Alexander shakes his head indifferently. "He had one. The old man had the largest tree in Manhattan. I haven't had one since I moved out at twenty-two."

My brows shoot up. "You haven't had a tree in ten years?"

He shakes his head.

I step to the side and grab my coat and purse off the hook by the front door. "Put some clothes on. I just decided what I'm buying you for Christmas."

We went and bought our first Christmas tree together. When we walked to the corner tree stand, Alexander's face lit up. I could see he wanted to buy the biggest one they had. Unfortunately, my apartment can barely fit the two of us, let alone a large piece of pine.

Luckily, the man also sold small tabletop trees for people who live like we do. It is so small, Alexander was able to carry it home in one hand. We stopped at the pharmacy and picked up a small package of lights and some ornaments. When we got home, we had our tree up and decorated in fifteen minutes.

It's not much of a Christmas gift but seeing the look on Alexander's face makes it worth it. The man could have a sixteen-foot tree in his uptown apartment but here he is with a look of complete satisfaction looking at his tabletop tree.

He is also wearing a look of satisfaction because we are currently lying naked on the chesterfield eating Thai food.

"Naked Thai is now my favorite takeout of all time," he says, using his chopsticks to pop in a bite of pad thai.

I laugh and my back vibrates against the arm of the chair. We are each on an opposite end of the couch, our toes resting near the other's side, a blanket thrown over us. The room is completely dark except for the twinkling lights on the tree. "It looks like Charlie Brown's Christmas Tree."

"It's perfect," he says and offers me a bite of his food. I lean forward and take a bite.

I settle back in my spot and find peace with the moment. Now if only he would say those three little words, life would be better. Is that weird? A twenty-five-year-old woman needing to hear the words "I love you" in order to feel validation. It's not enough he is here every night and has declared himself "all in" numerous times. There is something about hearing the words that brings a form of security.

It's only been three weeks.

Yes, but its also been five months.

My head is always a freakin' mess when it comes to him.

Alexander raises his toe and nudges my side to get my attention. "Earth to Emma."

"Sorry. Just daydreaming," I say, and Alexander looks back at me with a smirk as if asking "*About me?*"

"Always about you," I add.

He laughs and takes a final bite of his food before putting the carton down on the coffee table. "May I ask you a question?"

"Anything."

"Why won't you ask your sister if I can go to the wedding?"

Ugh, anything but that. I squeeze my palm and think of the million reasons why I have been putting off asking Leah if I can bring him to the wedding. I want him to meet my family but I'm not ready for their opinions and glares. Going home is going to be hard enough. I don't need Alexander witnessing the uncomfortableness that is me being in the same house as my parents. Even still, the real reason, the only reason that matters is, simply, Leah.

"It's her big day and you are not on her list of favorite people. This is the one time in her life that is all about her and I'm not going to ruin it by making it about me. I've done enough of that this year. Hell, she postponed her first wedding date because I was too mentally unstable. I'm not doing that to her again."

“You’re a grown woman, you should be able to bring a date to your sister’s wedding.”

I let out an unattractive huff. “You’re not just anyone. You’re the yacht sex guy who deserted me in a foreign country without saying good-bye.”

“Yacht sex guy?” Alexander asks with a puzzled look. He would have no idea if that term is a compliment or a criticism. I never told him how we saw him having sex with another woman the day before we met him. It’s actually something I’ve been avoiding.

“It’s not a good thing. I have something I need to ask you and I want you to be honest.”

Alexander crosses his arms over his broad bronzed skin, ready for the question.

“The day before I met you, Leah and I saw you with a woman on your boat. We didn’t know it was you at the time. Leah had these, crazy binoculars and . . . anyway, that doesn’t matter. She recognized you when she met you. Not as Alexander Asher but as the guy on the boat.

“When she found out you were lying to me about who you were, she painted this picture of you in her head as this awful person. A womanizer. Later I did too. She said she’s seen you in articles since with other women and, well, she just doesn’t like you.” When the last words are out of my mouth, my shoulders are so tense they’ve risen up to my chin. We’ve come so far, I don’t want to rehash the past and make him feel awful but he deserves to know why Leah doesn’t want him in Cedar Ridge this weekend.

Alexander’s mouth is set in a grim line yet he’s looking straight at me, piercing me with a look of sheer determination. “She’s right. I was a womanizer. *Was* being the operative word. I used women and they used me right back.”

I let down my shoulders. You have to give credit to a man who can admit his mistakes. “Malory was the woman I saw you with on the boat, wasn’t she?”

Alexander lowers his head and grunts. “Yes.” He looks back up and his pupils dilate. I know it’s because he can see mine are wide as well. “Emma.” His voice is thick and desperate with meaning. “I haven’t been with anyone since I met you. Even when we were apart.”

I open my mouth to say something but he cuts me off.

“Going to a party and being photographed with someone doesn’t mean we were together. You ruined me in Italy. I haven’t been able to think of anyone else. I was just too stubborn to go after you. Then fate brought you to me, and that’s when I knew for sure. Anything that happened before us is obsolete. I need you to believe me.”

Fate is a tricky bitch. What would life be like if I’d never come to New York? If I decided to stay close to my parents and let them dote on me? I might have never seen him again.

If I want to get real morbid I could think that if Parker never dumped me, Luke would still be alive, and Leah wouldn’t have called off her wedding, and I never would have met Alexander at all.

I can’t go there. The reality is I did meet him and here we are trying to move forward, but constantly being pulled back.

“I believe you. I do. This weekend is just not the time to bring you home. My family . . . they worry. They have questions and they hover and they—”

“You don’t think they’ll approve of me?” Alexander pushes the blanket away from him and rises. His glorious body is naked and hard with anger.

“That’s not what I mean—”

“You’re in or you’re out, Emma. Why won’t you fight for me?”

I sit up on the couch. “You are asking me to choose between you and my family. I can’t do that. Not after all that’s happened. I want you with me. I want you on my arm but not at the expense of hurting my sister. She knows how

I feel about you but she has no idea what your intentions are. All she knows is what she's seen so far and she doesn't exactly trust my judgment these days."

Alexander walks back to the bedroom and starts pulling pants up his legs. I grab the blanket and wrap it around my naked body, following him toward the room.

"Where are you going?"

"I need to think," he says, his arms sliding into a long-sleeved crew-neck shirt.

He needs to think?

Thinking is bad. Thinking means doubts and thinking leads to questioning your judgment.

"Can't you think here?" My voice cracks. I breathe steadily to will myself not to get emotional.

Alexander is sliding on his loafers and running a hand through his hair. "No. I think I'll spend the night uptown. Get used to not seeing you for a few days."

This time it's my turn to clench my jaw and go grim and broody.

"You're running. Figures. It's what you do best." My words are cold and callous. I turn around and walk back to the living room and take a seat in the chesterfield, pulling the blanket tightly around me. I wince at the sting in my hand that grows the tighter I pull.

The room is still dark except for the damn tree. It looks so festive yet the air is crinkling with anything but holly and joy. Instead I feel anger and resentment.

I should have known our bubble of bliss would be short-lived.

Alexander is not leaving as quickly as I thought he would. In fact, his movements have slowed quite a bit. Out of the corner of my eye I can see his shadow lurking in the hallway. He's so damn tall and commanding, it's hard to ignore his presence.

I fix my gaze on the bookshelves in front of me and try to ignore the urge to turn and run into his arms.

He takes a couple of steps toward me, seemingly unsure if he should approach. I let out a loud sigh and he takes that as his cue to walk over to me. Alexander lowers himself to his knees so we are eye level.

Even in the dark, in the twinkling lights, I fall into the damn rabbit hole like I always do. I lift my hand and brush his forehead, cupping his beautiful face in my palm. He relaxes into my skin and lets out a sound of defeat.

"I don't want to run anymore."

"I don't want you to run anymore."

"I'm still mad."

"That's okay."

He is so afraid of being alone and unwanted. At the first sign of an argument he goes running. But here we are, reconciling like two adults. We may be okay after all.

At least I desperately hope so.

chapter TWENTY-EIGHT

Today has been a strange day. Alexander left early for the office. It was the first time he didn't wake me before he left. We didn't talk anymore last night. I let him "think" on the chesterfield while I went to bed. When I woke up at seven, he was gone.

He also cancelled his lessons today, saying he had some important meetings uptown that couldn't be rescheduled. If there is one thing I found to be true about Alexander Asher it is that the Juliette Academy is the most important thing in his life.

The fact he cancelled classes is alarming.

I left the school early today to make my flight. Alexander wanted me to take his private plane home but I told him it was a gross waste of money. I can fly commercial just like the rest of the world. I did, however, concede to letting his assistant Cecilia book my ticket for me. I have a five o'clock flight out of Newark on United.

A little after two, I walked my suitcase down the stairs and onto the curb in order to hail a cab. I shouldn't have been surprised to see Devon there, but I was really hoping he wouldn't be. Instead of arguing, I handed him my suitcase and climbed into the front seat.

So, here I am with Devon driving us through the Lincoln tunnel and we emerge in New Jersey. I don't know my way around the Garden State but when I started seeing signs for Teterboro Airport instead of Newark, red flags go off in my head.

"Where are we going?"

"To the airport," Devon answers in a straightforward manner.

I scowl at him. “Which airport?”

Devon bites down on his lip and doesn’t answer.

I cross my arms and push my back into the leather seat and huff in frustration. I have a really good idea where we are going. My suspicions are confirmed when we pull into the private flight terminal outside Teterboro and end up next to a private plane with the name ASHER on the side.

“No. I can’t—” I look at the time. “I have a flight at Newark in two hours.”

Devon shakes his head and opens the door. “No, you don’t,” he says before exiting the car.

I can’t believe him. It’s bad enough the man has been ignoring me all day. Now I know he lied to me about the commercial flight and is making me take his very extravagant private plane.

Okay, I understand how this sounds.

Ungrateful.

I hear it in my own voice.

I pull out my phone to text Alexander but don’t know exactly what to write. It’s not like he’s been communicative today. In fact, it’s been radio silence. I put the phone away and step out of the car when Devon opens my door.

A woman greets me at the bottom of the stairs leading onto the plane. I give her a shaky smile and climb up the staircase. When I’m inside the plane I’m completely taken aback. Creamy ivory leather seats line the cabin, eight in total. A shiny birch veneer dining table matches the veneer accents throughout making it feel like I’ve stepped onto Air Force One. I peek in the back of the plane and see a bedroom with a full-size bed and a bathroom.

I take a seat in one of the eight passenger seats by the window. When the captain comes over to greet me, I ask him where we’ll be landing so I can text the information to my family. I don’t know who is picking me up. It was supposed to be Leah but she has an emergency wedding thing to take care of.

I keep my phone on for the flight as the plane is equipped with wi-fi and wait for Alexander to text or call . . . or something. I suppose I could text him a thank-you but I didn't ask for this and my stubbornness keeps me from contacting him.

We are two people who were burned by the past. When you have been hurt before it is difficult not to bring the pain with you into the present.

Parker left me for the possibility of something better. How am I not to assume someone else will feel the same way he did and leave me? Alexander loved a woman who loved him only for his money and another who was in love with someone else.

Rascal Flatts wrote a beautiful song called "Broken Road." It was about how every breakup and broken heart paves the pathway to finding your true love. The verse they forgot to write was about the midnight fight over trust issues.

I understand why he is upset. In a relationship, you should put the one you love first. When it comes to my family, I am having a hard time doing that.

When Parker left me, I was devastated. I put my own desires first. My need for a thrill put Luke in danger. It doesn't matter he was driving. I egged him on. Too many lives were ruined in the process.

Am I punishing Alexander for Parker's mistakes? Am I punishing him for *my* mistakes?

My inner monologue on whether to call Alexander or not takes over the entire flight and before I know it, an hour and a half has passed and we are starting our decent to Columbus.

The plane lands and I gather my purse and thank the captain and stewardess for a lovely flight, feeling so awkward for having taken it at all.

Descending from the plane, I see my dad's Toyota Corolla waiting for me. My dad is standing at the foot of the car watching a man put my suitcase in the trunk of the car.

I walk over to my dad and put my arms around him, embracing him for the first time in months. When I pull back I see he's staring at the plane.

"Fancy boyfriend?"

I look back at the plane and then meet my dad's questioning look and shrug.

"He's a little bit fancy."

"Serious?"

"It's a little bit serious."

"Serious enough to let you take his private plane but not serious enough to bring to your sister's wedding?" he asks in that way that dads ask questions about boys and their intentions for their daughters.

"Serious enough to leave him home and not have you give him the third degree." I pull his arms and swing him around toward the car. "Come on, I want to go home and make taffy."

Dad stops in his tracks and I halt, too, my arm still clinging to his. I turn around and see his mouth is open in surprise but the heavy lids of his eyes are sloped in. "You want to make taffy? You haven't wanted to make it since—" He stops for a second and I'm staring at him with my brows piled high, waiting for him to finish his sentence. "Never mind. Lets go home and make taffy."

"Is that my baby girl?" Mom comes barreling out the house before I even have a chance to get out of the car. I close the door just in time to get the full body Pamela Paige embrace. She smells like baked ham and cookie dough. Just like my mom should.

I sink into her hug and return it. She pushes me back and holds me at arm's length to properly evaluate me. Her eyes look for the three things they always do: my weight to make sure I'm eating, my hair to ensure I'm eating right, and my eyes to make sure enough of those foods are vegetables.

My stomach forms knots just waiting for the worrying to start.

"You look good," she says and I can feel my eyes widen in surprise. She takes a strand of my hair and holds it in her hands. "You got your hair done. I like it." Her smile is as wide as my eyes.

I stare at her for a second and wait for the "but" to come but there is none. She has nothing to add. No concerns, no worries.

"I'm making the trays for the rehearsal dinner tomorrow night. Why don't you put your bags up in your room and rest for a bit. You can come down when you're ready," she says but dad steps in.

"Emma and I are gonna make taffy." His voice comes up at the end as if he is ending the statement in a question.

I turn toward him and then back to my mom, who is looking at him in surprise. "Is that right? Well, there is plenty of room in the kitchen for everyone. Let's get inside."

Mom puts her arm around me and I walk with her into the house, dad carrying my bag behind us.

Mom, Dad and I stayed up until one in the morning making dinner and taffy for the rehearsal dinner tonight. I told them stories about the Juliette Academy and my life in New York. Dad shared some of his new lectures with me and mom introduced her newest kitten, Camilla, named for

Matthew McConaughey's wife. I was quite surprised Leah would name a cat after the devil woman who stole her man but I suppose since she is getting married, it's only right to let go of her hold on the great McConaughey . . . at least where his marital status is concerned.

It was close to midnight when mom finally worked up the courage to ask me about my own love life. I could tell a few times she was dancing around the topic. I know Leah told them I was dating someone and dad saw the plane. How much information they actually know about the guy I'm dating, I have no idea.

If I wasn't so unsure about where Alexander and I stood I would have offered up the information myself. The problem is, he still hadn't called. I kept my phone on ring but left it in my bag. I wasn't going to stare at it all night.

So I told them I was dating someone but it was casual. If I told my parents I had fallen in love with an emotionally unavailable man who keeps secrets hidden in a manila envelope, they'd panic and suggest I see Dr. Scheuler. No, thank you.

When I finally made it to bed, I looked at my phone and saw there were still no calls, no texts, nothing. I turned my phone off and stared at the ceiling until I passed out.

"So, that's what's been going on in my life," I say to the piece of stone in front of me. It's beautiful, about four feet tall, and made of red granite. Angel wings adorn the top and the name Luke Robert Paige written in large font. There is space below his name where mom and dad have vowed they want to be buried as well.

I came to the cemetery this morning. It's my first time since that cold day in January when we laid Luke to rest. It's just as cold today as it was then, but I came prepared with a blanket, thermos of hot coffee, and some of the taffy dad and I made last night. It's too early to be eating sweets but I don't care. Today is the kind of day that needs to start with eating something bad.

I've been here for a little over an hour, telling Luke everything that happened since the day of the car accident. Turns out he's a better listener than Dr. Schueler. He lets me get all my thoughts out without interrupting. Okay, it's a morbid thought but there is truth. Sometimes you just need to say what you're feeling out loud without someone else asking questions or telling you why you feel the way you do. A person just needs to feel without analysing it.

"I know it's crazy to love someone like Alexander. But, you see, Luke, he is sweet and loving and funny and passionate. I know you and Leah think music guys are lame but he is far from lame. You two would have gotten along so well. He has a motorcycle. I know you would be out on it in a second. He also knows celebrities and models." My inside coil at the thought of some of the ones he's dated. Leah filled me in on a few. Talk about not measuring up. I look like a wildebeest compared to some of them. I shake it off as Leah would and carry on. "He definitely would have hooked you up with a model or two. Imagine what your frat brothers would've said."

The thought makes me sad. The words *would have* are terribly depressing.

"I miss you little brother." I roll my eyes up in order to keep the tears from falling but they are stinging from the inside. I inhale a shaky breath. "It's hard to believe you're not here. I try to do that thing where you pretend the person who died is away at war or something and will return any day. The truth is, you're not coming back." My eyebrows feel heavy on my forehead and fall down toward my eyelids. "I have been trying to avoid coming here for so long. It's like, if I don't come here, then you're not really here and none of it happened."

My hand curls up to feel that familiar burn that has kept me from moving on. Funny thing about it, it doesn't hurt as much as it did almost a year ago. It's become a part of me. Something I am learning to tolerate.

"Everyone thinks my depression was from losing my ability to play the violin. As if losing you wasn't enough, it was the music that sent me over the edge." I shake my head at the though. "Fuck the violin." I say it again louder. "Fuck. The. Violin.

"If God gave me a choice that night and told me it was your life or my entire arm, I would have said, take the arm. Hell, I would have said take my life! It was never about the damn violin. It wasn't about my fucking career. It was about you. It was always you."

My heart is beating rapidly and my body shivers, not from the cold but from the nerves of the feelings in my blood, running through my veins.

"For so long I've been wallowing, pretending I was depressed about my damned hand when I really couldn't care less. I just want you back. That's right, Luke, I want you back and I have been too scared to say it out loud."

Large, fat tears run down my face as I break down in front of a piece of stone. The ground beneath my knees is cold and the air against my wet cheeks is freezing but it doesn't matter. I am crying for my brother. Crying for the life he lost. Crying for the future he'll never have. Crying for the dreams he'll never see.

"I am missing you like crazy, Luke." I brush the tears from my face and look up at his name. "You'd hate these tears." I laugh a little. "Oh, well. You never did understand how Leah and I got so emotional over things. Guess that's just girls for ya." Wiping my nose on my sleeve, I stand and wrap the blanket around my shoulders.

"I'm leaving some of daddy's taffy here for you. I know its silly, but whatever." I place the bag next to the headstone and pick up my thermos, not before placing a kiss on the hard, cold granite.

"I miss you little brother."

I stay at the cemetery for another hour just staring at the headstone and running my fingers inside the etched lettering of Luke Robert Paige. My thoughts and feelings that have played throughout the last eleven months are so heavy on my head, I can't leave.

By the time I get in my car it's close to one in the afternoon. I drive home as slow as possible, driving through my old neighbourhood and passing all the places Leah, Luke, and I used to frequent as kids. Our school, the local McDonald's, old lady Crandel's house where she would yell at us for playing on her lawn, and Jenny Fowler's house that had a chicken coop in the back. I pass the old music store that is now a Chinese takeout and the old Blockbuster that has been turned into a Party City. We were here every Friday night. Dad loves movies so we took turns on who could pick out the movie for the week. Going out to pick out the movie was part of the excitement.

Pulling into my parent's driveway, I see the tree house in the backyard. When the car is in park, I get out and stare at it for a moment. There were a lot of great memories in that tree house. Maybe Leah and Adam will have kids soon and they can come here and make some new memories.

I feel my face smiling.

Yeah, kids around here would be great.

chapter TWENTY-NINE

"I'm getting marrriieeedddd!"

I am having a serious case of *déjà vu* right now.

My mouth is dry and I know when I speak I'll have man-voice.

"Get up, get up, get up! I'm getting marrriieeedddd!" Leah is bouncing on my bed, and the entire thing squeaks and shakes.

"Dear, Lord, woman. As if anyone could forget." I throw myself back under the covers and put my head back in the darkness.

Leah pulls the blanket down and off my entire body. I reach for the pillow and place it over my head. I try to hit her as if I'm hitting the snooze button on an alarm clock.

"Ten more minutes," I mumble from under the pillow.

"Fine, I'm coming back in ten with a glass of ice water," she threatens and the thought wakes me up. I have no doubt she is telling the truth.

She leaves the room and I slowly start to roll out of bed by placing one foot on the floor. I'm not used to waking up at the crack of dawn. Alexander gets up this early and then gives me soft kisses before leaving the apartment.

Ugh, Alexander Asher.

He still hasn't called.

I haven't called him, either for that matter.

If he isn't done thinking soon then I'll give him something to think about and it won't be pretty.

Placing another foot on the floor, I roll the pillow off my face and look up at the ceiling, adjusting my eyes to the bright light that Leah turned on. I look at the clock and see it's six in the morning. Hair and makeup people are coming at eight so everyone has to be showered and in their Spanx by then. Since mom and dad only have one full bathroom in the house, it could take a while.

The ceremony isn't until noon but Leah wants to take pictures before then. Then of course, there are more pictures after and the reception starts at three. Leah and Adam even have an after party planned at McConaughey's.

Man, this is going to be a long day.

I walk over to my drawer and pull out my undergarments for the day. I hear the shower running so I have to wait my turn. My dress from last night's rehearsal dinner is resting on the rocking chair in the corner of the room. My parents hosted the party here at the house.

I spent a good portion of the evening retelling the same story.

No, I don't play the violin anymore.

Yes, I moved to New York City.

No, it's not just like Sex and the City*"* (At least for me, its not.)

Yes, I am working at a school.

Yes, I am seeing someone.

No, he is not coming to the wedding.

My grandmother was the most probing. She wanted to know about the "young man I've been seeing." I assured her he's thirty-two years old and has a full-time job. Never married, no kids . . . you know, the typical things grandmas want to know.

"Well, if he's such a catch, why hasn't he been snatched up yet?" she asked.

Because he has serious trust and abandonment issues.

But I didn't tell her that.

Needless to say, last night was mentally exhausting but not unbearable.

I am gathering my toiletries from my bag when I look up to see Leah walk into my room with a glass of ice water in her hands and look disappointed because I am up and getting ready for my shower. She turns on her heel and exits the room.

I knew she wasn't bluffing.

Leah and Adam's wedding is absolutely stunning and completely romantic. Standing by her side in my crimson chiffon dress, I cried during the service because those two romantic fools wrote their own vows and if you didn't believe in love, just watching Leah and Adam would have you writing sonnets to the first person you saw.

The look on their faces as Leah was walking down the aisle and Adam waiting impatiently for her to get to him was breathtaking. As excited as she was all morning, Leah was nothing but calm and composed at the thought of marrying the man she loves. Adam had tears in his eyes as she came toward him, the two wearing matching grins. When she made it to the altar they grabbed onto each other's hands and I swear they've been glued to each other since. Eighty guests watched them exchange "I dos" and promise forever to each other.

Everyone should be loved as much as they love each other. Have I ever been? Lord knows I have felt more loved by a man in the last few weeks than I have in my entire life. He may not have uttered the words but Alexander has shown it repeatedly.

Maybe I was wrong for not fighting for him. Alexander's never had someone fight for him. The man has abandonment issues and I did the worst thing—I abandoned him.

As soon as pictures are over and we make it to the reception hall, I run up to the bridal suite. I have to call him. I need to tell him I was wrong.

While Leah and Adam mingle with guests at the cocktail hour, I lock myself in the bathroom of the bridal suite and take out my phone. I let it ring.

And ring.

And ring.

Until I get voice mail.

He didn't pick up. He always picks up the phone when I call him. Am I too late? Has he given up on us?

This isn't something I was planning on saying to his voice mail but I am so inspired right now by Leah and Adam's love and the complete feelings of forever I have for Alexander I can't hold back. When the beep comes on the other line I start to talk.

"Alex. I . . . I'm so sorry. I should have brought you with me. I should have fought for you. I have been blaming you for leaving me in Italy but I did worse to you. It's so much worse because . . . I love you. This is probably the least romantic way to tell you but I am in love with you, and I wish you were here. I'm miserable. I need you, and I want you. You should be here with me. I just—call me back. I need to hear your voice." I am about to hit the red end button when I throw in, "It's Emma by the way. Okay . . . bye." I hang up and then feel like a total fool.

So much for the controlled Emma. I am seriously losing it.

I make my way to the banquet room and stand in line outside the doors with the rest of the bridal party getting ready to be introduced. I am paired with Adam's brother, Landon, and when our names are called we walk in with our arms raised, dancing to the music and the crowd cheers. We take a spot on the dance floor and clap along to the song playing as the DJ introduces "for the first time, Mr. And Mrs. Adam Reingold."

The room erupts in louder applause as the bride and groom come in arm-in-arm with foolish grins, fist pumping in the air. The music goes from a fast-paced dance beat to a slow country love song they chose for their first dance.

My mind keeps on wandering to thoughts of Alexander. I wish I had my cell phone with me. I left it upstairs in the bridal suite and now I can't stand the thought of possibly missing his call. My arm is pulled and I look over to see Landon motioning for me to join him on the dance floor. Apparently the bridal party was called to dance. I am so lost in thought I didn't even hear the DJ make the announcement. I take his hands and start to dance. Around us the dance floor starts to fill with more people and soon almost all the guests of the wedding are on the dance floor.

I feel so awkward dancing with Landon. His height is too short and his hands are too rough. His hand on my back feels tense and he has these light eyes that are so far from the beautiful golden ones I fell in-love with.

Golden eyes that are staring back into mine and tapping Landon on the shoulder.

"May I cut in?" Alexander asks from behind Landon who turns around and has to look up to answer him.

Without saying a word, Landon lets me go and backs away from the dance floor.

My mouth is wide open.

Alexander Asher.

He's here.

He is standing right in front of me on the dance floor of my sister's wedding. Wearing a black suit that showcases his perfect frame, hugging his broad shoulders and coming in at a tapered waist. A crisp white shirt offsets his gorgeous bronzed skin and a silver tie polishes off his extraordinary look. He is magnificent and powerful, commanding and exotic.

It is too much to take in.

He takes my limp hands that have fallen to my side and raises them, resting on his shoulder and cradles the other close to his heart as his other arm snakes around my waist and pulls me in.

I feel him sigh in relief as our bodies join.

I look up at him, still in disbelief that he's really here. Maybe I'm dreaming. I move my left hand from Alexander's shoulder to my neck and give my skin a squeeze.

The action causes him to laugh as if he knows what I'm doing.

I look back at him, tingles running up my back at what this all means.

"You're here."

"I'm here," he agrees. His voice is in that smooth, deep baritone that makes me melt.

I swallow and continue to stare, now at his beautiful square jaw and full lips. "How?"

"There is this thing called an airplane—" he says in a sarcastic tone, but I cut him off by hitting his shoulder.

"I know all about that airplane. It's beautiful by the way. I should be mad at you."

"But you're not." His lip turns up in a smirk.

I smile back. "No. I'm not." My arm moves around his neck as I pull him into my body so tight until we can't get any closer. "God, I missed you."

Alexander releases our hands and puts his other hand around my waist, holding me tightly. I bring my other arm around his neck, resting my cheek on his broad chest.

He kisses the top of my head and whispers, "I've missed you more."

Leah and Adam's first dance song ends and then a faster song plays. I am temporarily broken from the spell that is Alexander Asher and then realize where we are. We are at Leah's wedding. She didn't want him here yet here he is anyway. I have to approach her. I have to tell her that I am in love with him and if she loves me, she has to love him too.

But when I look over at her, I see she is smiling. Not just in wedding bliss, and not at me. She is looking directly at Alexander and smiling.

I look back at him as he pulls me back in and we start dancing to the fast beat. He is a really good dancer. In between spins and dips, I ask him, "She knew you were coming?"

"She did."

"And she wasn't mad."

"She was a little mad."

"How did you get her to change her mind?"

Alexander pulls me into his chest. Our feet stop moving. His honey-wheat eyes gaze into mine, and his lips part to say the sweetest words I'll ever hear.

"I told her I'm in love with her sister."

My hearts stops beating. Like, really, heart? Are you in there?

Lungs, you can breathe too.

Alexander moves a stray hair behind my ear. "I love you, Emma."

My smile is so wide I think it will break my face. I want to kiss him. Instead, he takes my hand and is pulling me off the dance floor. We walk away from the room and his head looks from left to right in search of a place to talk. I pull him down the hallway and into the bridal suite.

As soon as we are inside the door, I try to throw myself on top of him and kiss him but he is holding me back.

"Are you serious? I need to maul you right now!" I am eager to get to him.

He laughs and holds me in a way that we are embracing but I can't kiss him. "Emma, wait, I have to say this first and then I plan to do more than kiss you."

I groan in anticipation at the thought but I let him talk.

"I have always gotten what I want. Ever since I went to live with my grandfather, I have prided myself on getting exactly what I wanted when it came to business, luxuries, women . . ."

I make a sour face at the mention of other women but he ignores that.

"I wanted you and I got you. But the way I felt for you scared me so I ran, and I promised I wouldn't run again. I thought a lot about what you said the other night. I never gave you a reason to trust me. I wanted you to fight for me but I never did the same.

"So I called your sister and I told her how I feel about you. I even told her how you put her feelings before mine and she cried."

I shake my head, "When was all this?"

"Yesterday. Emma, I can't live without you. I didn't follow you once and it almost ruined us. I wasn't about to let it happen again and not without their blessing."

"Their?" I ask.

"I spoke to your mom and dad too."

"Oh, God." I place my hand on my forehead and try to comprehend the conversation I am going to have with them about Alexander.

Alexander takes my hand away from my head and lowers his eyes so they grab my attention. I give him my most disapproving look. "Why did you talk to my parents?"

He shrugs his shoulders and says, "I needed somewhere to stay while I was in town."

My inside release and I laugh out loud. "You're staying at my parents' house?"

Alexander nods. "I am."

"You know there is zero privacy in my parents' house and there is no way they're letting you stay in my room."

"I know. I have Leah's room,' he says with a face of mock fright. I laugh and he pulls me into him.

His hands come up to my cheeks and he holds my head as if it's the most precious thing in the world. "I love you,

Emma. I should have told you before. This. Is. It. For. Me. I'm all in."

"I love you too."

He smiles at my words. "I know."

I tilt my head in confusion.

"I got your voice mail," he says just before leaning forward and brushing his lips against mine. They are smooth and strong and feel like heaven. Our lips entwine, melding together like branches of a hundred year old tree and my entire body melts into his embrace.

His tongue slides along my upper lip and the warmth of it runs a chill up my spine. When my own mouth opens further to welcome him, our kiss grows deeper. As our tongues meet, I swear we both exhale in bliss and need. Hungry for more, my hands are pulling at his suit jacket, desperate to have more of him.

We kiss for an ungodly long time and just when I reach for his belt buckle, Alexander puts his hand my own and moves it away. I look up at him in shock and surprise

His breathing is ragged as he put his forehead against mine and catches his breath.

"Baby, there is nothing more I want than to make love to you right now but your sister's wedding just started and if I'm correct, you have a toast to make."

A toast?

Oh my God. I am in no condition to make a toast right now. I scoot back and away from him and start to make myself look presentable. I grab my purse from where I left it in the bathroom and look into the mirror. My face is flush, my lips are bright red from the scruff of his jaw and my hair is out of place from his strong hands grabbing at it.

"You're beautiful."

I look over to Alexander who is leaning against the wall with his hands in his pockets, looking at me like a man in love.

My shoulders rise and I let out a sigh. If only he knew what his words do to me.

I put some lipstick on and fix my hair just enough to look presentable. When I am done, Alexander takes my hand and together we walk downstairs just in time for the toasts.

Thankfully, I wrote my speech out so I can recite it verbatim. When I am done, Leah and Adam hug me, thank me for the beautiful words, and I take my seat. At my table, I see Alexander has a place beside me. When I look back at Leah, she winks at me and I thank her with my eyes for accepting Alexander into her life. It is the most Leah-like thing she has ever done. Her methods may be unorthodox but then again, that's what makes Leah, Leah.

Alexander is an exceptional wedding date. He has been dancing with me all night, is patient when I have to leave him to do my maid of honor duties, doesn't give me a hard time when I choose to avoid catching the bouquet at all costs, and gives Leah and Adam the most spectacular wedding gift: an all expenses paid trip to Capri.

I am talking to Adam as he, drunkenly, gives his blessing on my new relationship when I look over and see my dad pulling Alexander over for a chat.

I hug Adam and let him go back to enjoying his party and stand here, on the edge of the dance floor watching my dad and Alexander interact. Dad is a few inches shorter and narrower but he's trying his best to be as intimidating as the man standing in front of him.

I am biting my thumbnail, watching the two of them talk. It's foolish I would be nervous. I guess they just mean so much to me I want these men to get along. This is my future. The man who raised me and the man who completes me.

"Is that the young man you were telling me about?"

Grandma has slowly crept up next to me. All four feet, eleven inches of her. She's a silver fox-tress, as Leah calls her, and is very proper. Everyone in the family says I'm just like her.

"Yes, Grandma." I answer yet my eyes are still on dad and Alexander. Dad has a serious look on his face and Alexander is simply nodding at whatever he is saying.

"Well, if that boy doesn't light your fire, your wood is wet!"

My head on a swivel rolls in Grandma's direction to assess the old woman as she walks away with her cane and a smile.

Can't say I disagree with her.

Looking back at dad, I see he is crying. Oh, God, dad and his tears.

"It's fine, honey. He just wants to meet the man who is in love with you." My mom has sidled up next to me this time. My hands find my stomach as I brace for the forewarning. *Be careful, Emma. You are strong, Emma. Take care of yourself first, Emma.* "I like him. I think he's good for you," she says.

I relax my hands and turn to face her. The lines around her eyes are wrinkled in and they're slightly wet from the tears that are filling up her eyes. "It's good to have you back, honey."

Mom pulls me into a hug and I hold right on to her. We haven't shared a good hug in way too long.

I look back at the men in my life. My dad extends his hand to Alexander, who shakes it back and then my dad pulls Alexander in for a hug. I'd be lying if I said Alexander didn't look wildly uncomfortable with the gesture but he is going along with it anyway.

After the reception is over we make our way to McConaughey's for the after party and I am relieved to switch my wedding heels for a pair of slippers. Alexander loosens his tie but leaves his suit intact. Instead of the usual scotch, he orders a pint with me and together we sway and sing to the music blasting from the speakers as Leah leads us all in a song.

When we head back to my parents' house, Alexander and I are tipsy as we walk through the back door, clawing at each other's bodies and making out like teenagers and being entirely too loud. My parents are still up, wearing their robes and talking in the kitchen. When we see them, Alexander and I halt our laughter and remove our hands from one another.

Dad looks uncomfortable with the situation, his eyes darting to the floor. "Alexander, you'll be in Leah's room tonight. Pam made up the bed for you this morning."

Alexander offers him a "Yes, sir" and it causes me to snicker at the idea of Alexander being schooled by his girlfriend's dad. From the grin on Mom's face, I can tell she finds this amusing as well.

Dad walks over and gives me a kiss on the cheek. "Good night, darling," he says about to turn around but then faces me again, "It's so nice to see you smiling."

I place my hands to my mouth and feel the smile across my face.

My parents head out of the kitchen and I push Alexander's back so he's following them up the stairs.

When we get to my room, Alexander offers me a sweet kiss on the cheek and then disappears across the hall to Leah's room.

I take my time in the bathroom, showering off the caked-on makeup and washing out the massive amount of hairspray in my hair. When I emerge, the hallway is dark and the house is quiet. I glance at Leah's bedroom door and contemplate paying a visit to the man who traveled here to tell me he loves me.

I've never had a boy stay at my parents' house. I've never snuck one in and I've definitely never fooled around with a boy under my parents' roof.

I'm twenty-five years old and finally about to break the rules.

I walk to my room, thinking about what I can slip on that would be sexy yet easy to take off. I open my bedroom door and when I close it I almost scream as a large shadow is standing in the middle of my room.

I fall back against the door, my hand to my chest attempting to calm my rapid heartbeat.

"Jesus Christ, you scared the hell out of me!" I yell in a whisper.

Alexander quietly laughs. "Scared you? Try sleeping in Leah's room. It's like a time capsule to 2005 in there. I thought she only liked McConaughey, but there's Leto, Gosling, Damon . . . their eyes just stare at you in your sleep!"

I bite down on the inside of my lips, clamping them down to stifle my laughter. "Are you afraid of the dark?"

"No!" he says too defensively.

My sweet Alexander who doesn't like to be alone. He doesn't like the dark. It's like he had a nightmare—*Oh, wait.*

Could it be possible Alexander Asher is afraid of the dark? Yes, it could be. I know everything about him. I know about his childhood and the night his parents died. He was with them for hours, waiting for some to come while the two perished before his eyes.

I walk to him and place my hands on his waist letting them travel under the fabric of his white shirt. His muscles are taut under the heat of his skin. Leaning forward, I place a soft kiss over his heart.

"I will never abandon you."

Instead of answering me, Alexander's hand find that perfect spot on each side of my head. He lifts my chin and gently brushes his lips across my own. I close my eyes and feel the kiss straight down to my toes.

He unravels the towel around my chest and his thumbs finding my nipples hard and ready for him. His touch is powerful but not hurtful. The hold he has on me is one of a man claiming what is his, what he knows is his reason to never be alone ever again.

I place my hands around his neck, my fingers skimming through the golden strands of his hair, pulling them gently. This is my way of letting him know I will never let him go.

He pulls me toward my bed and I try to stop him before his body hits the frame and the bed lets out a frighteningly loud squeak. Alexander hops up quickly and turns around to look at the offending mattress.

I fall to the floor on my knees and pull him down by the hem of his pants. "Old house. Old beds." When he was on his knees as well, I start undressing him. "Ever make love to a girl on the floor?" I ask and then quickly add, "Scratch that. I don't want to know. I'm sure the answer is yes."

Alexander unbuttons his shirt, his perfectly sculpted chest and well-defined stomach glistening in the moonlight coming through the window. I admired this body in Capri, at a time when I never believed it would be mine.

"Emma," he says when his shirt is freed from his body and I can finally touch his velvet skin. I look up and see his gorgeous face looking down at me. I am naked but he isn't looking anywhere but directly into my brown eyes. "Everything I do with you is a first. Yes, I've been with a woman on the floor before but you are the first woman I have ever made love to. You are the first woman I have ever been in love with. So everything I do with you is brand new because it's with you."

Be damned the first love and be damned the second love.

I am the last girl he will ever love.

And I am so breaking the house rules tonight.

chapter THIRTY

Knock, Knock.

"Hmmhmm?"

"Emma, breakfast is ready."

"Okay."

"And, Alexander . . . Bob is taking you to the airport."

I shoot up like a jack-in-the-box but am pulled back down by the strong arms of Alexander Asher.

"Thank you, Pam," he says and then nuzzles himself back into my neck.

I push him off and sit up. My voice is in a harsh whisper. "You have to go. My mom just caught you in my room." This is so embarrassing. My mom knows I had sex with a man in my room.

He is laughing into his pillow and trying to pull me back down. "Baby, damage is done. They're gonna have to get used to me staying in here when we visit."

Leaning on my elbow, I glance down at the perfect cut, masculine jawline that has a bit of scruff coming in. "You want to stay here when we visit my parents?"

His hand takes the hair that is falling in front of my face, places it behind my ear and then rubs my earlobe with his thumb and forefinger. "Yeah, I like it here."

"You like the fact there is one bathroom?"

"Yes." His perfect white teeth gleam in the sunlight coming through the window.

"And that there are six cats living here and everything gets hair on it."

"No, I hate that part. But I do like being where you grew up. This room, it's a piece of you."

"Even the squeaky bed?"

Alexander smiles brighter and pulls me in, cradling his hands around my behind. "I love the squeaky bed." As if on cue, the bed makes a loud noise and we freeze in place, laughing into each other's necks.

Alexander suddenly turns very serious and pulls back to get a good look at my face. I tilt my head and wait for him to ask a question.

"Did you enjoy growing up here?" he asks. I have no idea where the question is coming from.

Taking in the room, I look around at the yellow walls, decorated with the awards I won at recitals and concerts. A picture of the Eiffel Tower over my dresser and boudoir-type mannequin bust in the corner where I hang my costume jewelry. Even as a teenager I was trying to exude class when I should have been drooling over boys in movie posters and running silly like Leah.

I had a great childhood. Playing in the tree house in the backyard and having movie night on Fridays, life was good. It was peaceful.

"Yes, I loved growing up in this house. We had everything we needed," I reply.

"And what was that?"

"Love. We have a lot of love in this house."

Alexander takes in my answer and seems to be assessing it. I lay my hands on his chest and look at him, waiting for him to give me some insight into what he's thinking. Instead I just watch him absorb what I said.

After a minute or so, he looks back at me and runs his finger down the length of my nose. "Let's go have breakfast with your parents. I'm sure your dad is in tears at the thought of his baby girl upstairs in bed with a man!"

My face forms into an honest look of dread but instead of dwelling, Alexander pulls me to my feet and the two of us get up. He steps out to Leah's room for his overnight bag and some clean clothes. When we are both dressed, we make our way downstairs and, thankfully, Leah and Adam are here so we all flow easily into a conversation about last night's wedding.

Mom invited Alexander to stay for Christmas but he said he couldn't, that he had a deal that was closing on Christmas Eve. I hate the idea of him being alone for the holiday so I announce to the table I'll be heading home in a few days to spend Christmas with Alexander. My mom looks disappointed and my dad seems like he's going to cry but I just squeeze Alexander's hand under the table and smile at him.

The time for Alexander to head back to New York comes in the blink of an eye. Dad is insisting on bringing him to the airport, and Alexander surprises me by liking the idea, so the two of us say good-bye in the foyer of my parents' house. I am going to stay for a few more days and then I'll take a flight home on the twenty-third, just in time for us to celebrate Christmas together.

When he is out the door, I walk to the kitchen and Leah takes her wedding veil from the garment bag she brought over and places it on my head.

"What are you doing?" I ask, feeling the comb of the veil dig into the back of my head.

"Trying it on. Looks like you're gonna be wearing one pretty soon," Leah says, and my mom starts nodding and smiling.

I take the veil off and throw it at Leah, who is now laughing. I give her an eye roll and walk back to my room and think about what it would be like to be Mrs. Alexander Asher.

chapter THIRTY-ONE

I am beyond excited to see Alexander. The last forty-eight hours without him have been torture. I guess that's a product of being in love.

Stepping off the plane, I am greeted by Devon, standing by the black SUV holding the front passenger door open. A part of me was hoping Alexander would be here to greet me but I'm sure he is waiting for me at home.

The giant greets me with a smile. "Good evening, Emma. How was your flight?"

"Next time I'm booking my own flight to ensure I fly commercial. Where's Asher?" I climb into the car and Devon shuts the door behind me.

When he gets into his side of the car he answers, "He has a meeting and asked me to bring you to his office."

"Sounds good." I buckle my seat belt and lean my head back as Devon drives us back into Manhattan.

I came to this city four months ago hoping for an escape. Instead I found myself face-to-face with the thing I was running from. Myself.

I was afraid of who I was without the ability to play music. I found a new place for myself in a world of teaching others to play.

I was afraid of letting someone into my heart for fear of it being broken. I learned I am strong enough to withstand any loss. And when I finally allowed my heart to be opened up, I found a love that shines so bright, I want to burn in it.

Devon drives us inside the garage to Asher Industries and parks alongside an elevator. We get out at the same time and meet at the elevator. When it arrives, Devon puts his building pass into the panel. He's about to hit the button for Alexander's office floor but I put my hand on top of his.

"I'd like to go to his apartment." I have a far better idea for how my night is going to go and it doesn't start off inside an office of Asher Industries. I'm thinking naked Thai.

When the code is punched in, Devon excuses himself from the elevator car and leaves me alone. It's a long way to the top but the elevator is pretty fast. A concerto doesn't do it. Instead, I play a dance tune on my fingers. My head bobs to the beat that plays in my head.

The elevator doors open and I am inside the vestibule of Alexander's apartment. It dawns on me I don't know the code to get in. I take out my phone and type him a message.

Wanted to surprise you.

Epic fail.

I need the code to your apartment.

That is a nice surprise

1-2-3-6-9

I need ten minutes and I'm all yours :)

I look at the code on the screen. I know the one and twenty-three are for his birthday. But he is definitely not born in the year nineteen-sixty-nine.

I roll my eyes. *Boys*.

I punch in the code and open the door. The lights inside are on and before I can even think about how it's a waste of electricity leaving them on when no one is home, I realize, someone *is* home.

What the . . .

"What are you doing here?"

Malory Dean is standing in the middle of the great room with her arms crossed, a black folder in her hands and a very serious expression on her face.

"I should be asking you the same thing. How did you get up here?" I ask.

She scowls at me as if I should know the answer to that. I don't, so I scowl back.

"Why won't you leave him alone?" My question is slow stated, each word emphasized.

This causes Malory to half-laugh and lift her chin in pride. "Before whatever escapade the two of you have been on, I am the one who kept his bed warm at night. For three years I was the one who kept his fucking head on straight."

I know better than to let an old flame ruin what Alexander and I have. "You're a bitter ex-girlfriend. Why should I listen to a thing you say?"

Malory's cheeks flush. She is not happy with my defiance. "Because in eight days he is about to make the biggest mistake of his life and it'll be all your fault." Her words hit me like a brick. I have no idea what she is talking about and it is killing me. "He didn't tell you, did he? Asher and his fucking games. He thinks he has something to prove to this goddamn world."

She releases her arms from around her chest and then leans on her hip. Her stance is open as if she is trying to explain something to me yet sighs as if explaining it to me is beneath her. "Did he tell you his real name?"

I nod.

"According to Edward Asher's will, Alexander Gutierrez will no longer exist. In order to inherit Asher Industries he has to legally drop his surname. The old man would have made him change his first name, if he could."

My head sways from left to right. That is not something Alexander would ever do. He loves his parents. Even though he could never speak of them, they were held so tightly within his heart, he could never let them go. And he won't now. "I don't get it. His grandfather died over a year ago. Why would Alexander change his name now?"

Malory tisks at me. "Because then he loses it all. Don't you get it? Edward Asher wrote in his will that Alexander had eighteen months to change his name or else he inherits nothing. You see this?" She motions dramatically to the space around us. "If he doesn't sign those papers in five days, he loses *everything*. I don't understand what the big fucking deal is. It's just a name. It doesn't change who you are."

A name might not mean anything to Malory but to Alexander, it means the world. He has to choose between being his father's son and his grandfather's heir. From everything I've heard about the old man, it's proof he is as cold as I thought he was. He took in a ten year-old boy and didn't let him speak of his parents. He wouldn't even refer to him as Alexander, but rather by his middle name, Asher. Of course that made Edward happy. He was being called Asher all this time. Being brainwashed into being what the old man wanted him to be.

Makes you wonder why Edward Asher didn't just change Alexander's name all those years ago when he had the chance. No, this way is far more powerful. He is making Alexander choose on his own, as an adult, what is more important to him. Wealth or family.

It is quite possibly the most evil thing I have ever heard.

And I want nothing to do with it.

"What does it matter what I say? This is his decision. Not mine."

Malory rubs her lips together and takes her time before she utters these words. "I think it's time you dropped the charade. You and I both know you're only in it for one thing. One *billion* things."

My teeth clench at the insinuation. "I don't want his money. I'd love him if he had nothing."

"Well, then, you're an idiot. Asher is not capable of love. And he is certainly not capable of existing without this lifestyle. If you let him do this he will wake up one day and regret it. I promise you he will hate you for the rest of his life. Is that what you want? A man who can't stand the sight of you?"

"Then he doesn't have to give it up. If this is what he wants—"

"So you don't want him to give up the empire?"

"I never said that."

"You just did."

"I . . . stop putting words in my mouth! Whether he keeps it or doesn't makes no difference to me." I'm irate and in a rage.

Malory on the other hand is satisfyingly cool. "Oh, Emma. Don't you see? It could never work between the two of you. If he gives up the empire, he'll resent you. If he keeps it, he'll always wonder if you are with him for the right reasons."

"Why do you care what he chooses? It's not your money?"

"Before you came along he was going to share it with me! I am the only one who understands him. There is no such thing as love in this world. All we have is respect. Alexander Asher is going to rule the world and I will be the one by his side.

"Now he's thinking about giving it all up. And for what? To prove to himself you really love him for who he is and not what he has? It won't work. You will leave him or he will leave you. When your relationship falls apart, and it will, I will be the one to pick up the pieces. I am always the one to pick up the pieces. But if you leave him, and he has nothing, well, then I'll have no reason to help him back up will I?"

Taking one panther-like step toward me, Malory's words are harsh. "I am giving you one chance to walk out that door right now or I will make your life a living hell."

I am just about to tell Malory off when a loud bang echoes through the room. Alexander walks in and stops when he sees me standing in the living room with Malory.

"What the fuck is going on here?"

His eyes meet mine and he realizes Malory told me about the terrible decision he has to make.

I swallow back and turn to Malory, letting her know that she should leave. Malory sees the angered look in my eyes but doesn't move. It turns out she's just getting started.

Malory lifts the black file folder and hands it to Alexander. "I wasn't planning on doing this in front of the little harlot but I suppose it serves her right to watch as you find out who she really is."

My head swivels over to Alexander and watches as he opens the folder and looks through its contents. The hard, masculine structure of his face morphs from anger and determination to hurt and betrayal.

"Emma, tell me this isn't true," he says, his voice begging but his eyes frightened of the answer I may give.

I stare back at him, dumfounded at what could possibly be inside the folder. What could he possibly think I've done for him to look at me the way he is right now?

Malory saunters over to Alexander's side and explains. "I did my own investigation in Italy. Turns out Emma, here, hired a boat captain by the name of Raphael and paid him to stage the boat escapade. She fell in front of Devon on purpose, knowing he'd rescue her. It was all an opportunity to get to you and it worked."

My mouth falls open at the ludicrous fabrication.

"You tricked me?" Alexander asks me. I am shocked he would even believe this nonsense.

"No!" I shout. How in the world could he possible think I was capable of this? I want to run to his side and beg him to believe me but this is Alexander. My Alexander. The man who closed his heart off for fear of being used. His worst nightmare is coming true. It all feels like a bad dream "You can't believe this—"

"Believe it," Malory says. "Don't you think it was all too convenient? The sister gets sick, not once but twice? I bet Emma's hand isn't really injured. Probably just a ploy to get to your *wounded soul*."

I turn to Malory. She is stunning in her vindictiveness. What Alexander has is worth far more to her than I ever imagined. She went through a lot of trouble putting this affidavit together. "How do you even know how we met?" I ask in any attempt to find an explanation for what is happening. Realization suddenly strikes. A memory of a woman in fancy shoes, dark sunglasses and wide brimmed hat. "I saw you. At the hotel, I saw you."

My mind is reeling, placing intricate pieces of the puzzle together. Malory left the magazine under the doorway.

"You were going to frame me back then. You wanted Asher to catch me with the magazine as if I knew who he was the entire time. You were going to fake this affidavit back then but you didn't have to. Adam pinged the boat and sent Alexander into his own frenzy. You thought I was gone forever."

She was so concerned about her investment and supposed future with Alexander Asher, she wanted to keep us apart before we even started.

And she succeeded.

"Who hurt you so badly you want to destroy other people's lives?"

Her mouth clenches tight and her nostrils flare as she breathes in hard. "You know nothing about me! Asher, you cannot let her fool you any longer. You have to see—"

“Get out!” Alex shouts. To whom I’m nervous to find out. “Malory. Get out!”

Malory cowers a little and I almost feel sorry for her. “Asher, no. She is using you! She’s like the rest of them. She faked that drowning scene. Why do you think she’s here? This has all been a ploy to get to you!”

“I said—Get. The Fuck. Out!” Alexander roars like a lion. Malory’s chest is panting as the shock of his words resonates. From a sharp pant to mild gasps and then slow and steady breaths, she goes from wounded to proud over a few short moments.

Her chin rises in indignation. “You’re making the biggest mistake of your life.”

Malory walks past me and then Alexander, her eyes straight ahead. That confidence she carries is held high. She has no shame for what she has done here tonight.

When the door is closed and Malory is gone, I turn to Alexander who is still furious. “Please tell me you don’t believe her.”

“I don’t know what to believe.”

I take a deep breath and try not to cry at the knife he just rammed into my heart. “She told me about your grandfather’s will.” No sooner are the words out of my mouth than he is spitting foul words out of his.

Alexander walks over to the mantel, lifts a heavy glass figure and smashes it onto the floor. His back is heaving as he takes exasperated breaths to try to control himself. It’s not working.

“Your grandfather hated your father. He wants you to drop your father’s name. If you sign those papers you will no longer be Alexander Gutierrez. You’ll just be an Asher. Is that what you want?”

My words cause him to turn around and face me. He swallows, hard, his Adam’s apple bobbing and his jaw clenching. “If I don’t sign I lose everything.”

“You’ll lose even more if you do sign.”

Asher looks at me, finally looks at me for the first time since he walked into the apartment. The black folder of heinous accusation is still in his hand. He looks down at it and his mouth coils back as if his heart is sinking. "Emma, I . . . I don't know how to trust."

"There's only one way to find out."

He walks toward me and then stops as if in fear or what he wants to do. His hands rise up in that way they do before his fingers find their most perfect spot on the sides of my head and slide into my hair. But they don't do that. They just stop midair and then fall to the sides.

I look up into his mesmerizing honey-wheat eyes and watch the brown flecks disappear as despair settles over his face.

"Is that what you want, Emma? If you want me to give it up, I will. If you want me to keep my father's name, I will. But if you want this world, I'll sign. I can show you magnificent things. Together we can change the world. Imagine what we can do with all that money. Tell me what you want."

Just tell him what I want.

What do I want?

It's a lose-lose situation.

"I can't answer that." My hands tremble slightly at the position he is putting me in and the idea of what it means to our future. I hate Malory Dean but there is no denying she was right about one thing. "If I tell you to keep it, than you'll always wonder if I love you for who you are or for the world I'll inherit being with you. You'll always wonder if Malory was telling the truth about me. And if I tell you to get rid of it, you'll resent me for the life you'll have to live in return."

"I won't resent you—"

"Yes, you will. You will because you want to keep it. You've had eighteen months to make this decision. If you wanted to honor your parents you would have done so a long time ago. The truth is you want to keep it and you're looking for an excuse to do so. Whatever you choose, I can't be your reason."

What I want to tell him is to burn those papers. If he signs, he won't be Alexander anymore. He'll be Edward. The empire will be more important than anything in his life. This is what he was brought up to do. Slowly, the lessons he learned from his grandfather will take the forefront and my sweet Alexander will be gone.

And my love for him . . . he'll always question it. Every time I enjoy a luxury of his lifestyle or spend a dollar, that little voice inside his head will always wonder if I am with him for the right reasons.

My suitcase is sitting by the door. I walk over to it and undo the zipper, pulling out a package I wrapped back in Cedar Ridge.

"Merry Christmas." I say, handing him the gift.

"Its not Christmas yet."

"I know, but I'm going back to Ohio."

"Baby, no—"

I place my thumb on his lips, feeling the scruff on his jaw and halt his words from coming out. "You have to make a decision soon and I can't be with you when you make it."

I turn around and pull the handle on my suitcase up and tilt it toward me. He's not moving so I think he understands why I have to turn away from him right now.

"Is there a possibility you won't want me after I decide?" he asks, his voice nearly breaking.

My eyes close as the tears stream down my cheeks. I don't turn around because I know what happens every time I look into his eyes, rabbit hole be damned.

"Come find me when you make your decision."

Those are the last words I say before walking out that door and out of his life.

chapter THIRTY-TWO

It's been a month. An aching, antagonizing month.

When I got back to Cedar Ridge, flying commercial, my dad was at the airport with open arms. I didn't want my parents to hate Alexander so I told them the story. I know it wasn't my story to tell but they deserve to know why their daughter is upset. More importantly, I needed them to see this wasn't breaking me like I was a year ago. My inner strength gives me the resiliency to stand tall, no matter what happens.

I spent the Christmas holiday with my parents and watched the snow fall over Cedar Ridge.

Every day I waited for my phone to ring.

It didn't.

I waited for the knock on the door.

It didn't come.

I waited for my bed to squeak.

It did, but only by me.

On January third, my family gathered at the cemetery.

I can't believe my year from hell is over.

I made it.

In one year, I had (what I thought was a) heart-wrenching breakup with the man I thought I was going to marry. Now, I laugh at the idea I was ever upset about the douche with a flute.

In one year, I suffered the devastating loss of my baby brother. My soul still aches for him, but I cry less and I can now say his name out loud.

In one year, I am starting not to think of the accident as the day my dreams ended. They just changed. I still squeeze my palm and feel the burn tingle up my hand but it hurts less. The therapy I've been keeping up has helped a lot. I'll never play professionally again. That still makes me sad. But I have found a love for teaching.

The day after Luke's anniversary, I came back to New York. For the last few weeks I've been working hard. Classes resumed after the winter break. Crystal resumed her classes at night. Every day I open the door to my office and look for a rose tucked neatly in my notebook.

Sadly, there hasn't been one.

With each passing day, I find more solace in my new city. Even in the cold, I sit in Washington Square Park and listen to Allyce play "La Vie en Rose," just for me. Mattie still comes down for dinner once in a while and makes me laugh with his wild stories of a young twenty-something in New York City. And, yes, I still have to rescue him when he's locked out.

Crystal and Lisa have taken turns spending time with me after hours. From tea at Balthazar with Crystal, to trips to the Museum of Natural History with Lisa and her kids, they've helped me navigate this new chapter of my life. They don't know why Alexander and I are taking a break but they sense I need the company, and I accept it.

It was no surprise that when they learned today was my birthday they offered to take me out but I opted out. For some reason, I just feel like going home, drinking a glass of wine on the chesterfield, and listening to music. It doesn't sound like much but, to me, it's the perfect way to turn twenty-six.

I lock my office door and then Crystal's classroom door, stopping for a second to recall how wonderful it was to watch Alexander teach. He was the most brilliant lecturer of music I'd ever seen. Shame he'll be too busy to teach again.

Yes, I'm assuming he chose the empire.

Let's face it. It's been twenty-three days since he had to make a decision. Our love affair was short but it was intense. He could have told me about the monumental decision he had to make. He probably never truly trusted where my intentions were. Even so, I can't believe he didn't come for me, to tell me what he chose.

Better he didn't. He should have known by the gift I gave him where my heart was. For Christmas, I gave Alexander a photo of his mother playing the cello at Julliard. My mom came up with the idea after he left. I called the school before they closed for the holiday break and someone was kind enough to find a photo of her in their archives. I had it framed and matted for him.

Wrapping the gift, I had no idea how symbolic it would be when I presented it to him. I wanted him to choose his family.

Swinging open the heavy stairwell door, I walk down the stairs and nearly stop at the sound of music playing from the concert room on the first floor. It's not the orchestra sounds I heard a few months ago when Alexander brought the philharmonic here. This is different. The sound is a lonely sound. A single sound. The dance of a piano.

I open the first floor stairwell door and walk through the lobby, the piano heard cleared the closer I get. The tune is familiar, a song I've heard before. A song I heard played in this same room.

My palms rise up against the oak door that leads to the concert hall. Tacked up against it is an envelope.

My Emma

My heart skips a beat, my lungs fall into my stomach. Can it be?

Please, God, tell me I'm not dreaming.

Opening the door to the room, I take in the site in front of me.

Alexander, in the center of the stage, alone. He is seated at the grand piano, the same he played this song on. This time it is just him. A man and his piano and a song that I pray is meant for me.

Cascaded by the low light hovering over the stage, he is luminous. His golden strands and bronzed skin make him look like an angel. The cut, masculine lines of his face under velvet skin, his eyes closed, feeling the truth in the melody. His broad shoulders, hovering over the keys as he plays with passion, those strong fingers working the keys with conviction.

And, around him, bouquets and bouquets of yellow roses with red tips.

Falling in love.

With the envelope in hand, I open the fold and slide out a simple white paper. On it are words I've read before.

Halos casts down beyond the glass
In the darkness is where I stand
She is a beacon summoning me to shore
My siren. My light.

Her eyes are closed. The water is calm.
From my soul it's a raging sea.
I've traveled alone for so long
Forgetting what it was I was looking for.

Flames rise on this dark soul.
And the angel is staring back at me.
A kiss. A moment. Entwined hands. A beating heart.
The planks light up in flames.
I go down with the sinking ship.

Like a mirage she is gone.
And I coast alone.
No soul. No hope.
No beacon to call me home.

The lyrics to the song are as beautiful as the melody.

The heavens opened up. Her light shining from the sea.
Out from the dark I can finally breathe again.
She found me. She saved me.
My light. My love. Rescued my weary soul.

Yet, the most powerful words are those written at the bottom of the page.

Written by Alexander Gutierrez

His name. He kept his name. He chose family over fortune.

I don't wait for him to finish. I run quickly up to the stage, taking the steps up two at a time and stopping in front of the grand piano. His eyes open and when he sees me, there is little surprise on his face. It's as if he knew his song would lure me to him.

"You're here," I say as his fingers work the last chords of the songs, softly now.

"I am," he says with a smile. I place my hands on my belly in anticipation of what he's about to say. What his decision was, what he plans to do with his life next, what this means for us . . . My mind is a mess.

"Sorry I took so long. I had a few things I had to take care of." Alexander is now standing in front of me.

I hold up the white paper and take a deep breath. My mouth is dry so my words come out a little course. "Does this mean you made a decision?"

"It means I did the right thing," he says, his hand dipping into his pocket.

I don't know what "the right thing is" so I just stare at him waiting for clarification. He doesn't offer me any. Instead he is lowering himself . . .

. . . down.

To the floor.

On his knee.

He's on his knee?

He's on his knee!

"Oh my God!" The words fly out of my mouth as he pulls his hand out of his pocket and produces a ring. A gorgeous, solitaire diamond on a metal band. It's simple and beautiful and so much more than I ever could have asked for.

"Emma Paige . . . Today is a day my life began and ended. It's a day I looked on in sadness. But then one day, the most beautiful woman I have ever seen, with blonde hair and beautiful brown eyes in nothing but a bathrobe stunned me with a song. I fell for you the second I saw you. And every time I learned something new about you . . . about your passion, your strength, your joy . . . I fell harder and deeper.

"Fate meant for us to find each other. The day I dreaded is also the day you were brought into this world. How can I hate such a day that created the most perfect vision on the planet? So I waited for today, the day that I no longer want to look on with sadness but as the day my life begins again.

"Will you marry me? Will you make me the happiest man by being the first person I see at the beginning of the day and the last person I kiss at night? Will you be my wife and be my family? Will you, Emma Paige . . . will you be Mrs. Alexander Gutierrez?"

Io sono il suo.

I am his.

I practically fall to the ground and into his arms. Taking his head in my hands I kiss him. I kiss his eyes and his nose and his mouth and his chin. I kiss him all over and with each kiss I say the words. "Yes.Yes.Yes.Yes."

Those full, lush lips widen into a gorgeous smile as he takes my mouth into his, sealing the moment. He holds up my left hand and slides the ring onto my finger. I look down at it and can't believe how stunning it is.

"This is too much. We can't afford it," I say and my heartbeat comes down from its historic elevation.

"Why can't we afford it?"

"Because you kept your name. You gave up the business," I say and then stagger back. "Didn't you?"

He plays with the ring on my finger. “This looks perfect on you—”

“Alex—”

“I did. Are you mad?”

“Mad?” I blink back. “No. I’m relieved. But, you didn’t do this because you thought it’s what I wanted, did you?”

He slowly shakes his head, his hands holding me from behind, the warmth of them enveloping me. “No, I did it for us. Before you, I never believed anyone would want me as the poor kid from Pittsburgh. I never wanted any of it. I just needed someone to believe in me in order to give it up.”

“I do believe in you. I want to be your wife even if that means we have nothing.”

“I wouldn’t say we have nothing—”

I sit back on my knees and rest my hands on my thighs, my head tilting up at him for an explanation. So he gives me one.

“I signed the company over to the board of trustees, claiming my name and seizing everything that was bought under Asher Industries. But, I still got to keep a few things.”

“Huh?” Yeah, that’s all that I can muster.

“There’s Black Dog,” he says pointing to me as if I’m familiar with it, which I am. “I also own a production company and then there’s stock I purchased with my own money and a trust fund from my great-grandfather that’s untouched.”

“Oh.” My lips purse together in confusion. “Alex, that’s not considered poor.”

“It is when you consider the fact I just signed over a billion-dollar business.”

I laugh and shake my head at my sweet Alexander. He is going to have to give up his three thousand–dollar scotch. The plane is definitely gone too. I hope he likes shaving his own beard.

"How were you able to keep the recording studio? Wasn't that an Asher property?"

"Actually, It's an Emma Paige property. I transferred it to your name the day I saw you teaching that boy how to hold a violin. I fell in love with you in that very moment. Something changed in me. All the anger I was holding, all the doubt I had vanished. And when you threw that violin at me in the back of the car? That was when I knew I was going to spend the rest of my life chasing you until you came back to me."

I feel like the Grinch whose heart grew three sizes because mine is about to explode. I'm not going to lie. I'm scared. I am absolutely petrified that this is too good to be true. Frightened how tomorrow it could all fall apart. I could lose Alexander and I could lose myself.

But I'm not going to let the possible hurt keep me from experiencing happiness. Never again. I am going to live and I am going to love and I am going to burn.

"What about the school? Will the Juliette Academy have to close?" The sudden guilt at what his decision means to the future of the greatest school I've ever known his me hard.

"The school is fine. They gave it to me as a parting gift. Looks like no one on the board wants to be bothered with it. What do you say, wanna run a school with me?"

"I'd love nothing more." And it's the truth. It's not the life I chose but it's the one that I was meant to live. "Thank you for choosing us."

"Thank you for choosing me."

EPILOGUE

ALEXANDER

A glass of Glen in my hands and the sun on my back. Not a bad way to start your day.

Especially when it's going to end with Emma Gutierrez in your bed.

My hands are wrapped around the hand of the only woman I have ever truly loved. And she looks radiant.

Her hair is down and loose like the first time I saw her. She asked if I had any special requests for our wedding day and this was it: to have her hair down.

I remember that day like it was yesterday. I had just sent Malory back to the mainland when Mateo, our deck hand, alerted me of Devon's arrival. I was looking for him when I heard a song coming from the one room on the ship no one was allowed. My music room was my space for personal reflection. The one place I could be me, the real me.

When I heard music coming from that room, I was livid. Knuckles ready for a fight, I stormed in there to find out who could be so defiant. Imagine my surprise to find an angel.

Long blonde hair, sun-kissed skin, and a mouth so lush and plump, she was the most beautiful woman I had ever seen in my life.

I was Odysseus and she my siren, calling me in from the sea.

The light from the two-story glass windows poured in and cast a glow upon her as she swayed to the music. Her eyes were closed and as much as I wanted to see the soul behind them, I begged her with my breath not to. I knew when she opened them she'd see. She would see me. And she did.

The most mesmerizing pair of brown eyes looked back at me and I knew they would be able to look right through me and down deep into my dark soul.

She looked at the worst part of me and healed it. She saved me and I will spend the rest of my life proving to her I was worth saving.

"What are you thinking about?" Emma whispers into my ear, her hair blowing in the warm Mediterranean breeze. She looks exquisite in her white gown. Just over an hour ago, she walked toward me on the arm of her father. The sight of her brought me to tears.

Yes, I am man enough to admit I cried at the site of my bride walking down the aisle in a pair of white Sperry Top-Siders. Yes, my bride is wearing boat shoes and I wouldn't have it any other way. While everyone was looking at her, as they should be, she was staring at me. With each step she took, she held my soul with every ounce of her being. And I gave it up freely.

Today she is mine. And I am hers.

It also helps that my wife looks gorgeous and way too sexy to be in the presence of God. She chose a form-fitting lace gown that hugs her gorgeous ass and narrows at her waist, the one I love to grab when she's on top of me, riding me, loving me. I can't wait to peel that dress off her tonight. Her supple breasts are about to pour out the top and it's killing me not to bite down on them.

Yes, I am still a man. I can say those things about my wife.

My wife. Jesus Christ, she's really mine. And she married me without the Asher name. She married me for me.

And I am so goddamn in love I'd die if she ever left me.

She's still looking at me, waiting for an answer. I could go for sweet and I could go for lewd. Instead I'll go for a kiss. Leaning down, I tug a hair behind her ear, wrap my hand around her jaw and kiss her, hard.

Emma responds easily, wrapping her lips around mine and lets her tongue glide across mine, caressing, loving, tempting—

Clink, Clink, Clink, Clink

Our moment is disrupted by the clanging of spoons on glasses as is customary at weddings when the bride and groom kiss. Emma laughs and buries her head into my chest. In return, I wrap my arm around her and hold her into me, laughing myself at the joy of the moment.

"Get a room!" Leah chants from the other side of the room, her swollen belly keeping her from drinking the limoncello.

"Oh, hush, you!" Pam play slaps her daughter.

"You can't hit a pregnant woman!" Leah chides and rubs her arm as if she was just beaten. She turns to Adam for comfort. "Honey, tell her she has to be nice to me. I'm carrying her grandchild."

Adam just shakes his head. "I won't let anyone be anything but perfect towards you, baby. I got you." He kisses his wife and rubs her stomach. They're expecting a little boy in a few months. His name will be Matthew. No one was surprised to hear that.

Looking around the room, I feel at peace. The open-air restaurant overlooks the Mediterranean Sea, overlooks the very spot where Emma nearly drowned and was recused by Devon. If it weren't for her inability to trust strangers with her belongings I never would have met her. She is still crazy about her belongings. She bought a white fanny pack to go with her wedding dress. Leah wouldn't allow it.

Emma leans her head into my side and her nose nuzzles the skin of my neck. I lean down into her. "Are you sniffing me?"

“Yes.” She says, her lips skimming my ear. “You smell of sea and soap. It brings back beautiful memories.”

When I proposed to Emma, I knew there was only one place in the world we would be married: on the island of Capri. As I don’t have any family and no one other than Devon I’d care to invite, Emma and I opted to keep it small. So we flew eight of our closest friends and family to Italy to share this moment with us.

Seated at a rectangular table are Emma’s parents, her grandmother, Leah and Adam and Devon. Lisa couldn’t leave the kids but Crystal and Mattie are here. They offered to pay their own way but I wouldn’t allow it. They have both been incredible friends to Emma, especially during our weeks apart.

On the table in front of each guest is a vase of yellow roses with red tips, the same ones I gave her time and time again portraying one true meaning: *Falling in love.*

And I fall, every day, further and further every day.

A warm, smooth hand, tugs at mine. I look over at Emma who is pulling me toward the veranda. I follow her, away from our guests to a secluded spot, feeling as if the two of us are the only people on earth.

She is smiling at me, looking like the cat that ate the canary. I bow my head and squint at her, wondering what my little minx is up to.

“I have a secret to tell you.” Her brow rises up in a dare.

“What kind of secret?” I ask, tempting her to tell me.

Her teeth skim her lip and I swear if we didn’t have another hour left of this dinner I’d throw her over my shoulder and carry her up to our room.

“You have to promise you won’t tell a soul. At least not for another four weeks.” The full pout of her lips spread. She is obviously quote excited about her secret.

“That’s a very specific amount of time. Why can’t I tell anyone for four weeks?”

"Because I can't let my father know I was pregnant at my wedding."

As if all the air in my body has been sucked out of me, I fight to speak but there are no words.

A baby. We're going to have a baby.

I am going to be a father.

For the second time today, I cry.

I cry for the child that will be coming into the world. I cry for the gorgeous creature in front of me who is giving me the greatest gift. I cry for my parents who will never know their grandchild. And I cry for the family that I have, after searching for so long. A family that is mine. A family I will do anything to protect.

"Baby, are you okay?" Emma asks, placing her hands on my face and looking deep into my eyes looking for the part of me that runs.

But I'm not running. I vowed to her long ago I'd never run from her again. And I never will.

I take her hands off my face and hold them in mine, up close to my heart. "A long time ago I asked you a question. When was the last time someone gave you a gift so monumental it made you cry? This is my gift. You have given me the greatest gift."

"What is that?" she asks.

"Love. You gave me love."

ACKNOWLEDGMENTS

To Autumn Hull of the Autumn Review and Wordsmith Publicity. I love a villain but couldn't quite get this story just right. Thank you for pushing me to achieve believability. Your guidance is immeasurable and I will forever value your friendship.

To Jamie Chavez, editor extraordinaire! I learned so much from you while writing Pure Abandon and brought that knowledge to this next novel. Thank you for your detailed copy editing and making me look like a rock star on paper!

To Sarah Hansen, of Okay Creations, a visionary in book cover creation and Jovana Shirley, of Unforeseen Editing, for making the inside pages a work of art!

To the online blogging community for making my first-time self-publishing experience amazing, especially Maryse Black of Maryse's Book Blog, Jennifer Ristic of Collector of Book Boyfriends and Maria Barquero of Maria's Book Blog.

To JCol's Army of Roses who share the love of #TeamAsher and #TeamGabriel. Shout out to Giovanna Bovenzi Cruz, Laurie Breitsprecher, Aubrie Brown and Wilmari Carrasquillo-Delgado, Anna Alonso and Natalie Padro – I worship you! Thank you to all the readers who contacted their favorite blogs to tell them about Pure Abandon and Reckless Abandon, especially Andrea Strauss Strohecker and Nancy Parken. Your support is amazing!!!

To all the amazing authors I've met along the way and welcomed me into this wonderful circle of Indie Authors, especially, Lauren Runow, Elisa Marie Hopkins, Cynthia Rodriguez, AJ Compton, Martha Sweeney, Nicole Hart, AM Johnson, Ramzi Holmes, Lucia Franco, Leddy Harper, SL Ziegler and L. Harvey. It has been awesome connecting with each of you and working together to share our work.

To my sister Nicole Romano and my best friends Jennifer Windstein, Nicole Lancellotti and Tara McCormick for being my Beta Babes.

To my friends and family who have provided unending support including Nanci Weaver, Jill Meister, Nicole Parsons, Anne Hogan, Noreen Suzor, The Distefano and Salzano Families. To my Nanny for teaching me to always exude confidence in myself and my work, and to my Poppi who won't read my books because they "seem a little spicy."

To my Mom who is the greatest person I know. She continues to put herself second so her daughters can fulfill their dreams. We love you, we value you and cherish every moment we have with you.

To My husband Bryan who this book is dedicated to. I always hated when people referred to their spouse as their "best friend." You are not my best friend. You are My Bryan. That title far surpasses any friend, lover or soul mate I could ever have. When we are gone from this world, our ashes will be scattered together on the island of Capri. A place where we connected far more than any place on this earth. A magical place that inspired this novel.

And, of course, to the two tiny people who I pray never give up on their dreams. No matter how silly they may seem.

Contact me! I'd love to hear from you!

(at least the nice things anyway ☺)

Jeanninecolette.books@gmail.com

I'm also on Facebook, Twitter and Instagram

Can't get enough of Reckless Abandon?

Check out my blog for photos, inspiration and random thoughts behind the book.

www.jeanninecolette.com

Made in the USA
Middletown, DE
27 December 2015